THE TRAITOR'S HAND

The most famous commissar in the galaxy has to choose his friends wisely...

COMMISSAR CAIN AND his regiment of Valhallans are sent to the planet Adumbria to bolster the Imperial lines and repel an impending invasion by the foul forces of Chaos.

However, nothing ever goes to plan for Ciaphas Cain and his hopes to sit on the back lines relaxing are thrown into disarray. Even for the forces of Chaos, the enemy is behaving oddly. Cain must unravel the mystery unfolding on this strange planet, while battling bigotry and suspicion within the ranks of the Imperial Guard itself.

The third Ciaphas Cain novel from Sandy Mitchell, *The Traitor's Hand*, is packed with action, tension and dark humour.

This book may be returned to any Wiltshire Library.
To renew this book, phone or visit our website:
www.wiltshire.gov.uk/libraries

Wiltshire Council

For Mary, for Grunts, and the quotation on page 57.

A BLACK LIBRARY PUBLICATION

First published in Great Britain in 2005 by
BL Publishing,
Games Workshop Ltd.,
Willow Road, Nottingham,
NG7 2WS, UK.

10 9 8 7 6 5 4 3 2 1

Cover illustration by Clint Langley.

A CIP record for this book is available from the British Library.

ISBN 13: 978 1 84416 187 4
ISBN 10: 1 84416 187 0

Distributed in the US by Simon & Schuster
1230 Avenue of the Americas, New York, NY 10020, US.

Printed and bound in Great Britain by
Bookmarque, Surrey, UK.

See the Black Library on the Internet at
www.blacklibrary.com

Find out more about Games Workshop
and the world of Warhammer 40,000 at
www.games-workshop.com

IT IS THE 41st millennium. For more than a hundred centuries the Emperor has sat immobile on the Golden Throne of Earth. He is the master of mankind by the will of the gods, and master of a million worlds by the might of his inexhaustible armies. He is a rotting carcass writhing invisibly with power from the Dark Age of Technology. He is the Carrion Lord of the Imperium for whom a thousand souls are sacrificed every day, so that he may never truly die.

YET EVEN IN his deathless state, the Emperor continues his eternal vigilance. Mighty battlefleets cross the daemon-infested miasma of the warp, the only route between distant stars, their way lit by the Astronomican, the psychic manifestation of the Emperor's will. Vast armies give battle in his name on uncounted worlds. Greatest amongst his soldiers are the Adeptus Astartes, the Space Marines, bio-engineered super-warriors. Their comrades in arms are legion: the Imperial Guard and countless planetary defence forces, the ever-vigilant Inquisition and the tech-priests of the Adeptus Mechanicus to name only a few. But for all their multitudes, they are barely enough to hold off the ever-present threat from aliens, heretics, mutants – and worse.

TO BE A man in such times is to be one amongst untold billions. It is to live in the cruellest and most bloody regime imaginable. These are the tales of those times. Forget the power of technology and science, for so much has been forgotten, never to be re-learned. Forget the promise of progress and understanding, for in the grim dark future there is only war. There is no peace amongst the stars, only an eternity of carnage and slaughter, and the laughter of thirsting gods.

Editorial Note:

To my great surprise, not to mention personal satisfaction, the first two volumes of material from the Cain archive which I have prepared for circulation among those of my fellow inquisitors who may care to peruse them have been quite widely read; although it must be said that many of my colleagues appear to regard them as light entertainment rather than the more serious food for thought I originally intended, finding it hard to believe that an imperial commissar could fall so far short of the ideals he was meant to embody. Given his public reputation I find this incredulity easy to understand, but thanks to our personal association, I can assure my readers that he was indeed very much as he depicts himself in these memoirs. I would point out, though, that perhaps as a result of his own awareness of these shortcomings, he does have a tendency to judge himself a little more harshly than he might actually deserve.

Hitherto I've concentrated my efforts on some of Cain's encounters with alien enemies of the Imperium, although in the course of his long career he crossed swords with all manner of warp-spawned monstrosities as well, confounding the dark designs of the Ruinous Powers and their mortal minions on numerous occasions. It seemed fitting, therefore, especially given the interest in the previous volumes from inquisitors of ordos other than my own, to select one such incident to prepare for wider dissemination.

I was aided in this decision by the fact that it follows on chronologically from the previous two extracts, although Cain's tendency to record his memoirs piecemeal, as different anecdotes occurred to him, means that the original material forms a somewhat extended digression. This happened in his account of the famous incident during the 13th Black Crusade, when he was dragged out of retirement to defend an entire world with little more than a handful of his Schola Progenium cadets. That will have to wait for a subsequent volume, of course; in the meantime, I believe I have successfully filleted the material relevant to the Adumbria campaign and present it here as a reasonably coherent narrative in its own right.

Like the earlier extracts, these events took place during Cain's service with the 597th Valhallan and cover the fledgling regiment's first encounter with the forces of Chaos. A particular point of interest is Cain's description of the ordinary troopers' reaction to the Great Enemy and the form its machinations took, which I hope will sound a much-needed note of caution to those of my readers who might fall prey to the pernicious tenets of Radicalism.

Since, as usual, Cain is infuriatingly vague about most things which don't affect him personally, I have continued to insert extracts from other sources where necessary in order to present a more rounded account of events on Adumbria and in the system surrounding it. Unfortunately, as before, some of these are the logorrheic meanderings of Jenit Sulla, for which I can only apologise in advance; were any other alternatives available, you can be sure I would have used them.

In accordance with the previous volumes, I have broken Cain's largely unstructured narrative into chapters for ease of reading, and once again I have been unable to resist prefacing them with a selection from the collection of quotations he maintained for the instruction and amusement of his schola students. Other than this I have confined my interpolations to the occasional footnote, leaving Cain to tell his story in his own inimitable manner.

Amberley Vail, Ordo Xenos

ONE

*'The wider he smiled and called us friend,
the tighter we clung to our purses.'*
– Argun Slyter *'The Wastrel's Stratagem,'* Act 4 Scene 1

I'VE HAD MORE than my fair share of unpleasant surprises over the course of a century or so of fighting the Emperor's enemies, whenever running away and hiding from them wasn't an option, but the sudden appearance of Tomas Beije in the corridors of the *Emperor's Beneficence* is one I still can't recall without flinching. Not because the situation was particularly life-threatening, which I suppose made it unusual enough given the kind of surprises I usually got, but because of the associations the memory of it still triggers: a curious amalgam of anger at his subsequent pig-headed stupidity, which almost ended up handing an Imperial world to the Ruinous Powers neatly gift-wrapped with a pretty pink

11

bow, and, more importantly, could have resulted in my ignominious execution had events not turned out as they did; and the flood of unpleasant memories his presence stirred up in me at the time. I hadn't liked him when we were commissar cadets together at the Schola Progenium and I suppose I would have disliked him still if I'd spared him so much as a single thought in the years since we were judged fit to inflict ourselves on a regiment somewhere and sent off elsewhere in the galaxy. (Or in my case, I strongly suspect, handed a scarlet sash and politely shown the door because it seemed the easiest way of keeping my tutors from resigning *en masse*.)[1]

'Ciaphas.' He nodded a greeting, as though we'd always been on good terms, and a smile as sincere as an ecclesiarch distributing alms in front of the pictcasters smeared itself across his pudgy features. 'I heard you were on board.'

That didn't surprise me. By that point in my career, my reputation preceded me wherever I went, smoothing the way in a fashion which often made my life a great deal easier, and, as if to balance things out in some way, periodically dragging me into life-threatening situations of bowel-clenching terror. No doubt by now, three days out from Kastafore[2], the entire ship would be aware that Cain the Hero of the Imperium was aboard,

---

1. In point of fact Cain's record as a schola student is best described as unremarkable. His academic results are, by and large, on the low end of average; the only areas in which he did better than this being sports and combat techniques. His disciplinary records are surprisingly free of infractions, which, given his character, probably means the one thing he truly excelled at, even in those days, was not getting caught.

2. An Imperial world recently cleansed of an ork incursion. For once Cain and the 597th had been out of the thick of the fighting, seeing relatively little action, and his brief anecdotes about the exceptions needn't concern us at this juncture.

and either pretending not to be impressed by that sort of thing or trying to find some way of scraping an acquaintance in order to further their own careers by coat-tailing on mine. Well good luck to anyone daft enough to try the latter, I thought.

'Beije.' I returned the nod curtly, irked by his use of my given name. We'd never been friends at the schola and I resented the presumption now. Come to think of it, I don't recall that he'd ever had any friends, just a small group of cronies as pious and self-righteous as he was, always whining on about the grace of the Emperor or running to the proctors with tales of the minor infractions of other students. The only time anyone was ever pleased to see him was on the scrumball pitch, where he got tackled enthusiastically at every opportunity whether he had the ball or not. 'I had no idea you were part of this little jaunt.'

The smile curdled a little as he registered the snub, but he was bright enough to realise that making an issue of it in public wouldn't be a good idea. The corridors were filling with senior Guard officers, the black coats and scarlet sashes of a handful of other commissars among them, all drifting towards one of the recreation halls where the lord general himself was expected to brief us in a few minutes' time. Not in person, of course, as he'd be travelling in some style aboard the flotilla's flagship, but the tech-priests had apparently rigged up some method for him to pictcast all the vessels in the task force simultaneously before we made the transition to the warp.

'I'd hardly describe facing the enemies of humanity as a jaunt,' he said stiffly. 'It's our holy duty to preserve the Emperor's blessed domains from the merest taint of the unclean.'

'Of course it is,' I replied, just as unable to resist teasing the pious little prig now as I had been nearly thirty years before. 'But I'm sure he wouldn't mind if we had a bit of fun while we're doing it.' Of course, facing whatever horrors might be waiting for us wherever we were going was about as far from my idea of fun as it was possible to get, but it was the sort of thing a hero was supposed to say and it went down well with the crowd around us, most of whom were trying very hard to look as if they weren't listening to the conversation.

'I'm sorry to interrupt your socialising, commissar.' Colonel Kasteen cleared her throat and glanced at her chronograph with studied nonchalance. 'But I believe it would be impolite to keep the lord general waiting.'

'Thank you, colonel,' I responded, grateful for the intervention and conveying that fact with a glance no one else present other than Major Broklaw, her second-in-command, would have been able to pick up on. Our years of service together[1] had given us a rapport which came as close to friendship as our respective positions allowed and which helped no end in the smooth running of the regiment.

'This is your colonel?' Beije asked with undisguised incredulity. Kasteen's jaw knotted with the effort of reining in her instinctive response, which from long experience I expected to be short, pithy, and anatomically improbable.

Happy to return the favour she'd just done for me, I nodded. 'She is indeed,' I said. 'And a damn good one too.' Then I laughed and patted Beije on the back,

---

1. *By this point, roughly five years after the adventures on Simia Orichalcae presented in the previous volume, Cain was almost a third of the way though his period of service with the 597th. His activities in the interim are recorded elsewhere in the archive, but are irrelevant to the present account.*

which I remembered from our days at the schola was something he'd always detested. 'Surely you haven't forgotten how to read rank insignia?'

'I hadn't noticed them,' he muttered, his face slowly crimsoning. Well, maybe that was true. Kasteen had quite a spectacular figure, in a trim, well-muscled sort of way, and perhaps he hadn't bothered to look that high. 'She was standing behind you.'

'Quite,' I said, unable to resist prolonging his discomfiture a little longer by making introductions. 'Colonel, may I present Commissar Tomas Beije, an old classmate of mine.' Kasteen nodded a formal greeting, which Beije echoed a little over-eagerly, trying to make up for his lapse in good manners. 'Beije, this is Colonel Regina Kasteen, commanding officer of the 597th Valhallan. And Major Ruput Broklaw, her executive officer.'

'Commissar.' Broklaw stuck out a hand for Beije to shake, which he did after a moment's hesitation, wincing as the major closed his grip. He'd tried the same thing on me the first time we'd met and I'd been grateful for the augmetic fingers on my right hand. 'Any friend of Commissar Cain is always welcome in our quarters.'

'Thank you.' Beije retrieved his hand, although whether he was astute enough to realise Broklaw's tone effectively ruled him out of that general invitation was unlikely. Trapped by social convention, he flapped it vaguely at the two men flanking him. 'Colonel Asmar of the Tallarn 229th, and Major Sipio, his second-in-command.'

I glanced back at Kasteen and Broklaw, amused at the contrast between the two groups. While the Tallarns were both short and dark-complexioned, swathed in the loose tunics of their desert home world, the Valhallans were about as physically different as it was possible to be. Kasteen was wearing her red hair drawn back in a pony tail, blue eyes as clear as the skies above the ice fields of her home world, while Broklaw's flint-grey gaze perfectly mirrored the night-dark hair which framed it. In deference to what they considered to be the stifling heat outside the areas assigned to us, which, as usual, they'd had refrigerated to temperatures which left the breath smoking, they were dressed in simple fatigues, only the rank pins on their collars denoting their status. So to be fair, I suppose Beije could have been forgiven for not realising who they were at first, but that wasn't going to stop me enjoying his embarrassment.

'A pleasure.' I nodded to the two officers. 'You have a formidable reputation as warriors. I look forward to hearing of the glorious victories of the Tallarn people.'

'We prevail by the grace of the Emperor,' Asmar said, his voice surprisingly mellifluous. Beije nodded, a little too eagerly.

'Yes, absolutely. Faith is the strongest weapon in our arsenal, after all.'

'Maybe so,' I said. 'But I'll still take a laspistol to back it up.' It wasn't the wittiest remark in the galaxy, I'll admit that, but I was expecting at least a smile. Instead, to my surprise, the Tallarns' expressions hardened imperceptibly.

'That would be your choice, of course.' Asmar bowed formally once and turned away, followed by his number two. Beije hesitated a moment, as if debating whether to go with them straight away, but just couldn't resist getting the last word in.

'I'm afraid not everyone shares my appreciation of your sense of humour,' he said. 'Our Tallarn friends take their faith very seriously.'

'Well good for them,' I said, beginning to understand why no one had shot him by accident yet. By luck or somebody's good judgment, he'd been assigned to a regiment of Emperor-botherers as humourless as he was. Of course, at that point, I didn't know the half of it; they had Chaplains like the rest of us had Chimera drivers, all of the kind that make Redemptionists look well-balanced by comparison[1]. Had I realised the consequences that were to flow from the impulse to irritate Beije and unwittingly offending his friends in the process, I suppose I'd have held my tongue, but at the time I remained in blissful ignorance and went into the briefing feeling rather pleased with myself.

Because of the delay in the corridor, Kasteen, Broklaw and I were among the last to arrive, but once again my reputation worked to our advantage and a trio of seats had somehow been kept clear for us despite there being not quite enough to go round. Beije and his Tallarns, I noticed in passing, were among those squeezed in at the back, standing uncomfortably and gazing resentfully at us as we made our way down to the front of the auditorium.

There were five regiments in all aboard the *Emperor's Beneficence*, an antedeluvian Galaxy-class troopship which seemed to be kept functioning entirely by the constant activity of her tech-priests and enginseers, and the senior command staff of all of them came to a tidy

---

1. *Cain is exaggerating a little on both counts. Tallarn regiments do tend to have an inordinate number of Chaplains compared to most others, often attached as low down the command structure as individual squads, but few of them are quite as fanatical as the members of the Redemptionist cult. It cannot be denied, though, that their entire culture is remarkably pious, and few natives of that world are prepared to take any significant decision without consulting a cleric for guidance as to the will of the Emperor in the matter.*

total; most had sent their entire complement to save the
effort of repeating the exercise later on, and I was able
to spot all of our own company commanders and their
immediate subordinates scattered among the crowd
before I sat down.

Apart from us and the Tallarns, the ship was carrying
a Valhallan armoured regiment whose Leman Russes I
had been delighted to see stowed in the hold next to
ours (and who in turn seemed equally pleased to have
found themselves travelling with another unit from
their home world) and a couple of infantry regiments
newly raised on Kastafore. The officers from there were
easy to spot, thanks to the newness of their uniforms
and the expressions of alert interest they directed at
everything which caught their attention (most of which
seemed to be the women from the 597th).

The cogboys[1] had been busy, there was no doubt
about that. Wires and cables snaked across the floor of
the chamber, being tended to by white-robed acolytes
chanting the appropriate rituals of activation, terminat-
ing in what I recognised as a hololithic display unit of
remarkable size and complexity. At the moment, it was
projecting a rotating image of the Imperial eagle, which
hazed and sputtered in the familiar fashion of all such
devices, accompanied by jaunty music of staggering
vacuity.

'Did anyone remember the caba nuts?' I asked,
reminded of a public holotheatre, and a few of the
nearby officers chuckled sycophantically. After a
moment, the hum of conversation died away as the
lights dimmed, the senior tech-priest ceremoniously
kicked his control lectern and the familiar face of Lord

---

1. *A slang term for tech-priests, common among the Imperial Guard,
apparently derived from the cogwheel insignia of their calling.*

General Zyvan replaced the aquila, looming down at us like an out-of-focus balloon. After a moment of heated discussion among the tech-priests, somebody yanked a couple of wires out of their sockets and the music stopped abruptly, enabling us to hear him.

'Thank you all for your kind attention,' the balloon said, its voice sizzling with static. It had been some time since I'd spoken to the lord general in person, our paths having crossed rarely since our first meeting on Gravalax about six years before, and most of those occasions had been fraught to say the least, occurring as they did in the middle of either a war zone or a diplomatic crisis. Nevertheless, we'd always got on tolerably well and I respected his concern for the welfare of the men under his command, which, since they included me, I thought was a decided asset in a military leader. 'No doubt you've been wondering why we've mobilised in such a hurry following the success of our campaign against the orks on Kastafore.' A few of the officers from there raised a cheer, which trailed off into embarrassed silence.

'Here it comes,' I murmured to Kasteen, who nodded grimly. Normally we would have expected to remain on the newly-cleansed world for some months at least, helping to rebuild the bits the greenskins had put a dent in, making sure the local PDF was back up to strength, and generally enjoying a bit of a breather before moving on to the next war. But instead we'd been hurried aboard the *Emperor's Benificence* almost as soon as we'd reached our staging area, the first shuttles already waiting to ferry our vehicles up to orbit as we'd arrived. One of the new Kastaforean regiments had already preceeded us starside. Fortunately they were too green to have staked out the most comfortable quarters and accessible mess halls for themselves and were easily displaced by the veterans of the 597th, so our troopers were as happy with the situation as it was possible to be. Which wasn't much: a mobilisation that rapid had to mean trouble had blown up without warning in a relatively close system and we were being sent to deal with it. That meant we'd be going in hot, with little idea of what we'd be facing, and already caught on the back foot. Not a situation any warrior likes to be in.

Zyvan wasn't too happy about things either, I could tell, although I suppose being personally acquainted with him gave me an advantage in that regard. He was hiding it well, though, his usual air of bluff competence barely impeded by the distortions of the hololith. Certainly most of the people around me were buying it.

'Ten days ago we received an astropathic message from a naval task force hunting a flotilla of Chaos raiders on the outer fringes of the subsector.' As I'd expected, Zyvan's face disappeared to be replaced by a map of the local star group. Kastafore was off to the bottom left, almost at the edge of the display, and a small cluster of contact icons overlapped it, marking the positions of our fleet.

I drew in a deep breath. If I'd read the runes correctly, we were the only troopship on the move, accompanied by a handful of the warships. The rest were still sitting in orbit, twiddling their thumbs, no doubt feeling mightily relieved that for one reason or another they weren't quite ready to go. That meant we were the spearhead, first into whatever might be waiting for us, which in turn meant we were likely to soak up the bulk of the casualties. My stomach tightened at the thought. I didn't have long to digest the implications, though, as the display lurched suddenly, skipping a couple of parsecs to the right and dumping Kastafore ignominiously into the void outside the projection field. A couple of tech-priests started arguing in urgent undertones and one of them disappeared under the lectern, his mechadendrites twitching.

'They've been tentatively identified as a group calling themselves the Ravagers,' Zyvan's voice continued, blissfully unaware that the starfield in the hololith was now bouncing like a joygirl on overtime. The image steadied itself as a shower of sparks erupted from the control lectern and the tech-priest emerged from beneath it, looking slightly singed. After a final wobble, it zoomed in on a cluster of contact icons bearing the runes of Chaos forces.

The hairs on the back of my neck prickled at the sight. Emperor knows I've faced a lot over the years, but the thought of the Great Enemy still disturbs me more than most. Perhaps it's because I've seen so much of what they can do, but I think it's their sheer unpredictability which makes them so worrying. Most enemies are rational, at least in their own terms: tyranids want to absorb your genetic material, orks want to kill you messily and loot your corpse, and necrons just want to kill every living thing in the galaxy[1]. But Chaos is random, by its very nature, and even if you can work out what it is the enemy's after, half the time only the Emperor knows why they want it in the first place.

'They've been hitting isolated systems and merchant convoys sporadically for the last few years,' Zyvan went on, while a red line considerately tracked the path of their depredations. 'Typical Chaos tactics, hit and run mostly, inflicting the maximum number of casualties,

---

1. *Actually just the sentient ones. So far as we know.*

then withdrawing before the fleet arrives to give them what for.'

'Sounds like a Khornate cult,' I whispered to Kasteen and Broklaw, who looked a little puzzled, before remembering they hadn't encountered any minions of the Ruinous Powers yet and I was probably the only one in the room with much idea of the divisions within the ranks of the Great Enemy. That was some degree of comfort, anyway. In my experience they were the easiest type of renegade to deal with, having little ambition beyond getting into combat as quickly as possible and killing as many of our people as they could before being cut down themselves. That made them particularly susceptible to ambushes and flanking attacks, which would work to our advantage, particularly if we could stick the Kastaforeans out in front as bait.

'The Navy finally caught up with them on the fringes of the Salomine system, inflicting severe losses on their fleet,' Zyvan continued. I wasn't surprised, recognising the blue icon of a tau colony world, where the Ravagers were sure to have met far stronger resistance than they expected. That would have given the fleet time to catch up and join in slaughtering the heretics in the name of the greater good. The tau would have loved that, I was certain, until it dawned on them that they now had an Imperial fleet squatting on their doorstep instead, and the heretics had already weakened their defences. 'Several vessels did manage to flee into the warp, the exact number and type remain to be determined.'

'Which affects us how, exactly?' Broklaw murmured, with the groundpounder's typical distain for anything the Navy might be doing. A Guardsman to the core, his only interest in starships was how quickly and comfortably they could move the regiment to the next planet we were supposed to kick nine shades of hell out of to maintain peace and stability in the galaxy.

As if to answer his question, Zyvan reappeared, pointing to an insignificant dot which looked to me pretty much like any other system.

'Our navigators consider it highly probable that they'll end up here, in the Adumbria system, especially if their warp engines have been damaged. Apparently the warp currents are particularly strong and turbulent around Adumbria Prime and they're likely to be drawn there.' He shrugged. 'Unless they're setting course for the place on purpose, which the fleet navigator thinks is quite possible, given their previous heading. What they might be after on a backwater like that is anybody's guess. It could just be the next convenient target on the list.' His voice hardened in the manner that I knew from experience meant he'd made up his mind about something and wouldn't be dissuaded by anything short of a direct command from the Emperor himself (or possibly a quiet word from the Inquisition). 'In any case, when they arrive, they're going to be in for a surprise. If the warp currents remain favourable, we'll be there ahead of them. If we're really lucky, the rest of the task force will have had time to catch up too.'

I don't mind admitting it, the last sentence sent a chill down my spine. What he meant was that barring a miracle, we'd be on our own, facing anything up to a full-scale invasion fleet with just five regiments and a handful of ships.

'And if we're not?' Kasteen asked quietly, clearly coming to the same conclusion I had.

'Then things are about to get very interesting,' I said, keeping my voice steady by a preternatural effort of will. As it turned out, that was to be one of the biggest understatements of my life, although even in my most pessimistic imaginings I never thought we'd find ourselves embroiled in a plot so diabolical as to threaten the very fabric of the Imperium itself.

Editorial Note:

Although Cain makes sufficient references to the peculiar conditions prevailing on Adumbria to enable an astute reader to deduce them, he never bothers to elucidate them explicitly. I've therefore appended the following extract, which I hope will make everything clear and help to explain much of what follows.

From *Interesting Places and Tedious People: a Wanderer's Waybook* by Jerval Sekara, 145 M39.

ADUMBRIA IS ALMOST unique, even among an assemblage of worlds as vast as our beloved Imperium, being as it is rotationally locked to its sun. This in itself is not so unusual, of course: the point of interest being that, unlike most examples of such planets, Adumbria falls within the primary biosphere of the star around which it orbits. The net result of this is that one side, a howling wilderness of blizzards and ice, is condemned to perpetual night, while its bright twin is seared by the pitiless heat of the sun without respite.

Unsurprisingly, the vast majority of the population live in the so-called Shadow Belt, a narrow strip running from pole to pole where temperatures remain tolerable. Here you will find cities to rival those of most civilised worlds, boasting bars, restaurants and places of entertainment of a standard ranging from the positively opulent right the way down to 'Society for the Assistance of Travellers recommended'.

Away from the centres of population, you may find such scant agriculture as the planet supports and two inland seas, fed by the snowfields of the dark side and surrounded by pleasant resorts. The prices are, of course, higher the closer you get to the sunward side, since the temperature of the water is correspondingly greater, as are the ambient light levels. Discerning holidaymakers generally make for the so-called 'sunset strip,' where the sun is so close to the horizon as to leave the sky permanently reddened in an ever-changing display of breathtaking natural beauty...

[Several paragraphs of extraneous travelogue omitted]

The sunward and dark sides of Adumbria have little to offer the discriminating wanderer, consisting as they do of little more than life-threatening extremes of temperature. Nevertheless, a few hardy (or perhaps foolhardy!) individuals manage to scrape a living there, hunting the native wildlife, which has adapted to such extremes, scrabbling minerals from the rocks and generally pursuing such labours as occupy the time of the artisan classes.

TWO

'One thing you can say for enemies;
they make life more interesting.'

– Gilbran Quail, *Collected Essays*

AT FIRST, DESPITE the apprehension which continued to
gnaw at me as the *Emperor's Benificence* ground its way
through the warp, it looked as though things might actually be going our way after all. We made the transition
back to the material universe without incident, to find the
Adumbria system completely free from heretical marauders. The only vessels to greet us were a somewhat surprised
patrol cutter and the merchantman they were pursuing,
who just had time to offer to sell us a variety of recre-
ational products of dubious provenenace before the cutter
crew boarded them and confiscated the entire cargo.

In short, by the time we made orbit round Adumbria
itself, I'd almost allowed myself to be lulled into that

sense of false security my innate paranoia generally keeps firmly at bay.

'Interesting place,' Kasteen said, joining me at the observation window of the portside recreation deck. I nodded, still lost in the contemplation of the planet below. I'd seen a fair few worlds in my years of rattling around the galaxy and was to see a great many more before finally making it through to an honourable retirement, but not many of them stick in my memory the way Adumbria did. It wasn't that it was beautiful, not by a long way, but it had a kind of defiant grandeur about it, like a faded dowager refusing to acknowledge the passing of the years.

By this time our troopship had joined the cluster of merchant vessels which naturally accreted at the point where the equator crossed the shadow belt, hanging just a few kilometres above the planetary capital[1] which rejoiced in the uninspiring name of Skitterfall[2]. To my surprise, the eye was drawn naturally away from the glare of the bright face, which I'd expected to be the focus of attention, to the unexpectedly subtle attractions of the dark side. Far from being wrapped in impenetrable blackness, as I'd expected, this shone with the faint blue lustre of reflected starlight, bouncing back from the plains of ice and snow which covered the entire hemisphere. The more I stared, the more I

---

1. *The equivalent point on the opposite side of the planet was occupied by one of the landlocked seas, making this one the obvious site for the largest starport on Adumbria.*

2. *A local dialect word describing the exact degree of twilight prevailing at that particular location. The Adumbrians have over thirty nouns for semi-darkness, each one more improbable-sounding than the last, and deliniating a subtlety of difference which could only matter to a people with far too much time on their hands.*

became aware of a thousand subtle shades and stipplings in that apparently uniform glow, resulting from the light rebounding unevenly from mountains, canyons and who knew what other geographic irregularities.

'It'll be good to get down there,' Kasteen said, following the direction of my gaze. That was a matter of opinion, of course; I've always disliked the sort of intense cold my Valhallan colleagues seemed to thrive in and was already anticipating the bone-crushing temperatures awaiting us on our deployment with less enthusiasm than the approaching Chaos fleet. But to be fair, I'd never heard a Valhallan complain about the excessive heat they felt they encountered pretty much wherever they went and I wasn't going to undermine my reputation, not to mention my leadership, by seeming less stoic than they were.

'I'm sure the troopers would agree,' I said instead. We'd been through some winter seasons on temperate planets in the last few years, but hadn't visited an ice world since our brief and abruptly truncated sojourn on Simia Orichalcae. The dark side of Adumbria wasn't quite the same thing, but it would be cold enough to feel like home as far as they were concerned.

A faint vibration shook the deck plates beneath our feet, too familiar even to register consciously, and we watched one of the dropships slipping away towards the planet below. Its engines flared brightly for a second as it corrected its course, and then it disappeared among the countless number of other shuttles coming and going from the starport beneath us. Sharp, distinct pinpricks of light in the distance would be the larger vessels they tended, merchants for the most part, as Zyvan had left the bulk of our warships to form a picket line in the outer system. Apart from the *Emperor's Benificence*, the only vessel from our relief flotilla to have made it all the way to Adumbria itself was the *Indestructible II*, an Armageddon-class battle cruiser the lord general had chosen to carry him and his senior command staff[1]. When I'd first arrived on the observation deck I'd amused myself by trying to pick it out, but at this distance the effort was futile and I'd rapidly abandoned the game in favour of studying the world we were here to defend.

'It seems as though our Tallarn friends are equally eager to get down there,' Kasteen commented, watching the shuttle disappear. Her tone was studiously neutral, but the implication was clear; she was glad to see the back of them, and so was I. In the month or so we'd been transiting the warp, the regiment had passed the time in all the traditional ways, including challenging the others to a variety of sporting competitions. The 425th Armoured had thrown themselves into socialising with all the enthusiasm you might expect of a regiment which had discovered not only that they had the good fortune to be sharing a troopship with another unit from home, but that it consisted largely of women, while the Kastaforeans had done their best to hold their own against a regiment of battle-hardened veterans and acquitted themselves tolerably well, all things considered. The Tallarns, on the other hand, had remained aloof, their idea of a good time apparently consisting of innumerable prayer meetings of unimaginable tedium.

Relations hadn't turned really frosty, however, until they'd refused to take part in the inter-regimental unarmed combat competition because the 597th had

---

1. *Presumably because none of the capital ships were ready to break orbit in time.*

included some of our women in the team. This, Colonel Asmar curtly informed us, was 'unseemly.' To no one's surprise except Asmar and probably Beije, their regimental champion was promptly and informally challenged to an impromptu bout the next time he wandered into the recreation deck. I have to report with a certain degree of satisfaction that he was subsequently pounded flat by Corporal Magot, a cheerfully sociopathic young woman who barely came up to his chin. (Which made little difference, as it only took her about a tenth of a second to bring it down to the level of her knee.)

Beije, of course, had been beside himself, and came storming into my office demanding to know what I intended to do about it.

'Nothing at all,' I said, smiling disarmingly and offering him the least comfortable chair. 'I've already dealt with the matter.' I turned to Jurgen, my odiferous and indispensable aide. 'Jurgen. Would you be so kind as to fetch Commissar Beije some tea? He seems a little agitated.'

'Please, don't bother on my account.' Beije paled quietly, having been exposed to the full effects of my aide's aroma while I left him to stew in the anteroom for as long as I thought I could leave it before he gave up and left. No doubt his appetite had been somewhat impaired by the experience.

'It's no bother,' I reassured him. 'I normally have a little break for some refreshment at about this time. Two bowls, please, Jurgen.'

'Commissar.' Jurgen saluted as awkwardly as ever and slouched out, somehow contriving to look as though his uniform never quite touched his body, which given his casual attitude to personal hygiene and perpetual eruptions of psoriasis, you could hardly blame it for. Beije watched him leave with an expression of stark incredulity.

'Why in the name of the Emperor,' (and damn me if he didn't make the sign of the aquila as he pronounced the Holy Name), 'do you tolerate such a slovenly lack of standards? That man should be flogged!'

'Jurgen's something of a special case,' I said. Quite how special I had no intention of disclosing, of course, as Amberley had impressed upon both of us the necessity of keeping his peculiar abilities as quiet as possible[1] and I had no wish to attract the attention of any inquisitors other than her. Beije looked sceptical, but commissarial etiquette demanded that he defer to me in all matters concerning the regiment whose morale I was entrusted with safeguarding, so he would just have to lump it. No doubt he'd assume some nefarious or discreditable reason, though, which he might be tempted to gossip about, so I decided to give him a little of the truth.

'Despite his appearance, he's a remarkably able and efficient aide, and his loyalty to the Emperor is as fervent as that of any man I've ever met.' More to the point, he was the only man in the galaxy I completely trusted to watch my back, and his vigilance had saved my life on more occasions than I could recall without effort. 'I think that matters rather more than the fact that his uniform's a bit untidy.'

All right, calling Jurgen a bit untidy was rather like saying Abaddon the Despoiler gets a bit cranky in the morning, but I knew adopting a casual attitude would be the surest way to get under Beije's skin. I knew my man well (as you'd

---

1. *Jurgen, as I discovered shortly after my first meeting with Cain, was a blank; an incredibly rare ability which effectively nullifies any psychic or daemonic forces in the immediate vicinity.*

expect given the number of times I'd left unpleasant surprises in his bunk at the schola), and noted the faint tightening of his lips with well-concealed satisfaction.

'That would be for you to decide, of course,' he said, as though trying to ignore a bad smell. A moment later he actually was, as Jurgen returned with a tray containing a couple of tea bowls and a gently steaming pot. I waited while he poured, enjoying the way Beije flinched before taking the bowl my aide proffered, then took my own. 'Thank you, Jurgen. That will be all for now.'

'Very good, commissar.' He indicated the data-slate he'd brought in with the tea and placed on my desk. 'When you have a moment, there's a message there from the lord general.'

Beije nearly choked on his tea as Jurgen and his aroma left the room.

I nodded sympathetically. 'I'm sorry, I should have warned you. Tanna's a bit of an acquired taste.'

'Aren't you even going to look at it?' he asked.

I glanced at the screen. 'It's not urgent,' I assured him.

Beije looked at me censoriously. 'Everything the lord general decrees is urgent.'

I shrugged and spun it around where he could see it. 'He just wants to know if I'll be free for a bite to eat and a game of regicide after we land,' I said. 'I don't think it's very high on his list of priorities.'

The expressions which chased themselves across Beije's face were priceless: shock, disbelief, naked envy and finally carefully-composed neutrality. 'I wasn't aware you were personally acquainted.'

I shrugged again, as casually as I could contrive. 'We've bumped into one another a few times and we seem to hit it off. I think he just enjoys the chance to unwind with someone outside the chain of command, to be honest. Hardly fitting for him to socialise with Guard officers, after all.'

'I suppose not,' Beije muttered. In truth, I suspect that really was the main reason Zyvan took an interest in my career and made a point of inviting me to dinner now and again[1]. He took another cautious sip at the tanna and regarded me through the steam. 'I have to say you surprise me, Ciaphas.'

'How so?' I asked, denying him the satisfaction of showing any irritation at his use of my given name, and savouring the bitter aftertaste of my own drink.

'I'd expected you to have changed more.' His chubby face took on a puzzled frown, making him look uncannily like a colicky infant. 'All those honours, the glorious deeds you've done in the Emperor's name...' Well actually they'd been done in the name of keeping my skin in one piece, but of course no one needed to know that, least of all Beije. 'I heard about them, of course, but I never quite understood how a wastrel like you used to be could have achieved half of them.'

'The Emperor protects,' I quoted with a straight face.

Beije nodded piously. 'Of course he does. But you seem especially blessed.' The frown deepened, as though he was about to bring up a posset of milk[2]. 'I

---

1. Cain is probably being too modest here. Zyvan had a healthy respect for his tactical sense and Cain's position outside the chain of command meant he could express his opinions rather more freely than most of the lord general's subordinates would. His eventual appointment as the commissarial liaison to the lord general's office was at Zyvan's instigation and his role there was as much as an independent advisor as it was as a commissar.

2. Cain's apparent familiarity with the habits of infants is not explained anywhere else in the archive. However, he was serving with a mixed-sex regiment at the time, so it's quite likely that the inevitable occurred on more than one occasion. If so, as the regimental commissar, he would have been responsible for ensuring the welfare of all concerned.

know it isn't for us to question divine providence, but I don't understand…'

'Why me?' I finished for him, and Beije nodded.

'I wouldn't put it quite that way, but… well, yes.' He spread his hands, spilling tanna tea on his sleeve. 'You've seen so much divine grace, the hand of the Emperor has been extended to you so often, and yet you still have the same flippant attitude. I'd have expected more piety, to be frank.'

So that was it. He was morally outraged that his old enemy from the schola had achieved so much success and glory while he was stuck in a dead-end posting with a bunch of Emperor-botherers as humourless as he was. Green-eyed jealous, in other words. I shrugged.

'The Emperor doesn't seem to mind. I don't see why you should.' I sipped my tea and favoured him with my best open, friendly, frak off now smile. His mouth opened and closed a few times. 'Was there anything else?'

'Yes.' He produced a data-slate for me to have a look at. 'Copies of the disciplinary proceedings against Trooper Hunvik.' The name didn't mean much until I read the charges at the top of the sheet and realised that this must be the man Magot had pounced on.

'Assaulting a superior officer?' I asked mildly.

Beije scowled. 'The… the soldier from your regiment was a corporal.'

Funny how he couldn't bring himself to say 'woman,' I thought. Somehow that must have rankled even more than the simple fact that their regimental champion had been bested. I nodded. 'She still is.' His eyes narrowed as I continued to skim through the slate. 'I see you didn't apply the death penalty on that charge though.'

'There were extenuating circumstances,' Beije said, a hint of defensiveness entering his voice.

I nodded. 'Quite. Knowing Magot, she undoubtedly threw the first punch.' And probably the next couple too. Mari Magot was a woman for whom the word 'overkill' was inherently meaningless. 'I trust the infirmary is making him comfortable?'

'As much as they can,' Beije said tightly.

'Good. Can't flog a man for brawling while he can't stand up, can you? Wish him a speedy recovery from all of us.' I downloaded the file to my desk, as though I could be bothered to read it, and added another to Beije's slate before handing it back.

He glanced at it and his jaw knotted. 'That was how you dealt with it? Reprimanded and returned to duty?'

I nodded. 'Magot's the new ASL[1] in her squad. They're just getting used to her. Reorganising them now, just as we're entering a war zone, would undermine their efficiency to an unacceptable extent.'

'I see.' His eyes hardened. 'She's another special case.'

'She is,' I agreed. Again I had no intention of telling him just how special she was, since the official line on the Simia Orichalcae fiasco was that it was a glorious though somewhat pyrrhic victory over the nasty grubby greenskins, and Amberley had made it very clear that the wrath of the Inquisition would fall on anyone who so much as breathed a word of what else we'd found there. And I knew her well enough to know that she never made idle threats. But the fact remained that Magot, then just a trooper, had walked through a

---

1. *Assistant Squad Leader, a junior non-commissioned officer trained to take over if the leader becomes a casualty. When, as was the case in the 597th, squads are routinely split into fireteams, the ASL takes command of the second team when they operate independently.*

necron tomb beside me and emerged from it at least as well-balanced as when she went in (however much that might have been). The Guard needed soldiers of that calibre, and if I had to bend a few regulations to keep them standing between me and whatever the warp might be about to vomit up at us, I'd make origami out of the rulebook without a second thought.

'Then our business is concluded.' Beije stuffed the data-slate back inside his greatcoat, no doubt deducing a highly improper relationship between trooper and commissar which probably added to his evident jealously of me. (Completely erroneously, of course. For one thing, I've never been that stupid, for another, Magot's preferences ran in an entirely different direction, and most importantly of all I've only got room for one lethally dangerous woman in my life.)[1]

'I suppose so,' I said, dismissing him completely from my mind. If I'd realised at the time how much animosity I was stirring up in him and by extension the Tallarns, I'd have been a great deal more diplomatic, you can be sure. However, I didn't, and the consequences of that conversation were still lurking some weeks in the future, so all I felt watching that shuttle depart was a sense of relief at the fact that I'd managed to avoid Beije for the rest of the voyage and was unlikely to ever have to set eyes on him again.

But, as I've remarked on more than one occasion, the Emperor has a nasty sense of humour.

THE FIRST STAGE of our disembarkation went as smoothly as a mouthful of fifty year-old amasec. We were the second regiment to be ferried down, and the

---

1. *Which I choose to take as a compliment…*

dropships began loading troopers and equipment as soon as the Tallarns had cleared their holds. Within moments the hangar bay took on a reassuring reek of burned promethium as our trucks and Chimeras began chugging up the loading ramps, and the high space echoed to the profanity of NCOs doubling their squads into the passenger compartments. Sure that, as always, Jurgen had packed our personal possessions with his usual matchless efficiency, I found myself able to relax and enjoy the spectacle.

And what a spectacle it was. For sheer impressiveness there's little to match the sight of a well-drilled Guard regiment on the move: almost a thousand people bustling around stowing gear, moving it, losing it, finding it again, and generally getting in each other's way in some arcane fashion which still lets things get done with almost superhuman efficiency. From the vantage point I'd adopted on a gallery overlooking the main hangar floor, I could see vehicles and troopers milling around on a vast plain of steel, receding almost a kilometre into the distance, where the dropships standing in a patient line were diminished by perspective so that the most distant were reduced to the scale of toys.[1]

'I've stowed our gear on the lead shuttle, commissar.' Jurgen's voice, preceded by his remarkable bouquet, broke in on my thoughts.

I nodded absently. 'Thank you, Jurgen. Are they ready to depart?'

---

1. *One of the reasons the Galaxy-class troopship remains so popular, even though none have been built since the Age of Apostasy and the means to do so are now thought lost, is that it has sufficient hangar space to embark an entire regiment under optimum conditions. Of course this assumes that it would have sufficient dropships aboard for the task, which few do, the slow-moving shuttles being easy targets in a war zone, and difficult to replace.*

'Whenever you are, sir.'

'Might as well get to it, then,' I said, trying to still the faint flutter of apprehension which rose in my stomach. Here, in the belly of a starship, it was possible to believe in the illusion of safety, and once we hit dirtside we'd be twiddling our thumbs waiting for the war to start (or so I thought at the time). But I'd had too many vessels shot out from under me not to be aware of how vulnerable they'd be once the heretics' war fleet arrived and I knew my chances would be a great deal better on the planet below. I activated my comm-bead. 'Colonel. I'm embarking now.'

'Emperor speed, commissar.' Kasteen sounded distracted, as she was bound to be by now, juggling a dozen minor crises at once. 'See you on the downside.'

'We'll be waiting,' I assured her.

She or Broklaw would be on the last shuttle down, making sure the departure went smoothly, while the other would take the first one possible once the pressure began to slacken. (Protocol forbade the colonel and her number two to fly on the same dropship unless something went hideously wrong; otherwise it would only take one lucky shot for the enemy to effectively decapitate the entire regiment.) By long custom I would be on the first shuttle to land: partly because it fitted my reputation to appear to be leading from the front, but mainly because that would give me a head start in procuring the best quarters wherever we were going to be billeted.

'Commissar.' Lieutenant Sulla, the most eager and irritating of the platoon commanders[1], saluted as

---

1. *Though she was later to rise to a position of great prominence in the munitorium, being the first (and so far as I'm aware only) woman to gain the position of Lady General, Cain appears to have been blind to her potential; in fact he seems to have found her consistently annoying throughout their service together.*

Jurgen and I trotted up the boarding ramp. I returned it casually, threading my way between two rows of Chimeras which had been neatly parked and secured. Absently I noted in passing that they'd been turned to face the exit, ready for a rapid deployment, and nodded approval. If nothing else the woman was efficient.

'This is a pleasant surprise.'

'I might say the same,' I said, as diplomatically as possible. 'I thought fifth company was taking point this time.' Each of the four infantry companies would normally take it in turns to be first down, officially so that none of them would hog the glory of being first into combat every time, and rather more pragmatically so that none of them would suffer significantly higher attrition rates. That would be bad for morale and would degrade the unlucky company's overall efficiency as it absorbed a higher than average number of fresh recruits.[1] Third company, our logistical support arm, would normally wait until the landing zone was properly secured.

Sulla shrugged. 'Something's gone wrong with their lander. Tech-priests are still taking a look at it.' I craned my neck past the line of vehicles, catching a

---

1. *Like most Guard units, the 597th returned to their home world every few decades to replenish their ranks; in the meantime a steady trickle of fresh troopers was provided by the Munitorum recruiting stations back on Valhalla. Thanks to the inertia of the Administratum and the fact that they were originally formed by the merger of two severely depleted regiments, they were fortunate enough to receive double the usual allocation of fresh soldiers, no one in the upper echelons of the munitorium having noticed that the 296th and 301st no longer existed. This bureaucratic quirk not only accounts for the regiment remaining at full strength throughout Cain's association with it, but also the fact that the numbers of male and female troopers stayed roughly equal.*

glimpse of white-robed figures scuttling around through the open cargo door. 'It'll take forever to offload everything, so they're sitting tight until it's fixed.'

'And this was the next shuttle due to go,' I finished.

Sulla nodded eagerly. 'Lucky for us, eh?'

'Quite,' I said, passing through the bulkhead and into the passenger compartment.

Contrary to what you may be thinking, the first thing which strikes you on boarding a fully-loaded dropship is the smell. Having Jurgen around for so long had given me an unusual degree of tolerance for such things, but two hundred and fifty troopers cooped up in a confined space can thicken the atmosphere nicely, let me tell you. Especially when they're Valhallans in what to most people would be a mildly warm environment, and nervous to boot. As I walked up the aisle between the rows of seats and crash webbing I had to fight to keep my face straight.

The second thing you notice is the noise, a murmur of conversation in which little or nothing can be distinguished, but which is loud enough to drown out anything being said to you unless you can see the lips of whoever you're trying to converse with. Nevertheless, I made a point of catching the eyes of a few random troopers as I passed and spouting off a few platitudes about honour and duty, and the mere fact that I seemed to be bothering started to spread little ripples of calm and reassurance throughout the shuttle like small rocks dropped into a pond. Wherever I looked I saw men and women holding on to their kit-bags, checking lasguns and dipping into their primers for inspiration or amusement. A few hardy souls were slumped in their restraints, getting a little extra sleep, or pretending to, which I suppose is one way of keeping the gribblies[1] at bay.

I managed to ditch Sulla as we passed her platoon and she dropped into her seat, and I settled into my own at the front of the passenger compartment, close to the door of the cockpit. I didn't anticipate having to go up there, but since our abrupt arrival on Simia Orichalcae I'd got into the habit of sitting close enough to the flight deck to be able to intervene in person if the pilot got jittery.

'Commissar.' Captain Detoi, the company commander, nodded a polite greeting and resumed discussing administrative trivia with his subaltern. I returned it and fastened my crash webbing. A moment later a faint vibration transmitted itself through the hull and the frame of my seat and I aimed a reassuring smile at Jurgen.

'We're on our way,' I said. He nodded, his knuckles white. There was very little in the galaxy which seemed to perturb him, but travelling by shuttle or atmospheric flyer most definitely qualified. I found it mildly ironic that a man who'd stared into the faces of necrons and daemons without flinching could be so thoroughly put out by something so mundane, but I guess everyone has their weak spot. Jurgen's was a tendency to motion sickness, which made itself manifest every time we hit atmosphere. Fortunately he generally breakfasted lightly before a drop, seeming to feel that throwing up in front of the rest of the troopers would undermine the dignity expected of a commissar's aide.

The familiar lurching sensation in the pit of my stomach told me that we'd dropped clear of the troopship at

---

1. *Nerves, persistent worries. One of the many Valhallan colloquialisms Cain acquired during his long association with the natives of that world.*

last, and a moment later the main engines ignited, nudging me gently in the small of the back.

With nothing better to do, I thought I might as well get whatever rest I could and closed my eyes, only to be roused a few moments later by what at first I took to be the usual buffeting which always shakes a shuttle entering an atmosphere.

'Commissar.' Detoi was shaking me gently by the arm. 'Sorry to disturb you, but I think you should hear this.'

'Hear what?' I asked, the palms of my hands beginning to tingle, as they often do when things are about to go horribly wrong. By way of an answer he tapped the comm-bead in his ear.

'Open channel D,' he suggested. I raised an eyebrow. That was the Tallarns' assigned command frequency and normally we'd have no business monitoring it.

'I wanted to know how their deployment was going, so they wouldn't be getting in our way once we got down.' Detoi seemed completely unabashed, clearly having formed as low an opinion of the desert fighters as the rest of us. At least they'd be stuck on the other side of the planet once we deployed, though, so that would be something.

'And?' I enquired, retuning my own unit as I spoke.

Detoi flipped a strand of lank blond hair out of his eyes. 'Most of them have cleared the starport. But the stragglers seem to have run into some kind of trouble.' By this time I was able to hear for myself and was forced to agree with his assessment. It sounded as though Asmar's command team and a fair few others were in the middle of a firefight. Who with, though, was anybody's guess.

'Better prepare for a hot drop,' I said, and Detoi nodded. While he began issuing orders I retuned the comm-bead to the starport control frequency, which seemed to be choked with panicking voices.

'Say again?' Our pilot sounded incredulous, always a bad thing in a Navy veteran with Emperor knows how many combat drops to his credit.

A quavering voice, unsteady with stress, responded. 'I repeat, abort your landing. Remain circling until we know what we're dealing with.'

'Frak off.' My relief at the pilot's pithy response was profound. If we followed that instruction we might just as well be towing a sign saying 'shoot me down now.' Our best chance was to hit the ground fast, where we could deploy the troops and find something for them to shoot at.

'You will comply, or face charges.' The voice sounded on the edge of breaking; no doubt whoever it belonged to was having a very bad day. Well tough, I was about to make it worse. I cut into the channel, using my commissarial override.

'This is Commissar Cain of the 597th,' I said. 'Our pilot is acting with the full authority of the commissariat. We are landing, and any further attempt to prevent us from engaging the enemies of the Emperor will be regarded as treasonous. Is that clear?'

'Absolutely,' the pilot agreed cheerfully. Words apparently failed the traffic controller, as transmissions from the tower suddenly went dead. 'Better hang on back there, we're going in hard and fast.'

'Acknowledged,' I said, making sure my crash harness was fully fastened and cutting into the general comm-net to warn everyone else to take the same precaution. Jurgen was looking even less happy than usual, so I checked his too, just as the dropship lived up to its name and began a vertiginous plunge towards the planet below. 'Any idea what the problem is?'

'The Tallarn command team and one of their platoons is pinned down here,' Detoi said, producing a data-slate on which a plan of the starport was displayed. 'They seem to have been ambushed as they left the main cargo handling area.'

I studied the plan. It was a good site for an ambush, there was no denying that. The Tallarns were pinned between the perimeter wall and a complex of warehouses, which would split them up and force them into a series of freefire zones if they tried to break out. I tapped the line of the wall.

'Why don't they just blast through this and retreat across the landing pads?' I asked.

Detoi shrugged. 'It's thirty metres high and ten thick. It's supposed to contain the explosion of a shuttle crash. Nothing they've got could even dent it.'

'Great,' I said. That meant if we came down on a pad ourselves we couldn't go to their aid without being bottlenecked by the same gate they'd been ambushed at. We'd blunder straight into the same trap. But my high-handed dismissal of the starport drone had committed us. By now the news that the celebrated Commissar Cain was on his way to rescue the stranded troopers would most likely be halfway round the city, so leaving Asmar and his men flapping in the breeze wasn't an option. Not if I wanted to stay on the lord general's invitation list at any rate, and being permanently deprived of his chef's cuisine would be a severe blow, so I had to think of something else fast. I scanned the surrounding terrain. 'What's this?'

'It's a monastery,' Detoi said, looking puzzled. He pulled up some data on it. 'The Order of the Imperial Light.' A faint grin appeared on his face. 'Rather ironic, considering the local conditions.'

'Quite,' I said. 'What's this around it?'

Detoi shrugged. 'Vegetable gardens, according to the plan of the city in the briefing slate. Didn't you read it?'

I hadn't, having found better things to do with my time aboard the *Emperor's Benificence* (which generally involved a pack of cards and other people's currency).

'Open ground, in other words.' Well, relatively open. I relayed the co-ordinates to our pilot, who received them with undisguised enthusiasm. 'I think we've just found our drop zone.'

'Works for me,' Detoi said. He switched frequencies again, to our general command channel. 'Listen up everyone, we're hitting dirt in two. It'll be hot, so look alive.' A flurry of activity broke out across the passenger compartment as troopers donned their helmets and snapped fresh power cells into their lasguns. In deference to the temperatures we expected to find when we landed, they'd left their greatcoats and fur hats in their kitbags, but most, I was relieved to see, had kept their flak armour on through force of habit. That was good. It showed they were still on the ball despite having expected a routine deployment. Whatever was waiting for us on the planet below was in for a big surprise, I reflected grimly.

Come to that, so were the monks. Our shuttle lurched a couple of times, making Jurgen swallow convulsively, then the sudden pressure of the landing thrusters kicking in hit me in the base of the spine. My aide's knuckles whitened even more, although being Jurgen it would probably be a little more accurate to say they became a paler shade of grey. Then the whole hull shook, a couple of deafening bangs and a metallic screech echoed through the passenger compartment, and we came to rest.

Loud metallic clangs and a rush of cool, sweet air told us the boarding ramps were down, and with a roar like surf crashing on a beach, second company rushed to meet the enemy.

THREE

'Incoming fire has the right of way.'
                    – Old artilleryman's maxim

MY FIRST IMPRESSION on leaving the shuttle was one of
confusion, although to the credit of the troopers they
all snapped into their immediate action drills as
smoothly as if we were on exercise. Squads of them
were fanning out, looking for trouble, ignoring a
herd of squawking crimson-robed anchorites who
were milling around as though the sky was falling
(although, to be fair, I suppose from their perspective
it just had). I could only hope they'd all had the presence of mind to run as soon as the shuttle appeared
overhead instead of standing there waiting to be

squashed like the rather unpleasant pulpy thing I'd just put my boot through.[1]

'Third platoon mounted up and ready to go,' Sulla reported, as a roar of engines heralded the appearance of half a dozen Chimeras which bounced down the port aft loading ramp and made a terrible mess of what was left of the crop we'd just landed on. Her head and shoulders were visible protruding from the turret of her command vehicle, easily distinguishable from the others by the cluster of vox antennae on top of it, and she waved cheerfully as she caught sight of me and Detoi. I raised a hand in return, though more to forestall any precipitate action on her part than to be social, and glanced at the captain's data-slate again.

'The hostiles appear to be concentrated here and here,' he said, bringing up icons to indicate their positions, and I nodded. The Tallarns were still boxed in, but making a fight of it for all that, and the messages we were receiving on their tac frequency were a good indication of where the enemy, whoever the hell they were, had set up their firing positions. 'They've called for reinforcements, but the bulk of their forces left by the main gate, so...'

'They're still at least twenty minutes away,' I finished, and Detoi nodded.

They could shave a good five minutes off that by cutting straight across the starport, of course, but they'd run straight into that damn gate and just make sitting

---

1. *Probably a local vegetable known for some reason as a 'squinch' which remains a popular crop on Adumbria, though more for the fact that it's one of the few edible plants capable of surviving in the perpetual twilight than that it's actually palatable. Medicae records for the district show no fatalities among the anchorites, although several were subsequently treated for minor injuries apparently related to treading on hastily-discarded gardening tools.*

ducks of themselves. I considered the layout of the streets, and could tell by the faint grunt of satisfaction he emitted that Detoi had come to the same conclusion as I had.

'We'll take them here and here,' I said, indicating the two main streets the heretics had effectively turned into shooting galleries. It was a fair bet that they'd set up their trap intending to butcher any Tallarns trying to break out, and that they'd be completely unprepared for a counter-attack in the opposite direction.

The captain nodded. 'We'll need to secure the flank too,' he pointed out. I concurred, having already seen the danger. If they became aware of our forces approaching from behind they might try to break away to the left, into the city, before being caught between us and the Tallarns. The other way was effectively blocked to them by the wall of the starport, which was actually working for us in this instance.

'Send Sulla,' I suggested. 'Her people are ready to go.' The flanking force would take a couple of minutes longer to reach their objective, so it made sense to send the platoon which was already mounted up and ready to roll. More to the point it would keep her sidelined, I hoped, where her tendency to reckless bravado would have less chance of getting somebody killed.

'Works for me.' Detoi nodded crisply and transmitted the data from his slate. 'Third platoon, secure the flank. First and fifth, you've got the main boulevards. Second, take the side streets by squads, sweep up anyone trying to get past our main thrust. Fourth, secure the perimeter, don't let anyone out who isn't one of ours until the noise stops. Hold anyone who looks like a civilian for questioning, shoot anyone bearing a weapon. Any questions?'

He was good, I had to give him that. The platoon commanders acknowledged, a faint note of disappointment just discernable in Sulla's voice, and Detoi turned to me.

'What about you, commissar?'

'I'll take the flank,' I said, having considered my options carefully, raising my voice above the howls of third platoon's Chimera engines as they ploughed their way out of the monastery garden. There was no sign of a gate, but then there wasn't much left of the wall either, the minor earthquake caused by a couple of kilotonnes of dropship impacting the ground having taken care of that quite nicely. Most of the shrine appeared to be intact, though, which I was pleased to see, as hacking off the ecclesiarchy tends to lead to more doleful sermonising than I care to sit through. The tracks of Sulla's command vehicle bit into the rubble and scattered it, and then she was gone, her quintet of squad transports bouncing in her wake.

Detoi looked doubtful. 'If you're sure that's wise?' he said.

'I am,' I assured him. 'Sulla's a good officer, but inclined to be impetuous.' He nodded, all too aware of this tendency. 'I'm not saying she might do something rash, but it's vital she holds position in case the enemy bolts. Knowing I'm around might prove to have a moderating influence.' More to the point, it was going to be a great deal safer sitting things out on the flank than it appeared, if our assessment of the enemy's state of preparedness was wrong. Charge headlong down a narrow fire lane? Not if I could avoid it.

'You'll need to move fast to catch up,' Detoi said, clearly conceding the point.

'Not a problem,' I said, tapping my comm-bead. 'Jurgen. We're moving out.'

By way of an answer the roar of a powerful engine echoed from inside the cargo hold and a Salamander bounced down the exit ramp, slewing between the Chimeras like a predator among grazers. Jurgen swung it to a halt beside me, raising a spray of mud and vegetable slime which caused the nearest monks to dive for cover just as they'd plucked up the courage to approach us and ask what the hell was going on, and crushing what remained of a small greenhouse to splinters under its tracks.

'Right here, commissar,' he said, phlegmatic as always, only a faint grimace that might have been the prototype of a smile betraying his relief at being back on terra firma.

'Good,' I said, clambering into the rear compartment and checking the pintle-mounted bolter I normally try to ensure is fitted to whatever vehicle is assigned to me. It might not seem like much, but the extra firepower has saved my neck on more than one occasion, and if nothing else it lets me look as though I'm doing something positive while getting away from trouble as fast as possible. 'We're attaching ourselves to third platoon.'

'We'll catch them,' Jurgen promised, gunning the powerful engine and sending the little scout vehicle hurtling in pursuit with all the alacrity of a startled pterasquirrel. Inured by years of experience to his unique and enthusiastic driving style I kept my feet, striking a heroic pose at the bolter for the benefit of the troopers who had still to mount up.

'I don't doubt it,' I said, clinging a little harder to the pintle mount as we bounced over the line of rubble which used to be a wall, and made the easier going of the street.

It was only then that I had time to take stock of our surroundings and got my first good look at the capital of Adumbria.

My first impression was one of gloom, which was hardly surprising given the perpetual twilight which held sway here. The buildings seemed to hang low over our heads, deep shadows falling between them, accentuated by the warm glow of light from a few of the windows. It was only as I got used to the conditions here that I came to realise that most of them were as elegant and well-proportioned as those of any other Imperial city, and that it was merely the endless evening which produced that illusion.

The streets seemed surprisingly empty until I checked my chronograph and realised that, despite the half-light which pervaded everything, it was the middle of the night according to the local custom.[1] That was something anyway; there would be fewer civilians around to be caught in the crossfire. Come to that, anyone still in the area after hearing the all-too-obvious sounds of battle in the distance was probably involved in the insurrection in any case, so we wouldn't have to worry much about collateral casualties. My spirits lifted at the thought; every innocent servant of the Emperor killed by mistake diminishes the whole Imperium, and, more to the point, would dump a pile of extra paperwork on my desk.

'There they are.' Jurgen accelerated past a startled-looking local praetor on a motorcycle who seemed commendably, though foolishly in my opinion, eager

---

1. *Since ambient light levels were completely unchanging wherever you were on the surface, the Adumbrians had adopted a local convention of sleep and work periods which held true for the entire world, thus avoiding the shifting time zones common to most inhabited planets.*

to investigate the source of the disturbance, and I waved casually as we moved ahead of him. No doubt the sight of a clumsy-looking armoured vehicle overtaking him, let alone one with an Imperial commissar in the back, was something of a shock, but the scout Salamander wasn't my vehicle of choice for nothing. Its powerful engine gave it a respectable turn of speed which, allied with Jurgen's formidable driving abilities, could get me out of trouble almost as fast as my reputation could get me into it in its more inconvenient moments.

Fortunately, there seemed to be little other traffic and most was moving in the other direction at speeds which would no doubt have attracted the notice of our praetor friend under any other circumstances, but they'd be netted by fourth platoon's cordon before they got much further so I paid them no mind. In any case, I doubted that they'd prove to be anything other than what they seemed: local workers and cargo handlers on the late shift who'd noticed what was going on and were getting as far away from it as possible. A couple of groundcars were pulled over at the side of our carriageway, the dents in their bodywork and the angry expressions of their drivers mute testament to Sulla's single-minded determination to close with the enemy, and I began to think that I'd made the right decision to hold her leash in person.

Jurgen swung us into place at the rear of the convoy, slowing our pace to match that of the Chimeras, and a moment later the praetor howled past us, his siren going. For an awful moment I thought he was going to cut in ahead of Sulla's command vehicle and try to flag her down, which would only result in him becoming an unpleasant stain on the blacktop, but to my relief he kept going, no doubt sticking to his orders to report back on whatever was going on.

'Commissar.' Sulla's voice in my comm-bead sounded surprised and pleased. From this distance I couldn't make out her facial expression as she turned in the turret to look at me, her blonde pony tail fluttering in the wind like a battle standard, but I could picture the toothy grin quite well enough. 'I guess we're about to see some action after all, if you're here.'

'That remains to be seen,' I said levelly. 'But if the heretics break they'll only have one place to go. Making sure they don't get away has to be our highest priority.'

'You can count on us,' she assured me, that cocky tone I'd learned to dread colouring her voice, and I sighed inaudibly. She was going to need watching closely, I could tell.

As we neared our assigned deployment zone the troop transports began to peel off, heading down side streets and through courtyards to take up their positions, and before long our convoy had been reduced to three: Sulla, ourselves, and one squad of troopers.

'This is it,' I said at last, and Jurgen spun the little Salamander on its tracks, slewing us to a halt broadside on, effectively blocking the entire carriageway and swinging the autocannon to point in the vague direction of where the enemy ought to be. Sulla's command vehicle coasted to a halt rather more sedately, a few dozen metres ahead of us, and began to reverse, its engine little more than idling. The troop transport swung sideways to bump over the central reservation, blocking the road in the opposite direction and rotating its turret-mounted bolter to face any oncoming traffic (which fortunately seemed to be non-existent by this time). After a moment, Sulla's driver backed her Chimera neatly into the gap, plugging the entire thoroughfare.

'No one's getting past us,' she said with some satisfaction.

'They'd have to try pretty hard,' I agreed, glancing round at the position we occupied. We were on an elevated stretch of highway, the ground below was a broken wasteland of rubble and discarded refuse. A few fires glowed, betraying the existence of a scavvy[1] tribe or some local equivalent, but other than that there was no sign of life.

'Platoon one ready to go.' A new voice broke into the tactical net, the familiar one of Lieutenant Voss, as cheerful as if he were ordering a round of ales in a bar somewhere. A moment later it was echoed by the rather more restrained report of Lieutenant Faril, commander of fifth platoon, who confirmed that his troopers were ready as well.

'Good. Move in.' Detoi was as crisp as ever. 'The Emperor protects.' I waited tensely, swinging the bolter I still leaned against round to face the direction from which we expected the enemy to come.

'Better disembark the troops,' I suggested to Sulla, and even from here I could see the faint frown of puzzlement on her face.

'Wouldn't it be better to leave them in the Chimera?' she asked. 'In case we have to move in to support the others?' That was the whole point, of course; if they were on foot she couldn't order an impetuous charge on the spur of the moment, but I made a show of considering her words.

---

1. *Marginal members of most hive societies who live quite literally at the bottom of the social order, salvaging whatever they can from the debris which falls from the higher levels. Cain makes frequent allusions to having been a hiveworlder by birth, and certainly possessed an uncanny affinity for tunnels and similar underground habitats, but firm details about his origins remain a mystery.*

'That's true,' I said. 'But we'd only lose a few seconds embarking them again. And if the enemy does try to get past us I want everyone ready.'

'You're right, of course.' She nodded, almost masking her disappointment, and the squad began to deploy, taking up positions behind the vehicles and whatever other cover they could find. I made a point of nodding to Lustig, the sergeant leading them, whose professionalism I knew from long experience that I could rely on absolutely.

'Sergeant.'

'Commissar.' He returned the nod and went about the business of ensuring the readiness of his subordinates with the quiet efficiency I always found reassuring. 'Jinxie, get your people set up on the right. I want overlapping fire lanes with first team.'

'Sarge.' Corporal Penlan nodded and started dispersing her fireteam. Recently promoted in the same round of advancements that had elevated Magot, she was shaping up well as ASL despite the reputation for being accident prone which had led to her nickname. In fact, troopers being troopers, morale in her team was unusually high, her subordinates appearing to believe that she'd attract any bad luck in the vicinity and leave them unscathed.

With nothing else to be done we waited, while the crackle of weapons fire in the distance intensified and my nervousness increased. The signals traffic in my comm-bead told me things seemed to be going well, the first and fifth platoons taking the traitors completely by surprise and the Tallarns gaining fresh heart from our intervention. For a moment I thought things had gone as I'd hoped and they'd be annihilated without involving me at all, but of course I'd reckoned without the fickle workings of chance.

'Contact, moving fast,' Penlan called, and I swung the bolter round a few degrees to bring the rapidly-moving dot in the distance squarely into the sights.

Sulla raised an amplivisor, stared through it for a moment and shook her head as she lowered it again. 'It's just the praetor.'

'And he's got company,' I added, making out a line of equally fast-moving motes a short way behind him.

Sulla snapped the amplivisor back up and tensed. 'Hostiles, closing fast. Prepare to engage.'

Lovely. It was obvious what had happened, of course. The praetor had blundered into the firefight, been spotted, and a unit of the enemy had been dispatched to keep him from reporting back. And now they were swarming down on me.

'Try not to shoot the praetor,' I added. If he had any pertinent information he might as well share it.

By this time he'd drawn close enough to be clearly seen, and his pursuers were beginning to come into focus as well. There seemed to be about a dozen, a motley collection of groundcars and light cargo haulers for the most part, and I began to relax, sure of our ability to take them. Not only did we have them comfortably outnumbered, we had overwhelming superiority of firepower on our side to boot.

'Fire at will,' I ordered, and opened up with the bolter at the line of vehicles beyond the praetor. The others followed suit with enthusiasm and a fusillade of lasbolts arced off into the semi-darkness, glowing brightly as they went. A second later the full-throated roar of the autocannon joined them as Jurgen clambered up beside me to trigger it.

The results were most gratifying, the leading vehicles in the fast-moving convoy breaking and scattering, one of them leaking smoke. The range was still extreme, of course, so we were lucky to hit anything, but these were civilian vehicles rather than the armoured targets we usually shot at, so even a glancing blow would be enough to put them out of commission.

'That'll give them something to think about,' Sulla said with some satisfaction, as the praetor slid to a halt next to us, his face white. I looked down at him and introduced myself.

'I'm Commissar Cain, attached to the 597th Valhallan,' I said, trying to look as friendly as I could. 'If you have any information about what's going on I'd be pleased to hear it.'

'Kolbe, traffic division.' The praetor pulled himself together with a visible effort. 'There's a major disturbance going on down by the starport, some gang fight we think. Our riot squads are responding, but...'

'It's worse than that,' I told him. 'Heretic insurgents have attacked a Guard unit. But it's all under control.'

I hoped it was anyway. There seemed to be a lot more activity at the other end of the bridge than I'd anticipated, and with a shiver of apprehension I realised that each of the groundcars which had been pursuing Kolbe contained several people. It was hard to be sure at this distance, especially in the twilight, but they seemed to be dressed for some kind of carnival. I revised my initial estimate of their strength upwards, trebling it at least. Sporadic return fire began, wildly inaccurate for the most part, but a las-bolt struck the armour plate protecting our crew compartment. I ducked reflexively, dragging Kolbe into more solid cover. 'Jurgen, if you would...'

The autocannon roared again, to be joined by the heavy bolters of the two Chimeras. This gave the heretics facing us serious pause for thought and they scurried for cover with gratifying speed. Gratifying, but worrying. This wasn't the sort of behaviour I'd expected from confederates of the Ravagers, who if my guess about their patron power was right, should have been charging forward obligingly ready to be cut down by our massed firepower.

'We've got them,' Detoi reported suddenly, his voice loud in my comm-bead. 'Complete surprise on both streets. The Tallarns are mopping up the survivors.'

'Good.' That was something at any rate, even though I was aware of the irony; if I'd gone in with the main attack I'd have been safe by now. There was no time for regrets, though, as the heretics seemed to be recovering a bit of courage, and some rather more purposeful fire began to pepper our armour plate. Jurgen responded enthusiastically and it was a second or two before I could reply. 'We're meeting a little resistance out here on the flank.'

'No problem, commissar,' Sulla cut in. 'I'm bringing first and third squads round to flank them.' I was relieved to hear it, if we could keep our assailants pinned just a little while longer we'd have them bottled up nicely.

It was at that point that Kolbe spun round, a bloody crater opening in his chest, and I turned to see a bizarre figure aiming a laspistol into the open crew compartment of the Salamander. It was a young man, the cut of his clothes leaving very little doubt about that. He was swathed in silks of a vivid pink which did nothing for his colouring. He was flanked by a similarly armed young woman with dyed green hair, whose costume seemed to consist of little more than leather straps (and damn few of those), and an elderly gent in a crimson gown clutching a stubber, whose pomade verged on chemical warfare. Other shadowy figures were in the gloom beyond them, clambering up from below the bridge.

'We've been flanked ourselves!' I yelled, swinging the bolter around, but by now they were too close and I couldn't depress the barrel far enough. I dived to one side just as the trio opened fire, but fortunately they lacked any real idea of how to handle a weapon and their shots went wild. I hit the rockcrete of the roadway, rolled by instinct, and came to my feet drawing my trusty chainsword. That might seem a bad choice against guns, but under the circumstances I thought it best. From such a close range I'd have little chance of aiming my laspistol on the fly, and the more I closed the distance the less likely my opponents would be able to either.

By sheer chance I was close enough to bring the blade up, already thumbing the activator as I gained my feet, and took the girl's left leg off at the thigh. She fell, fountaining arterial blood, and giggled. No time to worry about that, people do strange things in extremis after all, and I already had another target – pink boy was aiming his pistol at Jurgen, who had given up on the autocannon and was beginning to bring his standard issue lasgun up to fire from the hip. He wasn't going to make it in time, so I gave him the extra second he needed by lopping his would-be killer's hand off at the wrist, letting the gun fall harmlessly to the ground.

'Oh, yes!' The man was clearly deranged, an expression of ecstasy spasming across his face. 'Again!' Then his head exploded as Jurgen found his aim.

'No! It's my turn!' Greenhair called, slipping in the pool of her own blood as she scrabbled towards me.

She raised her laspistol, but before she could pull the trigger the pomade bomb stepped in between us, raising the stubber.

'Age before beauty, my love.'

'Frak this. You're all insane!' I kicked him in the stomach, sending him sprawling back over the girl, and drew my laspistol with my other hand. A quick burst of rapid fire saw to both of them, and I turned, expecting to see a full battle raging, but it had all gone quiet again. Roughly a score of bizarrely-dressed corpses lay on the rockcrete, most of them bearing the telltale cauterised craters of lasgun wounds. Sporadic firing from the other end of the bridge and the familiar growl of Chimera engines were enough to tell me that first and third squads had arrived and were enthusiastically engaged in mopping up the rest of our assailants.

'How's Kolbe?' I asked, after making sure none of our troopers were down.

The squad medic glanced up at me, her expression impatient, and went back to tending him. 'He'll live. His armour took most of it.'

'Good. We'll need to debrief him.' I glanced at the scattered corpses around us. 'I don't suppose there'll be many of these frakheads left to interrogate.' As if to underline the point, the firing at the other end of the bridge suddenly ceased, and Sulla gave me a cheerful thumbs up.

'All clear,' she reported. 'No casualties.'

'Good.' I was just beginning to relax again when I became aware of a faint rumbling in the rockcrete beneath my feet. I glanced up, back down the highway, and saw a dozen more Chimeras approaching at speed. 'Now what?'

The lead vehicle slowed as it approached and a familiar figure appeared at the top hatch, waving us imperiously out of the way.

'Clear the road.' Beije yelled. 'Our colonel's under attack.'

'Already taken care of,' I told him, stepping out of the shadow of the Salamander so he could get a good look at me and I could savour the expression of pop-eyed astonishment that spread across his face. 'Check your command channel.' He listened to his comm-bead for a moment, his jaw clenching. I smiled. 'No need to thank us,' I added.

Editorial Note:

Given Cain's usual disinterest in the intricacies of the political sit-
uation then prevailing on Adumbria, or indeed anything else which
didn't concern him directly, I felt the following would prove help-
ful in placing much of what follows into some kind of context.

Unlike most popular histories of this kind, it's substantially
accurate, the author having been given access to as many of the offi-
cial records as were deemed fit for public consumption as part of the
planet-wide commemoration of the twentieth anniversary of these
events, and having taken the time and trouble to interview as many
of the surviving participants as he reasonably could.

* * *

From *Sablist[1] in Skitterfall: a brief history of the Chaos incursion* by Dagblat Tincrowser, 957 M41.

THE DEATH OF Governor Tarkus on 245 936 M41 could hardly have come at a worse time, expiring as he did little more than a year before the Great Enemy made their move against us. Indeed it has been suggested by many commentators that this was too fortuitous to have been entirely coincidental, and much time and ink has been expended on fruitless speculation about whether a conspiracy actually existed to assassinate him, who the participants might have been and why no evidence of who to blame has been uncovered in the two decades since. This last fact, in particular, has been seized on by the more rabid of the conspiracy theorists as a kind of proof in itself of their wilder speculations, since they seem to believe that the complete absence of anything concrete to confirm their suspicions merely proves the efficiency of the ensuing cover-up.[2]

Confining ourselves to the incontrovertible, therefore, we should merely note that Governor Tarkus died of what at the time were recorded as natural causes entirely consistent with a man of his advanced years who had a wife and two known mistresses all over a century younger than he was, and move discreetly along.

In most cases of this nature, the succession of his heir would have been a mere formality. Unfortunately,

---

1. *Another Adumbrian dialect word, meaning a state of almost total darkness with a barely perceptible glimmer of light still visible. Adumbrian readers would have found the title a witty play on words, the rest of us merely irritating.*

2. *Or the agents of the Ordo Malleus, who would surely know the truth of this if anyone does.*

Tarkus died without having provided one, provoking a discreet but ferocious free-for-all among the noble houses of Adumbria, a situation exacerbated by the fact that, thanks to almost two centuries of energetic fornication by the erstwhile incumbent, all were able to present candidates with some plausible claim to being related by blood.

In order to prevent the day-to-day business of running the world from grinding to a halt entirely, a compromise of sorts was eventually reached: the highest-ranking member of the Administratum on Adumbria was appointed Planetary Regent, with wide-ranging executive powers, pending the eventual resolution of the welter of claims and counterclaims to the vacant throne. Since the Administratum were doing most of the actual work, this left the situation pretty much as it had been, except that the Regent was expected to refer for approval all matters of policy to an ad-hoc committee made up of all the rival claimants before taking a final decision. Since few of them could be persuaded to agree on anything and most disliked each other intensely, it will be readily appreciated that achieving anything significant became virtually impossible.

And into this quagmire of inertia came the news that a Chaos raiding fleet was about to attack the planet, followed shortly be the arrival of five regiments of Imperial Guard and a squadron of warships.

It would hardly be an exaggeration to say that panic ensued.

FOUR

'If you don't expect gratitude you'll seldom be disappointed.'
    – Eyor Dedonki, *Memoirs of a Pessimist*. 479 M41

'THERE'S NO DOUBT about it,' Lord General Zyvan said, pausing for emphasis and sweeping his gaze around the council chamber. 'The threat to your world is even greater than we feared.' The assembled great and good of Adumbria, or to be more precise the rich and power-ful, which in my experience is less often the same than it ought to be in a fair and just galaxy, reacted pretty much as I'd expected. Some looked as though they'd developed severe indigestion, some went pale and the majority just stared at him with the same expression of bovine incomprehension which I'd seen so often before in people so used to sycophancy that they simply lacked the intellectual capacity to take in bad news delivered in plain language. There were about a dozen of them, all drawn from the local aristocracy so far as I could tell, although what qualification they had other than that to be there was beyond me; the lack of a chin, perhaps.[1]

The only exception was the man chairing the meeting, who had been introduced as the planetary regent; that was a new one to me, but I heard enough to gather that he was in effect the acting governor of this Emperor-forsaken backwater, so I smiled affably at him when he caught my eye. He smiled back and nodded, so either he was a lot less stuck-up than the collection of aristocratic by-blows surrounding us or he was aware of my reputation. Surprisingly, he was wearing the gown of some high-ranking bureaucrat, but at least that meant he had some idea of how things actually worked, so I resolved to keep an eye on him. His name, I gathered, was Vinzand, and being handed the job had come as something of an unpleasant surprise to him, which I found comforting, as in my experience the last people who should be given any real power are the ones who actually want it.

'You're referring to the attack on your soldiers, of course.' He nodded, smoothing back the white hair which still hung thickly around his face and hitching up the arms of his crimson robe, which seemed to be a couple of sizes too big for him. I was incongruously reminded of Jurgen and suppressed a smile, which seemed wholly inappropriate under the circumstances. 'I trust the wounded are recovering well.'

'Fine, thank you,' Colonel Asmar said, scowling at me. I had no idea why he should be so sniffy about having his bacon saved, other than that he might have been embarrassed by feeling beholden to another regiment,

---

1. *The summary of the local political situation was no doubt one of the things he'd neglected to read in his briefing slate.*

but that was just stupid. Under the opposite circumstances we'd have welcomed the assistance, and if he'd
rather have ended up as traitor bait, more fool him. It
went deeper than that, of course, but at the time I didn't
have a clue what was biting him.

'Commissar Cain's timely intervention undoubtedly
turned the tide,' Zyvan said, to my great satisfaction,
and Kasteen grinned at me. We were seated together
with the other regimental colonels and their commissars at a long table along one side of the council
chamber, leaving Zyvan and his staff to take the place of
honour on a small stage in front of the delegates, who
all sat behind data lecterns like a bunch of overgrown
and overdressed schola students. The other Valhallans
were next to us, of course, on our right, then the two
Kastaforean regiments, with Asmar and Beije at the
other end, as far away from Kasteen and I as they could
possibly get. This suited me fine, as it happens.

Vinzand was sitting almost opposite us, where he could
watch the lord general and his own aristocratic parasites
with equal attention, surrounded by low-ranking Administratum drones who seemed to be taking copious notes
of everything said and done. The only other person there
who seemed to stand out was a lean looking fellow in
military attire, a plain grey uniform unornamented by
anything other than rank pins I was too far away to read,
who watched everything with pale eyes of a similar hue to
his clothing.

'There have been protests from the Order of the Imperial Light,' Vinzand said mildly, 'concerning damage to
the fabric of their property and the loss of a great many
squinches.'

Having tasted the things at almost every meal since
our arrival, I felt that to be no great loss, but tried to

look as if I cared. 'Please feel free to convey my strongest regrets to them,' I said. 'But under the circumstances I felt I had no other choice.'

'No other choice?' Beije bristled at me, his face purpling. 'You desecrated a holy shrine! What in the Emperor's name were you thinking?'

'I was thinking that your colonel and his men were about to be butchered by heretics,' I said. 'How could a loyal servant of his divine majesty stand back and let that happen?'

'We would rather have perished than have our survival bought at the price of blasphemy,' Asmar said, his voice censorious.

I fought down a flash of disbelieving anger. 'We'll know better next time,' I said as blandly as I could, and had the quiet satisfaction of seeing his jaw clench at the same time as Zyvan suppressed a grin.

'Our sappers are already over there repairing the damage,' Kasteen put in helpfully, not wanting to miss the chance of giving Asmar another poke in the ribs while she could. 'Perhaps you could spare a few of yours to help them?'

'We have little time for fortifications,' Asmar said, 'other than the citadel of our faith in the Emperor. We do not trifle ourselves with mere physical barriers.'

'Fair enough.' Kasteen shrugged. 'We'll get the priests to bless a few of the bricks in your name if you like.' Her face was so straight even I wasn't sure if she was joking for a moment, and after glaring suspiciously for a second or two Asmar nodded.

'That would be acceptable.'

'Good.' Zyvan nodded. 'Then if we could get back to the main point, it seems we could be facing a war on two fronts. As the raiding fleet approaches, we can expect more attacks from their confederates aimed at hindering our ability to respond.'

'How great a threat are these insurgents?' Vinzand asked.

By way of reply Zyvan gestured towards me. 'Commissar Cain is probably the best man to answer that. He's fought more of the agents of the Ruinous Powers at close quarters than anyone else in my command.'

I stood, shrugging laconically. 'I've had help,' I said, playing up to my reputation for modest heroism and enjoying the ripple of amusement which swept through the room. 'Usually from an army. Nevertheless, I suppose it's true I've seen heretics and their machinations more often than most.' I stepped out from behind the table so that the gormless aristos could see me properly. Most of them looked agog at the prospect of a briefing from a Hero of the Imperium.

'Then I'm sure your observations will prove most enlightening,' Vinzand said in a tone of voice which didn't need to add 'so stop playing to the back row and get on with it.' I began to suspect that there was more to the regent than just a fancy title.

'By all means.' I nodded. 'Chaos cults are insidious, and they can spring up practically anywhere, sucking in the basest and most degenerate specimens of humanity. Their greatest threat, however, is that as they grow they bring in more recruits who may remain unaware at first of precisely what it is they're joining; they may think it's a street gang, a political movement, or a social club for those with a particular kind of sexual deviancy. Only as they grow more corrupted by their patron power do they realise the full extent of what they're now a part of, and by that time the lies and illusions are too strong. They've become damned and they don't even care.'

'Then how do we know the difference?' the grey man in the corner asked. 'We can hardly bring in every social and criminal organisation in the city for questioning.'

'That's a good point, sir,' I said. Even though I still didn't have a clue who he was, he sounded like someone in authority, and he'd had the sense not to speak until he had a specific question. Under the circumstances, I felt it best to be polite. 'But believe me, the problem won't be confined to the city. Chances are the cults will be established in every major population centre by now. If they're showing their hand openly it's because they think they're strong enough not to fear retaliation.'

'Or they're panicking,' Beije interrupted. 'Knowing that the wrath of the Emperor's servants is about to fall upon them–'

'Ought to drive them even deeper underground,' I pointed out mildly. He glared at me and shut up.

The man in grey nodded. 'That much seems evident.' He turned to Vinzand, pointedly ignoring the rabble of aristos. 'I'll need to consult with the Arbites[1] and see if they've noticed anything out of the ordinary.'

'Of course, general,' Vinzand said, and I blessed the impulse to have been polite; this must be the commander of the local PDF. No doubt they'd be as undisciplined as most of their kind, but at least their leader looked as though he knew what he was doing.[2] Vinzand turned to Zyvan. 'Might I also suggest General

---

1. *Having ultimate authority over matters of law enforcement, the Arbites representatives on Adumbria would have access to the relevant records for the entire planet.*

2. *Like most Guard officers, Cain had a low opinion of the average Planetary Defence Force.*

Kolbe liaises with your people too? Your greater experience of these things might well prove helpful.'

'Indeed.' The lord general turned to me. 'Perhaps Commissar Cain could be prevailed upon to make the arrangements, since he and the general already have an acquaintance in common?'

Well you might think I'm pretty dense, but it was only at that point that the coin dropped, and the significance of the general's name became clear to me.

'How is your son?' I asked, hoping my guess was accurate. It was, as it turned out, gently enhancing my reputation for being on top of the little details.

Kolbe senior nodded. 'Recovering well, thank you.'

'I'm glad to hear it,' I said. 'He showed exemplary courage under extremely trying circumstances.'

General Kolbe swelled a little with paternal pride. I was to learn later that his youngest son's decision to join the praetors rather than the military had rankled for some time, and that the incident at the bridge had initiated a reconciliation that both would have been too stubborn to try for under other circumstances, so at least some good had come out of it. (Other than a pile of dead heretics, of course, which always brightens the day.) Out of the corner of my eye I could see Beije all but grinding his teeth at the sight of me hitting it off with yet another high ranker, which made the moment all the more enjoyable.

'Then that's settled,' Zyvan said. 'We'll arrange a joint intelligence committee to pool what information we have. The regent will be appraised of what we can determine at the appropriate time.'

'That's entirely unacceptable,' a new voice cut in as one of the overdressed fops stood up to lean on his lectern. Up until that point I'd almost forgotten they were there, to be honest; it was as if one of the chairs had had the temerity to interrupt.

Zyvan frowned at him, like an eminent tragedian peering over the footlights to try and identify a drunken heckler. 'And who might you be?'

'Adrien de Floures van Harbieter Ventrious, of House Ventrious, rightful heir to the...' A sudden clamour of outrage from all the other parasites drowned the rest of his sentence and continued until Vinzand pointedly called the meeting to order.

'One of the members of the Council of Claimants,' he corrected, and Ventrious nodded tightly, conceding the point.

'For the moment, yes,' he said. 'And therefore entitled to be kept appraised of all that affects our world. Especially in the current dire circumstances. How else are we to reach a swift and effective consensus about what is to be done?'

'A point of order, if I may.' A pale, colourless youth in turquoise hose and a shirt trimmed with fur rose to his feet, his acne flaring with embarrassment. He caught Zyvan's eye and bowed awkwardly. 'Humbert de Truille of House de Truille. Um, I know I haven't been to many meetings and all, but, um, well, aren't there supposed to be, you know, emergency powers and stuff? So the regent can act without convening the council in, well, emergencies I suppose.'

'There are.' Vinzand nodded in confirmation. 'And your point is?'

Humbert flushed even more deeply. 'Well, it seems to me, um, this is sort of an emergency. Shouldn't you, you know, invoke them or whatever? So things don't get bogged down like they usually do?'

'Out of the question!' Ventrious thundered, striking his lectern, while several of the other drones nodded in approval. 'That would strike at the very heart of the reason for the council's existence. How am I...' he corrected himself hastily, 'is the eventual appointee supposed to govern effectively after being sidelined during the biggest crisis our world has ever faced?'

'A lot more effectively than he would after being slaughtered by heretics,' Zyvan said, his voice all the more resonant for not being raised. 'The lad's suggestion should be adopted.'

'Absolutely not,' another periwigged halfwit chimed in. 'House Kinkardi will not stand for it.'

'Nevertheless the proposal has been made,' Vinzand said mildly. 'All those in favour please indicate in the usual way.' The silken rabble prodded at runes on their lecterns, and an ancient hololith sparked into life over the stage, projecting three green dots and a rash of red ones into the air. Zyvan nodded slowly, taking in the result.

'Before you commit yourselves to your final vote, please bear in mind that the alternative is the imposition of martial law. Make no mistake, I have no desire to take so drastic a step, but I will do so if the alternative is to leave our forces hamstrung by a lack of clear leadership.' His voice had that 'damn the plasma bolts' quality again, making several of the councillors quail visibly in their seats. Gradually the red dots began to change to green, although a few remained glaring defiantly red. Looking at Ventrious's face I had no doubt that his was one of them.

'The motion is carried,' Vinzand said, tactfully refraining from gloating at the result. 'Supreme executive authority is hereby transferred to the regent for the duration of the emergency.'

'Good.' Zyvan permitted himself a wintry smile. 'Then if you would be so good as to clear the chamber we can get to work.' A howl of outrage rose from the assembled aristocracy as it suddenly dawned on them that they'd voted themselves out of the loop.

'Gentlemen, please!' Vinzand tried vainly to restore order. 'This is most unseemly. Will the delegate from House Tremaki please withdraw that remark.'

'Allow me.' Zyvan gestured to our table. 'Commissars, would you be so kind as to escort the councillors into the foyer? They seem to need some fresh air.'

'With pleasure,' I responded, and three black-coated figures rose to their feet to back me up. Beije, I noted, was noticeably slower, trailing after the rest of us as we shepherded the aristos out of the room and closed the door on them, abruptly attenuating the noise.

'Good.' Zyvan relaxed for the first time since we'd arrived and sat back in his chair with every sign of satisfaction. 'Now let's hunt some heretics.'

FIVE

*'When the traitor's hand strikes,
it strikes with the strength of a legion.'*

– Warmaster Horus (attributed)

To MY GREAT delight, the extra duties Zyvan had so casually dropped in my lap kept me in Skitterfall for the better part of two weeks, making the most of the equitable temperatures, while Kasteen and Broklaw took the regiment off to our assigned staging area in the frozen wasteland of the dark side. As I'd expected, the troopers were in something of a holiday mood at the prospect of being back in sub-zero temperatures again, and this exuberance manifested itself in a steady stream of minor infractions which kept me busy enforcing discipline and placating a succession of bar owners, praetors, and aggrieved local citizens whose sons and daughters apparently found something irresistible about the contents of a Guard uniform. Fortunately, as always, the ever-reliable Jurgen proved to be an invaluable buffer between me and the more onerous aspects of my job, politely inform-ing most of my callers that the commissar was unavailable and would be dealing with whatever they were upset about at the earliest opportunity.

The positive aspect of all this was that, in the interests of appearing to be both interested and conscientious, I was able to visit a wide selection of bars and gambling dens in the guise of investigating these complaints while my aide dealt with the paperwork, and was thus able to discover a few congenial places to while away my leisure time far more quickly than I might otherwise have done.

Fortunately, by the end of the first week the troops had all been deployed, which left me free to concen-trate on the more important matters of filtering the reports from the joint intelligence committee and tak-ing full advantage of my impromptu recon sweeps. There was no way a single regiment could be expected to hold down an entire hemisphere on their own, so they were being held in reserve at a mining complex close to the equator where the dropships from the *Emperor's Benificence* could, in theory, rush them to wherever the approaching raiders looked like touching down before the invaders got there. Assuming the Tal-larns or Kastaforeans didn't ask for them first, of course; that was a real headache for Zyvan, who kept harrying the rest of our task force to get their act together and join us as quickly as possible in an increasingly terse series of astropathic messages. Five regiments with which to defend an entire planet[1] was

---

1. *He seems to completely discount the PDF, which outnumbered the entire expeditionary force by at least four to one, as an effective fighting force. As later events were to show, this does them a considerable disservice.*

beginning to seem like a bad joke, less and less funny as the punch line got closer.

The Tallarns naturally got the hot side to deal with, and I have to admit I was heartily pleased to see them go. I hadn't encountered either Beije or Asmar since the briefing in the council chamber, but the knowledge that they were the other side of the planet from our own regiment was a great relief. At least the sand-shufflers' abstemious habits meant that they were unlikely to turn up in the bars and bordellos frequented by our grunts, any more than a trooper from the 597th was likely to waste any of their R&R time going to church, so the brawls I'd been dreading never broke out. (At least not with the Tallarns. It went without saying that I was swapping datafiles with my opposite numbers at the 425th Armoured and the two Kastaforean regiments with monotonous regularity. Or I would have done if Jurgen hadn't been keeping on top of it for me, citing the pressing need to collate intelligence reports for the lord general to cover my absence.)

The 425th, to their evident disappointment, were stuck in Skitterfall for the foreseeable future instead of joining our people out on the glaciers, as Zyvan wanted the tanks to defend the capital when the raiders arrived. I couldn't fault his logic, as, at the time, it seemed to be the most likely target for the invaders to strike. The Kastaforeans, too, were deployed around the shadow zone, bolstering the PDF wherever they looked particularly weak (which to my apprehensive mind meant practically everywhere).

As things settled down, however, I began to find the assignment as congenial as could be expected. Whatever state of readiness his men might be in, and time alone would answer that, General Kolbe at least seemed competent enough. True, he'd never seen any actual combat, apart from a few occasions when the PDF had been mobilised by the Arbites to put down the sort of civil disorder that flares up from time to time pretty much anywhere in the Imperium, but he was methodical, incisive and bright enough to listen to advice. It was at his suggestion that we went back through the archives with the benefit of hindsight, trying to see if there was any possible link between some of those previous incidents and nascent cult activity.

'At least if we can find a connection, that'll give us some idea of how long they've been active on Adumbria,' he pointed out.

Zyvan nodded slowly. The three of us, Vinzand and Hekwyn, the senior arbitrator on the planet, were cloistered in a heavily-shielded conference suite in the high-class hotel Zyvan had commandeered as his headquarters. If nothing else the place was extremely comfortable, as befitted his status, and I'd lost no time in grabbing a room for myself there too. After all, I was supposed to be liaising closely with his staff, so it made perfect sense for me to hang around there now that my regiment was half a hemisphere away.

'Up to a point,' he agreed. 'Although it would be safest to assume they've been infiltrating here for a generation at least. Possibly several.' The three Adumbrians looked shocked at that, even more so as I concurred.

'It might be worth checking the starport records for the last century or two as well. Chances are that the local cult was founded by a handful of heretics arriving from offworld.'

Hekwyn, a stocky man with a shaven head and the pallid complexion of most Adumbrians, paled even further. 'That would be millions of names,' he said.

Vinzand nodded. 'Possibly as much as a billion,' he agreed drily, with the indifference to large numbers common to Administratum functionaries. He made a note on his datapad. 'I'll have my staff look into it. But frankly I'm not hopeful.'

'Neither am I,' I admitted. 'But right now we're critically short of hard data. Even a shred would help.'

'I'll have my people follow up from their end,' Hekwyn offered. 'We monitor the cargo areas closely, checking for contraband. It's possible we might have netted a heretic or two along with the smugglers.'

'Excellent.' Zyvan nodded. 'Any leads from your street sources?'

Hekwyn shrugged. 'Vague at best. There have been a few incidents, gang fights and the like, but if there's an agenda behind it the pattern's hard to read.'

'I'll take a look at it,' I said. My years of paranoia have given me the ability to sometimes see connections that others with a less finely honed survival instinct might miss. I turned to Kolbe. 'Any unusual incidents involving the PDF?'

'If you mean have we been infiltrated, nothing's come up so far to suggest that.' His voice was level. 'But given the amount of time these heretics may have been active we have to assume that cultists have penetrated the command structure.' My respect for the man rose even more. Most PDF commanders in my experience would have been outraged at the idea, vehemently denying the possibility and refusing to allow a proper investigation.

'I meant have any of your units come under attack?' I said. Since the strike against the Tallarns four days ago we'd been braced for more similar incidents, but the second boot resolutely refused to drop. Of course we'd tightened security since then, so the heretics wouldn't find so soft a target again, but somehow I thought that was unlikely to deter them. With the Guard regiments on a state of alert and the PDF providing a plentiful supply of easy targets spread out across the entire shadow zone, they ought to be next in the firing line by any reasonable logic. Of course reason and logic aren't exactly high on the entry requirements for a Chaos cult, so second-guessing them is never going to be easy, unless you're as bonkers as they are.

Kolbe shook his head.

'Since you've raised the matter,' Zyvan said mildly, 'what precautions are you taking against infiltration?'

'We're running thorough background checks on every officer, starting at the highest level and working back down the chain of command.' He essayed a wintery smile. 'I'm pleased to report that so far I appear uncompromised.'

'And who investigated the investigators?' I asked, the palms of my hands beginning to tingle as a bottomless spiral of mistrust and suspicion began to open up beneath my feet.

Kolbe nodded. 'A good question. So far they've been investigating each other, two teams independently verifying the loyalty of a third. It's not infallible, of course, but it should go some way towards preventing fellow cultists covering for one another. If there are any there in the first place, of course.'

'Of course. And in the meantime they've got us chasing our own tails, diverting Emperor knows how many resources and man hours...' I broke off, suddenly sure that this was the main reason for the cultists alerting us to their presence by attacking the Tallarns in the first place. But if that was their agenda, we had to go along with it; any other course of action would be impossible. I voiced my suspicion and Zyvan nodded.

'I'd come to the same conclusion.' He shrugged. 'But that's Chaos for you. A hidden agenda in even the most irrational-seeming action.' He sighed in irritation. 'Why is there never an inquisitor around when you actually need one?'[1]

I kept quiet at that remark, having discovered more about the Inquisition and its methods than I'd ever wanted to know, since becoming Amberley's occasional cat's-paw, but reflected that just because you can't see them it doesn't necessarily mean they're not there. A thought which brought little comfort, stoking as it did the sense of paranoia that had already got me in its grip.

'We'll just have to do the best we can with what we've got,' I said, unsure as ever just how much Zyvan knew about my tangential activities as a reluctant agent of the Inquisition. He must certainly have been aware of the personal relationship between Amberley and myself, and he was definitely astute enough to realise that it probably went further than the merely social, but had never asked and I wasn't about to volunteer the information.[2]

'Quite so.' Zyvan stood and stretched, walking around the conference table to the small one at the side of the room holding a pot of recaff, some tanna tea for me (which nobody else would touch, but he knew my fondness for the stuff and was considerate like that) and a selection of snack foods. It was a common enough thing for him to do, especially as the conference had

---

1. *Not entirely true, as our earlier encounter on Gravalax quite clearly demonstrates.*

2. *Zyvan was wise enough to know that there were things he didn't want to know, and to direct his gaze accordingly.*

already been going for over an hour, but this time it was to save his life. 'Can I get anything for anyone else while I'm up?'

Before I could ask for some fresh tanna, the sludge at the bottom of my cup having turned unpalatably tepid, the window erupted in a hail of bolter fire which shredded the seat the lord general had vacated a moment before. I dived for cover, heedless of the shower of glass splinters still falling all over the room, knowing the explosive projectiles would wreak havoc with any of the furnishings I might seek refuge behind. The only option was the wall itself, beside the shattered window, and I flattened myself against it, drawing my faithful old laspistol as I did so.

I didn't have to wait long for a target. A rising whine outside the building abruptly terminated in a *crump* of impact which left my ears ringing, and the nose of an aircar ploughed through the gap of the window frame, wedging itself fast. It was an open-topped model, I noted absently, the interior luxuriously appointed in furs and fine leather, the metal of its bodywork filigreed with gold decoration, mangled beyond recognition by the impact with the side of the hotel. The driver slumped over the brass handle of the grav regulator as I shot him through the head, making a real mess of his elaborate coiffure, and his front seat passenger bounded over the wreckage like a man possessed, brandishing the bolter.

I looked round for my companions, but only Zyvan and Kolbe were reacting, both drawing bolt pistols and seeking a target. Vinzand was huddled in a corner, his face a bloodless mask of shock, and Hekwyn was down, bleeding heavily from the stump of where his left arm used to be.

'Help him!' I shouted, and the paralised regent moved forward to try and stem the flow of blood before the arbitrator expired from shock. I had no more attention to pay to either, though, as bolter boy brought up the cumbersome weapon as smoothly as if he were wearing Astartes armour. I fired, the las bolt blowing a bloody crater in his bare torso and obliterating a tattoo which had made my eyes hurt. I expected him to drop, but to my astonishment and horror he just kept coming, giggling insanely.

'Frak this!' I dropped and rolled as he aimed the bolter at me, staying ahead of the stream of explosive projectiles by a miracle as they gouged a line across the wall. The firing abruptly ceased with the bark of two bolt pistols almost simultaneously; the man with the bolter seemed to explode, spraying bloody offal around the room and doing the expensive wallpaper no favours at all. 'Thank you,' I added for the benefit of the two generals, and drew my chainsword to meet the charge of the rear seat passengers, who had spent the second or so it took to dispatch their comrade clambering over the driver's corpse. A space this confined was no place for firearms in a general melee, the chances of hitting a friend instead of a foe far too great.

Not a consideration for the heretics, of course, who all seemed completely out of their skulls to begin with, on 'slaught unless I missed my guess, the distended veins in their flushed faces being a dead giveaway. I sidestepped a rush by a woman naked except for a leather mask, gloves and thigh boots, and kicked her in the back of the knee, bringing her down just as she aimed the stubber in her hand at Zyvan. No time to worry about her after that, as a fellow built like a Catachan in voluminous pink silks swung a power maul at my head. I ducked it, blocked with the chainsword and took his hand off at the wrist. By luck or the Emperor's blessing the maul kept going, pulping the head of the stubber girl as she rose to her feet, and I spun round to take the third assailant in the midriff, a willowy youth of indeterminate gender in a flowing purple gown and far too much makeup.

He or she came apart in the middle, giggling gleefully and scrabbling forward on blood-slicked hands, trying to recover the laspistol that had fallen to the floor as they dropped. I kicked out, driving the sundered torso back, my boots slipping in the spreading lake of blood, but even enhanced with combat drugs, the human frame can't last too long in that state: the eyes rolled back in their sockets and after a few more twitches the hermaphrodite lay still.

Which left only one, the muscleman in pink. Catching a flicker of movement out of the corner of my eye I ducked, drove my elbow back into a midriff which felt like rockcrete, and reversed the humming blade in my hand to stab backwards under my own armpit. It spitted him nicely, opening up his entire ribcage as I withdrew the blade and turned, swinging the weapon to take his head off. This was a bit of a grandstanding gesture, to be honest, but probably necessary for all that. I'd seen before what 'slaught could do, and it was quite possible the fellow would have continued to fight until he bled to death in spite of his wounds.

'Commissar!' Zyvan called, from over by the door, and I looked up to see the other four on the verge of leaving the room. Gradually it dawned on me that the whole fight had been over in less than a minute. 'Are you all right?'

'Fine,' I said, as nonchalantly as I could, holstering my weapons. 'How's Hekwyn?' Not that I cared particularly, but it wouldn't hurt my reputation to seem more worried about someone else now that I was safe again.

'Vinzand's stemmed the bleeding.' Zyvan was looking at me oddly, and for a moment I wondered what I'd done. 'I'll be recommending you for a commendation for this.'

'Absolutely,' Kolbe chimed in, while I tried to mask my astonishment. All I'd done, as usual, was try to save my own neck. 'I can see your reputation for selflessness is richly merited. Holding them off single-handed like that, so we could attend to Hekwyn...' So that was it. My impulse to seek shelter by the wall had put me between the heretics and the others, and they thought I'd done it on purpose.

I shrugged as modestly as I could. 'The Imperium needs its generals,' I said. 'And you can always get another commissar.'

'Not like you, Ciaphas,' Zyvan said, using my given name for the first time. That was truer than he knew, of course, so I just looked embarrassed and asked after Hekwyn again. He was looking grey, even for an Adumbrian, and I was mildly relieved to see a medic among the squad of Zyvan's personal guard who were doubling along the corridor towards us, hellguns at the ready.

'You can stand down,' I told them. 'The lord general's safe.' No point in not gently underlining my supposed heroism while I had the chance.

The Guard commander looked a little embarrassed, having taken almost two minutes to respond to the first sound of gunfire, but the hotel was huge and Zyvan had insisted on seclusion for our conference, so I suppose it wasn't really his fault. In any event, he made up for it by dispatching Hekwyn to the medicae with commendable promptness and insisting that Vinzand went too: by now the regent was showing signs of shock, which I couldn't really blame him for, being a civilian and not really used to this sort of thing.

'How did they get past our security cordon?' Zyvan asked.

The Guard commander had a short, somewhat intense conversation with someone on the other end of his comm-bead. 'They were broadcasting the appropriate security codes,' he confirmed after a moment. Kolbe and Zyvan exchanged glances.

'I suppose that answers the question of whether the PDF has been compromised at any rate,' I put in.

The Guard commander frowned. 'I'm sorry, sir, perhaps I wasn't quite clear. The codes identified the vehicle as belonging to a member of the council of claimants.'

'Find out which one and have him arrested,' Zyvan ordered. The commander saluted and trotted away. The lord general turned back to Kolbe and me. 'This is just getting better and better.'

'It doesn't make sense, though,' I said, the palms of my hands tingling again. We were missing something, I was sure of it. 'If they have someone that highly placed it would be madness to expose them simply to carry out such a risky attack. They must have known their chances of success were minimal.' And that was putting it mildly. Five untrained civilians, however fanatical, could never have prevailed against a roomful of soldiers. True, the death of Zyvan would have crippled our command structure, but even so...

'Clear the building!' I shouted, the coin dropping. This was a diversion, it had to be. The main attack would be somewhere or something else, and the instinctive paranoia jabbering at the back of my skull told me what that was most likely to be. Despite the clear breach of protocol, I shoved the two generals heavily in the small of the back. 'Run like frak!'

'Evacuate the building,' Zyvan said levelly into his comm-bead and started running down the corridor.

After a moment Kolbe followed, with an astonished glance in my direction. I might have felt a moment of satisfaction at the sight, as there are precious few men alive who can say they've given orders to a lord general, let alone had them obeyed, but I suppose he was a bit more inclined to listen given my commissarial status.[1]

As I watched them go, every fibre of my being urged me to sprint after them, or ahead if I could barge my way past in that narrow corridor cluttered with expensive nick nacks on delicate tables, but I forced myself to remain where I was. If I was wrong about the threat I perceived and the whole idea had been to force us out into the open, I'd be running headlong into a trap, and I didn't dare take that chance; despite the risk, I had to be sure. I turned and ran back in to the conference suite.

The room was as big a mess as I remembered, the wreckage of the aircar filling my vision as I clambered over the splintered remains of the conference table, slipped in some spilled viscera and scrambled into the shattered vehicle. The dead driver was in the way, so I grabbed him by the scruff of the neck and pitched him backwards out into space, where he fell the thirty or so floors to the rockcrete below. Belatedly I remembered that Zyvan's entire headquarters staff would be milling around down there by now, and hoped he didn't hit

---

1. *Typically, it doesn't seem to have occurred to Cain that Zyvan was reacting out of the regard he held for him personally.*

anyone, least of all the lord general; that would have been the crowning irony. (As it turned out, he burst harmlessly on a porch roof, so that was all right.)

No point trying to pop any of the maintenance hatches, as the metalwork was buckled beyond all hope of repair, so I thumbed the selector of my chainsword to maximum and sliced through the thin sheeting with a fine display of sparks and a screeching sound that set my teeth on edge. Heedless of the raggedness of the tear and the concomitant risk to my fingers (the real ones anyway), I levered the makeshift flap aside, taking as much of the pressure on the augmetics as I could.

I stared into the engine compartment, my bowels spasming. My guess was right.

'The powercells have been rigged to blow,' I said into my comm-bead. 'Get me a tech-priest – now!' There was no time to run, of that I was certain; I'd never make it out of the building in time. It was even debatable whether I could have made it if I'd fled with the others, who would barely have made it as far as the fire stairs by now.

'This is Cogitator Ikmenedies,' a voice said in my ear, with the flat unmodulated cadences of an implanted vox unit. 'How may I assist you?'

'I'm looking at a timer,' I told him, 'attached to what looks like the promethium flask of a flamer. They've both been taped to the powercells of the aircar which rammed the building. The timer has less than a minute to run.' The wire connecting it to the powercells had been jarred loose by the impact, I noticed with a sudden thrill of horror. If it hadn't been for that it would probably have detonated almost as soon as the heretics hit the building. As it was, the timer was running in intermittent jerks, counting off a few seconds then pausing for a couple before resuming its inexorable march towards zero. 'I need you to tell me how to deactivate it.' For an instant I found myself wondering if the fault would give me enough time to get clear after all, but logic overrode the impulse to flee with the stark truth that doing so would just get me far enough for my shredded corpse to be entombed under most of the building when it collapsed.

'The mysteries of the machine god cannot be lightly revealed to the unconsecrated,' Ikmenedies droned.

I gritted my teeth. 'Unless you want to explain that to him in person in less than a minute that's precisely what you're going to have to do,' I told him. 'Because if I can't defuse the bloody bomb I'm going to use the last few seconds of my life to organise a firing squad.'

'How is the timer powered?' Ikmenedies asked, as tonelessly as ever but with almost indecent haste.

'There's a wire to the powercells. It's already loose.' I reached out a hand towards it. 'I can pull it out quite easily.'

'Don't do that!' Somehow the tech-priest managed to inject a frisson of panic into his level mechanical drone. 'The power surge could trip the detonator. Are there wires leading to the promethium flask?'

'Yes, two,' I said, trying to still my hammering heart and giving thanks to the Emperor that at least I still had two fingers which failed to tremble in reaction to my near-fatal mistake.

'Then it should be simple,' Ikmenedies said. 'All you have to do is cut the red one.'

'They're both purple,' I said, after a moment's inspection.

I heard a muffled curse, then there was a short pause. 'You'll just have to use your best judgement.'

'I don't have any!' I practically shouted. 'I'm a commissar, not a cogboy. This is supposed to be your department.'

'I'll pray to the Omnissiah to guide your hand,' Ikmenedies said helpfully. I glanced at the timer, seeing only a handful of seconds left. Well, a fifty-fifty chance of survival is a lot better than some of the odds I've faced over the years, so I picked a wire at random, wrapped my augmetic fingers around it, took a deep breath, and closed my eyes. For a moment fear paralysed my arm, until the survival reflex kicked in and reminded me that if I didn't do this I was dead for sure, and I tugged spasmodically at it with a whimper of apprehension. It came free surprisingly easily.

'Commissar? Commissar, are you there?'

I became aware of the voice in my ear after a moment and let my breath out in a single gush of relief. 'When you see the Omnissiah, say thanks,' I said, sagging back into the overstuffed upholstery.

'Ciaphas?' Zyvan's voice cut in, concern and curiosity mingled in it. 'Where are you? We thought you were behind us.'

'I'm still in the conference suite,' I said, noticing for the first time that the refreshment table had somehow survived the melee. I clambered out of the aircar and staggered towards it, avoiding the larger pieces of heretic. The tanna pot was still warm so I poured myself a generous mug. 'After all that excitement I feel I could do with some tea.'

Editorial Note:

While Cain was keeping himself occupied in *Skitterfall*, the rest of his regiment had been successfully deployed in and around *Glacier Peak*, a mining town situated conveniently close to the geographical centre of the dark face, or 'coldside' as the Adumbrians succinctly termed it. Since this process had gone as smoothly as could reasonably be expected, the details of it need not concern us here: what is important is that they had seen action unexpectedly early, an encounter which would, with hindsight, prove to be a vital turning point in the campaign as a whole.

As we might have expected, Cain has virtually nothing to say about this, displaying his usual disregard for anything which didn't affect him personally, so I have felt it incumbent upon me to insert an account of the incident from the perspective of an eyewitness. Unfortunately, this comes from the second volume of the memoirs of *Jenit Sulla*, which, as you'll no doubt realise within a sentence or two, is no more readable than the first. As ever I feel I should apologise for including it, but offer the shred of consolation that it is at least mercifully brief.

From *Like a Phoenix on the Wing: The Early Campaigns and Glorious Victories of the Valhallan 597th* by General Jenit Sulla (retired), 101 M42.

THOSE OF MY readers not fortunate enough to have been native to an iceworld, as we were, can scarce imagine the fashion in which our spirits rose to find ourselves once more treading the permafrost which, with every bootfall, would send our blood thrilling with the visceral memory of home. Not that nostalgia was our ruling passion of course; far from it. That, as always, was our duty to the Emperor, which every woman and man of us held so dear, even to the shedding of our own precious blood in his glorious name.

We had not been long in Glacier Peak, a picturesque spot surprisingly little blighted by the shaft heads and hab domes erected by the miners who worked so hard to scrabble a precarious living[1] from the veins of merconium[2] so far beneath our feet, when the chance we all longed for to fulfil that duty came at last.

I was summoned to the command post set up by Colonel Kasteen early one morning (although in the constant night in which we now found ourselves living, such distinctions were all but irrelevant), to find myself entrusted with a mission of the utmost importance. Our

---

1. *In actual fact the work was well paid and highly sought after.*

2. *A naturally-occuring substance most notable for its ability to bond irremovably with almost anything.*

perimeter sensor net was being constantly disrupted by the seismic disturbances of the miners as they went about their work, and, as she gravely informed me, no junior officer seemed so suited to the task of ensuring our security from heretic infiltrators as myself. It is no exaggeration to say that my heart swelled within me to hear so fulsome a vote of confidence from my commanding officer, and I accepted the assignment eagerly.

As can be readily appreciated, this required the undertaking of periodic patrols to check the proper functioning of the sensors, for which the tech-priests assigned to our regiment as enginseers thoughtfully provided us with the appropriate rituals. Despite my natural trepidation that such things were best left in the hands of the duly ordained, they declined to accompany us on our excursions, assuring me that the prayers and data downloads would prove equally efficacious if performed by the highest ranking trooper present, and indeed this proved to be the case. In order to be even more certain of our success in this vital task I took to accompanying each patrol myself, reasoning that as the highest ranking member of the platoon I would thus ensure the greater favour of the Machine God.

And so it was that I found myself present with the women and men of fourth squad in what at the time I took to be a mere skirmish. Only hindsight and the tactical genius of Commissar Cain were to later reveal just how significant that minor incident would prove to be.

My first intimation of trouble appeared as our Chimera came to a halt some half a kilometre from the site of the sensor package we'd been sent to bless, and stood there, its engine idling, for some time. At length, Sergeant Grifen, an experienced trooper who had earned the respect of the commissar (which was no easy task as those of us who had done so could attest), approached me, raising her voice slightly to be heard over the rumble of our engine.

'I think you should take a look at this, L.T.'[1] she said. Knowing that she was unlikely to be perturbed without good reason I followed her, savouring the chill which struck through the weave of my greatcoat as I descended the boarding ramp.

It wasn't hard to see what had so excited her curiosity. A few metres ahead, cutting across our own course, was a twin line of tracks, clearly left by a vehicle of some kind. I commended the vigilance of our driver, for spotting them would have been no easy task in the constant darkness which enveloped us. I stooped to examine them.

'They're heading for the settlement,' Grifen concluded, and I was forced to agree; the constant wind was eroding the marks even as we watched, and over to our left they were all but obliterated already. Time was clearly of the essence: if we were to follow, and follow we surely must if only to assure ourselves of the innocence of these mysterious travellers, we had to set out quickly before their trail vanished before us like smoke in a gale.

A quick call to the command post confirmed that no other units were out here and no civilian traffic had been cleared through our perimeter, so as we commenced our pursuit I urged our women and men to be ready to face

---

1. *A familiar form of address between a senior NCO and the lieutenant commanding them, in the same way that their own subordinates might abbreviate their title to 'sarge'. It seems that whatever Cain may have thought of Sulla she at least had the respect and confidence of the troops she led.*

the enemies of the Emperor. True to form, they were
enthused at the prospect and immediately fell to checking their lasguns and other equipment while our faithful
Chimera closed the distance rapidly.

'There's a light ahead,' our driver reported, an instant
before any doubts we may have had about the intentions
of the vehicle we followed were answered by a pattering
of stubber rounds against the armour of our hull. Our
gunner swung the turret and unleashed a hail of retalia-
tory bolter fire.

Unable to resist seeing for myself what was going on, I
clambered up to the top hatch and stuck my head out,
shielding my eyes from the flurrying snow with the
unconscious ease of reflexes ingrained since girlhood. A
mining crawler stood crippled before us, great rents torn
through its thin unarmoured body, its crew piling out to
engage us with a variety of small-arms. They would no
doubt have proved poor opponents for the doughty warriors under my command, but even as I opened my
mouth to give the order to disembark and engage them
the crawler exploded in a vivid orange fireball which
reduced it to smouldering wreckage in an instant, immo-
lating in the process the heretics who had dared oppose
the Emperor's will.

SIX

'Paranoia is a very comforting state of mind. If you think they're out to get you, it means you think you matter.'

– Gilbran Quail, *Collected Essays*

'THE QUESTION IS,' I said, 'what were they doing out there in the first place?'

Kasteen nodded and handed me a steaming mug of tanna, which I accepted gratefully. 'Carrying weapons, we think. I had Federer go over what was left of the crawler, and he says he found traces of fyceline among the wreckage.' I had no trouble believing that. Captain Federer, the officer in command of our sappers, had an enthusiasm for all things explosive which bordered on the unhealthy and if there were traces of the stuff to be found he would undoubtedly be the man to uncover them. 'He says it looks like the bolter shells penetrated the cargo compartment and cooked off whatever was in there.'

'I suppose it would be too much to hope that just for once Sulla left us some survivors we could interrogate?' I asked, sipping the fragrant liquid and savouring the sensation of warmth it ignited on the way down. I'd just arrived in Glacier Peak, our main staging area, and found it even less inviting than it sounded. Not only was the coldside living up to its name, as I'd steeled myself to expect, the perpetual night was beginning to get to me, and I'd only been there for an hour.

Well, technically at any rate, we'd left the shadow zone some six hours before that, the pervasive gloom I'd got used to in Skitterfall gradually deepening over the preceding two, and I'd grown sleepy as the monotonous snowscape crept past the window. To my thinly-disguised dismay there were no air transports available, and I'd had to make do with a compartment on one of the railway trains transporting miners and their supplies back to the outpost we'd no doubt overrun with our own people.[1]

Despite the three carriages coupled to the rear of the freight wagons being crowded in the extreme, with several passengers being forced to sit on their luggage in the corridor, Jurgen and I were left with an entire compartment to ourselves. At first I thought this was due to the respect our Guard uniforms commanded, but after observing the way the crowd parted whenever my aide

---

1. *In actual fact, Glacier Peak was a fair-sized town, with a population of around thirty thousand. Only about a third of these were directly involved in the mining operation, the rest being made up of storekeepers, tavern owners, and other service sector workers, not to mention the families and dependants of the economically active local citizens. The abrupt arrival of a thousand or so Guard troopers would have had an impact on the community, no doubt, but not the overwhelming one Cain seems to imply. Then again, as the regimental commissar, his perceptions were almost certainly coloured by the inevitable exceptions he would be required to deal with.*

left his seat to use the sanitary facilities I was forced to conclude that this had more to do with his distinctive aroma than it did with my charisma. Used as I was to this, and pleased as I might otherwise have been to have the extra legroom, after eight hours with him in a confined space I was beginning to think they had a point.

The upshot of all this was that by the time I'd arrived at our destination I was tired and irritable, and in no mood to hear that Sulla had taken it upon herself to bag a crawler-full of heretics without bothering to find out what in the warp they were doing out here in the first place.

'All blown to frak, along with the crawler,' Kasteen said. She shrugged. 'On the plus side, I suppose at least that's one batch of weapons the heretics won't be getting their hands on.'

'Assuming they don't have a whole lot more where they came from,' I said.

The palms of my hands were tingling again, but for once I couldn't tell if it was from apprehension or returning circulation. The cold outside was every bit as bone-chewing as I'd anticipated, and chill as it was here in Kasteen's command post, where I could still see our breath puffing visibly with every word or exhalation, it felt almost tropical by comparison. She and Broklaw had their sleeves rolled up to the elbows, and the vox operators and other specialists coming and going were similarly lightly clad.

All, I was pleased to note, still wore their flak armour though, the lord general's strictures on remaining alert still being in effect. (I still had the carapace armour I'd been given on Gravalax concealed beneath my greatcoat, as I generally did whenever things looked like they might get uncomfortable without warning; it was

getting a bit battered by now, but as far as I was concerned that just reinforced the wisdom of forgetting to
return it to the stores in the first place.)

'Quite.' Broklaw nodded, his eyes thoughtful, and kicked
the portable hololith with all the assurance of a tech-priest.
It hummed into life, projecting a topographic recreation of
the surrounding countryside. (I use the word loosely,
although no doubt the Valhallans could appreciate sub-
tleties in it denied to me.) 'I think we can safely assume that
whatever they had planned though, we were the target.'

'Almost certainly,' I agreed. The crawler had been
heading for Glacier Peak, that much was certain, and we
were the only significant military presence there, so it
hardly needed an inquisitor to join the dots.

I gazed at the image, something nagging at the back
of my mind. The ring of red icons around the town
would be our sensor packages, of course, and the thin
line snaking its way through the valleys was the railway
which connected us to the civilised delights of the
shadow zone. There were no roads, as the constant
snow would have rendered them permanently impass-
able, so the ribbon of steel was the only way in or out
apart from the occasional flyer. If you needed to go anywhere else, like an outlying settlement or mining claim,
the only way to do it was by crawler.[1]

'The skirmish happened here,' Broklaw added helpfully, adding a contact icon more or less where I'd

---

1. *Since these are alluded to repeatedly, but never described, in both the
Cain archive and Sulla's scribblings this seems as good a place as any to elucidate. Crawlers were locally manufactured vehicles which came in a variety
of forms, the main characteristic of which was the wide tracks which
enabled them to move reasonably efficiently across snow and ice at a brisk
pace and in as much safety as might be expected under the circumstances.
Most were about the size of a Chimera, the vast majority with enclosed passenger or cargo bays.*

expected it to be. The heretics' intended course was clear enough, following a valley down towards the edge of Glacier Peak, at which point they'd simply have merged into the traffic on the streets and vanished.

'They must have had contacts somewhere in the town,' Kasteen said.

I nodded slowly. 'That seems likely. Even if they were planning to carry out the strike themselves, they'd need somewhere to hole up while they were preparing it. That means confederates.'

'We're liaising with the local praetors,' Broklaw said, forestalling the next inevitable question. 'But so far they don't have much to go on. Not even a missing person report.'

'Outsiders then, almost certainly,' I agreed. 'The question is, where did they come from?' There weren't that many outposts of civilisation on the coldside, and the others were all a long way from here; too far to make the trip by crawler anything other than insanely risky. Of course these were heretics we were talking about, so insanity was pretty much guaranteed, but even so I felt we were missing something.

I tried to trace the path of the crawler back from the point at which Sulla had encountered it, and felt a nagging sense of wrongness about the topography. The valley was broad and long, but surrounded by mountains and with no sign of a pass leading into it. I voiced my concern. 'That looks like a dead end to me.'

'You're right,' Kasteen said, dropping her head to examine the projection from eye level. She glanced at Broklaw for confirmation, seeing in his almost imperceptible nod that he'd reached the same conclusion. 'There must be a cache of weapons out there somewhere.'

'Sounds likely,' I said, unable to think of another explanation. 'Our heretics must have been on a supply run.' The thought wasn't comforting. For the crawler to have blown up like that implied that it was carrying a lot of ordnance, and that in turn probably meant there was a lot more of it out there. Certainly no one would bother taking a single crawler-load out to bury, then bring it all back again in one go. No one sane, in any case. Once again I reminded myself that we were dealing with the minions of Chaos here, and that nothing could be taken for granted.

'Where did it come from in the first place?' Broklaw asked.

I shrugged. 'The starport. Hekwyn said they had a problem with smugglers. The weapons must come in hidden among the cargoes and then cultists in the city distribute them. They probably arrived in Glacier Peak disguised as mining supplies.'

'Not that difficult if you think about it,' Kasteen agreed, pouring herself a fresh mug of tanna. 'There are legitimate shipments of explosives arriving on practically every train.'

'Then we have a place to start, at any rate,' I said, feeling a sudden flare of hope that we might just be getting one jump ahead after all. I turned to Broklaw. 'We need a list of everyone in the mines with access to explosive shipments. And who might have a chance to tamper with them while they're en route too.'

He nodded. 'I'll get on to the Administratum,' he said. 'They should have all the records we need.'

And a lot more besides, if I knew them. 'While you're doing that, I'll contact the Arbites in Skitterfall,' I said, the optimistic conviction beginning to grow in me that the key to all this lay in the planetary capital. With a bit of luck I could find an excuse to be on my way back there by the time the next train left. 'They must have some idea of how this stuff is getting through the starport.'

'It's an elegant theory, commissar.' Hekwyn's head floated in the hololith, nodding pleasantly, as if reluctant to batter my deductions with anything as crude as solid facts. He was looking a lot better than the last time I'd seen him, even allowing for the slight instability imparted to his virtual presence by the equipment. His image was partially overlaid with Zyvan's, since I felt the lord general should be kept informed of the latest developments, and the pair of them looked like some strange piece of two-headed warp spawn. I hit the projector the way I'd seen Broklaw do, and to my vague surprise the images from the two pictcasters separated, at least some of the time, flicking apart and back together at irregular intervals. 'But it's just not possible for large quantities of weapons to be coming through the starport.'

'You told me yourself that you have a smuggling problem,' I riposted, unwilling to let such a neat chain of reasoning go without a fight. The arbitrator nodded and scratched his chin with his new augmetic arm, not quite getting the distance right; I remembered similar problems adjusting to my new fingers back on the Reclaimers' battle barge[1] in the Interitus system all those years before.

'We do. With a port that size it's almost inevitable. But believe me, arms and explosives would almost certainly

---

1. *Cain was attached to this Astartes Chapter as the Imperial Guard liaison officer for a while during his previous assignment at brigade headquarters. His activities during this period are described elsewhere in the archive.*

be detected. In the quantities you describe, they'd be found for sure.'

'I've known psykers pull some pretty slick disappearing acts,' I said, grasping at the last straw I could think of. 'And we are looking for Chaos worshippers. If they've got a witch or two in tow they could walk past your inspectors with a baneblade and no one would notice.'

'Except for our own sanctioned psykers,' Zyvan pointed out mildly. 'I've had a couple posted at the starport ever since we arrived. No one's used any witch talents there, you can be sure of that.'

Great. I watched the best lead I'd been able to construct crash into ruins in front of me, along with my ticket back to somewhere my blood wouldn't freeze. I sighed heavily.

'Ah well,' I said. 'My apologies for wasting your time then.'

'You've hardly done that,' Zyvan assured me, more from politeness than strict accuracy, I strongly suspected. 'It was an astute piece of deduction.' He smiled. 'But I'm afraid even you can't be right all the time.'

'But we're right back where we started,' I said, fighting the impulse to pinch the bridge of my nose. Now that the consuming sense of urgency to communicate my reasoning to the high command had been punctured, the weariness I felt from my journey was beginning to make itself felt again.

Hekwyn scratched his chin once more, a little more accurately this time.

'Not quite,' he pointed out, and Zyvan nodded in agreement. 'We know that your regiment seems to represent a particular threat to them.' I felt a shiver of apprehension running down my spine, already sure of the lord general's next words.

'Precisely. Of all the targets on the planet they could have struck at, they seem to be going to inordinate lengths to prepare an attack on you. Have you any idea why that might be?'

'None at all,' I said, hoping I hadn't answered too hastily. The only thing which made the 597th any different from a million other Guard regiments was the presence in it of Jurgen, whose peculiar gift of nullifying psychic or warp-derived sorceries had saved my life (and probably soul) on a number of occasions. If the heretic cult was aware that there was a blank somewhere on Adumbria, and had psykers among their number, they'd stop at nothing to eliminate so potent a threat, and the chances were that I'd be standing right beside him when they struck. After all, I could hardly start avoiding my own aide (however tempting the notion became when the temperature rose above the moderately warm). Then again, his strange ability was a secret known only to the two of us, Amberley, and presumably at least some in her retinue,[1] and I was damn sure no one on that select little list was in the habit of chatting with heretics.

'Perhaps there's something about the town which is significant to them,' I suggested, partly to deflect the conversation away from this sensitive area, and partly to try and allay my own fears, 'and our presence here is merely incidental.'

'Perhaps.' Zyvan looked unconvinced. 'But we're not going to know until you get some hard evidence.' I

---

1. Only two, in point of fact: Mott, my savant, who would undoubtedly have deduced it for himself if I hadn't told him, and Rakel, who, being a psyker, had most decidedly noticed the fact. Indeed it was her hysterical reaction to Jurgen's presence at our first meeting which had initially piqued my interest in him.

noted his use of 'you' with intense foreboding, but nodded as sagely as I could.

'We're following up all the leads we can,' I said. 'If there's a heretic cell anywhere in Glacier Falls, you can rest assured we'll find it.'

'I don't doubt that for a minute,' the lord general said. 'But it's just as possible that the answer lies elsewhere.'

'I can be back in Skitterfall by tomorrow,' I started to say, but choked myself off after the first syllable as a familiar topographic projection superimposed itself over the two men in front of me. As luck would have it, the wretched machine was keeping their images separate at the time, or the combined interference would probably have rendered the whole thing incomprehensible.

Zyvan gestured at the valley next to the mountain ridge his head and torso were protruding from like some strange geological wart. 'You say that this valley is a dead end.'

Already sure of what was coming next, I nodded numbly, my mind racing to find an excuse and failing miserably. That's what happens when you call senior and influential people without sufficient sleep or recaf, and why I strongly recommend against it.

'It certainly appears to be,' I conceded.

'Then by your own logic there must be some trace of the heretics' arms cache out there,' Zyvan went on cheerfully, while Hekwyn nodded in agreement. 'Possibly more weapons we can trace back to their source.' He shrugged. 'Who knows, maybe even some hard evidence we can use to identify the ringleaders.'

'We can lend you a forensics team,' Hekwyn offered. 'You'd be surprised how many traces people leave behind, even when they think they've covered their tracks completely.'

'Thank you,' Zyvan responded, as though he'd just been offered a cyna bun. 'That would be very helpful. And we can bring in one of our spooks[1] to give the site the once-over too.'

'Assuming we ever manage to find it,' I said, my eyes drawn again to the vast expanse of snowscape represented by the hololithic valley.

Zyvan turned his head to stare straight into the pict-caster. 'You're a remarkably resourceful fellow, Ciaphas. I'm sure you won't let us down.'

Well what else was I supposed to say after that? Frak off, you're out of your mind? Tempting as it was, and don't forget that technically as a member of the commissariat I could have done just that, it really wasn't an option. My fraudulent reputation left me with only one possible response, and I gave it, nodding gravely as I did so.

'I'll get right on it,' I said.

To be honest, the thing I really got right on as soon as I finished my far from satisfactory conversation with the lord general was my bunk, where I remained for the next several hours sleeping off the rigours of the day's journey. Technically by now, I suppose, it would have been the previous day's journey, but the unvarying darkness outside made it hard to keep track, and I really didn't care much in any case. Being an old hive boy I'd grown up believing that light levels (or lack of them) were pretty much constant in any given location, and had found the whole business of day and night something of a wonder the first time I'd found myself on the surface of a planet somewhere; not to

---

1. *An Imperial Guard slang term for sanctioned psykers, less pejorative than most, but still surprising coming from a man of Zyvan's rank.*

mention thoroughly disconcerting until I'd got used to it. So all in all I suppose I found the curious conditions on Adumbria rather less of a strain to adjust to than most of my companions (with the probable exception of Jurgen, who accepted them as phlegmatically as he did everything else).

The result of all this was that by the time I awoke, feeling a great deal better about things and with my aide's distinctive odour wafting into the room laced with the rather more inviting one of fresh tanna, the problem I'd been handed last night seemed a lot less intractable. (Which I like to think proves the wisdom of my course of action. Rushing off to try and organise things while my mind was still clouded with fatigue wouldn't have got us anywhere, or at the very least would have got us to the same place with a great deal more stress and irritation to all concerned.)

'Good morning, sir.' Jurgen's voice joined his odour, and I cranked my eyes open in time to see him place the tray of tea things beside the narrow bed. The room he'd found for me was comfortable enough, as I'd have expected given his almost preternatural talent for scrounging things, but it was a far cry from the standard of luxury I'd grown used to while hanging around in Zyvan's headquarters. (On the other hand, it was a considerable improvement on some of the accommodation I've occupied over the years. Believe me, once you've experienced the hold of an eldar slavers' ship even the most spartan of conditions seem perfectly tolerable.)

'Good morning,' I responded, although the darkness beyond the window was as absolute as ever, relieved only by the faint gleam of arclights in the compound below. The reassuringly familiar sounds of Chimera engines and shouted orders drifted in, even through the double thickness of thermocrys, which at least kept the temperature in here at a reasonable level. 'Any news on the heretic hunt?'

Jurgen shook his head dolefully as he poured the tea. 'No progress to report, sir. Major Broklaw was quite definite on the point when I asked on your behalf.' I could well believe it. Broklaw was a man who'd never seen the point of internalising his frustrations.

'Well, let's see if we can improve his mood,' I said, savouring the first mouthful of tanna. 'The lord general has suggested a rather interesting approach.'

'I'M NOT SAYING it can't be done.' Broklaw stared at the hololithic image of the valley as though wishing he could somehow strangle it. It seemed Jurgen hadn't been exaggerating about his mood; but then, knowing his propensity for literal-mindedness, I'd hardly expected him to be. 'I'm just saying it'll take a long time. Searching an area that size could take weeks, even with an entire platoon on the job. Which we can't spare,' he added hastily, in case I thought that was reasonable.

To his visible relief I nodded. 'I quite agree,' I said. 'Even if we were desperate enough to try it, the chances are the enemy fleet would have arrived here long before we found anything.'

'Then what do you propose?' Kasteen asked levelly. She'd probably had no more sleep than her executive officer, but still managed to project an air of calm authority.

By way of an answer I pointed to the little red dot almost overlapping the contact icon which marked the spot where Sulla had terminated the renegades' journey with such lethal emphasis. 'Sulla was on her way to bless this sensor package, yes?'

Kasteen and Broklaw nodded, not seeing the connection. 'That's right. They've all been malfunctioning since the day we got here.' The colonel looked at me curiously, no doubt wondering if I still needed a few more hours of sleep to clear my brain. 'What with the mining charges going off all the time, and the vibrations from the railway every few hours, I'm amazed we're getting any usable data from them at all.'

'Exactly,' I said, and the two officers glanced at one another, clearly wondering what the procedure was for notifying the Commissariat that my elastic had finally snapped and could they have a sane replacement please. 'And both those things are known events. The mines have records of when their charges were set, and the trains run to a timetable. More or less.'

Expressions of dawning comprehension broke across their faces as they finally realised what had occurred to me in the curious state between sleep and full wakefulness, when the mind makes connections it might otherwise have missed.

'So if we filter out the known interference from the data we've recorded, we might pick up some sign of activity that'll point us in the right direction,' Broklaw said, looking happier than I'd seen him since I'd got up. I nodded.

'We just might,' I said.

Of course it was all far easier said than done, and it took most of our enginseers most of the day to carry out the appropriate rituals. Long before they were finished the drone of their chanting and the choking clouds of incense around their data lecterns had driven all but the hardiest of us from the command centre. Nevertheless, by the evening I was able to report to Zyvan that we'd tentatively identified about a dozen sites where anomalous readings might, just possibly, indicate human activity where no human was meant to be.

'Why did your people miss this in the first place?' he asked, not unreasonably.

I stifled a sneeze, my eyes still sore from the acrid smoke, and tried to look composed. 'They had no reason to look for it. The data was being swamped by other readings, and they were only looking for anomalies on or near the perimeter. Until Lieutenant Sulla ran into that crawler, no one even suspected there might be heretics lurking that far out in the wilderness.'

'Fair enough,' the lord general conceded. Then he smiled. 'I look forward to hearing what you find. I'm sure you're itching to get out there and get stuck in.'

At those words my blood ran as cold as if I was already being exposed to the biting winds that were sure to be howling through the mountain passes, and I suppressed a shiver. If I'd managed to cling to a vestige of hope that I'd be able to stay safe and warm in the command centre while I palmed the dirty work off on some deserving candidate (and I had the perfect one in mind, you can be sure), Zyvan's pleasantry torpedoed it as thoroughly as a battleship swatting a destroyer. If I didn't seem to be leading from the front now I'd lose his confidence, which meant no more bunking up in the lap of luxury the next time I was able to wrangle my way into his headquarters, and no more pleasant social evenings enjoying the genius of his personal chef. So I nodded soberly, like the stoic old warhorse he took me for, and tried not to cough.

'As eager as I always am,' I told him truthfully.

SEVEN

*'The most dangerous thing on the battlefield
is a junior officer with a compass and a map.'*

– General Sulla

GIVEN THE LORD general's personal interest in our little
recon sweep and the number of potential sites we had
to check, I found it easier than I'd expected to persuade
Kasteen and Broklaw to assign a full platoon to carrying
it out, along with our entire troop of sentinels. After all,
we now had a definite mission to complete. It wasn't as
if we'd be wasting our time out there for days on end,
casting around searching for nothing in particular.

After some consideration (or at least the show of it)
I'd picked Sulla's platoon for this assignment. After all,
she'd got us into this mess, so she might as well clean it
up too. Not that she saw it like that of course, prattling

on about how much she was looking forward to gutting more heretics until I felt like strangling her. Feeling that, on the whole, it would be unwise to give in to the impulse, I decided to risk sticking my head out of the Chimera despite the cold – right then pneumonia seemed distinctly preferable to much more of her conversation.

It was my first real view of the coldside, and despite the sensation of having my face flayed by flying razor blades the moment my head cleared the rim of the top hatch I found it curiously captivating. Up until then all I'd seen of it had been from inside well-lit windows, which the all-pervading blackness turned into mirrors, or within the precincts of Glacier Peak. There, of course, the streets were permanently lined with luminators, supplemented by the light spilling from every building, and all that had done was intensify the darkness surrounding them until it seemed the entire town was enveloped in suffocating velvet.

Out here, though, there was nothing apart from the spotlights of our vehicles to get in the way, and I found myself staring at a night sky littered with stars in a profusion I had seldom seen from the surface of a civilised world. They burned, too, with a cold, hard brightness, which struck from the snows all around us, imparting a faint blue glow to our surroundings.[1] So uniform was this illumination that it cast no shadows except in the deepest of crevices, which appeared by contrast to be maws of the uttermost darkness, exuding a sinister fascination; after all, anything could be lurking inside them undetected. As I considered this I caught sight of a flicker of starlight reflecting from the metallic shell of

---

1. *Adumbria had no moon, which no doubt made them appear even brighter by contrast.*

one of our sentinels, keeping easy pace with us and shining its spotlight into each of the crevices we passed, and the knowledge that we were unlikely to be ambushed by unseen lurkers put my mind as much at ease as was possible under the circumstances. And even if we were, I suppose we wouldn't have had too much to worry about; the firepower of the three walkers and second squad's Chimera a score or so metres behind us, would be more than enough to even the odds.

After some consideration, Kasteen had decided to split our recon force into three, in order to minimise the amount of time it would take to check out all the possible sites we'd identified. That had seemed reasonable enough to me: two full squads and their Chimeras, with a squadron of sentinels for backup, ought to be more than enough to handle the handful of heretics we might expect to find out here. And if we were wrong about that, they'd certainly be strong enough to disengage without any problems and keep the traitors pinned for long enough to call in some backup.

Despite the obvious drawbacks, I'd decided to attach myself to Sulla's command squad for the duration of the mission. For one thing there were only five of them, which meant that even with all the extra vox and sensoria equipment cluttering up the passenger compartment there was still a lot more room for Jurgen and myself than if we'd been jammed in alongside half a score of troopers, and for another I thought we might actually acquire some useful intelligence if I was around to restrain her generally commendable impulse to slaughter everything in sight that was not wearing an Imperial uniform. I suppose we could have tagged along in the Salamander, which would probably have helped my mood, but only at the expense of frostbite.

One look at the open-topped vehicle was enough to resign me to Sulla's company as by far the lesser of two evils.

'Rooster one to mother hen,' a voice crackled in my comm-bead. After a moment I recognised it as Sergeant Karta, whose recent elevation to the leadership of first squad had opened the way for Magot's problematic (and probably temporary, knowing her record) promotion. 'Objective two's a bust. Proceeding to three.'

'Acknowledged, rooster one.' Sulla sounded vaguely affronted, as though the heretics were somehow cheating by not coming out to play according to the plan. It was no surprise to me, though; conditions were hellish out here, the landscape unstable, and the first site on our list had turned out to be nothing more than an icefall of quite epic proportions. Our third group, squads four and five, had had no more luck than the rest of us, and the young lieutenant was visibly champing at the bit. (An analogy which occurred quite naturally to me, since her long narrow face bore a distinct resemblance to an irritable horse at the best of times.) I have to say, though, had I realised just how soon her craving for action would be satisfied I would have been considerably less casual about my next remark.

'Stay sharp,' I cut in, more to remind everyone that I was there than because I had anything useful to say. 'Every site we eliminate brings us closer to the real one.' As I spoke I narrowed my eyes against the swirling snow, sure I'd caught a glimpse of yellow light out here where none should be. It could have been nothing, of course, but I didn't get to my second century and an honourable retirement by ignoring the slightest presentiment of danger.

I switched frequencies to the local tacnet, bringing in Sulla, Sergeant Lustig in the other Chimera, and the three sentinel pilots. 'Kill the lights,' I ordered.

'Commissar?' Sulla sounded curious, but the spotlight of our own vehicle went out immediately, as did the one on second squad's transport and the sole sentinel I could still see. I peered through the obscuring flurry of whiteness, seeing nothing for a moment, and had almost convinced myself I'd imagined it when the momentary gleam came again.

'There's something out there,' I said, ducking back behind the armour plate, and regaining the blessed warmth of the passenger compartment. (All right, the temperature had been adjusted by Valhallans, so it was still pretty cool by most objective standards, but after a moment or two outside it felt positively hot.) 'Two o'clock relative, moving slowly.'

'Got it,' the auspex operator confirmed after a moment. 'Big, metallic, heading for town. Doing about forty klom per hour.[1]'

'Captain, if you wouldn't mind?' I asked the commbead.

'My pleasure.' Captain Shambas, commander of our sentinel troop, ordered his squadron into the attack with the gusto I'd come to expect from him. 'You heard the man. Last one to bag a heretic buys the beers. And try to leave a couple alive for the commissar to interrogate.'

'Yes, sir.' His flankers acknowledged, and I watched the screen of the auspex tensely as the three dots of the fast-moving sentinels peeled away from us to intercept the contact.

---

1. *Kilometres per hour.*

'Tea, sir?' Jurgen appeared at my shoulder, pouring a cup of steaming tanna from the flask he'd produced from one of the equipment pouches he was habitually festooned with. I took it and sipped the warming liquid gratefully.

'Thank you, Jurgen,' I said. The auspex operator flinched away from him, momentarily blocking my view of the display, so I heard rather than saw the engagement begin.

'It's a crawler,' Shambas reported, to my total lack of surprise. 'Looks like an ore truck. Jek, take the tracks.' The distinctive crack of ionising air told me he'd triggered his own multi-lasers an instant ahead of his subordinate's lascannon.

'On it,' Jek acknowledged. A moment later his voice took on a smug note. 'Tracks frakked.'

'They're popping hatches,' a female voice added, an instant ahead of a confused babble of noise. A moment later she was back. 'Sorry commissar. They had a rocket launcher.'

'Can't be helped, Paola,' I said, pleased that the momentary hesitation before I recalled her name had been so slight. But then there were only nine sentinel pilots in the entire regiment, and, in the nature of things, their names tended to cross my desk rather more frequently than most of the other troopers.[1]

The third sentinel in the squadron carried a heavy flamer, so there was no point in asking if there'd been

---

1. *Sentinel pilots are recon specialists, used to acting away from the supervision of their superiors to a far greater extent than most Guard troopers. This tends to breed a casual attitude to correct procedure which, on occasion, can spill over into outright insubordination. A wise commander or commissar, which Kasteen and Cain most definitely were, will recognise their value and accordingly cut them a little more slack.*

any survivors; the gout of burning promethium would have flooded the cab, incinerating anyone inside. 'Better them than one of you.'

'My sentiments exactly,' Shambas said, the bright dots of the sentinels peeling away across the auspex display to rejoin us. A moment later the stationary blip disappeared and a dull *whump* punched its way through the hull to reach our ears.

'Oops,' Paola said, with the flat tone of someone who doesn't really mean it.

I shrugged. 'Well I guess that answers the question of whether they had any more weapons back at the cache,' I said.

'And where it is.' Sulla had been busy at the chart table behind us, and directed my attention to the hololithic image displayed there.

My heart sank. Our position was on a line almost directly between Glacier Peak and the next objective on our list. There could be little doubt that we were heading directly for the heretics' outpost.

'I think you're right,' I said, doing my best to sound casual. I shrank the scale of the holomap to the point where the other two groups appeared, far too far away to have any hope of joining us until long after we'd reached the objective. Sulla watched curiously.

'Do you want me to bring the others up to join us?' she asked. I nodded as though I'd been thinking about it, which of course I hadn't. We knew for certain there were heretics where we were going, so waiting an hour or so to assault them with a full platoon instead of two squads, one of them half strength,[1] was the only sensible

---

1. *Typically command squads in the Imperial Guard consist of an officer and four troopers, as Cain has already mentioned, instead of the ten soldiers of a line squad.*

thing to do as far as I was concerned. Mildly embarrassing if the outpost turned out to be deserted, of course,
but I thought that would be something I could live with.

'That might be prudent,' I said, as though her raising
the point had been the thing to make up my mind.
'Normally I'd be inclined to push on and see what's
there, just as we planned, but now that we know there's
a heretic stronghold of some kind up ahead I'd like to
be sure we've got them properly surrounded before we
move in. No point in letting any of them slip away if we
can avoid it.'

'Of course,' Sulla said, slouching over to the vox unit
as though I'd just insisted she finish her homework
before she could go out. She gave the orders as crisply
and efficiently as any other officer, though, and I was
relieved to see both icons respond by changing course
to join us. Group three (fourth and fifth squads along
with sentinel squadron three) was the closer and had
the advantage of clearer terrain to boot, with any luck
they'd be with us in half an hour or so. Group one had
a crevasse field to negotiate so would take at least twice
as long.

As I listened to the brief exchange of messages, however, another thought struck me. Surely there hadn't
been time to get another crawler out here, loaded, and
halfway back to town in little more than a day? The
shipment we'd intercepted was probably a replacement
for the one Sulla had destroyed, which meant the
heretics manning the outpost had somehow known
that it had failed to reach its destination and had dispatched a replacement. And that meant...

'Scan all the frequencies,' I ordered the vox operator,
rounding on him so suddenly he visibly started. He
hastened to comply, while Sulla watched me curiously.

After a moment the man began to nod. 'I'm getting some traffic,' he said. 'Hard to pin down, but it's local. They're trying to contact someone called Andros.'

'The heretics,' I said. 'They must be trying to raise the crawler.' Which at least meant they hadn't got a call off before Paola toasted them. But since they were too busy being dead to reply, it wouldn't take their friends long to realise something had gone seriously ploin-shaped. Sulla looked at me, an expression of eager expectation on her face, and I nodded slowly. 'We've run out of time.'

'Move in,' she ordered, and the Chimera jerked violently as the driver floored the accelerator. I grabbed the chart table for support and enlarged the scale again to the point where we, the other Chimera, and the trio of sentinels appeared as separate runes. She started to hoist herself up into the cupola, then hesitated. 'Commissar. Would you care to…'

'Ladies first,' I said. 'And I wouldn't want to inhibit your ability to command in any way.' Not to mention stick my head out from inside a nice solid box of armour plate while we engaged Emperor knew how many heavily-armed heretics.

'Thank you.' She shot me a grin and scrambled up into the top hatch. I glanced at the tactical display again. The walkers were pulling ahead, splitting to flank the heretics' position and transmitting what data they could back to our command transport. Grainy images began to form on three pictscreens above our heads, snow and static mingling to render them almost incomprehensible.

'I'm picking up heat sources,' Shambas reported after a moment. 'Could be humans.' Or something like them, I found myself thinking. Not all followers of Chaos qualified any more, if they ever had to begin with. 'No sign of habitation though.'

'I'm guessing it's that.' Jek's pictcaster twisted to settle on a large snowdrift, far too regular to be a natural formation.

One of the Valhallans next to me snickered and hefted her lasgun. 'Shoot the camo party,' she said. I could understand her amusement. If even I thought the mound looked suspicious, to the natives of an iceworld the heretics might just as well have painted it orange and put up a neon sign saying 'We're over here!'.

'I'm sure somebody will,' I assured her, getting a wide grin in return.

'Could just be,' Shambas responded to his subordinate. 'Paola, find anything?'

'They've been busy.' She was over on the other flank, with Jek between her and the captain, which explained why he'd seen the mound first. 'Don't ask me why, but there's a cleared space here the size of a shuttlepad.' Her pictcaster showed me she hadn't been exaggerating – someone had gone to a lot of trouble to clear a large area of rock and level it off. Of course it was knee deep in drifting snow by now, which on a sentinel is roughly up to the chest, but even so it had obviously been prepared with great care. Determining why it had been done, though, would have to wait until we'd taken the place.

We struck with a gratifying amount of surprise, the two laser-armed sentinels striking the dome from the flanks while both Chimeras opened up with their heavy bolters. As the covering of snow boiled away, flashing instantly to steam from the laser hits, I could see the unmistakable outline of a prefabricated hab dome identical to Emperor alone knows how many others scattered across civilised space.[1] Jagged rents were

---

1. *This, of course, is because they're one of the STC artifacts found pretty much anywhere there's a need for them.*

appearing in the rockcrete surface as our bolter shells gouged and chipped away at it.

'Found the main entrance,' Paola voxed, the image from her pictcaster showing a swarm of thickly-bundled figures boiling from it like ants from a kicked-over nest. A bright orange flare of burning promethium gouted from somewhere below the imager, sending them scattering and plugging the gap. I found myself hoping that there was nothing too inflammable beyond it, like another ammo dump. That would be all we needed, another pile of smouldering wreckage in lieu of answers.

'It won't be the only one,' I cautioned, having seen enough of the structures facing us to be familiar with its layout. There would be four in all, equidistantly spaced around the circumference, access to the cargo area opposite the main personnel door Paola had just blocked and two auxiliary ones between them. All, I knew, would be heavily defended; a guess which was confirmed a moment later as our Chimera slewed to a halt, small-arms rounds pattering from the armour plate of its sides. Our turret-mounted bolter traversed to return the favour and the familiar dull roar echoed through the interior of the transport.

'We have to get inside,' Sulla voxed. 'Second squad, disembark and prepare to assault the side entrance.' She was right, unfortunately, the success of our mission depended on penetrating the building and recovering what intelligence we could, but the price was going to be high. Lustig's troopers were going to take some heavy casualties getting past the guards on the door. Worse still, I'd have to go in with them or lose the good opinion of the lord general. I debated internally for a moment whether to join them now and hope I could hang back enough to keep out of the way of the worst of it, or try to make some work for myself in the command Chimera until they'd cleared the way and risk giving the heretics a chance to regroup while I floundered through the snow once the noise had stopped.

Then my nose caught the familiar scent of Jurgen, approaching to retrieve his tanna flask, and a third alternative occurred to me. He was carrying a melta, as was his custom whenever we were expecting to run into trouble (which seemed to be most of the time these days).

I cut into the command circuit. 'Wait a moment,' I said. 'I've had an idea.' After a brief exchange of words with Sulla and the sentinel pilots, I steeled myself as best I could and piled out into the bitter cold, pausing barely long enough to adjust my snow goggles. (I'd been caught in the open without them once before, on Simia Orichalcae, and I wasn't about to make that mistake again.)

The shock of it punched the air from my lungs and left every exposed part of my face stinging like the aftershock of a neural whip, but I kept going by sheer force of will, slogging through the knee-deep snow as if my life depended on it (which of course it did). Jurgen waded after me, sure-footed as only an iceworlder could be in these conditions, and I found his presence as reassuring as always. I glanced around, seeing the looming bulk of second squad's Chimera a few metres away, which felt like kilometres to traverse, and plodded doggedly towards it. So focussed had I become on reaching my goal that I had almost forgotten the presence of the heretic defenders, until a gout of snow flashed into steam a few centimetres ahead of my foot.

I whirled, drawing my laspistol and seeking a target, grateful for once for the black uniform of my office, which would be nicely blurred in the all-pervading darkness. A flicker of motion caught my eye as a heavily-muffled heretic raised a lasgun and I shot him or her through the chest. The heretic fell back, wounded or dead, I couldn't tell and didn't care, and a moment later I gained the lee of the Chimera and the welcome cessation of that pestilential wind.

'We're ready when you are, commissar,' Lustig said, his voice attenuated by the perpetual howling of the gale and the crackle of small-arms fire which told me the sentinels were doing a bang-up job of keeping the defenders busy. I'd got them circling the dome, moving fast so they'd be difficult to hit, and laying down fire as they went. Chances were they wouldn't hit much (except possibly Paola), but that wasn't the point; they'd keep the heretics' heads down nicely, well dug in by the doors, sure they could keep us out indefinitely, which they probably could, under most circumstances. Unfortunately for them we didn't need a door to get inside.

'Whenever you're ready, Jurgen,' I said, after a short dash (for the Valhallans anyway, my progress was a bit slower and a lot less elegant) had brought us level with the gently curving wall.

'Commissar.' He levelled the melta and triggered it, while the rest of us flinched back and protected our eyes from the actinic flash of activation as best we could. The rockcrete burst into vapour, leaving a rapidly-cooling hole just wide enough for a trooper to get through.

'Pyk, Friza.' Lustig directed a couple of troopers through, and they took up position inside covering the corridor in each direction. Nobody shot them so I was next into the building, grateful for the sudden warmth despite the agonising cramps of returning circulation as my sluggish blood rushed back to my extremities. I began to take in our surroundings.

I wasn't sure what I was expecting to find inside, but this certainly wasn't it. Soft carpets covered the floor, growing soggy from the snow flurrying in through the gap, and the walls were covered with murals depicting acts of sensuous depravity which left my mouth momentarily hanging open in stunned surprise. Most of the troopers seemed hypnotised by them, with the single exception of Jurgen; which, given his fondness for porno slates, was quite an astonishing feat of self-control.

'I don't believe that's possible,' Penlan said, with a trace of envy.

'It's not,' I assured her, 'and even if it was it would be against regulations.' A thick, cloying scent was in the air, wrapping itself around my senses like the flimsiest of gossamer scarves, and a nagging sense of familiarity began trying to surface at the back of my mind. As my aide raised the melta and took up his accustomed place at my side, I found my head beginning to clear, although whether this was due to him masking the narcotic musk with his own earthier bouquet or his innate gifts blocking some insidious miasma of warpcraft I couldn't be sure. In either case the priority now was to get the squad moving, and Jurgen was the key.

'Stay close,' I ordered, getting everyone organised around us, so that however Jurgen was doing it we all got the benefit. As a bonus, that put a fireteam on either side of me, so I wouldn't be the first in the firing line whether the heretics hit us from the front or behind. I got them moving fast enough after that, albeit with a few furtive glances back at the pictures as we left, and to my relief they began to focus on the mission again. 'And stay sharp. We could be facing warpcraft in a place like this, so be ready for anything.' As I'd expected, the prospect of facing sorcery had them so keyed up that I don't think they'd have been distracted by the living embodiment of the murals other than to chuck a frag grenade into the room.

'This reminds me of something,' Jurgen remarked as we advanced cautiously along a corridor decked with soft, colourful wall hangings. 'There's an odd smell in the air I think I recognise.' As always the irony of his words was lost on him. 'Can't quite place it, though.'

'Slawkenberg,' I said, with a sudden rush of realisation. The scent in the air was like the perfume Emeli the Slaaneshi sorceress had worn the night she tried to feed my soul to the monstrosity she worshipped, and a cold chill of dread squeezed my heart. Even after more than a decade (or now, after more than a century, if I'm honest) I still woke from my slumbers occasionally with images of that baleful seductress trying to lure me to my doom resonating in my head, as if the tendrils of Chaos were still reaching out to try to draw me in. I hadn't had that dream in months, though, and an irrational flash of petty resentment at the prospect of further nightmares rippled through my mind.

'Clear.' Penlan ducked back into the corridor after investigating a room full of cushions and pillows which had no discernable function that I could see,[1] and motioned us onwards. I'd been heading directly for the centre of the dome, on the assumption that whatever was going on here would be well protected, and the lack

---

1. *For a man of the galaxy, as he undoubtedly was, I feel Cain is being a little disingenuous here.*

of resistance so far had me on edge. Of course that could just mean that our diversion was working far better than I'd expected it to, but in my experience battle plans seldom survived contact with the enemy.

'That's it. Nothing.' Penlan waved us forward into an empty storage area, bare save for a single luminator and the stained glass mobile beneath it which shifted with the air currents sending ripples of rainbow light around the room. It had clearly been used quite recently, though, as it was free of dust.

'Damn.' I hovered by the doorway, mildly irked to find my deduction proven hollow, and nagged by a vague sense of something being wrong about the shape of the room.

It was probably this moment of indecision which triggered what happened next, as I was in Penlan's way as she stepped back, still keeping the space covered like the good soldier she was. Lost in thought and trying to decide which new direction to try, I failed to move out of her way fast enough, nudging her elbow. Her finger tightened reflexively on the trigger of her lasgun, sending a hail of las bolts flying across the room and the rest of the squad diving for what cover they could.

'Sorry.' Her face flamed scarlet, bringing out the old flash burn scar she'd acquired on Gravalax, while her subordinates scrambled to their feet, grinning at the sight of her living up to her nickname.

'No need,' I said, seeing the need to restore her authority without delay. 'It was my fault entirely.'

From somewhere up the corridor I could hear the sound of running feet as someone came to investigate the noise. Great. So much for sneaking around and getting what we'd come for without anyone noticing. 'Everyone inside!'

I spoke not a moment too soon, as las bolts and stubber rounds began to pepper the rockcrete around the doorway and the troopers deployed to meet the new threat. A knot of armed cultists either extravagantly dressed or hardly dressed at all spilled out of the side corridors, getting in each other's way to a most satisfying extent and providing us with a target-rich environment of which my companions immediately took full advantage.

'Overlapping fire lanes. Keep their heads down and we can hold out here indefinitely,' Lustig said.

'That's a comfort,' I told him. 'But I don't think we're going to have to.'

Judging by the voices in my comm-bead, fourth and fifth squads, along with their escorting sentinels, had finally arrived to join the party outside. With the cultists drawn away from the doors to meet the unexpected threat within, Grifen and her troopers were already sweeping aside the sporadic resistance left around the main cargo bay and pouring into the dome.

I motioned to Jurgen. 'If you wouldn't mind clearing the corridor?'

'With pleasure, commissar.' My aide grinned at me as he levelled the melta. 'I'm afraid I forgot the marshmallows again, but heretics toast better anyway.' He squeezed the trigger and a gout of thermal energy ravened its way down the narrow passage, vaporising everything in its path in a most satisfying manner. The few surviving heretics shrieked and ran, and a moment later a crackle of lasguns told me they'd stumbled into fourth squad.

'Try to take a couple alive,' I reminded everyone again, and was reassured a moment later by Magot's cheery tone.

'Don't worry, sir. Got one here in one piece. She's leaking a bit, but she'll survive.'

'Good,' I said, feeling that things were finally beginning to go our way. Lustig and the troopers were already following up the opening Jurgen had made, running up the gently steaming passageway heedless of the damage the occasional greasy patch of heretic residue was doing to their boots, eager to fall on the defenders at the main door from behind. I was happy to leave them to it; I had no intention of putting myself in the way of any stray rounds at this stage of the game if I could help it.

I was just turning away to follow a little more sedately when I noticed something odd about the wall where Penlan's las bolts had hit. They'd penetrated it completely, whereas the las-bolts the heretics had been shooting at us had been stopped completely by the outer wall of the room. Suddenly the nagging sense of wrongness I'd felt about the shape of the space made sense to me; there was a false partition here, designed to conceal something.

Dismissing my first impulse to let Jurgen solve the problem with his melta, in case it took any crucial evidence directly to the Emperor along with the wall, I cast about carefully for some kind of panel or catch, feeling absurdly like the hero of a haunted house melodrama. I could find no trace of one, however, and at last I motioned him forwards, hoping that the weapon wouldn't do too much damage to whatever was behind the partition.

'Wait,' I said, just as he raised the melta and prepared to fire it. For some reason, perhaps the way his shadow fell across the wall, the outline of a panel had suddenly become visible.[1] I looked at it more closely, wondering

---

1. *More likely he was masking some concealing sorcerous illusion. No doubt someone from the Ordo Malleus could explain the principles, if anyone cares.*

how I could possibly have missed something so obvious, and within moments had determined the method of opening it.

'Emperor on Earth!' We both reeled back, gagging from the stench which poured out of the narrow space, and after a moment spent recovering our breath we leaned forward cautiously to peer inside. Jurgen produced a luminator from somewhere and shone it round the room thus revealed.

The first things we noticed were probably the bodies, how many we couldn't tell, flesh and bone seared and warped by sorceries I didn't want to imagine. Most disconcerting of all was that what remained of the faces bore expressions of what I can only describe as insane ecstasy. Jurgen, imperturbable as ever, swept the luminator beam around the walls, picking out arcane sigils which made my eyes hurt and compelled my gaze to skitter away like waterfowl bouncing from a frozen pond.

'Don't think much of the decor,' he said, with commendable understatement.

I nodded, swallowing hard. 'There have been foul sorceries done here,' I said. 'The question is, what and why?'

'I'm afraid I wouldn't know, sir,' my aide replied, taking the remark as literally as he did everything else.

'Neither would I, thank the Emperor,' I said. This was a job for Zyvan's tame psykers, and no business of honest men. Or me. I turned away with a sense of profound relief. 'Close it up and leave it for the experts.'

'With pleasure, sir,' Jurgen said, leaving the chamber of horrors as rapidly as he could and helping me manhandle the access panel back into place with almost indecent haste. Recalling the trouble I'd had finding it in the first place, I unwound the scarlet sash of my office from around my waist and wedged it into the gap before closing it, so that it hung from the wall like a jaunty flag.

'There,' I said. 'That should do it.' To my surprise the simple job had left me trembling with reaction, as though exhausted.[1] I had little time to muse on this, though, because Sulla was yelling in my comm-bead.

'Commissar! They're abandoning the dome.'

'Say again?' I asked, unable to credit what I'd been hearing. There was nowhere else for the surviving heretics to go out here, and insane as they undoubtedly were, choosing to freeze to death rather than surrender or die fighting didn't make any sense at all. Then the idea of a suicide bomb flashed into my mind, and I was running full tilt for the nearest exit. 'Everybody outside!' I yelled. 'They may have rigged the place to blow!'

In fact they hadn't, but the fear of it leant wings to my feet so that I was outside in time to be as startled as the rest of us.

'Incoming arial contact, closing fast!' the auspex operator cut in, his voice tense. I narrowed my eyes against the flurrying snow, fitting the goggles into place and wiping them clear with trembling fingers. A small knot of heretics was wading through the drifts towards the clear area, exchanging sporadic fire with fifth squad and trying to keep the swooping sentinels at bay with what looked to me like a couple of krak missile launchers. They weren't having much luck, but they were managing to hold them back out of effective flamer and multi-laser range and I could see why Shambas hadn't ordered his pilots to close the distance. The traitors were

---

1. *More likely this was due to the psychic shock of being so close to the residues of sorcery.*

obviously finished now, and they might as well wait for them to run out of rockets before moving in.

The shriek of powerful engines tore through the skies overhead, and a vast, dark shape blotted out the starlight as it passed.

'It's a cargo shuttle,' Jurgen pointed out unnecessarily. 'Where did they get one of those from?' It was a good question, but academic at the moment.

'Target their engines.' Sulla ordered, an instant before I could, but it would be a futile gesture at best. Even a civilian shuttle is ruggedly built, and a couple of las-cannons and a handful of heavy bolters won't do much more than scratch the paintwork.

'Frak that,' Shambas retorted. 'Jek, Karis, go for the flight deck.' The two designated sentinels reared back on their haunches for maximum elevation and spat luminescent death at the approaching shuttle. It was a desperate gamble, and for a moment I thought they might just do it, but the armourcrys protecting the cockpit is tough enough to take the stresses of re-entry; even a couple of lascannon bolts wouldn't be enough to penetrate it. One struck home, however, leaving a vivid thermal bloom across the previously transparent surface, and the two sentinel pilots began a good-natured argument about which one of them had inflicted it.

It was enough to break the shuttle pilot's nerve, however, and the engine noise rose in pitch as the main boosters ignited, powering it back up towards wherever it had come from in the first place. A howl of disappointment rose from the little knot of heretics as they watched their expected deliverance disappear as suddenly as it had arrived, then, as the followers of Chaos so often do, they began to argue bitterly among themselves. One group threw down their weapons and began to trudge wearily back towards the dome, their hands in the air, while the others began firing at the encircling troopers with even greater desperation than before. And, inevitably, some of them began to gun down those of their fellows who were attempting to surrender.

I watched for a few moments, until the inevitable conclusion had played itself out, before trudging back to the command Chimera more troubled than I would have believed possible before setting out on this assignment. True, we'd found what we were looking for, but instead of giving us answers, it just seemed to have opened the way to even more questions.

Editorial Note:

As so often in his memoirs, Cain's tendency to elide the details of what he regards as uninteresting threatens to deprive what follows of some much-needed context. I have accordingly felt the need to insert some additional material at this point, which I hope will prove illuminating.

From *Sablist in Skitterfall: a brief history of the Chaos incursion* by Dagblat Tincrowser, 957 M41.

DESPITE THE FEARS which understandably gripped most of the world in the weeks following the heretics' daring and unexpected attacks upon the newly-arrived expeditionary force, the traitors chose not to show their hand again for some time. With hindsight we can quite clearly see that this was simply because their short-term objectives had been met; the security forces were compelled to waste incalculable man hours and precious resources preparing for a campaign of guerilla warfare which never materialised, and the longer it failed to do so the more firmly convinced those in authority became that this was because the cults they were facing were small, weak and poorly organised.

This impression was abruptly dispelled by Commissar Cain's personal discovery of a hidden shuttle pad, cunningly concealed on the coldside within easy striking distance of Glacier Peak. It became instantly apparent that the conspiracy was far stronger and more organised than had previously been suspected, and that all they had done before was with the aim of diverting attention from this most insidious of threats. Who knew how many of their confederates had managed to infiltrate Adumbria undetected, and what manner of vileness they'd brought with them? Indeed, it would be no exaggeration to say that many within the Council of Claimants became convinced that the vanguard of the enemy fleet was already among us, awaiting their moment to strike.

Such a prognosis was, of course, needlessly alarmist, but there were few on Adumbria, and even fewer among the Imperial forces ranged in its defence, prepared to discount the possibility entirely.

To: The Office of the Lord General, by the grace of His Most Divine Majesty, protector of that part of the Holy Dominions known as the Damocles Gulf and Adjacent Sectors to Spinward.

From: Commissar Tomas Beije, charged by the Office of the Commissariat with the maintenance of True

Fighting Spirit among his most loyal and fervent warriors of the Tallarn 229th.

My lord general,

I have received this day, 273 937 M41, your recent communiqué regarding the discoveries made by my colleague Ciaphas Cain and his rabble of a regiment, and perused it with interest. You may rest assured that in the opinion of both myself and Colonel Asmar, there is absolutely no likelihood of a similar rebel foothold being established on the so-called 'hotside' of Adumbria under the very noses of His Divine Majesty's most loyal and fervent warriors.

Nevertheless, as you are at pains to point out, additional caution is never a bad thing; I have accordingly given my approval to Colonel Asmar's proposal to widen the range of our perimeter patrols by up to five kilometres and have urged the priests of our company to say additional benedictions invoking the Emperor's guidance of their footsteps. In the unlikely event of such heretical deviants polluting that part of the divinely-appointed realm given over to our charge, our soldiers will undoubtedly be led straight to them by The Emperor's Grace as a result of this intercession.

I trust that this will prove sufficient to ensure the success of our Holy task.

Tomas Beije, Regimental Commissar.

Thought for the day: Faith is the strongest shield.

EIGHT

'Hope for the best, but prepare for the worst.'

– Imperial Guard tactical manual

IT WAS A grim little group we made as we convened in a conference suite at the lord general's headquarters, virtually identical to the one we'd been using when our last meeting had been so rudely interrupted. Fortunately the hotel he'd commandeered possessed several, so the partial demolition of the other one during the heretics' botched attempt to assassinate Zyvan had turned out to be a minor inconvenience at best: in the manner of plush hotels across the galaxy it was almost impossible to tell the difference between the two rooms. Even the little side table of refreshments was in the same place I remembered it.

There were a number of significant details which had changed, though, the most noticeable one being the fact that we were now on the ground floor and a battery of Hydras were parked outside with orders to shoot anything that crossed the perimeter no matter how authentic its clearances seemed. The sight of the anti-aircraft guns reminded me of the earlier incident and I asked how the enquiries into that were progressing.

'Slowly,' Zyvan admitted, helping himself to a cyna bun from the table in the corner. Famished from the trip back from Glacier Peak, which had been undertaken with gratifying speed aboard a flyer dispatched to collect me by the lord general himself, I lost no time in following his example. 'We arrested the owner of the aircar, of course, but he maintains that it was stolen without his knowledge.'

'I suppose he would,' I said. 'Anyone we know?'

'Ventrious,' Zyvan said, to my complete surprise. The aristocrat had struck me as a pompous idiot, of course, and a damn sight too eager for power, but that pretty much summed up the entire breed in my experience, and try as I might I couldn't picture the red-faced buffoon I'd seen throwing a tantrum in the council chamber as a Slaaneshi cultist. He'd have looked ridiculous in pink, for a start.

'And you're satisfied with his story?' I asked.

Zyvan nodded. 'Our interrogators were very thorough. If he knew anything he would have told us.' I didn't doubt it, and said so. Zyvan smiled bleakly. 'Under any normal circumstances I would have agreed with you. But we were dealing with the possibility of warpcraft, remember. I had to be sure his memories were real ones.'

'I see,' I said, shuddering in spite of myself. I nodded cordially to the colourless young man in neatly-pressed fatigues devoid of insignia who Zyvan hadn't bothered to introduce. Hekwyn, Vinzand and Kolbe were all seated as far away from him as they reasonably could be, and I must say I didn't blame them. I'd met psykers before, and it had rarely ended well. Luckily I'd dispatched Jurgen to prepare my quarters immediately on our arrival, so there was no possibility of his secret being abruptly revealed by accident; I made a mental note to keep him as far away from the lord general's staff as possible, since there was no telling how many other mind-readers he had lurking about the premises.

'His mind was intact,' the young psyker assured me. 'At least to begin with.' He must have read something of what I was thinking on my face, because he smiled without humour. 'I was as careful as I could be. He'll recover, more or less.'

'Sieur Malden is one of the most capable sanctioned psykers on my staff,' Zyvan said.

I nodded again. 'I'm sure he is,' I agreed. Like I said, I've met several, albeit not exactly socially in most cases, and Malden (I noted the use of the civilian honorific as protocol demanded)[1] was clearly one of the sharpest blades in the scabbard. Rakel, Amberley's tame telepath, for instance, was as barmy as a jokero and made about as much sense most of the time.[2]

---

1. *Like commissars, enginseers, and other specialists attached to Imperial Guard forces, sanctioned psykers are technically not part of the military command structure. This is probably because no sane officer would be willing to take responsibility for them.*

2. *In defence of my psyker I have to say that Cain exaggerates a little. Rakel isn't the easiest of people to get along with, and her conversation, not to mention her thought processes, do take some getting used to, but she's not completely insane. Besides, her medication is generally quite effective. As to the jokaero, whether they're actually sentient enough for the concept of sanity to be in any way meaningfully applied to them is still a subject of much debate in the Ordo Xenos.*

Now you might think that someone with as much to hide as I have would have been terrified at the prospect of sharing a conference table with a telepath, but one thing I'd picked up about them over the years was that they're not going to be listening to your deepest, darkest secrets. Not without trying very hard, anyway.

Rakel once told me in one of her more lucid moments that catching stray thoughts from the people around her was like trying to pick a single voice out of a crowded ballroom, and even then it was just the surface thoughts she could detect. Going deeper takes a lot of effort and concentration, almost as dangerous to the psyker as the person they're trying to read, and for someone as practiced as I was at dissembling there was nothing on the surface for them to pick up on anyway.

'I've been to the installation you found,' Malden told me, his voice curiously toneless, which at least matched his appearance. The only word which fitted him was 'nondescript'. I must have been in the same room as him scores of times over the years, but I still can't recall his height, build, or the colour of his eyes and hair. 'I found the experience… interesting.'

I felt a faint tingling in the air, like the charge before a thunderstorm, and the hololith flickered into life without anyone touching the controls. Vinzand and Kolbe both flinched, no doubt muttering prayers to the Emperor under their breath, and I noticed the faint smile, genuine this time, which Malden almost succeeded in masking. Only Hekwyn failed to react, no doubt inured to unpleasant surprises as a result of his duties with the arbites.

'That's not quite the word I would have chosen,' I said casually, determined not to give him the satisfaction of seeming in any way disconcerted.

'Really?' The young psyker's eyes drifted towards me. 'What word would you have used?'

'Terrifying,' I admitted. 'It reminded me…' I glanced at the trio at the end of the table, and Zyvan nodded.

'Under the circumstances you can take it that everyone in this room is cleared for any information you may wish to contribute,' he said. 'Even that pertaining to the nature of Chaos.' I nodded soberly, conscious of the expressions on the three men's faces; a peculiar mixture of curiosity and apprehension. They all knew they were about to hear things that few citizens of the Imperium were ever made privy to, and were not exactly sure that they wanted to know them.

'Some years ago,' I began, 'I encountered a coven of Slaaneshi cultists, who were attempting to create a daemonhost.'[1] Kolbe almost choked on his recaff and Vinzand went pale, even for an Adumbrian. Hekwyn raised an eyebrow a millimetre or two and began to look marginally more interested. 'There was something about that hab dome which reminded me of them.'

'What happened to the daemonhost?' Hekwyn asked.

I shrugged. 'Destroyed, I assume. I called in an artillery barrage and levelled the place.' Almost killing myself in the process, I might add.

Malden nodded once. 'That might work,' he said with a casualness which only intensified my unease.

'Excuse me.' Vinzand coughed hesitantly. 'When you say create a daemonhost, you mean…' he waved his hands vaguely. 'I'm sorry, I'm rather new to all this.'

'They were summoning a daemon from the warp and confining it in a host body,' I explained, trying not to remember that the body in question had been one of

---

1. *Cain's account of the incident forms one of the shorter fragments of the archive, and need not concern us at this juncture.*

the Guard troopers accompanying me. He still looked baffled, so after a sidelong glance at Zyvan for an almost imperceptible nod of approval I elaborated a little. 'Daemons are creatures of the warp, and draw their power from it. But dangerous as they are, they can't exist in the material universe for long without being drawn back to where they came from.' And a good thing too, if the ones I'd encountered before were anything to go by. 'Trapping it in a mortal body allows it to remain here, although its powers are diminished, and it's usually under the control of whoever summoned it in the first place.'

'Up to a point,' Malden agreed, and I deferred to his greater knowledge of warpcraft with relief. 'Any control over it is tenuous at best. You'd have to be insane to try it.'[1] He shrugged. 'But the commissar is substantially correct. The only other way for a daemon to interact with the materium for a prolonged period is to find a world or a region of space where the two realms intersect one another. Fortunately such places are rare.'

'The Eye of Terror,' I said, making the sign of the aquila as I spoke.

Malden nodded again. 'The vast majority are there,' he said. 'And the few exceptions are interdicted by the Inquisition.'[2]

'Who are far better qualified to worry about such things than we are,' Zyvan said, dragging the meeting

---

1. *Or a Radical member of the Ordo Malleus, which pretty much amounts to the same thing.*

2. *Unfortunately it's generally impossible to pronounce Exterminatus on a so-called daemonworld, since, being outside time and space in the conventional sense, tried and tested methods such as virus bombing are at best ineffective and at worst counter-productive; the last thing you want to do in such a case is give them ideas.*

back to the point at last. Knowing a little more about the Inquisition and its methods than he did I had my doubts about that, but if I voiced them it might have been bad for my health, so I said nothing and waited for Malden to turn back to the hololith. Just for once the image was still and crystal clear, and I found myself staring at a perfect miniature replica of the hideous chamber I'd discovered behind the wall.

'What are those symbols?' Kolbe asked, trying not to look too hard at them. I couldn't blame him for that as I was doing the same thing myself, although their hololithic representations were far less disconcerting than the real things had been.

'Some of them are wards,' Malden replied. 'If you wanted my best guess, I'd say that something had been confined in there. Something touched by the warp.' This time, I noticed, mine wasn't the only hand which moved reflexively to invoke the Emperor's protection.

'And the others?' I asked.

For the first time the young psyker seemed unsure of himself. 'I've never seen anything like them before,' he admitted reluctantly. 'My best guess would be to channel warp energy, perhaps to summon something.' He shrugged. 'The warp currents around here are strange enough at the best of times. You'd be better off asking a navigator or an astropath, to be honest. It's more their department than it is mine.'

'Perhaps they were trying to affect the flow of the currents,' Kolbe suggested. 'To speed up their invasion fleet or delay your reinforcements.'

'That would make sense,' Zyvan conceded, nodding slowly in a manner which told me just how much he didn't like that idea. 'I'll discuss it with the senior representative of the Navis Nobilitae.' It went without saying that the navigator of his flagship wouldn't lower himself to converse directly with the likes of us, and I have to say I was heartily glad of that fact. They're spooky little bastards at the best of times, and snobbier than a planetary governor with a pedigree going back to before Horus. And on top of that they can kill you with a look. Literally.

'What about the bodies?' Vinzand asked, looking at them with a visible effort.

'Lunch?' I suggested. 'For whatever was stuck in there?'

Malden favoured me with a smile which actually contained a modicum of warmth. 'Possibly,' he conceded. 'Or something to pass the time. But my guess would be a sacrifice. Heretics are big on sacrifice, especially when they're summoning things.'

'Maybe one of the prisoners we took can tell us,' I said.

We'd ended up with half a dozen relatively intact specimens in the end, which wasn't a bad haul, and Hekwyn's promised experts from the Arbites were crawling over the entire dome looking for Emperor knows what, so at last it looked as though we were getting somewhere.

'Perhaps,' Zyvan said.

I raised an eyebrow. 'I thought your interrogators would have extracted everything they knew by now.'

'They appear to be unusually resilient. Some of them even seem to be enjoying themselves.'

'In the meantime,' Hekwyn said, with an audible sigh of relief as the hololith clicked off, 'we have at least been able to start rounding up the smuggling ring from the Glacier Peak end.' He favoured me with a smile and a nod of the head. 'Despite my scepticism, it seems

Commissar Cain's assessment of the situation wasn't too wide of the mark after all. He just assumed the weapons were flowing into the town from Skitterfall instead of the other way round.'

'I'm pleased to hear your confidence in the security of the starport was justified,' I replied graciously.

'Up to a point.' The arbitrator frowned. 'The shuttle you scared off must have come from somewhere. My guess is it was one of the freighters in orbit.'

'We're already combing the traffic control records,' Vinzand chipped in. 'But with thousands of shuttle flights a day, it won't be easy to track. Let alone the previous landings.'

'If it's even one of those,' Kolbe suggested gloomily. 'Perhaps it came from one of the raiders, lurking in the outer system.'

'No.' Zyvan shook his head decisively. 'If there was a Chaos ship here already we would have detected it when we dropped out of warp. And our pickets would have intercepted anything emerging into realspace once we got here that wasn't in one of the shipping lanes.' I remembered the myriad of dancing lights I'd seen from the observation window of the *Emperor's Benificence*, and didn't envy whoever got the job of trying to identify which of them was our smuggler.

'Do we have any more of an idea when the raiders are due?' I asked.

The lord general shook his head again. 'Three to twelve days is the best estimate the navigators can give me. Assuming General Kolbe isn't right about their confederates on the coldside having found a way of speeding up the warp currents, of course.'

'Then we'd better assume they'll be here any time,' Kolbe said. He seemed surprisingly happy at the

prospect, until it dawned on me that all this talk of daemons and warpcraft had him thoroughly spooked and
he was grabbing the opportunity of returning the conversation to matters he understood with unconcealed
alacrity. 'I'll put all our PDF units on full alert the
moment I return to my headquarters.'

'A wise precaution,' Zyvan said, activating the hololith
the traditional way by pressing the runes on the lectern
and thumping it with his fist until it sputtered into life.
This time the image was as fuzzy as usual, which I
found vaguely reassuring, the almost preternatural clar-
ity of the images Malden had shown us bringing back
the sense of unease I'd felt in the habdome. A three-
dimensional image of the planet appeared, with
hundreds of green dots indicating the presence of the
PDF forces arrayed in its defence. Most were in the
shadow belt, of course, clustered most thickly around
major population centres and sites of strategic importance, although a few were scattered across the hotside
and coldside, where towns and other installations made
convenient spots to place a garrison in the unforgiving
landscapes.

After a moment of studying the coldside I was able to
find Glacier Peak and the reassuring amber rune which
marked the presence of my own regiment, although the
handful of similar icons making up the rest of our expeditionary force were all but lost in the rash of PDF
locations. The Valhallan tanks were easy to find of
course, being overlaid on Skitterfall, and the Tallarns
stood out reasonably clearly in the sparsely-garrisoned
hotside, but I had to search for some time before I
found either of the Kastaforean regiments. It was a
sobering moment.

'How long before the reinforcements arrive?' I asked.

'Five to eighteen days, according to the last message we received.' Zyvan hesitated a moment before going on. 'And that was three days ago.'

'Three days?' Vinzand asked, the quiver of apprehension in his voice fortunately drawing everyone's attention and saving me the bother of controlling my own expression. The palms of my hands were tingling, which never augurs anything good. 'I was under the impression that you received updates on their deployment every twenty-four hours.'

'Normally that's true,' Zyvan admitted, with the expression of a man sucking a bitterroot. 'But our astropaths have been unable to get through to the rest of the fleet.'

'They say there seems to be some kind of disturbance in the warp,' Malden chipped in helpfully, which did absolutely nothing to calm my fears, I can assure you. Clearly whatever the cultists had been up to in Glacier Peak (apart from stockpiling Emperor alone knew how much lethal ordnance, which was bad enough) had succeeded. What that was I had no idea, but I knew enough about the Great Enemy to know that it would be nothing good, and just hoped I wouldn't be the one to find out the hard way. (A hope in which I was to be grievously disappointed, as things turned out.)

'So we're on our own until further notice,' Zyvan concluded.

Kolbe squared his shoulders. 'My men won't let you down, lord general. They might lack the experience of your Guardsmen, but they're fighting for their homes. That makes up for a lot.'

'I don't doubt it,' Zyvan said, although probably only I knew him well enough to see that he wasn't entirely convinced.

'What worries me is that we're spread so thinly,' I said without thinking, then realising what I'd said I carried on as smoothly as if I'd never meant to pause. 'If we're going to back up General Kolbe's troops effectively, we'll need to deploy as soon as we know where they're coming under pressure. By the time the dropships get down to us, loaded and away, we'll just turn up in time to join in with the victory parade.' Or bury the bodies, more likely, but saying that wouldn't be tactful. I didn't have to anyway – Zyvan knew the score well enough to know what I meant.

'I've been thinking about that,' he said. The image of the planet in the hololith shrank to make room for a couple of icons in orbit above the capital. His flagship and the *Emperor's Benificence*, I assumed. I was correct as it turned out, as his next act was to point out the troop-ship. 'Holding the dropships in reserve as I'd intended won't help, as the commissar has just pointed out. They'll be sitting waterfowl in orbit once the enemy fleet arrives anyway.'

'So what's the alternative?' Vinzand asked, probably only just realising that all those civilian starships above us would be giving the raiders some easy target practice on the way in as well.

Zyvan sighed. 'Five dropships, five regiments. I'm attaching one to each. That way at least one company can be ready to deploy in a matter of moments. With a bit of luck they can ferry Guard reinforcements in to wherever they're needed, and return to the staging area for another load.' He looked at me, thinking he could read my reaction in my face, and shrugged. 'I know, Ciaphas. It's a messy option, but it's the best we can do.'

'I suppose it is,' I said, trying to sound grave. It would leave the lucky company in question out on a limb, of course, but a formation that size ought to be able to take care of itself until the second or third run arrived. More to the point, all I had to do was find an excuse to stick close to the dropship and I'd have a way off the planet if things went sour, which they looked very like doing at that point. All in all things seemed to be getting a bit brighter so far as I was concerned.

I should have known better, of course.

NINE

'His loyalty couldn't be bought at any price;
but it could be rented remarkably cheaply.'

– Inquisitor Allendyne, after the execution of
Rogue Trader Parnis Vermode for trafficking
in interdicted xenos artifacts

JURGEN, EFFICIENT AS ever, had managed to get my personal effects neatly stowed in the suite I'd occupied on my last sojourn in the lord general's headquarters, so once the conference finally broke up I lost no time in heading back there to avail myself of a hot bath, a good meal and a large soft bed, in that order. About the only thing missing was some feminine company, which would have rounded things off nicely, and as I drifted into sleep I found myself wondering what Amberley was doing at that moment.[1] That should have led to

---

1. *Shooting my way past a ridiculous number of inordinately persistent hrud, if I've worked out the dates correctly.*

some very pleasant dreams, but seeing that damned hololith of the chamber I'd found in the heretics' hab dome had apparently stirred up deeper, less pleasant memories, and my slumbers were to be far from restful.

As I've mentioned before, I still had occasional nightmares about my earlier encounter with a nest of Slaaneshi cultists. Usually vague, formless things in which I felt my sense of self slipping once again under the psychic assault of the sorceress Emeli, who would appear as an insubstantial wraith as a rule, urging me on to damnation until I would wake with a shudder, entangled in sweat-soaked bedding. This time, however, the dreams were lucid, and vivid, and remained with me on waking, so that even now I can recall them in some detail.

It began in her chambers, where she'd lured me with her sorcerous wiles, my mind clouded by the air of sensuous luxury which had quite disarmed my companions.[1] In the manner of dreams, the room was exactly as I recalled it, small details I had barely noticed at the time standing out vividly, but with the perspective curiously distorted so that it seemed to be without physical boundaries. Emeli was reclining on the bed, half out of the green silk gown which so closely matched her eyes, smiling at me enticingly, drawing me towards her as she had before. Unlike the reality, however, the ugly crater of the laspistol wound was already clearly visible, punched through her torso, where I'd broken the spell she'd placed on my mind by the most desperate and direct method I could.

---

1. *His account of the actual incident leads me to suspect that he wasn't quite as taken in as he says here.*

'You're dead,' I told her, aware as you sometimes are that you're dreaming, but somehow unable to reject the experience as entirely unreal.

Her smile widened. 'I'm coming back,' she replied, as though it were the most natural thing in the galaxy, and once again I felt drawn towards her, desire and revulsion mingling within me until I could barely tell them apart. 'Then I'll taste your soul as I promised.'

'I don't think so,' I said, reaching for my laspistol as I had in life, only to find that the holster had vanished, along with the rest of my clothing. Emeli laughed, the familiar enchanting trill of it drawing me in, and opened her arms to embrace me. I tried to pull away, panic flaring, and her face began to change, flowing into something I didn't dare to look upon but was powerless to turn aside from, more beautiful and terrifying than the mind was meant to perceive.

'Are you all right, sir?'

I woke abruptly, my heart hammering in my chest, to find Jurgen standing by the light switch, his lasgun in his hands. 'You were shouting something.'

'Just a dream,' I said, staggering to the decanter of amasec and downing a hefty slug, far more hastily than so fine a bottle deserved. I poured a second and drank it a little more carefully. 'About that witch on Slawkenberg.'

'Oh.' My aide nodded once, his own memories of the incident no doubt prompted by my words. 'Bad business, that.' And it would have been a great deal worse had it not been for his peculiar talent, which, at the time, we were both blissfully unaware of. He shrugged. 'Still. Dreams never hurt anyone, did they sir?'

'Of course not.'

I didn't feel like sleeping any more, though, and began to get dressed. 'Do you think you could find me some recaff?'

'Right away, sir.' He slung the lasgun over his shoulder and turned to leave the room, barely suppressing a yawn, and I realised for the first time that I must have woken him; he'd commandeered a sofa in the lounge of the suite, which I was using as an office and which was the other side of the bathroom. Some nightmare if he'd heard me from that far away, I thought.

'Better get some for yourself, too,' I added. 'You look as though you need it.'

'Very good, sir.' He nodded once. 'Will you be requiring breakfast?'

I wasn't sure, to be honest, still queasy from the nightmare and the amasec, which was beginning to look like rather a bad idea now that it had reached my head, but I nodded too. 'Something light,' I said, confident that he knew my tastes well enough and that I could trust his judgement better than my own at the moment. 'And whatever you feel like as well.' As he left and his distinctive aroma followed him from the room, I found myself trying to think of a reason to call him back.

This is ridiculous, I told myself firmly. I was an Imperial commissar, not a frightened juvie. I tied my sash tightly, placed my cap squarely on my head and tried not to feel quite so relieved when I'd buckled my weapon belt around my waist.

Nevertheless, as I walked through to the lounge area, fastidiously negotiating the litter of half empty plates around Jurgen's couch, I found myself wondering if what I'd experienced had been more than just a dream. Could some psychic residue of the cultists' ritual have crawled inside my head in the chamber I'd discovered?

The idea was so disconcerting I found myself on the verge of voxing Malden right then and there to ask if it was feasible. Then reason reasserted itself. For one thing, I'd had Jurgen with me the whole time, and I knew for a fact that nothing like that could possibly have happened in his presence, and for another raising the possibility was the surest way I could think of to have the young psyker rummaging around in my head before you could say 'The Emperor Protects.' And the thought of that, you can be sure, was enough to snap me out of my stupor post-haste. Apart from my own discreditable secrets, which I was keen enough not to have anyone else privy to, there was enough sensitive information about Inquisition resources and contacts cluttering up my mind to sign my death warrant ten times over[1] if they became known to anyone else.

Once I'd realised that it was quite enough to put a couple of bad dreams firmly into perspective, and by the time Jurgen returned pushing a trolley laden with comestibles (having taken my injunction to pick up anything he liked as literally as he did pretty much everything else), I was already at my desk wading through the routine paperwork. It might seem strange, given the momentous events I'd been discussing only a few hours before, but it continued to accumulate regardless. Troopers are troopers, after all, and if the enemy isn't obliging enough to keep them entertained they'll find their own amusements.

Now breakfast had arrived I found myself surprisingly hungry and managed to put a fair-sized dent in the stack of ackenberry waffles Jurgen had thoughtfully selected for me. Watching him eat was not an activity

---

1. *Once would have been sufficient.*

for the faint-hearted, so I returned to my desk where I could ignore everything but the sound effects, and was thus in a position to answer the vox myself almost as soon as the first chime sounded.

'Cain,' I said crisply, trying not to notice the choking sound as Jurgen attempted to mask his outrage at the breach of protocol. He took it as an Emperor-given right to filter my incoming messages, deflecting the vast majority with apparently inexhaustible patience and obstinacy, for which I was normally heartily grateful. This morning, however, I needed whatever distractions I could get, the echoes of the nightmare still leaving me on edge, and felt that for once he might as well finish his breakfast in peace.

'Commissar,' Hekwyn said, sounding surprised. 'I thought you'd still be sleeping.'

'I might say the same about you,' I said, wondering why he would be calling me this early in the day. Nothing good, I suspected.

'"The Imperium never sleeps"[1],' he quoted with a tinge of wry amusement in his voice. 'And something's come up I thought you might be interested in.' If I'd realised at the time just what this innocuous remark was going to lead to I would have cut him off with the first excuse I could think of and gone scuttling back to the relative safety of Glacier Peak, and to hell with the cold. At the time, though, I thought any distraction would do to lift my mood, and settled back in my chair to listen.

'Sounds intriguing,' I said. 'What have you been up to?'

---

1. *The catchphrase of Arbitrator Foreboding, a popular holo character of the time, who battled criminals, heretics and mutants with relish and a very big gun.*

'A bit of old-fashioned detective work,' Hekwyn said. 'Or at least watching the local praetors do some. They've picked up one of the middlemen in the smuggling operation you uncovered.'

'I'm impressed,' I said, meaning it for once.

Hekwyn's voice sounded quietly smug. 'It wasn't that hard. As you suggested, we took a look at people with access to the rail wagons going in and out of Glacier Peak. And frak me if there wasn't a freight dispatcher spending three times his annual income on obscura and joygirls.'

'And does this paragon of virtue have a name?' I asked.

'Kimeon Slablard. We've got him in a holding cell at the moment, thinking about all the terrible things that can happen to citizens who don't cooperate with the authorities in a properly public-spirited manner.' That made sense. If he was just a cat's-paw he'd probably spill his guts at the first opportunity, and making him sweat first would only help. If, on the other hand, he was part of the cult, he'd take as long to break as the ones we already had in custody and an hour or two's delay in getting started wouldn't make any perceptible difference. 'I thought you might like to sit in. Once he realises he's in the ordure with the Guard as well, he should snap like a twig.'

'It's worth a try,' I said. I risked a glance at Jurgen and decided he might as well finish his meal. It wasn't as if Slablard was going anywhere, after all. 'We'll be with you within the hour.'

In actuality it took slightly longer than that, the streets being choked by the citizens of Skitterfall setting off to work as though the day was perfectly normal and their

entire world wasn't about to be ravaged by a fleet of
Chaos marauders. But then I suppose that's a part of
what makes the Imperium what it is: the indomitable
spirit of even its most humble citizens. Or their incredible stupidity, which amounts to more or less the same
thing half the time.[1]

At any event the carriageways were full of groundcars chugging along at a pace which left them being
overtaken by the occasional energetic pedestrian, and
even Jurgen's remarkable driving skills weren't
enough to manoeuvre the Salamander through the
narrow gaps between the smaller, lighter civilian
vehicles. I was just beginning to think we should
have commandeered an aircar instead, despite my
aide's reluctance to fly, when he accelerated abruptly
up a flight of stone steps between two towering
buildings.

'Short cut,' he said, heedless of the gaggle of Administratum drones scattering before us spewing an
interesting assortment of profanity. He directed us
across a wide plaza cluttered with statues of noble
Adumbrian bureaucrats. A few vertiginous swerves
later and an equally precipitate descent down another
staircase apparently leading through a shopping district and a tram terminal, he drew up outside the
Arbites building in a space reserved for official vehicles.

A couple of officers stared at us suspiciously, but a
glance at my uniform and the heavy weapons aboard
our sturdy little vehicle seemed to disincline them to
challenge our right to be there.

---

1. *Cain is perhaps being overly cynical here. It's a common human reaction
to cling to the familiar in times of uncertainty, and many of the Adumbrians no doubt found sticking to their regular routines a source of reassurance.*

'Thank you, Jurgen,' I said, clambering out, unexpectedly grateful for the amasec I'd drunk earlier after all. 'That was very resourceful.'

'Couldn't have you missing your appointment, sir,' he said cheerfully.

Further conversation seemed superfluous, so I left him to deal with the praetors who seemed to have plucked up the courage to approach by now, and went inside.

'Commissar.' For a moment I failed to recognise the young praetor who stood inside the cool marble atrium beyond the heavy wooden doors, clearly waiting for me, then the nagging sense of familiarity clicked. Young Kolbe. With his helmet off the resemblance to his father was quite striking, although his build was taller and slimmer. 'It's good to see you again.'

'I'm pleased to find you so well,' I said.

Kolbe inclined his head in the same manner as his father. 'Your medic did an excellent job. I'm supposed to be on light duties, but under the circumstances...' his gesture took in the bustle surrounding us. Uniformed praetors were hurrying in all directions, many of them leading prisoners who were either cursing loudly or protesting their innocence according to temperament, and I even caught a glimpse of a couple of black-bodygloved members of the Arbites itself.

'Things do seem a little hectic,' I said as he escorted me across the echoing space towards the bank of elevators under a vast and tasteless mural of the Emperor scourging the unrighteous.

'We've been rounding up every low-life in Skitterfall who might have a connection to the heretics,' he told me cheerfully. 'And then there's the usual unrest you get in a civil emergency.' We side-stepped a redemptionist preacher and his congregation, still happily bawling his lungs out about the apocalypse about to descend on the unworthy in general and the riot squads who'd waded in to prevent them making an early start on the vice district in particular, despite their escort's frequent and enthusiastic application of shock batons. 'So arbitrator Hekwyn thought it might be a good idea to send me along to meet you.'

'Good idea,' I said, as we gained the sanctuary of the elevators and the relative shelter of the large stone eagles flanking them. Young Kolbe punched a couple of runes on one, and the doors clanked open, the brass filigree forming a pattern of interlocking eagles mirroring their large stone cousins.

'Sub-basement seventeen,' Kolbe said, looking up and drawing his own baton as the Redemptionist party collided noisily and violently with a group of joygirls on their way to an adjacent holding pen. 'If you'll excuse me?'

'By all means,' I assured him, grateful that here at least was a mess I didn't have to worry about sorting out, and watching him wade into the fracas with every sign of enjoyment. The doors creaked closed as I pressed the icon he'd indicated, and I began my descent into the lowest level of the building.

After about thirty seconds of tedium, made even worse by a scratchy recording of *Death to the Deviant* apparently performed by tone-deaf ratlings with nose flutes, the doors rattled open to reveal a plain anteroom with a scuffed carpet and an arbitrator in full body armour behind a desk pointing a riot gun in my direction.

'Commissar Cain,' I told her as casually as I could while staring down a gun barrel I could have comfortably fitted my thumb inside. 'I'm expected.'

'Commissar.' She put the clumsy weapon down and did something to a keypad on the desk. She must have had a comm-bead inside her helmet, because she nodded at something I couldn't hear, and waved me to a seat in the corner. 'The arbitrator senioris will be with you shortly.' I'd heard that one before and was beginning to think I should have brought something to read, but I'd barely had time to sit down before a thick steel door behind her swung open and Hekwyn emerged.

'Glad you could make it,' he greeted me, holding out a data-slate in his new augmetic hand. He seemed to be getting used to it now, judging distances as easily as he did with his original one. I took the slate, skimming through Slablard's record as quickly as I could. It was similar enough to the military charge sheets I was intimately familiar with for the job to take little time. By the time I reached the end we were halfway along a plain corridor, finished in unpainted rockcrete, in which blank metal doors were set at intervals, identical save for the numbers stencilled on them. The air was close, smelling of old sweat, bodily fluids and the unmistakable tang of acute fear which no one familiar with an eldar reiver slave pit can ever forget. 'He's in here.'

The door looked no different from any of the others around us, but Hekwyn seemed positive enough, tapping a six digit code into the keypad too rapidly for me to follow. The door opened, releasing the smell of flatulence, and I motioned the arbitrator through ahead of me politely.

---

1. From which we can conclude that Cain was now sufficiently past any residual trauma left by his nightmare to be fairly described as his old self again.

I was pretty sure our smuggler wouldn't have the wit or the determination to be waiting in ambush, in the hope of overpowering whoever next came through the door and making a run for it, but there was no point in taking any chances.[1] As it turned out, there wasn't much chance of that anyway, as he was quite firmly shackled to a chair in the middle of the chamber, and didn't strike me as the kind to chew his own arm off to escape. (Which I suppose pretty much ruled him out as Chaos cult material.)

I wasn't quite sure what I'd expected him to look like, but I knew I'd expected something a little more impressive. He was a small man with watery eyes which refused to make contact with whoever was talking to him and thinning brown hair; the net result was uncannily like a startled rodent.

'I want to see a legal representative,' he blustered as soon as we appeared. 'You can't just keep me here indefinitely.'

'What we want and what we get in life are seldom the same,' Hekwyn said regretfully.

Slablard squirmed. 'I want to talk to someone in authority.'

'That would be me,' Hekwyn said, stepping further into the room. Slablard's eyes widened at the sight of his uniform, then positively bulged when he saw mine. 'I have overall responsibility for the operation of the Arbites on Adumbria.' He paused a moment, giving this time to sink in, then indicated me. 'This is Commissar Cain, who you may also have heard of. I've invited him to sit in on our conversation as a matter of courtesy, since acts of treason also fall under military jurisdiction in a time of emergency.'

'Treason?' Slablard's voice rose an octave, sweat stains appearing under the arms of his coarse blue shirt as though someone had turned on a tap. 'I just moved a few crates!'

'Containing weapons subsequently used to attack His Majesty's Guardsmen,' I said as sternly as I could. 'And that's treason in my book.' Slablard looked desperately from one of us to the other, finally fixing on Hekwyn as the slightly less intimidating of the two.

'I didn't know.' he whined. 'How could I?'

'Perhaps if you'd asked?' Hekwyn suggested mildly.

The little man wilted visibly. 'You don't know these people. They're dangerous. You don't want to cross them, you get what I'm saying?'

'These people are heretics,' I said. 'Worshippers of the Ruinous Powers, sent here ahead of the invasion fleet to undermine our defences against them.' I leaned forward, fixing him with my best commissarial glare, which had made generals turn pale before now. 'Have you any idea how much harm you've done?'

'They told me it was just black market ore!' Slablard was practically in tears. 'You have to believe me, I'd never have dealt with them if I'd known they were heretics.'

'It's not me you have to convince,' I told him. 'It's the Emperor himself. You'd better just pray that your soul hasn't been corrupted by your association with the agents of darkness, or you'll be damned for eternity.' All claptrap, of course, but I delivered it as fervently as Beije would have done and felt quite pleased with my acting ability.

'That's hardly our judgement to make,' Hekwyn reminded me, as if he actually cared. I began to suspect that after years of data shuffling in the upper echelons he was relishing the chance to indulge in some hands-on arbitration. 'Once the threat of Chaos has been neutralised it will be for the Inquisition to determine who is or isn't tainted by the Dark Powers.'

That did it, as I'd been pretty sure it would. At the mention of the Inquisition Slablard broke down in hysterics, which threatened to go on for so long I eventually sacrificed part of the contents of my hip flask just to get him to calm down enough to talk. It was a shocking waste of good amasec even if his palate was refined enough to tell the difference (which I doubted), but there was plenty more back in my suite, and I had no doubt that Jurgen could find another bottle once that was gone.

I stepped gingerly round the puddle of urine spreading across the rockcrete floor, finally divining the purpose of the drain in the corner, and resumed my casual-but-dangerous pose leaning against the door.

'These people,' I began. 'Who are they, and where do we find them?'

TEN

'Competence on the battlefield is a myth. The side which
screws up next to last wins, it's as simple as that.'

– Lord General Zyvan

THE ONLY REAL problem we had with Slablard in the end
was shutting him up. I downloaded the list of names,
dates and locations he'd given us to the hololith in the
conference suite with the air of a conjurer at a children's
party producing an egg from an ear.

'If anything, we've got a little too much to go on
now,' I said. Zyvan and the senior Kolbe nodded, taking it all in as it scrolled up the display. Vinzand, I
noticed, was absent, presumably because this was an
operational matter and nothing he needed to be concerned with. Well, that suited me; the less debate there
was before we took action the better, so far as I was
concerned.

'My people should be able to pick up any of these individuals who slip though the net,' Hekwyn said. 'But under the circumstances we're a little stretched to be mounting simultaneous raids on half a dozen different addresses.'

'I see your point,' Zyvan replied, having evidently been keeping abreast of the situation in the city.[1] He turned to Kolbe. 'Perhaps the PDF could oblige us with the necessary manpower.'

He would rather have used Guardsmen I was sure, but we were so widely scattered it would have taken hours to bring sufficient troopers back to the city, and if the heretics noticed Slablard had disappeared in the meantime they'd be long gone by the time we were ready to deploy. The Valhallan tanks were already in place, of course, but I tried to picture a troop of Leman Russes moving stealthily through the crowded streets and had to suppress a smile; we might just as well vox ahead and let the cultists know we were coming.

'Of course.' Kolbe nodded, all calm efficiency, clearly confident in his troops' ability to deal with whatever awaited them. I hoped he was right. 'I can have a couple of companies at your disposal within minutes.'

'I'm sure that will be sufficient,' Zyvan said, straight-faced. That would give us practically two full platoons for each objective, which was as sure-fire a recipe for utter confusion as I could imagine; that number of troopers would be getting in each other's way more often than engaging the enemy. 'But perhaps we should assign personnel to the operations once we've determined conditions on the ground.'

---

1. *Not to mention the rest of the planet. The praetors in every major population centre were tied up with heretic hunting and the suppression of civil disorder, just as they were in Skitterfall.*

That took a while, as you'd imagine, but at last we'd worked out the optimum troop deployment for each of the objectives and Kolbe had issued the orders. I stretched, glanced at my chronograph, and found to my surprise that it was still a few moments short of noon.

'Well, that appears to be that,' I said, as Hekwyn departed for the Arbites building and the two generals stood, preparing to walk down to Zyvan's command post.

The lord general nodded. 'I suppose you must be eager to return to your regiment,' he said.

I thought of the bone-chilling cold of Glacier Peak and the endless tedium of the train journey before I reached it, and nodded with every appearance of enthusiasm I could muster.

'My place is with them,' I agreed, unable to find a plausible reason to delay my departure. One crumb of consolation was that I should be able to hang around here long enough to grab a decent lunch before I went, though.

Zyvan smiled, sure he could read my real thoughts. 'But you'd rather hang on here and see what the raids turn up, eh? After all, if it wasn't for you we wouldn't even have these leads.'

'I'm sure Arbitrator Hekwyn's people would have found them just as quickly,' I said, trying not to look too eager. If he meant what I thought he did, it looked as though I could hang around here in the warm, enjoying every comfort the place had to offer, for at least another day after all; maybe even longer if I drew out the process of appearing to evaluate the intelligence we gathered.

'I'm sure they would,' Zyvan said, sounding about as convinced of that as I had. 'If you don't mind delaying your departure for a while, it occurs to me things might go a little smoother this afternoon if we have a representative of the Commissariat along on the operation.' He shot a sidelong glance at Kolbe. 'No reflection on your people of course. It would just save us the necessity of forwarding a formal report to them afterwards.'

'By all means,' Kolbe said, no doubt happier at the prospect of his troopers' performance being scrutinised by me, rather than some rear-echelon data-pusher with the benefit of hindsight.

'It would be an honour to serve with your command,' I told him. 'Albeit briefly.'

If I'd known what I was about to get into, of course, my answer would have been very different, and I'd practically have run for the blasted train, but all I could see at the time was the prospect of another couple of days of good food and comfortable bedding.

So it was that, an hour or so later, I found myself rattling down a city boulevard in the back of the Salamander, half a dozen Chimeras behind me and my comm-bead full of excited chatter from PDF troopers all keyed up about their first taste of action.

'Vox discipline,' I reminded them, trying to make allowances, and the extraneous traffic died with gratifying speed. 'We're passing the outer marker.'

After some consideration, I'd attached myself to the group going after a house in the suburbs owned by one of the people Slablard had implicated, a woman called Kyria Sejwek, who Hekwyn claimed had tenuous links to a number of organised crime figures and probably ran a stable of high-rent joygirls. She also had a very good lawyer and connections to several members of the Council of Claimants, which meant that so far the Arbites had been unable to accumulate sufficient evidence for an arrest.

Taking on a handful of bodyguards and a house full of women seemed a lot safer than going in against the warehouse where the weapons had ended up, which was no doubt heavily guarded and stuffed with explosives to boot, although I hadn't shared those reasons for selecting this particular objective with the generals, of course.

'This is the obvious target,' I'd said, highlighting the warehouse on the holomap, and giving every appearance of being eager to storm the place single-handed. A few other icons glowed, picking out the secondary targets, and I pointed at the Sejwek house with just the right degree of a puzzled frown. 'But something about this place doesn't feel right.'

'How do you mean?' Kolbe asked obligingly, and I shrugged.

'I can't quite put my finger on it. But this woman's record – highly placed, intimations of vice – I'm probably reading too much into it, but…'

'It could be the centre of the Slaaneshi cult in the city,' Zyvan said, taking the bait.

I continued to look dubious. 'It's possible of course. But the warehouse is definitely our most promising lead.'

'Nevertheless,' the lord general said, the idea I'd planted clearly taking root in his mind, 'it's a possibility we can't afford to ignore. Perhaps you'd better accompany that platoon instead.'

'It might be wise,' Kolbe agreed. 'If there's evidence of sorcery there, the men would find your presence extremely reassuring.'

'Well,' I said, with every sign of reluctance. 'If you're both convinced of the need…'

By the time I'd finished protesting, of course, they were practically insisting I raided what I had no doubt was nothing more sinister than a high-class bordello, and I gave in with as much good grace as I could simulate.

'That must be it,' Jurgen said, indicating a high brick wall running along the edge of the pavement. It certainly seemed to be; the other houses, large rambling structures, their windows glowing warmly, were set back from the road behind lawns and shrubberies designed to emphasise the scale and ostentation of the buildings they contained. Only this one was sealed away behind what was beginning to look like a fortification, and my palms began to tingle with the intimation that perhaps this wasn't going to be the pushover I'd expected. Then again, given what we knew of her character and probable activities, Sejwek no doubt had a lot to hide in any case.

'It is,' I confirmed, after a surreptitious glance at the mapslate just to make sure. I activated the comm-bead. 'This is it,' I broadcast over the platoon tacnet, so everyone could hear me.[1] 'I don't have to tell you how important this is, for Adumbria and for the Imperium. I hope I also don't need to tell you that General Kolbe and I have complete confidence in you all, and know you won't let us or the Emperor down. Onward to victory!' It was one of the pre-battle speeches I'd been reciting by rote since the day I left the schola, but the PDF troopers had never heard it before and it did the job. Far better than I expected, as things turned out.

'You heard the commissar.' That was the platoon commander, an excitable young man called Nallion who

---

1. *The PDF troopers wouldn't be equipped with personal comm-beads, like the Guardsmen Cain was used to fighting alongside (or more likely behind if he could contrive it), but each squad would have included a specialist carrying a portable vox unit.*

looked barely old enough to shave, and who wore his officer's cap at what he no doubt thought was a rakish angle. 'Deploy to your positions!'

After a chorus of acknowledgements from the various squad leaders, the Chimeras split up, Nallion's command vehicle and first squad halting in front of the main gates (tasteless wrought-iron scrollwork with a hint of drooping lilies and far too much gilt) while the rest broke left and right, tearing up the lawns and flattening the shrubberies of the no-doubt outraged neighbours. Jurgen and I kept up with the left flank, which dropped a Chimera by the side wall before crashing through a boundary hedge to link up with another troop transport which had approached from the other side.

'Third and fifth squad in position,' I reported, more to remind everyone I was still there than because it was necessary. A ratling gardener was staring at us and the deep furrows across what had obviously once been a lovingly-tended lawn, with an expression of stupefied astonishment even more pronounced than was usual for his kind. As his eyes fell on Jurgen he started visibly and fled.

'Mister Spavin!' he cried as he went. 'Mister Spavin! The doom's come upon us at last!' He spoke truer than he knew, of course, but there was no time to worry about him or his employer now. I listened to a chorus of position reports in my comm-bead as the other squad leaders reported in, and Nallion gave the order to attack.

'All units move in!' he shouted in a voice which barely trembled from the tension, and with a roar of gunning engines the Chimeras moved forward, their heavy bolters opening up and blowing large sections of the wall to rubble. The Salamander jerked under my feet as we ploughed across it, but I kept my balance instinctively after nearly two decades of being driven by Jurgen, and I hoisted myself up behind the comforting bulk of the bolter. Gouts of dust and the rattle of heavy weapons fire in the distance were all the confirmation I needed that the other three elements of our assault were on the move, although to their credit the squad commanders kept their heads admirably and relayed a steady stream of status reports as crisply and concisely as a Guardsman would.

'Second squad disembarking,' their sergeant said, followed almost at once by similar messages from his counterparts in first and fourth. 'Resistance light.'

A crackle of small-arms fire could be heard from the direction of the house now, as the occupants responded to the unexpected attack. Absently I picked out the sounds of stubber fire from the sharper crack of the lasguns the PDF troopers bore, which confirmed that at the very least the occupants had access to illegal weaponry. Slugs began to rattle against the armour plate of the Salamander and I returned fire without thinking, hosing down the facade of the house as Jurgen continued to bear down on it across a lawn no less immaculate than the one we'd chewed to pieces next door.

Without warning, one of the Chimeras ahead of us lurched to a halt, the red flare of explosive detonation standing out starkly in the perpetual twilight, and panicked troopers began bailing out. A couple fell, caught by the blizzard of stubber fire.

'Third squad! Stay in cover, damn it!' I just had time to yell, before Jurgen swung the bucking Salamander hard to the left. Something shot past us no more than a metre away, leaving a trail of smoke, and detonated against what was left of the garden wall behind us.

'They've got missile launchers!' I voxed, trying to bring the bolter round to retaliate and reflecting that I could have been on a nice uncomfortable train by now instead of in mortal danger again. 'Leave the vehicles and move in on foot.'

'Acknowledged,' Nallion replied. 'All squads advance by fire and movement.'[1] He was on the ball all right, I had to give him that.

'Jurgen!' I called. 'Did you see where that rocket came from?'

'About one o'clock, commissar,' he responded, as calmly as if I'd just asked him to get some more tanna. I swung the pintel-mounted weapon around in that direction, and my bowels spasmed. There were at least two missile launchers being aimed at us from within a pair of tall glass windows, and what looked like a heavy stubber on a tripod. Most, to my vague surprise, were being wielded with considerable expertise by young women whose minimal state of dress left little doubt as to their day jobs.[2] Any second now we'd be joining the Chimera behind us, which was blazing away merrily by this time.

'Head for the nearest cover,' I yelled, squeezing the trigger and hoping to put their aim off just long enough for Jurgen to take us out of the line of fire. To my amazement he gunned the engine, accelerating even more rapidly towards the house.

'Very good, sir.' He triggered the hull-mounted heavy bolter, reducing a couple of the amazons to unpleasant

---

1. *A common infantry tactic, where half the squad lays down covering fire while the other half advances, then the first group of troopers provides covering fire for the rest to catch up.*

2. *Or night jobs, to be a little more accurate.*

stains, and before I had time to realise what he was doing he had roared up the patio, scattering some ornamental shrubs in the process, to ram us through the flimsy wood and glass partition behind which our assailants had taken shelter. One of the survivors disappeared under the tracks with an abruptly-curtailed shriek, and the Salamander slammed to a halt against the far wall of an opulent living room, reducing a marble fireplace to rubble in the process.

'Fifth squad! Follow the commissar!' The squad sergeant, Varant if my memory serves, bawled in the comm-bead, and before I knew it half a score of troopers had followed up our impromptu and precipitous entry, finishing off the rest of the defenders in the process, which at least saved us the bother. The survivors of third squad joined them a moment later, and everyone looked at me expectantly.

'Very good,' I said, adjusting my cap and stepping down from the Salamander as nonchalantly as I could. 'Let's get this done.'

'Yes sir,' Varant said, with an expression of awe on his face, and started organising the men.

I looked at my aide. 'Jurgen...' I began, then decided there wasn't any point remonstrating with him. He'd followed my orders after all, and things had worked out as well as they ever did. 'That was...' Words, for once, failed me.

'Resourceful?' he suggested, reaching back inside the driver's compartment for the melta, which, true to form, he'd brought with him.

'To say the least,' I said, drawing my laspistol.

'Second squad advancing,' their sergeant reported in my comm-bead, his voice calm as ever. 'No resistance so far.'

'Copy that,' Nallion responded. 'First squad report.' There was a pause, broken only by the hissing of static.

'First squad, respond.' My palms were itching again, a sense of forboding I could almost taste fluttering in my gut. The lieutenant's voice took on an edge of asperity. 'First squad, where are you?'

'Fourth squad,' a new voice cut in, a note of suppressed panic quite clearly detectable. 'We've found bodies. Could be them.'

'What do you mean, could be?' Nallion snapped.

'It's hard to tell, sir. There's not much left…' His voice choked off.

This wouldn't do at all. We'd clearly blundered into something very dangerous, and if anyone panicked now it would spread like a spark in a promethium tank. Which would cut my chances of getting out of here in one piece more considerably than I found acceptable.

'This is Commissar Cain,' I cut in. 'Stay alert. Stay focussed. Fire on anything that moves which isn't one of ours. Is that understood?'

'Yes sir.' It seemed to have done the trick anyway, the man's voice was shaking a little less. 'Moving on to the next mark.'

'Good,' I told him, hoping to bolster the squad's sagging morale. 'Remember, the Emperor protects.'

I never finished the platitude, the vox channel suddenly becoming swamped with sounds which, in an eerie, overlapping echo, carried to our ears through the air a fraction of a second later. Screams, the chatter of lasguns on full auto and a sound which raised the hairs on the back of my neck: melodious, inhuman laughter. A moment later, the sounds of the evidently one-sided battle ended abruptly.

'Fourth squad, report,' Nallion bellowed, but no answer came, and if he honestly expected one he was the biggest optimist in the system.

'What do we do, sir?' Varant asked, and after a moment I realised he was looking at me, ignoring the lieutenant's voice completely. I assessed the situation rapidly. Retreat, always a good choice in my book, was impossible. Apart from the fact that it would undermine my reputation, it would expose us to Emperor alone knew how much fire from the house as we made our way back across that wide open lawn, and I didn't intend to become a bit of easy target practice for some civilian tart with a new toy. I shrugged, trying to look nonchalant and speak through a mouth which had suddenly gone as dry as the hotside.

'We complete the mission,' I said simply. 'There's something foul in this place, and we need to cleanse it.'

It seemed painfully obvious now that my carefully contrived excuse for being here was no more than the truth after all, which I suppose at least proves that the Emperor has a well-developed sense of irony, and I'd seen enough sorcery over the years to know that confronting it straight away is the only chance you've got of survival. Not a particularly good chance, I grant you, but trying to run from it only gives it more time to grow in power and come after you on its own terms rather than yours.

'I do hope that's not a criticism of the cleaning staff,' a mellifluous voice chimed in. 'They do their best, you know, but it's such a rambling old place it's hard to keep on top of.'

The woman who spoke smiled easily as she strolled into the room, as though finding a score[1] of armed men

---

1. *If Cain is being literal here we can infer that only two men from third squad were actually incapacitated after their Chimera was destroyed; however, it seems more likely from his other remarks that he's simply going for an approximate round number and that they suffered more casualties than this.*

standing over the bodies of her associates was the most natural thing in the world. I began to bring my laspistol up instinctively, my finger tightening on the trigger, then froze, my heart pounding. I'd come within a hair of shooting Amberley! For a moment I was so startled that I was literally paralysed with astonishment, something which up until then I'd always assumed was merely a figurative cliché in the more undemanding kind of popular fiction.

Her smile widened as she looked at me and the knot of troopers whose lasguns all hung slack in their hands.

'I know you must be surprised to see me here,' she purred, the words sounding impossibly sweet and seductive. Something tried to push itself towards the front of my mind, but the vision of her, lovely as the last time we'd parted, the flower I'd plucked impulsively from the hegantha bush on the veranda still tucked behind her ear, filled my senses.

'Margritta?' one of the troopers asked, as though he couldn't believe his own eyes, and the burgeoning thought became clearer. Something definitely wasn't right…

'Yes, my love.' Amberley reached out a hand, caressing him gently on the cheek, and a surge of white-hot jealously erupted through me. Before I could react in any way, however, the trooper screamed, his body contorting, seeming to wither like a dried ploin before dropping to the floor.

'Commissar?' Jurgen tugged at my sleeve, an expression of puzzlement on his face. 'Are you going to let her get away with that?'

'She's an inquisitor,' I started to say. 'She can do what she likes,' but when I looked up again Amberley had gone. (Well she hadn't, of course, because she was never there in the first place, but you know what I mean.) In her place, standing over the crumbling corpse of the fallen soldier, was a dumpy middle-aged woman in an unwise pink gown which would have looked fine on someone ten years younger and as many kilos lighter. She looked directly at me, an expression of surprise and outrage beginning to suffuse her vaguely porcine features.

'Madame Sejwek,' I said, savouring the flicker of uncertainty which rose in her eyes, almost losing my aim from the surge of anger which left my hand shaking from its force. Fortunately my augmetic fingers were immune to such an emotional reaction and kept the muzzle of my laspistol centred firmly on her forehead. 'Impersonating an inquisitor is a capital offence.'

She just had time to look even more startled before I pulled the trigger, and her warp-tainted brain erupted from the back of her skull to ruin a wall hanging which had evidently been chosen for its subject matter rather than its aesthetic qualities.

'What happened?' Varant asked, looking slightly stunned. The rest of the troopers were snapping out of it too now, muttering in low tones, making the sign of the aquila and generally looking sheepish.

'She was a witch,' I told him, keeping things as simple as I could. 'She did something to our minds. Made us see…' I made what I assumed at the time to be the obvious deductive leap, but which Malden later confirmed was a known power of Slaaneshi psykers. 'Someone we care about.'[1]

'I see,' he said, looking confused. 'Lucky she didn't fool you.'

'Commissars are trained to spot that kind of thing,' I lied smoothly, not wanting to draw any more attention

---

1. *Which for Cain was positively effusive, and, I must admit, rather gratifying.*

than necessary to Jurgen. To tell the truth I was more than a little concerned that Sejwek had managed to get inside my head at all while he was so close. (To my relief, I learned later that he'd gone back to the Salamander for his lasgun while I was busy with the vox signals, taking me out of the range of his protective aura. It had belatedly occurred to him that his beloved melta might be a little counterproductive in such a potentially inflammable building; as always his pragmatism couldn't be faulted, although his timing left a lot to be desired.)

'Well, I suppose at least we know what happened to first and fourth squad,' the sergeant said, looking from the body of the witch to the desiccated husk of his erstwhile subordinate.

'Possibly,' I said. It didn't add up to me. Fourth squad had died quickly, in combat, not held by delusion to be picked off one by one. 'There's only one way to find out.'

And find out we did. The mortal remains of our comrades, and there were precious few of them left, were scattered around a ground-floor hallway at the foot of a huge wooden staircase, the banisters of which were carved in the semblance of fornicating couples in a bewildering variety of anatomically improbable positions. Blood and scorch marks spattered the walls, which were decorated with the kind of debauched murals that I'd seen before in the hab dome hidden away on the coldside, and a nagging sense of familiarity fought its way to the surface of my thoughts.

'The rest of the house is clear,' Nallion reported, looking slightly green as he took in the carnage, but determined not to throw up in front of the commissar. 'No sign of anyone else on the premises.'

'False walls, hidden chambers?' I asked, the memory of the hab dome still fresh, that strange scent that had flooded the air there still faintly detectable through the more pervasive one of butchery.

Nallion shook his head. 'No sign of anything like that,' he said. 'We can bring in some tech-priests with specialised equipment...'

'Don't worry about it,' I told him, to his evident relief. 'The Guard will take care of that. You and your men have done enough, and done it well.'

'Thank you, sir.' He took the hint and frakked off, with a perfunctory salute and an air of undisguised relief.

'Jurgen,' I said, pointing to the staircase. It was large and apparently solid, but we could have parked the Salamander in the space it enclosed. 'If you wouldn't mind?'

'Of course not, sir,' he assured me, and a moment later the familiar roar of the melta and an actinic flash through my tightly-closed eyelids told me he'd done as requested. Despite his fears of accidental arson (which he confided to me later, a little too late to have been much help if they were founded, but with Jurgen following orders always came first) the surrounding wood failed to catch light. A large, smoking hole was punched through the treads, looking uncannily like the entrance to a cave. I borrowed a luminator from one of his ever-present equipment pouches and took a cautious look inside.

'Emperor on Earth!' I reeled back, choking from the smell. If anything, it was worse than the chamber we'd found in the hab dome, although the details were depressingly familiar. The pile of twisted corpses, still grinning in infernal rapture, the sanity-blasting sigils on the walls… I backed away until I was on the other side of the hallway and contacted the lord general directly.

'It seems we were right about this place,' I told him. 'It was being put to unholy use.' I hesitated. 'And if I'm right,' I added, the knotting of my guts telling me I was, 'we got here too late. Whatever they were doing, they've already done.'

Editorial Note:

Given the course of subsequent events, the following communication may prove somewhat revealing.

To: The Office of the Commissariat, Departmento Munitorum, Coronus Prime

From: Tomas Beije, Regimental Commissar to the Tallarn 229th

Date: 285 937 M41

Astropathic Path: Blocked at this time. Delivery deferred.

Gentlemen and esteemed colleagues,

It is with a heavy heart I feel I must call into question the competence of a fellow commissar, not least because the officer in question was a classmate of mine at the schola progenium, and as we all know such ties remain strong. However, I would be derelict in my duty not to bring this matter to your attention, and must set aside my personal feelings for the sake of the Guard, the Imperium and the Emperor Himself. Truly our duty to Him must outweigh all else, and after much prayer and fasting I can see no alternative.

The individual in question is none other than Ciaphas Cain, the regimental commissar of the Valhallan 597th. I am aware that he has something of an inflated reputation, which may incline some of you to dismiss my concerns, but nonetheless I feel I have no alternative but to speak out. Indeed, it may be this very reputation which has led to his current sad decline as an effective commissar: how truly has it been said that the glory we gain blinds us first with its lustre.[1]

I have observed at first hand that discipline and proper order are practically non-existent in the regiment with which Commissar Cain has been charged, his own aide failing to reach the standards expected of a member of His Divine Majesty's blessed legions, while serious infractions and breaches of discipline are treated as minor matters barely worthy of his attention. Since arriving on Adumbria he has neglected his duties altogether, spending more time in the planetary capital than with the 597th, even going so far as to

---

1. A quotation from Caddaway's *Paths to Damnation*, a Redemptionist tract of dubious theology and even worse literacy.

attach himself to a local PDF company rather than rejoin the Guard unit he should properly have been most concerned with.

It might be claimed that his discovery of not one but two concealed nests of heretic sorcerers vindicates his actions, but consider: in neither case was he in time to prevent their fell purpose, whatever that was, and his interference in a PDF operation in which he had no official interest may well have led to sufficient delay to have ensured such a failure on at least one occasion. I draw no inference from this, of course, but merely suggest the coincidence was fortuitous for our enemies.

May the divine light of His Glorious Majesty illuminate your deliberations.

Your Humble Servant,

Tomas Beije.

Thought for the day: The traitor's hand lies closer than you think.

ELEVEN

*'I don't care how bloody sanctioned they are,
a psyker's a psyker, and anything to do with the warp
is more trouble than it's worth.'*

– General Karis

I WAS BEGINNING to get heartily sick of the sight of that
conference room by now. Every time I entered it, it
seemed, my life became more complicated. Even the
prospect of a hearty dinner and a comfortable bed,
which had been sufficient to keep me in Skitterfall that
morning, began to look like scant consolation, receding
as they both were into an indefinite future. The damn
place was getting steadily more crowded, too. Aside
from Zyvan and myself, and a couple of his aides whose
names hadn't stuck if anyone had actually bothered to
introduce us, Kolbe, Hekwyn and Vinzand were present, and all had decided to mark the urgency of the

situation by bringing a flunkey or two along themselves. Malden was there too, with the far end of the table pretty much to himself as usual, chatting to a woman whose sunken eye sockets would have marked her out as an astropath even without the distinctive robes she wore. The unease most of those present clearly felt at the sight of two spooks in the same room was palpable, although had I but known it the feeling was about to get a whole lot worse.

'Are you all right, Ciaphas?' Zyvan asked, and I nodded, trying to dismiss the image of the chamber we'd found from my mind. It wasn't easy, I can tell you that, and that struck me as slightly odd given the sheer number of horrors I'd faced in my career up to that point. It kept coming back to me, overlaid with the memory of the similar chamber we'd found in the hab dome and that damnable laughter I'd heard as the PDF soldiers died. That had a haunting sense of familiarity about it too, although how or why I couldn't put my finger on.

'I'm fine,' I said, picking up a mug of tanna from the refreshment table. As usual, I was the only one drinking it. I glanced around the conference room, which was filling up (except for the end where the spooks were), and tried to change the subject before he started asking any more questions. 'If that's everyone, I suppose we ought to get started.'

'Nearly everyone,' Zyvan said, helping himself to a smoked grox sandwich. Before I had a chance to ask what he meant by that, some kind of commotion erupted outside the door. Voices were raised, and I found myself reaching instinctively for my chainsword, but the lord general's relaxed demeanour forestalled the motion. (Not without an amused glance in my direction as he registered the movement, I might add.)

'Do I look as though I need to show your underlings my credentials?' The question was directed at Zyvan, as though there were no other people in the room, and to all intents and purposes there might as well not have been. A young woman, astonishingly petite but somehow managing to fill the entire doorframe with the force of her personality, strode past the quivering woodwork, the ashen faces of a couple of the lord general's personal bodyguards just visible in the corridor outside. Zyvan dismissed them with a gesture, and they hurried to close the door behind her with remarkable alacrity.

'Of course not.' Zyvan bowed formally. 'You honour us all with your presence.'

'Of course I do,' she snapped back irritably. 'And don't expect me to make a habit of it.' Her hair was dark and lustrous, the hue of open space, falling to the shoulders which her simply-cut gown left bare. The dress seemed to have been woven from fibres of pure gold, reflecting the light in a fashion I found almost dazzling, clinging to her pleasingly plump figure in a fashion which left very little of it to the imagination, and setting off the preternaturally pale skin of her décolletage to perfection.

The thing which held my eyes, and every other pair in the room, however, was the bandana around her forehead. It was woven from the same material as her dress, but in the exact centre of it the image of an eye had been embroidered in thread as dark as her hair. Without thinking I made the sign of the aquila, and believe me, I wasn't the only one.

'May I present the Lady Gianella Dimarco, navigatrix of the *Indestructible*,' Zyvan said, addressing the room in general, as though anyone present could possibly not have realised who she was (well, maybe the astropath, I suppose).

Dimarco sighed. 'Let's just get on with it, shall we?' She dropped into a vacant seat at the spooky end of the table, no doubt feeling she had slightly more in common with Malden and the blind woman than the rest of us.[1] Everyone else shuffled awkwardly into their chairs, leaving as wide a gap as possible between the psykers and themselves.

'By all means.' Zyvan inclined his head courteously. 'I'm sure we all appreciate you taking the time to join us in person.'

Well he might. I would have been just as happy with a written report and less of the superior attitude, assuming she had anything useful to contribute at all. (Which of course she had. And if I'd been thinking a little more clearly I would have realised she must have been scared witless to subject herself to the company of scruffy little proles like us in the first place.)

'Of course you do,' Dimarco said irritably. Her dark eyes swept the room, and despite knowing intellectually that they couldn't do me any harm, it was the one the bandana concealed which could kill in an instant, I shuddered, reluctant to meet them. 'But you're not going to like what I've got to say.'

That would have been true if we were discussing music or the weather, given what I'd seen of her personality (which, to be fair, was bordering on the amiable for a navigator), but even so I felt the familiar premonitory tingling in the palms of my hands.

'Nevertheless,' Zyvan said, inclining his head.

---

1. *Perhaps, or she may simply not have registered the distinction. Members of the Navis Nobilitae seem to regard anyone who isn't another jumped-up little mutant with a warp eye as scarcely more than orks with table manners, and treat them accordingly.*

Dimarco sighed. 'I'll keep this as simple as I can, so even a bunch of blinders[1] should be able to grasp it.'

She leaned forward, her elbows on the polished wooden table, and supported her chin on her steepled fingers, revealing an impressive amount of cleavage in the process. 'The warp currents around Adumbria are strong, but predictable. Usually.'

'Usually?' Vinzand asked, a note of alarm evident in his voice.

Dimarco looked at him with the expression of an ecclesiarch who has just heard one of the congregation fart loudly in the middle of the benediction (something you get used to attending services accompanied by Jurgen[2]).

'I'm getting to that,' she snapped. 'Do I tell you how to count paperclips?' After a moment of embarrassing silence she continued. 'They normally form a complex but stable vortex, centred on the planet itself. This, in part, accounts for the system's position as a major trading port.'

The Adumbrians present nodded with more than a trace of smugness. Dimarco shrugged, with interesting effects on her dress and what I could see of its contents. 'I couldn't tell you why this is, though.' She glanced almost imperceptibly at her fellow psykers.

'It seems to be something to do with the orbital dynamics,' Malden said dryly. 'The fact that the world is

---

1. *A term used by navigators to describe those without their dubious gift of warpsight. As it's among the least offensive we can infer that Dimarco was making what she no doubt thought of as a considerable effort to be gracious.*

2. *Which may seem surprising, given the cavalier attitude Cain usually expresses towards the pious and matters of faith. However, attendance at certain services would have been part of his commissarial duties, and therefore unavoidable; having his aide accompany him on these occasions would normally be a matter of protocol.*

rotationally locked sets up a resonance in the warp, which bends the currents.'

'Something of an oversimplification,' the astropath said, her voice surprisingly young. 'But unless you can feel them directly, it's the closest you're likely to get.'

'Wait a minute,' Kolbe said. 'You mean these currents are shifting?'

Dimarco sighed loudly. 'What have we just been saying? Of course they're frakking shifting!' As her voice rose in pitch I began to realise she wasn't just being a snotty pain in the arse, she was genuinely worried; probably more so than she'd been in a long time. (And when you consider she'd been serving on a battleship, which had undoubtedly been shot at a few times, that would be saying something.) 'Three times since we got here. Big, sudden shifts. Which, in case you haven't been paying attention, is something which definitely shouldn't be happening.'

'Three times?' I asked, before I could stop myself, and the woman's night-black eyes were on me again, spraying contempt like the barrel of a hellgun. Before she could say something trite and obvious, like asking if I was deaf, I nodded thoughtfully and continued to speak, overriding any sarcastic comment she might be about to make. 'Can you give us a precise time on that?' The effect was quite satisfying, I have to say: a faint moue of puzzlement flickered across her features, and she bit back the words she'd been preparing to fling with a faint choking sound.

'Not precise, no,' she said. She turned to the astropath. 'Faciltiatrix Agnetha?'

The blind woman nodded. 'Since the first one was what cut us off from the rest of the fleet[1], I can tell you

---

1. *From which we can infer that Agnetha was the chief astropath from Zyvan's flagship, rather than a local civilian.*

to the second. The others I'd need to check if you want more accuracy than within an hour or two.'

'That would be fine,' I said, a sudden sinking feeling telling me I'd just made an intuitive leap I really didn't want to be right about. Unfortunately I was: the most recent shift in the warp currents had happened earlier that day, shortly before our eventful raid on the Sejwek house. (The other attacks had all gone without a hitch, of course, including the one on the warehouse I'd been so keen to avoid: the heretics had already moved the weapons out, and the place was deserted when the PDF got there. The only consolation was that at least I'd survived the mess I'd got myself into, and had inadvertently boosted my reputation for sagacity and courage into the bargain.)

'So,' Zyvan said, looking as perturbed as I'd ever seen him, 'the heretics are doing something to affect the warp currents. The big question is why.'

'With respect, my lord,' Malden said, 'the big question is what. If they really are responsible for this, we're dealing with a level of power far greater than any mortal psyker could possibly wield.'

The growing sense of apprehension I felt curdled in my gut. There was an obvious answer to that, and I didn't want to be the one to state it. Nobody else seemed willing to verbalise the thought, though, despite the number of ashen faces around me who had presumably reached the same conclusion.

'When you examined the room we found in the hab dome,' I said at last, 'you said you thought some of the sigils there were part of a summoning ritual. Did you find any similar ones in the Sejwek house?'

'We did,' Malden said. 'Almost identical.' He permitted himself the ghost of a smile. 'It's hard to say if they were exactly the same, as your method of entry erased a few.' Along with the wall they'd been painted on, of course.

'In your opinion,' Zyvan said, clearly reluctant to hear the answer, 'could they have raised some kind of warp entity with sufficient power to affect the currents?'

'It's possible.' The young psyker nodded. 'There are daemons strong enough to do that.' An audible gasp of horror rippled around the room as he casually used the word everyone else had been so carefully trying to avoid. Dimarco looked as though she was about to be sick, and I could hear Hekwyn muttering one of the catechisms under his breath. 'I doubt you could hold on to one that powerful, though, at least for long.'

'Maybe they didn't have to,' Agnetha suggested. 'If it was cooperating with them voluntarily...' Her voice trailed away, leaving us all to contemplate the same uncomfortable thought. What possible bribe could tempt a daemon to work alongside human cultists, and what blasphemous goal could they conceivably have in common?

'Does that mean the thing's still at large somewhere?' Hekwyn asked, regaining his composure with a visible effort.

'They can't stay in the material world for very long,' I reminded him. 'It'll be back in the warp where it belongs by now.' I turned to Kolbe. 'Probably thanks to the heroic sacrifice of your troopers,' I added. 'From what I heard they were giving a good account of themselves.'

Actually it sounded like they were panicking and dying horribly, which was what you'd expect under the circumstances, but if we were really facing a threat that terrible the more I could do to boost morale the better.

'Until the next time they summon it,' Dimarco said limply, the arrogance well and truly knocked out of her by the realisation of what we were facing. (But not for long, of course – she was a navigator after all.)

'Assuming they do,' Zyvan said.

'Of course they will,' Dimarco rejoined, no doubt taking some comfort in being able to contradict someone. 'If they'd already succeeded in whatever they're trying to do we wouldn't be sitting around here discussing it, would we?' Which sounded like a fair point to me.

'Can any of you take a guess at what that might be?' I asked, trying to project an air of calm reassurance the way they'd taught me at the schola.

I certainly wasn't feeling either calm or reassured, you can depend on that, but the familiar routine of maintaining morale helped me at least look as though I was coping.

Agnetha narrowed her sightless eyes thoughtfully. 'Disrupting our communications, obviously,' she said. 'But they managed that the first time.'

'Cutting us off physically from the rest of the fleet,' Dimarco said, clearly fighting to keep her voice level. 'When I look at the currents directly, it's as if they're brewing up into a localised warp storm, centred on the planet. They're already getting too turbulent to navigate easily.'

'That doesn't make sense, though,' Kolbe objected. 'They'd be cutting us off from their own invasion fleet too.'

'Perhaps that's the idea,' I suggested. 'Let them in, and then close the door before our reinforcements get here.'

Malden looked dubious. 'That would require some pretty good timing,' he pointed out. 'And the warp isn't that cooperative.'

'Well, maybe they know something we don't,' Dimarco snapped, looking more like her old self with every passing minute.

'No doubt they do,' Zyvan said. 'But we know things that they don't, too.' He turned to Hekwyn and Kolbe. 'We need to track down every lead we can squeeze out of the sites you raided. The rest of the cult must have gone to ground somewhere.'

'We're already following up on that,' Hekwyn assured him. He exchanged a glance with Kolbe. 'We'll find them, don't worry.'

'I'm sure you will,' Zyvan said. 'But we're running out of time. If they really are trying to stir up a warp storm to bottle us in, we'll be sitting waterfowl for their invasion fleet.'

It was probably not the most tactful thing he could have said, under the circumstances. Vinzand and his civilian advisors started muttering among themselves, and Dimarco let out a strangulated squeak.

'Well let's make sure it doesn't come to that,' I said. Emperor help me, I was beginning to run out of soothing platitudes already, and the meeting looked like it was going to go on for hours yet. In reality, though, it was about to be abruptly terminated.

'Excuse me, sir.' One of Zyvan's aides approached him, a comm-bead visible in his ear and a data-slate clutched in his hand. 'I think you should see this.'

'Thank you.' Zyvan took it and studied the screen, his expression unreadable. My palms started tingling again. Whatever the news was, it had to be bad. After a moment he handed the slate to me.

'What is it?' I started to say, but the words choked themselves off as I glanced down the page, the breath freezing in my throat as surely as if I'd just stepped into a Valhallan shower.

'Ladies and gentlemen,' the lord general said gravely, 'I've just been informed that our picket ships are engaging the enemy in the outer system. As of this moment Adumbria is under martial law. All Guard and PDF units are to be placed on full invasion alert.'

Blast, I thought. After all I'd been through today, I wouldn't even get the dinner I'd been hoping for.

Editorial Note:

As usual, Cain takes little interest in anything which doesn't affect him directly, so his own narrative jumps rather abruptly at this point. Accordingly, I felt it best to insert some material from other sources in order to present a more balanced picture of the overall situation.

From *Sablist in Skitterfall: a brief history of the Chaos incursion* by Dagblat Tincrowser, 957 M41.

If the first blood of the ground campaign had gone to the Valhallan 597th, the credit for the first victory of the conflict in space must surely be given to the crews of the picket ships patrolling the outer reaches of the shipping lanes. To fully appreciate their courage and that of their squadron commander Horatio Bugler, we must bear in mind that they were hopelessly outnumbered by the approaching invaders, and knew it; their job was simply to report as much as they could of the size and disposition of the enemy fleet and escape with their lives if they could. That they did so much more is a shining testament to the fighting spirit of the Imperial Navy and Captain Bugler's outstanding qualities as a tactician and leader of men.[1]

With only two frigates at his disposal, his own *Escapade* and the equally lightly-armed *Virago*, he somehow managed to cripple three of the enemy vessels before withdrawing, having sustained only minor damage to both ships.

From *Flashing Blades! The Falchion-class frigates in action* by Leander Kasmides, 126 M42.

An interesting encounter occurred during the attempted invasion of Adumbria, a minor trading world on the fringes of the Damocles Gulf, by traitor forces in 937 M41. Two Falchions had been left on picket duty in the outer system when the main invasion fleet emerged from the warp. The *Escapade* under the command of Captain Bugler and the *Virago* under Captain Walenbruk were both all but untried at this time, having been attached to a task force sent to the Kastafore system a few months before directly from the shipyards at Voss. There they saw little action, having been relegated to extended patrol duties in lightly-contested regions; probably

---

1. *As most readers have no doubt guessed, this is an early incident in the long and glorious career of Fleet Admiral Bugler. Unlike General Sulla, however, he has yet to produce his own account of it, or anything else for that matter, for which we should probably be thankful.*

because, as a relatively new class of vessel, the fleet commanders had little idea of their capabilities, preferring to rely on the more familiar Sword-class ships at their disposal.

They were to prove their worth beyond any doubt in this engagement, however, being confronted by an armada of a dozen or so enemy vessels. Fortunately, the vast majority turned out to be armed merchantmen, carrying the ground forces intended to overwhelm the planet, but even so, the sheer weight of numbers would normally have been expected to overwhelm two lone frigates. By adroit manoeuvring, however, they were able to attack the enemy from behind, where none of the freighters could direct return fire, blowing two of them apart with torpedo volleys before concentrating their primary batteries against a third, gutting it completely. At this juncture, the escorting warships began to return fire, and the *Escapade* and *Virago* boosted away before they could close the range sufficiently to inflict any significant damage.

This might be considered unfortunate, as two of the enemy ships were positively identified as Infidel-class raiders; the very design which was stolen by traitors from the shipyards at Monsk, and the attempted reconstruction of which had resulted in the development of the incomparable Falchion class. A duel between these very different siblings would have been the first recorded clash of the two classes anywhere within the sector; as it was that epic confrontation would have to wait a little longer, until the Sabatine incident some seven months and over a hundred parsecs away...

TWELVE

'Hurry up and wait.'
– Guardsman's traditional summation
of the process of deployment

THE JOURNEY BACK to Glacier Peak was as tedious as
I'd expected, despite being relatively short, the lord
general having taken the trouble to put another flyer
at my disposal. Within twenty minutes of us having
become airborne, the rectangle of sky beyond the
viewport had darkened to the perpetual night of the
coldside, relieved only by the glimmering of the stars
above, and I watched the blue-tinted landscape
below us rippling away with a sense of ennui I could
only put down to the dispiriting realisation that the
crisis was finally upon us. Even the excellent amasec
in my hip flask, which I'd taken the opportunity of

replenishing from the lord general's private stock before we left, was insufficient to raise my mood. I found myself watching the skies for some sign of motion, despite knowing full well that the enemy fleet was still too far away for any of the vessels to be visible yet.

It was only as we began to descend towards the landing pad that I sat up and took notice of the scene below us, the vast familiar bulk of a dropship seeming to fill the entire field of compacted ice. Our pilot seemed competent enough, though, making a final approach and circling around the space-going behemoth in order to give us a better view of it. (Or so it seemed; no doubt he was merely trying to find somewhere to set down.) Under the constant glare of the luminators I could see a steady stream of vehicles the size of my thumbnail rumbling up the loading ramps, directed by arm-waving ants. At least Kasteen was on the ball. There was no point waiting until the traitors actually arrived before getting our rapid reaction force poised and waiting. I found myself nodding approval as our skids hit the permafrost at last and I went to rouse an ashen-faced Jurgen (who, true to form, had relished our short flight not at all).

'The dropship arrived about three hours ago,' Kasteen confirmed as I entered the relative warmth of the command centre, brushed a couple of centimetres of snow from the brim of my hat and sent Jurgen off to find me some tanna.

'As we didn't know how soon you'd be back, Ruput and I thought we should make the assignments without waiting for your input.' She was perfectly within her rights to do so, of course. Technically the regimental commissar is only supposed to scrutinise command decisions and suggest alternative courses of action if they have grounds to believe that the fighting abilities of the unit are being compromised. The habit we'd got into of including me in preliminary discussions and tactical meetings was a purely informal arrangement.[1]

'Quite right too,' I said cheerfully, masking a faint sense of being left out of things which vaguely surprised me. 'Which company did you pick?'

'Second,' Broklaw told me, looking up from the hololith, which was jumping just as badly as I remembered, presumably no one had bothered to get a tech-priest in to bless the thing in my absence. (Then again, our enginseers were probably too busy getting our vehicles into fighting trim to bother with trivia like that.) 'None of their platoons were assigned off-base when the dropship came in, and they've already had a bit of practice at rapid deployment here.'

He grinned at me, and after a moment I realised he was referring to our impromptu rescue of the Tallarns on the day of our arrival. So much seemed to have happened since, I found it hard to believe it had only been a couple of weeks ago.

'Good choice,' I said, turning as Jurgen's returning odour told me my tanna had arrived. I took the drink gratefully and let the mug warm a little feeling back into my non-augmetic fingers. (The pilot had had to set the flyer down some distance away, and it had been a long, cold walk back to the command centre.) 'I'm sure Sulla's got her platoon's Chimeras stowed already.'

---

1. *And a striking testament to the rapport he'd built up with Kasteen and Broklaw. Most Guard officers in a similar position would consider the regimental commissar a nuisance at best and keep him as far removed from most command decisions as possible.*

'And is offering helpful advice to the other platoon commanders,' the major confirmed dryly.[1]

'So what's the news from HQ?' Kasteen asked.

'We're neck deep in it, as usual.' I sipped the tanna gratefully, feeling the fragrant liquid warming me gently from the inside out. 'You've seen the latest sitreps?'

The colonel nodded, her red hair bouncing gently against her shoulders. 'Enemy fleet inbound, ETA around three days from now. Heretic sorcerers playing frak with the warp and possibly a daemon on the loose. Oh yes, and Emperor knows how many smuggled weapons in the hands of an as-yet undetermined number of insurgents hiding among the civilian population. Have I left anything out?'

'Not really,' I said. 'Unless you count the fact that the Navy doesn't seem to have enough firepower to stop the enemy fleet before it gets here.'

I hadn't envied Zyvan the call on that one. I didn't really understand the problem, naval tactics not being the kind of thing I generally paid attention to, but the main thrust of it seemed to be that the traitors had split their forces. In the kind of warfare I was familiar with, which was all about taking or holding ground, that would have been a fatal mistake, but it seemed things were different on a system-wide scale. Apparently it takes spacecraft so long to get anywhere that once they're drawn out of position they'll never get back to it in any reasonable time frame, so the sort of mobile

---

1. As a former quartermaster sergeant, Sulla would have had considerable expertise in logistical matters, which probably accounts for her skill in the stowage of vehicles which Cain has remarked upon before. How welcome her willingness to share this knowledge with her fellow officers may have been, we can only speculate.

reserves we generally relied on to bolster a sagging line wouldn't be an option.

When I left, the lord general was still discussing things with his captains, wondering whether to try intercepting one group at a time and risk some of them getting through, or to keep his handful of warships in orbit where the enemy could strike at leisure and almost certainly break through somewhere by concentrating on a weak point.

'Neck deep sounds about right,' Broklaw agreed cheerfully. He turned back to the hololith, bringing it into focus with a practiced thump, I was beginning to think he might have missed his vocation. 'Any thoughts on our own dispositions here?'

Well, I hadn't really, or at least none that he and Kasteen hadn't already had themselves, but the discussion was calming, and I eventually went off to bed feeling considerably happier than I'd expected to. Come what may, I thought, the 597th was as ready for action as it could possibly be, and everything else was in the hands of the Emperor.

AFTER THE RIGOURS of the day you'll no doubt appreciate I was pretty exhausted, and even my spartan quarters in Glacier Peak seemed pretty comfortable by the time I shed my clothes and collapsed into bed. I fell asleep almost at once, but my sleep was to be far from restful. I awoke some time later with a pounding headache, dazed and disoriented, my quarters suffused with a familiar odour.

'Are you all right, sir?' Jurgen asked from the door, and with a curious sensation of *déjà vu* I realised he was holding his lasgun ready for use. I blinked gummy eyes open, yawned loudly, and became suddenly aware that

I was holding my laspistol (which, from long habit, I had carefully stowed where I could draw it without leaving the bed[1])

'Bad dreams,' I said, trying to chase the elusive fragments of imagery which were scuttling away from my conscious mind as I became progressively more wakeful.

Jurgen frowned. 'The same as last time, sir?' he asked. The casual question hit me like a jolt of electricity. I nodded slowly, the dim recollection of green eyes and mocking laughter beginning to surface through the throbbing fog in my skull.

'I think so,' I said, becoming steadily more convinced that I had indeed been dreaming of Emeli again. I supposed this was hardly surprising after encountering another of her kind, but even so I found the notion unsettling. I tried to recall the details, but the harder I tried the more elusive they became. 'It was the sorceress again.' I shrugged. Unsettling as it was, it had just been a dream after all. Nevertheless, I found the idea of going back to sleep distinctly unappealing. 'Could you get me some recaff?'

'Of course, commissar.' Jurgen slung the lasgun across his shoulder and left the room, leaving me to drag myself into the shower.

At length, feeling marginally refreshed, I wandered back to the command centre. There was nothing really for me to do there, but as always the sense of waiting for the enemy to make the first move was subtly unnerving, and I found the bustle of troopers going about their business and the constant clamour of messages coming in and out reassuring; it meant that we were ready for

---

1. *A practice he stuck to whatever the circumstances, even in the most apparently secure locations.*

whatever might be about to happen. (Or so I thought at the time; as it turned out no one sane could possibly have predicted the magnitude of the threat we were actually facing, and a good thing too. If I'd had even an inkling of it I'd have been catatonic with terror.)

I wasn't the only one reluctant to rest either: as I snagged a mug of tanna from the urn in the corner and turned to face the room, a flash of red hair caught my eye and I made my way over to Kasteen's desk. She was sprawled back in her chair, her feet on the desktop, snoring faintly. Unwilling to wake her, I turned away, intending to catch up on some of the routine disciplinary reports which were no doubt cluttering up my own desk by now, but she was too good a soldier not to be roused by a nearby footstep.

'What?' She sat up straight, brushing her hair from her eyes with her left hand, the right hovering just above the butt of her bolt pistol. 'Ciaphas?'[1]

'It's all right,' I said. 'Sorry to wake you.' I handed her the mug of tanna, feeling she needed it more than I did. 'Haven't you got a bunk for that sort of thing?'

'I suppose so.' She yawned widely. 'I was just resting my eyes for a moment. Must have dozed off.' She grinned. 'I suppose you'll have to shoot me for sleeping on duty now.'

'Technically,' I pointed out, 'you should have been off duty hours ago. So I suppose I can overlook it just this once.' I shrugged. 'Besides, can you imagine the sheer number of forms I'd have to fill out?'

'I'd hate to put you to that much inconvenience,' Kasteen agreed gravely. She stretched and stood up. 'So, did I miss anything?'

---

1. *It's extremely unusual for senior officers to be on first name terms with their commissars, another indication of Cain's remarkable rapport with the regiment he was attached to.*

'Haven't a clue,' I admitted cheerfully. 'I've only just got here myself.'

Rather than get involved in a conversation I'd rather avoid, I resorted to a half-truth. 'I couldn't sleep.'

'I know how you feel,' Broklaw said, appearing round a partition with a half-eaten sandwich in his hand. 'It's the waiting that gets to you.' He seemed as edgy as the rest of us, in that curious adrenaline-fuelled state where you feel too tired to rest.

Despite myself I felt a smile beginning to spread across my face. 'Well, we're a fine example for the lower ranks,' I said. 'Jumpier than a bunch of juvies on Emperor's Day Eve.'

'Except it's the heretics who are going to get the presents,' Broklaw said, with undisguised relish. 'Death and damnation, gift-wrapped by the 597th.' I can only assume it was the lack of sleep we were feeling, because the remark struck us all as hilarious, and when the hololith flickered into life with the image of the lord general the first thing he saw was the three of us howling with laughter like a bunch of drunken idiots.

'I'm pleased to see morale in the 597th remains high,' he remarked dryly, as we sobered up and the two Guard officers tugged their uniforms back into shape. He raised a quizzical eyebrow. 'Although I'm surprised to see you all awake at this hour.' He wasn't, of course; he was an old enough campaigner to know exactly how we all felt.

'The feeling's mutual,' I said, being the only one of the three of us who could converse with him without being hamstrung by protocol. The palms of my hands were tingling again, whatever he wanted at this time of night, it wasn't a social call. 'What's happened?'

To my surprise, the image split, Colonel Asmar appearing on the opposite corner of the display. No doubt we had appeared in his at the same time, as his face betrayed a flicker of hastily-masked hostility before he could compose his features again.

'Commissar.' He nodded once, ignoring the others, which at least told me which one of us Zyvan wanted to talk to.

'The Tallarn 229th have discovered something perturbing in their sector,' the lord general explained. His own face took on an expression of barely-masked exasperation. 'A little late in the day, but I suppose we must be thankful for what we can get.'

'The Emperor provides what we need,' Asmar quoted from somewhere, 'not what we want.'[1]

Zyvan's jaw tightened, barely perceptibly. 'What I want are regimental commanders who undertake search and destroy missions when ordered to, instead of going through the motions and doing the least they think they can get away with, and commissars who aren't afraid to get their hands dirty.' My ears pricked up at that, you can be sure. I hadn't a clue what had riled him so much, but it was clear that Asmar, and probably Beije, had hacked him off in no small measure. Probably by spouting Emperor-bothering gobbledygook instead of following orders, if I was any judge. But if the Tallarn's skiving had been backed by his commissar there wasn't a whole lot the lord general could do about it, of course.

'We'll be pleased to help in any way we can,' I said, grabbing the opportunity to stir it as eagerly as you can imagine.

---

1. From Nordwick's Considerations of the Divine, *a chapbook of daily meditations (most of which are as platitudinous as that one).*

Zyvan nodded. 'I don't doubt it.' The implied rebuke to Asmar was about as subtle as an ork breaking wind, and the Tallarn colonel's face coloured slightly. 'I was hoping for your input on this, as you seem to have had the most experience of the enemy's sorcerous activities.' To my carefully concealed delight Asmar looked distinctly nervous at this point, and made the sign of the aquila.

'I've shot a few heretics and raided a couple of their hideouts,' I said, conscious of the unmerited reputation for modest heroism that Zyvan expected me to maintain. 'But I think any credit should go to the troopers with me. They did the bulk of the fighting, and not all of them were as lucky as I was.'

'Quite,' the lord general said, buying it wholesale. 'But you have the experience in intelligence assessment and you've fought the Great Enemy before.'

'True,' I said, nodding my head. 'So what's the information our gallant Tallarn comrades have uncovered?' Asmar looked a little suspicious at that, no doubt realising I was taking the frak, but prepared to take the question at face value. (No doubt he had some pious quotation to cover that as well.)

'One of our rough rider patrols encountered a nauga[1] hunter this morning,' he began. 'He mentioned seeing traces of activity near some caverns to the north of our position, so they went to take a look.' Zyvan's expression was hardening by the moment, I noticed. 'What they found there was...'

Words seemed to fail Asmar for a moment, and he made the sign of the aquila again. 'Unholy,' he concluded at last, his face paling.

---

1. *A species of animal indigenous to the hotside of Adumbria. Its toughened hide is highly prized for certain hard-wearing applications, particularly the covering of sofas in waiting rooms.*

'Let me guess,' I said. 'Bodies, twisted in some foul fashion, peculiar sigils painted on the walls?' Asmar nodded. 'Did your troopers encounter any resistance?'

'No,' Asmar said. 'The place was deserted.' If he made the sign of the aquila much more, I thought, his fingers were going to fly away. 'But the miasma of evil was palpable.'

'Lucky for them the daemon had already gone,' I said, unable to resist prodding him again. I was rewarded by an expression of unmistakable terror flickering in his eyes. I turned my attention to Zyvan. 'It sounds as though we've found the site of the third ritual.'

'That was my conclusion too,' the lord general agreed.

'This could be the break we've been looking for,' I went on. 'If Malden can examine a site uncontaminated by battle damage, he might be able to determine precisely what the heretics are up to.'

'He might,' Zyvan agreed. 'If Colonel Asmar and Commissar Beije hadn't taken it upon themselves to destroy the site before he had the chance.'

'It was the only thing to be done,' Asmar insisted. 'Is it not written in the *Meditations of the Saints* that the shrines of the unholy must be cleansed with the fires of the righteous?'

'And is it not written in the manual of common sense that trashing an enemy installation you've had the luck to capture intact before it can be properly examined for useful intelligence is the act of a cretin?' I responded, unable to credit that anyone, even Beije, could have been quite so stupid.

Asmar flushed angrily. 'I know my duty to the Emperor. When I stand before the Golden Throne to meet his judgement, my conscience will be clear.'

'Wonderful,' I said. 'I'm delighted for you.' I returned my attention to Zyvan. 'So in sum, all we know about the enemy's activities on the hotside is that they were definitely there.'

The lord general nodded. 'That's about it,' he agreed.

'Where is "there". exactly?' Kasteen asked.

By way of an answer, Zyvan leaned forward to manipulate some controls we couldn't see, and Asmar's face was replaced by a rotating view of the planet from orbit. A single contact rune marked the position of the heretic shrine, which, on this reduced scale, seemed to be on exactly the opposite side of the planet from Glacier Peak. She nodded. 'Hm. That's interesting.'

'What is?' Zyvan asked.

'It's probably just coincidence, but they form a triangle. Look.' She pointed out Skitterfall, where the other shrine had been. Sure enough, the planetary capital was equidistant between the two points.

'There's no such thing as coincidence where sorcery's concerned,' I said. 'It must be significant somehow.'

'Only if you draw the line from us to the Tallarns directly through the core of the planet,' Broklaw pointed out. 'Would that make a difference?'

'Emperor alone knows,' Zyvan said. 'We're dealing with warpcraft, so little details like a planet being in the way might not matter to them. I'll talk to Malden and the others, see what they think.' He nodded thoughtfully. 'Well spotted, colonel.'

He seemed on the verge of cutting the link, so I stepped in quickly.

'One other thing,' I said. 'Any word from the fleet yet?'

Zyvan shook his head. 'The warp's still too churned up for the astropaths to get a message through. When or if they arrive is in the lap of the Emperor.'

'About what I expected,' I said. He cut the link. Kasteen, Broklaw and I looked at each other in silence. After a moment, the major put what we were all thinking into words.

'I think it's just risen to our chins,' he said.

Editorial Note:

*Since the battle in space played a decisive part in what was to fol-
low, and Cain doesn't bother to mention it at all, another short
extract from Tincrowser's account of the campaign seems to be
called for at this point. He is somewhat imprecise on the details, as
one might expect from a civilian, but he covers the main points well
enough.*

From *Sablist in Skitterfall: a brief history of the Chaos
incursion* by Dagblat Tincrowser, 957 M41.

As the enemy fleet continued to make its way towards
Adumbria it fragmented, splitting into three groups, no
doubt in an attempt to evade the gallant defenders. Two
of these seemed relatively unthreatening, consisting as

they did of lightly armed vessels[1] while the third contained the majority of the transports and their escorting warships.[2]

Having shown their mettle in the first engagement and being the only vessels in a position to intercept them before they made orbit, the *Escapade* and *Virago* were each given the task of harrying one of the smaller flotillas; this they did successfully enough, although neither was able to prevent all of their intended victims from reaching the planet. The *Escapade* fared the better of the two, managing to destroy all but one of its targets and suffering minimal damage in the process, while the *Virago* destroyed one completely. Unfortunately, in so doing it was caught in a crossfire by the remaining pair, doing sufficient damage to its engines that it soon fell behind, unable to continue the engagement.

The main body of the enemy fleet continued to drift inwards towards Adumbria, daring the remainder of the Imperial Navy forces to intercept it, but they refused to rise to the bait. The *Indestructible* remained in orbit above Skitterfall, where it was joined by the squadron of destroyers[3] which had until then been patrolling the inner shipping lanes.

So it was that three vessels of the enemy advance guard were able to enter orbit and deploy the troops they carried, the first to pollute the soil of our beloved home world.

---

1. Three each of the armed merchantmen so casually dispatched by the Falchions in the earlier engagement.

2. The two Infidel-class vessels mentioned by Kasmides, a Desolator-class battleship and between five and eight transport ships. The records are a little hazy on this point due to the high volume of legitimate merchant shipping in the system at the time.

3. Three Cobras: the Gallant, Impetuous and Spiteful.

One at least was to regret its temerity, however, as the hotly-pursuing *Escapade* caught and overwhelmed it almost immediately, sending it plunging to a fiery doom in the upper atmosphere.

This would be scant comfort to the gallant defenders, however, as for the first time combat was joined on the surface. And, as before, the Valhallans were to find themselves in the forefront of the battle.

THIRTEEN

'If your battle plan's working, it's probably a trap.'
– Kolton Phae, *On Military Matters*, 739 M41

IRKSOME AS IT had been waiting for the enemy to arrive, once they did the monotony and tension which had suffused the last couple of days began to seem positively welcome in retrospect. I was in the command post with most of the senior staff at the time; Kasteen, Broklaw and all the company commanders who weren't deployed elsewhere, watching the contact icons lighting up in the hololith as the enemy troops made planetfall. I'd been expecting a concerted assault on the capital, but within moments it began to look as though the planet was suffering from a case of the underhive pox, red spots appearing all over the place apparently at random.

'What the hell are they up to?' Detoi muttered at my elbow, clearly chafing at the lack of any obvious troop concentrations to deploy rapidly against.

'Beats me,' I said, having fought the minions of Chaos too often before to expect much of what they did to make sense. With hindsight, it was explicable, but at the time we were still missing some vital pieces of the puzzle.

'It looks to me as though they're just getting the troops down as quickly as they can,' Kasteen said. 'They can't expect the transports to last long unsupported.' As if to emphasise her words, one of the three contacts in orbit flared suddenly and began to descend, spewing debris and shuttles as it went.

'Well, that's something,' I said, indicating it. 'Looks like the Navy's saved us a bit of spadework there.'

From the patterns of the landings and the occasions when I'd been part of a force moved by a freighter rather than a specialised troopship, I knew that the civilian shuttles they carried would have to make several trips back and forth to disembark all the warriors aboard. Of course, I wouldn't expect Chaos fanatics to worry too much about safety margins and overcrowding, but even so the descending fireball above us would only have had time to disembark about a third of the cannon fodder they carried. Normally a ship that size would be expected to carry a full regiment of Imperial Guard, but again there was no telling if the enemy had packed in more than that.

'The Tallarns are going to take a battering,' Broklaw remarked, not seeming terribly concerned at the prospect.

It was true that there seemed to be a concentration of enemy forces building close to their position on the hotside, but that was their problem. Ours was defending the population of Glacier Peak. I glanced at the hololith again, seeing the final wave of shuttles from the doomed freighter screaming down through the atmosphere towards us.

We were ready for them, our troops deployed around the town in what should have been an impenetrable cordon. Second company remained in our compound, as their vehicles were still stowed aboard the dropship, which I was suddenly aware would make a very tempting target if the enemy had any aerospace units. (As it turned out, though, that was a needless worry. The freighters only carried civilian shuttles, which were unarmed, gratifyingly easy targets for the PDF fighter pilots, who made sure that damn few of them were able to make more than a couple of drop runs.)

I turned to Detoi. 'Better make sure your people are sharp,' I said. 'We might need them to defend this position if they're not called on for support somewhere else.' I was only trying to encourage him at the time, knowing he'd rather be ordering their embarkation for some distant battlefront, but I spoke truer than I knew. In theory, first company had a couple of platoons in reserve to do the job, but Glacier Peak was a big enough place to take care of, and it was perfectly feasible that they'd find themselves otherwise occupied at the time.

He nodded dutifully. 'Incoming,' one of the auspex operators said, her voice tense. 'Five contacts, airborne, closing fast. They're widely scattered.'

'All units prepare to engage,' Kasteen said, as calmly as if she were ordering another mug of tanna. She glanced up at me. 'Commissar?'

I made some encouraging remarks over the open vox link, invoked the protection of the Emperor and turned to Detoi.

'If you don't mind, captain,' I said, 'I think I'd rather join your company while this is going on.'

This might seem a little odd, given that I was in a warm, bullet-proof building at the time, but as usual my paranoid streak was thinking about a number of uncomfortable possibilities. For one thing, we knew the heretics had had plenty of time to infiltrate the local PDF, even though nobody senior had been netted by Kolbe's investigators yet, and they certainly had some ears among the Council of Claimants (or at least their households). It wasn't entirely unfeasible that they knew where our regimental headquarters was, and if that was true and any of those incoming shuttles were armed, I was currently sitting in the middle of the most tempting target for a bombing run on the entire coldside. Out in the open, on the other hand, unpleasant as it was, I'd have a much better chance of surviving an aerial attack.

'Have fun.' Kasteen grinned at me, no doubt believing I was just eager to be in with a better chance of facing the enemy.

I directed a carefully composed smile in her direction. 'We'll try to save a couple for you,' I promised, as though she was right, and fell into step beside Detoi as we left the bustling room behind us.

'Commissar.' Jurgen was waiting outside, and had been for some time judging by the aroma of old socks which suffused the corridor. He pulled himself to a semblance of attention, his usual collection of mismatched equipment pouches rattling slightly as he shouldered his precious melta, which clanked against his lasgun. Detoi returned his salute crisply and without a trace of a smile. She was one of the few officers in the regiment who at least pretended to consider him a proper soldier.

'Jurgen.' I nodded a greeting, relieved to see him, and surreptitiously adjusted the straps of the carapace concealed under my greatcoat. Clearly we were both expecting trouble. 'We were about to take a small constitutional around the compound.'

'I thought you might, sir.' My aide burrowed in one of the pouches. 'So I took the liberty of making a flask of tea. Knowing how you feel the cold a bit.'

'Very thoughtful,' I said, forestalling the motion. 'But perhaps later.' The faint sound of engines was audible now, and if they were about to attack the building we didn't have much longer to get outside. I turned to Detoi. 'Shall we go?'

'By all means.' He led the way outside into the perpetual cold and night. I glanced up, the sky even clearer than usual now that the luminators had been doused in anticipation of an enemy attack, the stars burning down at us colder and harder than ever. A few of them seemed to be moving, the whine of their engines growing louder by the minute.

I tapped the comm-bead in my ear. 'Visual contact,' I said. 'I can see three of them, approaching from due east. High and fast.'

'That's odd,' Broklaw said. 'A couple of them are overshooting the town.'

'Heading for us, maybe,' Kasteen cut in.

'They're dispersing,' the auspex operator confirmed. 'They're in a landing pattern, but it seems uncontrolled.'

'Hardly surprising,' I said, taking the amplivisor Jurgen was holding out with a nod of thanks and raising it to my eyes. After a moment of searching, I found one of the shuttles and brought its magnified image into focus. 'With the amount of damage they've taken it's a miracle they're flying at all.' In the faint orange light of the early dawn I could make out jagged rents in the hull and a plume of smoke from its engines. It was juddering wildly and must have been hell to keep under control.

Well, good. If it crashed that would be one less bunch of lunatics left to deal with.

I lowered the lenses and handed the amplivisor back to Jurgen, who stowed it away somewhere. He was growing steadily more visible as the sun rose behind me, a faint shadow beginning to stretch from his feet. My own also became gradually visible on the hard-packed snow. Absently I found myself thinking it was the first time I'd seen it since we'd arrived on Adumbria…

'Emperor on Earth!' I said, the coin finally dropping, whirling round to stare at the fireball scorching its way across the sky above us. For the first and last time in Adumbrian history, the coldside was wanly illuminated by the death throes of the traitors' transport vessel, and the troopers around me raised a spontaneous cheer at the sight. Well, who could blame them? As it faded over the western horizon, setting as abruptly as it had risen, a scream of tortured air followed it, like the howling of daemons clawing free from the warp.

After that, an eerie silence seemed to settle across us, leeching the sound from the air as the light faded back to the constant faint blue of the endless starlight.

'That's going to make a dent when it hits,'[1] Detoi prophesied, and trotted away to find his command

---

1. It eventually impacted on the hotside, about a hundred kilometres from the nominal boundary of the shadow zone, gouging a crater a little over three kilometres in diameter. A half-hearted attempt to promote the site as a tourist attraction after the war understandably failed, since few citizens could be bothered to put up with the time and discomfort required to look at what was really nothing more than a big hole in the ground. The cara-vansari established for their use eventually became a holiday lodge for affluent city dwellers who fancied the idea of a weekend nauga hunt.

team. There was little time to waste on idle conversation after that, as the enemy were suddenly upon us.

'One contact down. No, three,' the auspex operator reported. 'One two kilometres to the south, another in the north-eastern suburbs.'

'We can see it,' a new voice I recognised as one of the platoon commanders from fourth company chimed in. 'First and third squads moving in to contain them.'

'Contact three down in the town centre,' the auspex operator continued.

'Fifth company, encircle and eliminate,' Kasteen ordered, while another platoon from fourth moved up to support their comrades in the suburbs. I was beginning to think about ducking back inside and following the action on the chart table, which would be a great deal preferable to freezing out here now the threat of an air attack was almost past.

'Contact four heading due west,' the auspex operator droned on. 'Looks like they're overshooting.'

'Engaging,' a lieutenant from first company cut in, her voice shrill with excitement. 'They're practically overhead.' Her words were almost drowned out by the roar of half a dozen Chimeras unloading both their heavy bolters at once, and I was hardly surprised to hear a faint cheer over the channel a moment later. With all that firepower they must have hit something, even by sheer blind luck. 'Got him! He's trailing smoke... Frak it, he's still airborne.'

I glanced up, seeing a dark mass scream overhead, vivid orange flames licking around its main engine before it disappeared into the distance in the vague direction of the hab dome we'd found. They wouldn't find any help there, I reflected grimly. Asmar had been right about one thing: a place that tainted couldn't be

allowed to exist. The difference had been that we'd
made damn sure we'd learned everything we could
about it before we'd let Federer out to play. All the
descending heretics were going to find (if they got down
in one piece, which didn't seem all that likely at this
point) was a scorched pile of rubble and third platoon,
fourth company, who'd been camping out there for
almost a week by this point and were just itching for
something to kill to relieve the monotony.

'Recon one, two and three heading out to contact
two,' Captain Shambas reported. 'Let's see what the
frakheads are up to.' That made good sense: the three
sentinel squadrons were designed for just such a task
and would get to the shuttle which had grounded to the
south far quicker than any other units we had.

'Good luck, captain,' Kasteen said, making it official,
although the sentinel pilots would be hard to dissuade
now the idea that they had a target-rich environment all
to themselves had had time to sink in. Any other
response would be far more trouble than it was worth.
Calling them off would be difficult and time-consum-
ing and probably involve an inordinate number of
freak vox failures, so on the whole it was probably best
to just let them get on with it. (Which they did, mopping up the entire group quite happily without needing
to call for backup.)

That just left one of the incoming shuttles unac-
counted for, and with a thrill of horror I realised that
the engine noise which so far had been a loud, consistent sound in the background was rising in pitch
alarmingly.

'Incoming!' I shouted, just as the auspex operator
managed to find her arse with both hands and a
map.

'Contact five inbound, closing fast,' she reported. 'Estimated LZ within half a kilometre.'

'It's a frak sight closer than that!' I shouted as the frozen air around us lit up with las bolts, the troopers spitting defiant small-arms fire at the descending ship. The heavy bolters mounted on the company Chimeras might have made a difference, of course, but they were still aboard the dropship, and I might just as well have wished for a battery of Hydras while I was about it. 'Prepare to engage!'

'Look out, commissar!' Jurgen grabbed my arm, urging me to duck as the ungainly shuttle swooped overhead, seeming close enough to touch, the wind of its passing grabbing the cap from my head and spinning it off into the darkness. A vice of cold clamped itself around my temples, driving needles of ice into my forebrain and the back of my eyes. I scrabbled instinctively after my tumbling headgear, which probably saved my life, as the snow around me began puffing into vapour under the impetus of multiple las bolt impacts.

'Frak this!' I drew my trusty laspistol, grabbing my elusive cap with the other hand and jamming it over my head. The migraine receded a little, and what felt like a couple of kilos of melting slush mashed itself into my hair and slithered down my neck. I turned in time to see the wounded shuttle hit the snow, skid and plough itself to a halt in a long groove of friction-melted ice, which began to freeze instantly around it. In the process, it shed the dimly-glimpsed figures which had been hanging out of the rear cargo doors firing wildly, coming so close to hitting me. They cart-wheeled through the air, striking the permafrost with an impact sufficient to shatter bone and liquefy flesh. And serve them right, I thought. None of them stirred again, merely acquiring makeshift shrouds of lightly-drifting snow as the battle raged about them.

For battle it was. There were plenty of their comrades left aboard, and they came boiling out of the steam-shrouded wreck like parasites fleeing a dying grox, firing wildly as they went. The Valhallans returned fire with all the disciplined professionalism I'd come to expect, dropping them by the dozen, but the survivors swept on, frenzied as an orkish war band.

'Something's not right about this,' I said, firing my pistol at the onrushing mob, then ducking for cover behind a snow-shrouded drum of some foul-smelling lubricant the enginseers had been using on a partially disassembled Chimera. The cultists we'd faced before had been fanatical, of course, but they'd shown a modicum of tactical sense.

'No kidding.' Corporal Magot jogged past, grinning happily, her fireteam in tow, lobbing frag grenades in the general direction of the enemy. 'It's almost too easy.' One of the troopers with her went down suddenly, a spray of fresh blood freezing almost instantly into a bright, hard scab across his chest.

'Medic,' I voxed, dragging the man under cover. It was a good excuse to keep my head down and it never hurt to seem concerned about the ordinary troopers. Magot shot me a grateful smile with an edge colder than the flensing wind.

'Thanks, boss.' Her voice rose. 'Are we going to let 'em get away with that?'

'Hell, no!' the rest of the team chorused in unison.

'Then let's frag one for Smitti!' With a roar that sounded almost like a mob of orks, they charged off into the snow looking for something to kill. I began to feel almost sorry for the enemy.

I busied myself looking after the wounded trooper until the medic arrived, then glanced back up over our makeshift barricade. The compound was in uproar by this time, small knots of traitors in flimsy crimson fatigues and black flak armour[1] engaging squads and fireteams almost at random. They fought with the fury of the possessed or the truly insane, heedless of their personal safety or anything resembling tactics, apparently intent on charging into close combat as quickly as they could.

'If they made it any easier they'd be on our side,' Jurgen said, triggering his melta for the third or fourth time and bringing down what seemed like most of a squad. The snow around them was littered with steaming chunks of meat where their predecessors had fared little better.

'Blood for the Blood God!' A red-uniformed trooper came screaming out of the endless night at me, his old-fashioned autogun held across his chest like a pole arm, apparently intent on using the wickedly-serrated bayonet clipped to its barrel. I assumed at the time that he was out of ammunition, but for all I know he was just carried away by bloodlust.

'Harriers for the cup!'[2] I riposted, shooting him in the face. His head liquefied under the impact of the las bolt and he fell heavily to the snow at my feet. I looked around, feeling that things were getting a little out of hand here.

---

1. *Presumably by this time the luminators had been rekindled, as these colours would have been almost indistinguishable under the starlight, or Cain may simply be writing with the benefit of hindsight.*

2. *A reference to a scrumball team in the subsector league (who were knocked out in the semi-finals that year, incidentally).*

'Captain Detoi, report.' Kasteen sounded calm enough, so at least none of the fanatics had made it as far as the command bunker yet. 'What's going on out there?'

'The captain's down,' Sulla reported. 'I've taken command.'

Wonderful, I thought, as if we weren't in enough trouble already. But she had the seniority, and interfering now would be seriously counterproductive, so I just cut in with some encouraging platitudes. 'We're containing them, but they're persistent little frakkers.'

'Well, we won't have to hold them much longer,' I pointed out, drawing my chainsword in time to bisect a persistent enemy trooper who was trying to interrupt me with a rusty-looking combat blade. His movements were slow and sluggish, the flesh of his face and hands pinched and blue. 'The cold's going to finish them off for us pretty soon.'

After that I shut up and let Sulla get on with it, just keeping an ear on the vox channel to make sure she didn't do anything too stupid, although to be fair she did a reasonable job of co-ordinating the different platoons and had the sense to put Lustig in charge of her own. By this time trooper Smitti had been carted off to the medicae receiving station, so I couldn't see any reason not to return to the command centre and let things play themselves out without me.

I tapped Jurgen on the shoulder. 'We're heading back inside,' I told him. 'It's all over out here bar the clean-up.'

I should have known better, of course. Sometimes I think that the Emperor's listening to me just so he can spring a little surprise every time I say something like that.

'Second squad, say again,' a voice was shouting in my earpiece, one I recognised as Lieutenant Faril, the officer in charge of fifth platoon. It was one of a dozen routine exchanges I'd barely noticed in the course of the battle, but there was an edge of alarm in his tone which sounded new. 'Second squad, report.'

'It's unstoppable!' another voice replied. 'Heading for the perimeter...' The report choked off with a scream. I flicked my head around, certain I'd heard the sound overlapping in the way that means the source of a vox transmission is close enough for the noise to carry naturally through the air almost simultaneously, and sure enough, the intensity of lasgun fire in the immediate vicinity was growing.

'Get some backup to them,' Sulla ordered crisply, and Faril dispatched another couple of squads.

Well, that was enough to persuade me that I needed to be back in the command centre right away, where I could find out just what the hell was going on, and I hurried around the disassembled Chimera intent on nothing more than getting back inside as soon as I could. Abruptly, though, I found myself surrounded by running troopers, as by great bad luck my path intersected with the reinforcements Faril had just ordered in.

'Commissar!' One of the sergeants glanced over in my direction, his face a mask of delighted surprise. A ripple of resolve shivered almost visibly along the score of troopers double timing in his wake and I cursed under my breath. I couldn't duck out now without denting their morale and doing who knew what damage to my reputation. I nodded a genial greeting and dredged the man's name up from the depths of my memory.

'Dyzun.' I shrugged. 'I hope you don't mind me sticking my nose in, but it sounds as though something interesting's going on.'

'Glad to see you, sir,' he said, with every sign of sincerity, and Emperor strike me dead if I'm exaggerating, but the whole lot of them started chanting my name like a battlecry.

'Cain! Cain! Cain! Cain!'

Maybe it was that which took our opponent off-guard for a moment, mistaking it for the chant of the followers of his own blasphemous god, because he turned his head slowly to look at us, drawing his attention reluctantly from the corpses of second squad which lay all around him. Only a few survivors still stirred, trying feebly to raise weapons or crawl to safety.

'Emperor on Earth!' I said, my bowels spasming. The man, if man he still was, was a giant, towering over us all. My months as the Guard liaison to the Reclaimers had left me familiar with the superhuman stature of the Astartes and with a healthy respect for the strength and durability of the armour they wore, but this was no paladin of the Emperor's will; quite the opposite. His armour was blood red and black, like the uniforms of the cultists still dying in droves around us, and chased with vile designs in burnished orichalcum. He carried a bolt pistol holstered at his belt, but apparently distained to use it. His hands, encased in massive gauntlets, gripped a curious weapon, like a battleaxe, but surrounded with whirling metal teeth like my own trusty chainsword.

'You swear by the corpse god?' The thing's voice was gutteral, from a throat constricted with rage, and so deeply resonant that I felt it reverberate through my very bones. 'Your skull will grace the throne of the true power!'

'Big red thing, five rounds rapid fire!' Dyzun ordered, remarkably calmly under the circumstances, and the troopers snapped out of their astonishment to comply. But the twisted parody of a Marine was fast, at least as agile as one of the true heroes he aped, and leapt aside, avoiding most of it. The few las bolts which struck his armour scored it, adding to the pockmarks already inflicted by the luckless second squad, and I felt vindictive laughter resonating through my bones.

As ill luck would have it, his leap carried him over the heads of most of the troopers, to land almost at my feet. I felt a bolt of sheer terror arc through me as the metal-clad giant tilted his head forward to look down at where I stood, and swung his chain axe with lightning speed. Which was his first mistake. Had he made any other attack he might well have killed me where I stood, still paralysed with fear, but the whining chain blades triggered my duellist's reflexes and I parried the blow with my own gently-humming chainsword without a second's hesitation. That snapped me out of it, you can be sure, and I began to fight for my life in deadly earnest.

'Is that the best you can do?' I taunted him, sure that in his arrogance he had expected an easy kill, and hoping to goad him into making a mistake. Not that I had any serious hope of besting him in a prolonged fight, of course; my unaugmented muscles would tire quickly, even without the strength-sapping cold, and his already superhuman endurance would be boosted by the power armour he wore. But if I could keep him pinned long enough for the troopers with me to line up a good shot and somehow disengage before they took it, I hoped I could wipe the smile off his face... if he still had one under that grotesque helmet.

I slashed at his chest, raising a shower of sparks from the abused ceramite. 'I thought the acolytes of Khorne were supposed to be warriors, not a bunch of pansies.'

'I'll feed you your own entrails!' the giant roared, slashing down again with his cumbersome weapon. This time I deflected it so that it struck his own leg, raising another shower of golden sparks and a cheer from the surrounding troopers.

'Like I've never heard that before,' I sneered, following through and getting right under his guard. I rolled in the snow, making as much distance as I could, seeing him turn out of the corner of my eye and raising the axe again.

He never completed the motion. The actinic light of Jurgen's melta stabbed the darkness, vaporising the middle of his chest, and he stumbled, dropping slowly to his knees. I scrambled hurriedly to my feet, having no desire to be crushed to death under all that falling metal, and holstered my weapons.

'Thank you, Jurgen,' I said, brushing the accumulated snow from my greatcoat.

'You're welcome, sir.' My aide lowered the cumbersome weapon as our defeated enemy slumped to the permafrost with a sound like an accident in a bell foundry. 'Will there be anything else?'

'Now you come to mention it,' I said, conscious of the rapt attention of the troopers surrounding us and straightening my cap with all the insouciance I could muster, 'I think now would be a good time for that tea.'

Editorial Note:

There were other engagements, equally hard-fought, across most of Adumbria, although naturally Cain doesn't think they're worth more than the most casual of references. Indeed, the attack on the regimental headquarters in which he was involved was arguably a minor sideshow to the main battle for Glacier Peak, in which the bulk of the regiment and the local PDF garrison acquitted themselves most creditably.

So once again we must rely on other sources to fill the gaps, and once again Tincrowser's populist account does a workmanlike job of sketching in the bigger picture.

From *Sablist in Skitterfall: a brief history of the Chaos incursion* by Dagblat Tincrowser, 957 M41.

To THE SURPRISE of many, Skitterfall itself saw relatively little action during this first incursion. In retrospect, this was almost certainly due to the presence of the warships in orbit above it, which would have made any direct approach almost suicidal. Indeed, the Cobra squadron and the triumphant *Escapade* made short work of the two remaining starships before either had the opportunity to flee back into deep space. But the damage had been done and several thousand enemy soldiers had landed by the time their transports had been repulsed.

The overall strategy of these raids, if there even was one, has been the subject of much speculation over the last twenty years. In very few cases did the enemy mass in sufficient numbers to pose a serious threat, and it seems most likely that they were there simply to allow their masters aboard the main fleet to gauge the strength of the resistance they were to expect when they arrived in force. Any damage they were able to inflict by these hit and run tactics would have been a welcome bonus, of course, and it cannot be denied that the psychological effect of their arrival was considerable; the panic and civil disorder in many of the major population centres certainly increased for a time, although this was followed by a period of relative calm, the populace no doubt reflecting that the worst of their fears had now come to pass.

As has previously been noted, relatively few of the enemy landed in Skitterfall itself, the defences around the starport proving a formidable deterrent for those few who tried. Indeed, so strong was the resistance here that the few shuttles which made it through were forced to land in the suburbs, far from the city centre, where the local PDF, ably assisted by the Valhallan tanks and Kastaforean infantry elements of the Imperial

Guard, were able to repulse them in pretty short order. Rumours at the time of patriotic citizens forming ad hoc militia units to meet the threat can now, with the wisdom of hindsight, be seen for the wishful thinking they undoubtedly were, but such tales undoubtedly played a part in boosting the resolve of the civilian population to resist the invader.

The largest battles of the first incursion occurred in the most unlikely of places: the town of Glacier Peak on the coldside and an area of wilderness on the hotside of note only for the fact that the Tallarn element of the relieving task force had established their headquarters there in the remains of an old botanical testing station.[1] Given that Glacier Peak was the headquarters of the Valhallan 597th, it seems probable that part of the reason for the incursion was an attempt to inflict damage on the two Guard regiments most isolated from their fellows. If that was indeed the case, the traitors were to be sorely disappointed.

The Tallarn 229th were to prove their reputation for the mastery of desert warfare was richly merited, driving off and slaughtering their attackers with almost contemptuous ease. In this they were undoubtedly assisted by their familiarity with the harsh environment they found themselves in, as the heretics were to find the conditions there debilitating in the extreme. Indeed, one contemporary account suggests that almost as many were to die of dehydration and heatstroke as at the hands and weapons of the Guardsmen.

---

1. *A relic of an ambitious, and quite clearly doomed from the start, attempt to establish some kind of agricultural industry in the perpetual sunshine of the hotside in the early years of the third century M41.*

The same could be said of the contingent which attacked the coldside, many of them succumbing to the freezing temperatures as readily as to the martial zeal of the Valhallans, who, as natives of an ice world, found them no handicap. The town of Glacier Peak offered many refuges from the killing cold, however, and the struggle there became one of prolonged attrition, driving the invaders out street by street, building by building. And, despite the best efforts of the Guard troopers, many civilians were to suffer and die in the crossfire. Their sacrifice was not to be in vain, however, as at length the last of the heretic scum were hunted down as they attempted to flee the town on foot, braving the freezing temperatures of the wilderness. This, above all else, points to their sheer desperation, as there was undoubtedly no shelter to be found there.

FOURTEEN

'Things can always get worse.'

– Valhallan proverb

'WELL, THAT WAS unexpected.' Zyvan nodded gravely in the centre of the hololith. His head, about a quarter life size, was surrounded by others, orbiting around him like the moons of a gas giant: the commanders of the other Guard regiments, their commissars, Malden, Kolbe and a couple of other faces I didn't recognise but who probably had something to do with the PDF. To my vague relief there was no sign of Vinzand, so things would probably go a little more smoothly; no doubt Zyvan felt we were getting into things no civilian, however exalted, needed to know. I noted the absence of the lady Dimarco with slightly mixed feelings, she was decorative enough and her presence would have been a welcome distraction from the collection of military men, but her corrosive personality went a long way towards negating that.

And talking of corrosive personalities, Beije was there, along with Asmar of course, trying desperately to look as though he understood what was going on. Well, I supposed I could always amuse myself by needling him if things got too tedious.

'Are you absolutely positive about this?' True to form, Beije couldn't resist sticking his nose in, heedless of the opinions of anyone else in the conference link. 'Not that I doubt Commissar Cain's veracity for a moment,' his tone quite clearly implying the opposite, 'but I'm sure I'm not the only one here who finds this story a little hard to swallow.'

Asmar nodded in agreement, although most of the others remained stone-faced and a few visibly bristled, especially the CO of the Valhallan tankies and his commissar. 'I know he has something of a swashbuckling reputation,' Beije prattled on, cheerfully oblivious to the reception he was getting, 'but the idea of any man defeating a member of the Traitor Legions in single combat has to be difficult to credit.'

'Indeed it would be,' I responded, 'if that were the case. But I can hardly take the credit for the actions of others.' Not if there was a chance I wouldn't be able to get away with it, anyway. 'I simply exchanged a couple of blows with the fellow. The kill was made by my aide and a couple of squads of our troopers. Who, incidentally,' I added to Zyvan, 'I would like to recommend for commendations.'

I was rewarded by a projection field full of nodding heads and benign smiles. That was the trick which had always worked best for me: appearing to be modest about my supposed heroism. Now the legend would grow out of all proportion, until half the troopers on the planet would indeed be convinced that I'd bested a tainted superman in a contest of blades. The only exceptions, of course, were Asmar and Beije.

'Are we even convinced that it was one of the accursed traitors?' Beije asked, worrying at the argument like a kroot with a bone, completely unable to grasp that the more he tried to undermine my supposed achievement the more he consolidated the fact in everyone else's mind. 'It could just have been one of the cultists of unusual stature.'

'Pretty convinced,' Zyvan said dryly, the image in the hololith changing to show the corpse of the dead Chaos Marine. I didn't need to see the expressions on the assembled faces at that point, as the collective intake of breath was perfectly audible. There was absolutely no chance of mistaking that monstrous corpse for anything else. After a moment the image returned to the mass of heads. 'We've positively identified him as a member of the World Eaters Legion.'

'Are we to infer, then, that the next stage of the attack will be carried out by a Traitor Legion?' Kolbe asked, managing to keep his voice steady with an effort someone less adept than I was at reading people would have found hard to spot.

Zyvan shook his head. 'With Chaos, of course, nothing is certain, but I doubt it. Were that the case, we would be facing a far greater fleet and the World Eaters would be proclaiming themselves openly rather than hiding behind the banner of the Ravagers.'

'Not very big on subtlety, Khorne cultists,' I chipped in helpfully, underlining the fact that with the possible exception of Zyvan, I probably had more experience of facing the various factions of Chaos than anyone else on the planet.

Kasteen looked at me curiously. 'I thought you said they worshipped something called Slaynish?'

'The heretics we've been fighting so far seem to be Slaaneshi cultists,' I said, emphasising the correct pronunciation almost imperceptibly. 'Which is odd, to say the least.'

'What's the difference?' Beije asked impatiently. 'A heretic's a heretic. We should just kill the lot of them and let the Emperor sort them out.'

'I quite agree,' I said, enjoying the brief flicker of astonishment and uncertainty which crossed his face. 'But it may not be as simple as that.'

'Quite.' Zyvan nodded. 'What Commissar Cain is aware of, and some of you appear not to be, is that Chaos is not a single, unified enemy. Not very often, anyway, thank the Emperor.' The few in the conference circuit who knew what he was talking about looked visibly perturbed, no doubt visualising the Gothic War or the last Black Crusade. (Perhaps mercifully, none of us was even able to guess at the magnitude of the next one, lurking a mere sixty years or so in our collective futures.)

'Quite,' I said. I addressed Zyvan directly again. 'I assume everyone here has the necessary security clearance to be discussing this?' Of course they would, or he would never have raised the subject, but he enjoyed a bit of melodrama as much as I did and nodded gravely.

'You may continue,' he said.

Well, that was a bit of a shock, I'd been looking forward to dozing through the meeting, rousing myself just long enough to tease Beije if the opportunity arose, but I've never been averse to being the centre of attention, so I nodded as though I'd been expecting something of the kind.

'There are four principal Ruinous Powers,' I began, 'at least as far as we know. Heretics worship them as gods, and of all the warp entities so far discovered, only they are strong enough to challenge the Emperor Himself for dominion of the immaterium.'

'Challenge the Emperor?' Beije was outraged. 'The very idea is blasphemy!' He leaned forward, apparently reaching for the controls of his pictcaster. 'I'll listen to no more of this heretical twaddle.' His face vanished from the collection of disembodied heads floating in the hololith. Asmar's remained, but looked far from happy.

'The rest of you may care to note,' I said, concealing my amusement with some difficulty, 'that I said "challenge", not "defeat". That would indeed be heresy, and is, of course, utterly unthinkable.' Most of the heads nodded gravely. 'The precise nature of these powers is a subject to be studied and considered by those far wiser than I,[1] but the salient point is that all four are essentially rivals. They may make temporary alliances from time to time, but in the end they all seek complete dominion for themselves alone.' That I knew from personal experience; the sorceress Emeli, who for some reason kept invading my dreams of late, had been part of a Slaaneshi cult locked in a deadly struggle with a Nurglite faction for control of Slawkenberg. 'And none are more deadly rivals than Khorne and Slaanesh,' I concluded. 'If they're acting in concert here it would be almost unprecedented.'

'Completely so,' Zyvan confirmed. 'The only examples ever recorded are during events like a Black Crusade,

---

1. *And the Ordo Malleus, of course. No wonder so many of them go off the deep end.*

when adherents of all four factions are somehow able to put their differences aside. Fortunately, they start stabbing each other in the back sooner or later, and the whole thing falls apart.'

'This is hardly on the scale of a Black Crusade,' one of the Kastaforean commissars pointed out mildly. I'd spent a bit of time in his company aboard the *Emperor's Benificence*, and felt the lad might have a reasonable future in front of him. He wasn't an overt Emperor-botherer, liked his ale and a hand of cards, and had a pretty good idea of when to be looking the other way instead of jumping on every minor infraction his troopers committed. 'More of a Black Skirmish.'

'Precisely,' I said, smiling at the witticism until a few of the others decided they'd better too. 'Which leaves us with two possibilities that I can see. One of which is that there's something on Adumbria both factions want to get their hands on.'

'What might that be?' Kolbe asked, looking understandably perturbed at the idea. It must be bad enough coming to terms with the fact that one of the Ruinous Powers is taking a special interest in your homeworld, never mind two.

'Who knows?' Zyvan said. 'Adumbria's been settled for millennia. That's a lot of time for someone to hide or lose a powerful artefact. Or it might be something that's been here even longer than the Imperium.' I suppressed a shudder at that thought, being reminded rather too forcibly of the necron tombs I'd stumbled across on Interitus and Simia Orichalcae. Still, I reminded myself forcibly, the metal monstrosities weren't the only source of archeotech, and it was possible some long-lost hoard of the stuff remained buried away somewhere on this peculiar planet.

'What about the other possibility?' Kasteen asked.

'The Khornates are here to prevent the Slaaneshi from doing something that'll tilt the balance of power between them,' I said.

'Like raising daemons and frakking about with the warp currents,' the colonel concluded.

I nodded. 'Given what we already know about the activities of the Slaaneshi cult here, that would be my guess. Although I haven't a clue what they're hoping to achieve, or why the Khornates would be so desperate to prevent it.' Which was just as well. If I'd had even the remotest inkling I would have been gibbering quietly under the table by now rather than talking about it.

'Any further along on what's happening with the warp currents?' Zyvan asked Malden.

The young psyker shook his head. 'As we said before, they're turning in on themselves. It's as if whoever's behind it is trying to create a very small, very intense warp storm centred on the planet. How or why is still hard to pin down.'

'Thank you,' the lord general said dryly. He shrugged. 'So I'm open to suggestions.'

'How about the pattern of the attacks?' Kasteen asked. She brought up the display from the hololithic chart table. 'The first wave hit the Tallarns. Then they struck at Glacier Peak.'

'They struck pretty much everywhere,' Asmar pointed out, clearly relishing the chance to shoot down whatever theory she was developing.

But Kasteen merely nodded. 'They did. Which is hardly surprising, given the amount of ground fire their shuttles were taking and the fact that at least one of their transports was destroyed before it could offload most of its troop complement. Most of their forces didn't so much land as crash.'

'A good point,' Zyvan conceded. 'But I don't quite see what you're getting at.'

'I've been looking at the movements of the enemy here in Glacier Peak.' Kasteen magnified the map of the town and its surroundings. 'Five shuttles came down here. Two hit the town, one hit us and the other two deviated. One landed here, to the south, and the other crashed out here to the west, near the hab dome the commissar discovered.'

'I've read the AARs,'[1] Zyvan said, a tone of curiosity mingling with mild reproof.

Kasteen nodded. 'So have I. It was only while I was collating them that something struck me. Once the heretics were down, they only advanced in one direction. Due west. We assumed at the time they were hoping to take the town or reinforce the units attacking our compound, but I began to wonder if that wasn't the real objective.'

'If that's so, then what was?' the lord general asked.

Kasteen highlighted the hab dome. 'What if it was the site of the ritual? The shuttle that almost made it didn't overshoot the objective, as we thought at the time, the others all fell short.'

'What would be the point of that?' Asmar asked scornfully. 'The heretics had already completed their foul sorceries long before these renegades even entered the system.'

'But maybe they didn't know that,' I said, the pieces of Kasteen's chain of reasoning falling into place so neatly I was convinced she was right. And even if she hadn't

---

1. *After Action Reports: a summary of an engagement, passed up the chain of command for subsequent assessment.*

been I wasn't about to let Asmar make her look stupid in front of the lord general. 'They attacked you too, didn't they? And you're practically sitting on the site of another heretic shrine.'

As I'd hoped, the reminder of that fact left him looking severely uncomfortable. 'Did any of them seem to be making for it?'

'It's possible,' the Tallarn colonel conceded after a moment, looking distinctly unhappy at the prospect. 'I'd have to check. Our traditional tactics rely heavily on hit and run strikes and rapid manoeuvre, so the heretics were scattering in all directions.'

'If you could let us know as soon as possible,' Zyvan said, making the simple request sound more like an order than if he'd visibly exerted his authority. Clearly the exchange I'd overheard before hadn't been the end of the matter.

Asmar nodded. 'By the grace of the Emperor, it will be done.'

'Good.' Zyvan's attention turned to Kolbe. 'Any hostiles approach the site in Skitterfall?'

'A few elements made it through,' Kolbe said. 'We assumed at the time they were hoping to find reinforcements there.'

'I see.' Zyvan nodded once. 'We'll have to improve our liaison channels with your people, obviously.'

'Which raises an intriguing possibility,' Malden said, in his usual drab monotone. 'The locations of the sites do indeed appear significant, as Colonel Kasteen suggested before, and this new enemy is as aware of their importance as the one we've been attempting to track.'

'Which helps us how, exactly?' Kolbe asked.

Malden spread his hands. 'The sorcerers clearly haven't been able to achieve their objective yet. This would imply that they need to perform their ritual at least once more, probably at a specific site or sites. If we analyse the pattern of the landings along the lines the colonel has pointed out, we might be able to locate it.'

'Excellent.' Zyvan nodded. 'I'll get our intelligence people on it right away.'

THE RESULTS WERE disappointing, however. After nearly two days of feverish activity by the analysts, during which time we twiddled our thumbs and reorganised ourselves to fill the gaps in our roster left by the recent engagements, Zyvan called us in person with the bad news.

'It looks like a dead end,' he told us gloomily. 'Colonel Kasteen was definitely right about the invaders aiming for the ritual sites, but that doesn't seem to help us locate the next one.'

'Why not?' I asked. By way of reply the image of his face in the hololith, which, thank the Emperor, one of our tech-priests had finally got around to doing something about, was replaced by the now familiar globe of Adumbria, which hardly juddered at all. As before, it was pocked with contact icons, the majority concentrated in the shadow zone.

'Most of the intruders don't seem to have moved with any real sense of purpose,' Zyvan explained, 'other than the groups she already pointed out.' The clusters around Glacier Peak, the Tallarns and Skitterfall glowed a little brighter to highlight them. 'The others just started attacking the nearest PDF, Guard unit, or civilian population.'

'Well that's Khornates for you,' I commented wryly, noting Kasteen's thinly veiled disappointment and hoping to lighten her mood. 'Show them something to kill and they just get distracted.'

'Quite,' Zyvan said, clearly as disappointed as the colonel; once again a promising lead had evanesced into nothingness before our eyes. 'Most inconsiderate of them.'

'Logically,' Broklaw put in, loyally backing up his CO, 'the next ritual site should complete a pattern. Surely your psykers can predict where it should be.'

Zyvan's face reappeared, looking pained. 'You haven't had much contact with psykers, have you, young man?' Broklaw shook his head, clearly quite satisfied with that state of affairs.

The lord general sighed. 'Then just take my word for it. Getting a sensible answer out of them isn't always as easy as you might think.'

I recalled my last few conversations with Rakel and nodded in sympathy. 'Malden seems relatively well-balanced for a spook,' I said.

Zyvan sighed again. 'A little too much so, if that's possible. He won't commit himself without more data, while the others on my staff are... more typical. The only other person with an opinion is the Lady Dimarco, who seems to think the only prudent course of action is to leave the system while the currents are still marginally navigable, and tells me so incessantly.'

'Is that actually an option?' I asked as casually as I could, wondering how best to get myself aboard the flagship if it was.

Zyvan shook his head vehemently, taking the inquiry as a joke. 'Of course not. We're here to defend this place, and that's what we'll do whatever the warp throws at us.'

'Some of these units seemed to be moving,' Kasteen said, still studying the heretics' deployment in our chart table display. She highlighted a few, apparently skirting the shores of the larger of the landlocked seas. 'Perhaps we should be searching the shoreline.'

'All sixteen thousand kilometres of it?' Zyvan asked mildly. Kasteen coloured slightly, never a good sign in my experience, and I stepped in hastily.

'The sea is directly opposite Skitterfall,' I pointed out. 'A fourth site there would complete a geometrical figure.'

'We've already considered that,' Zyvan said, smiling wearily. 'I'm not completely dense, you know, Ciaphas.'

'I was beginning to wonder after that last regicide game,' I joked. For one of the greatest tacticians in the segmentum, he was surprisingly easy to beat, a fact about which I pulled his leg constantly. I suppose the abstract game was just too simple for him compared to moving entire armies around the void, but he was a gracious host and good company.

'According to Malden, anywhere along the coast would be too far out of alignment with the other sites. A couple of the others suggested that one of the poles would be a possibility, but none of the enemy units seemed to take a particular interest in either.' This was hardly surprising, really: one was occupied by a provincial town which seemed to subsist entirely on the cultivation of squinch, and the other by a PDF training facility which was stuffed to the gills with troopers and which annihilated the single shuttle-load of cultists that landed there in pretty short order.

'How about an island?' Broklaw suggested. Zyvan shrugged. 'There aren't any, at least far enough out from the coast to make a difference.'

'Well that's it then,' I said. 'We're right back where we started.'

'Not quite,' Kasteen said. I looked at her curiously and she smiled without mirth. 'All we have to do is wait for the invaders to attack again, and see where they're going.'

'If we don't get a break soon,' Zyvan said bleakly, 'it might just come to that.'

Editorial Note:

As so often, we find ourselves having to turn to another source at this juncture for a fuller picture of events. And, once again, Tincrowser's account covers the salient points as well as any other.

From *Sablist in Skitterfall: a brief history of the Chaos incursion* by Dagblat Tincrowser, 957 M41.

The second onslaught began, as everyone had expected, with a clash in space between the two opposing fleets. By this point the invaders were committed, their course predictable, and the Imperial warfleet began to move out of orbit to engage them. The *Escapade* and *Virago*, the latter still limping from the wounds she had sustained earlier but eager for the fray nonetheless, boosted out to meet the enemy, accompanied by the squadron of destroyers.

Their orders were to avoid contact with the enemy warships as much as possible, concentrating their efforts on the transport ships, but this was to prove more difficult than hitherto. The enemy escorts had had time to deploy against the approaching defenders, and the destroyer squadron was soon caught up in a desperate struggle against a pair of raiders protecting the flanks of the flotilla.

They were ultimately successful, leaving one gutted and adrift in the void while the other turned and fled, grievously wounded, only to tear itself apart as its warp engines overloaded when it attempted to find refuge back in the foul domain from which it had sprung. This victory was bought at a high price, however, as all three sustained some damage, one being so severely mauled that it was reduced to a drifting hulk, its crew being forced to abandon it entirely.[1]

The victory of the others was to be short-lived, however. As they closed with the enemy fleet the vessel at the heart of it, no less than a battleship, moved ahead of the merchant vessels for the first time and opened up with the full awesome power of its forward batteries. Both surviving destroyers were crippled before they could even come within the range of their own guns, one[2]

---

1. The Spiteful was salvaged the following year and returned to service in 948, eventually meeting its end in a rather more heroic manner: this was the vessel which rammed the battleship Agonising Death at the blockade of Garomar in 999 M41, destroying it completely along with itself, and saving the lives of an estimated eighty thousand civilians in the refugee fleet it was escorting.

2. The Impetuous.

being reduced to little more than a cloud of drifting debris by the first salvo.

The two frigates were to fare little better, although they had succeeded in reducing the number of transports by three by this point.[1] The lance batteries aboard the terrifying behemoth licked out once, destroying the bridge of the *Virago* and crippling the engines of the *Escapade*, which was soon left too far behind to continue the fight.

All that stood between Adumbria and Armageddon now was the *Indestructible*, outnumbered and out-gunned. Some expected her to go to the assistance of the stricken escort vessels, but she remained on station above Skitterfall highport, standing resolutely between the heavily-armed leviathan and the swarm of merchant ships.

Effectively unhindered, the remaining transport vessels in the invasion fleet slipped into orbit and began dropping their cargo of heretical vermin on the planet below.

---

1. *One kill to the* Virago *and two to the* Escapade.

FIFTEEN

'You can never have too many enemies. The more you've got, the more likely they are to get in each other's way.'

– Jarvin Wallankot, *Idle Musings*, 605 M41

IN THE END, Zyvan wasn't so far wrong. We spent the remaining time until the enemy fleet arrived in a fever of preparation, knowing that the assault to come would make the one we'd beaten off before pale into insignificance. Fortunately, our casualties had been relatively light, at least compared to the Tallarns and the PDF, so the amount of reorganisation we had to undertake was less than I'd feared.

'Detoi's fit for duty,' Broklaw reported, helping himself to a refill from the pot of tanna Jurgen had brought into my office. It was a far cry from the opulent buffets in the conference rooms of the lord general's headquarters, but my aide had done his best to make the long

meeting bearable for us, and given his almost preternatural talent for scrounging, he'd been able to keep us
fed and watered well enough. I pushed the plate which
had contained a trio of palovine pastries to one side of
the desk to make room for the data-slate.

'I'm glad to hear it,' I said, skimming the medicae
report.

Fit for duty was stretching it a bit, he'd taken a las bolt
to the chest and was damn lucky the flak armour under
his greatcoat had absorbed most of the impact, but
there was nothing they could do for him now except
wait for him to recover naturally and for the ribs to knit
back together. Lying around in the infirmary wasn't
going to make him heal any faster, and no doubt the
thought that the longer he took to get up the longer
Sulla would be in charge of his company was a hell of
an incentive to discharge himself.

'Well, it simplifies the personnel reassignments,' Kasteen said, brushing a crumb of pastry from the corner of
her mouth. My office was crowded with the three of us
present, let alone Jurgen when he wandered through,
but it was a lot easier to work in there than in the command centre. What we were doing was sensitive and a
regrettable neccessity: reassigning personnel to fill the
gaps in our organisation left by our dead and severely
wounded.

In most cases, the best course of action was to do
nothing, as a squad light by a trooper or two would still
function reasonably well, and rotating people in or out
of a smoothly-functioning team would be more disrup-
tive to their efficiency and morale than just leaving well
enough alone. In a few cases, though, where NCOs and
officers were down, someone had to be brought in to
fill the hole they'd left, or designated the new leader

until they recovered. Which brought us to the delicate matter of first company.

'At least we're only looking for one new company commander,' I agreed. Captain Kelton had been unlucky enough to run straight into a group of heretics armed with rocket launchers, and a couple had penetrated the hull armour of her command Chimera with inevitable results. The platoon commanders had managed to hold things together reasonably well, but none of them had been clear about who had seniority and in the end Broklaw had had to take charge himself, directing them by vox from the command bunker. This was far from ideal and a striking example of why taking AFVs[1] into a cityfight against infantry is one hell of a risk.

'The question is, who do we appoint?' Broklaw said. 'After the last debacle, none of the lieutenants strike me as being up to the job.'

'I'm with you there,' Kasteen agreed. 'They're all good enough at platoon level, but someone should have taken charge on the ground as soon as Kelton was taken out. None of them had the confidence to step in, and that worries me.'

'Right,' I concurred, making it unanimous. 'At least Sulla showed some initiative when Detoi went down. And she did a reasonable job too, under the circumstances.'

Which was perfectly true. She might have been the most irritating junior officer in the entire regiment and a damn sight too reckless for my liking, but she got things done and the troopers seemed to like her for some reason. So despite my personal reservations, I felt I should give credit where it was due.

---

1. *Armoured Fighting Vehicles, a generic term used by the Guard to refer to anything from a Salamander to a Baneblade.*

'Sulla,' Kasteen said, a thoughtful tone entering her voice. Broklaw and I glanced warily at one another, already seeing where this chain of thought was taking us. But in all honesty I couldn't see a credible alternative.

Broklaw nodded slowly. 'She's been keeping second company together well enough,' he agreed cautiously. 'But she's been serving with them since the amalgamation and the other platoon commanders trust her instincts. Would a new company be quite so willing to work with her?'

'That's her problem,' I said bluntly. 'Either she's up to the job or she isn't. And there's only one way to find out.' I sighed. 'Besides, who else is there?'

'Quite,' Kasteen said. She looked thoughtful. 'A few of them are going to have trouble taking orders from another lieutenant, though. Especially as they match her in seniority.'

'Brevet[1] her up to captain,' I said. 'If she doesn't make the grade she can always have her old platoon back when we find someone else.'

'Fair enough.' Broklaw nodded his agreement. 'What do we do with third platoon in the meantime? Bump Lustig up to lieutenant?'

'He won't thank you for it,' I said, remembering some of the veteran sergeant's more trenchant comments about officers in general. 'Better just tell him he's confirmed as

---

1. *A form of battlefield promotion to be confirmed at a later date. Though entitled to wear a captain's insignia and be considered one in the chain of command, Sulla would remain a lieutenant for most administrative purposes until the change in her status was approved by the Munitorum. In theory, if she proved unable to do the job she could thus be returned to her original position and rank without the stigma of a demotion marring her service record.*

platoon sergeant for the time being, until he's had time to get used to being in charge, and make him up to lieutenant in the next round of promotions. That way if we have to put Sulla back in place no one loses face.'

'Good point.' Kasteen nodded decisively. 'Is his corporal up to running the squad on her own for the time being?'

'I'd say so,' I said. 'Penlan's a good soldier. She and Lustig should be able to pick a new ASL for themselves without any interference from us.'

'Penlan?' Kasteen looked thoughtful for a moment. 'Isn't she the one they call Jinxie?'

'Yes.' I nodded. 'But she's not nearly as accident prone as she's supposed to be. I'll grant you she fell down an ambull tunnel once, and there was that incident with the frag grenade and the latrine trench, but things tend to work out for her. The orks on Kastafore were as surprised as she was when the floor in the factory collapsed, and we'd have walked right into that hrud ambush on Skweki if she hadn't triggered the mine by chucking an empty food tin away...' I trailed off, finally listening to what I was saying. 'You know how troopers tend to exaggerate these things,' I finished lamely.

'Quite,' Kasteen said, keeping a remarkably straight face. 'Is that about it?'

It was, more or less. We spent a few more minutes on personnel assignments and dealt with a few logistical matters, and were just about to separate to go about our other duties when Jurgen entered the office. I didn't take much notice, to be honest, as he'd been in and out several times over the course of the afternoon to deal with routine paperwork and keep us supplied with refreshments. Then he coughed stickily, his inevitable prelude to delivering a message when he thought my attention was elsewhere.

'Begging your pardon, commissar, ma'am, sir, but there's an urgent message from headquarters. The heretic fleet has engaged the warships and the lord general expects them to start landing troops as soon as they can.'

'Thank you, Jurgen,' I said as calmly as I could, reaching for my weapons. One way or another, the battle for the soul of Adumbria was about to be decided, although quite how literally I still had no idea.

DESPITE MY FEARS, the initial reports coming in from the battlefronts made no mention of giants in crimson power armour, so it looked as though we were to be spared an onslaught of Chaos Marines at least. This wasn't so unusual; according to some highly classified files Zyvan had made available to me, the World Eaters Chapter[1] quite often sent out a few of their number to advise the hordes of wannabe warmasters infesting the galaxy. (But what advice a follower of Khorne would listen to other than 'Kill them all!' is quite frankly beyond me.) It was quite probable that we weren't facing any more than a squad or two in the whole invasion force, which was still a disturbing enough prospect I grant you, but rather less intimidating than an army of psychopathic supermen would have been, especially if I didn't have to deal with any more of them myself.

'Eight shuttles inbound,' the auspex operator called. Kasteen and I exchanged glances. The palms of my hands were tingling again, and my mouth suddenly felt dry.

---

1. *Technically Legion, as the traitors never underwent the reorganisation which followed the Horus Heresy.*

'We're taking a hell of a gamble,' I said.

The colonel nodded tensely. 'Well, it's too late to change our minds now.' We glanced at the dispositions of our forces in the chart table holo tank, and inevitably I felt a flutter of apprehension; if we'd made the wrong call things were about to get very ugly indeed.

After much deliberation, we'd decided to follow Kasteen's instinct and assume that the isolated hab dome would be their main target. Accordingly we'd deployed the whole of fourth and fifth companies in a wide ring around it, camouflaged as only Valhallans can be in a snowfield, hoping to close the noose around them once they were on the ground. Which, with second company still waiting to be deployed by dropship, left first to protect the town more or less unaided, unless you counted the handful of Hekwyn's people assigned there. Not for the first time I wondered if Sulla was really up to the job we'd handed her, and hoped I wouldn't get my answer in the form of a pile of civilian corpses.

This left the problem of ensuring the security of our compound. In theory, second company should be more than enough to do the job, as they had before, but this time they were already embarked aboard the dropship which stood, engines idling, awaiting the lord general's orders to deploy to Emperor knew where at a moment's notice.

We still had a couple of hundred warm bodies in third company, and being Guard troopers first and foremost they could shoot as well as anyone, but the thought of relying on a motley collection of cooks, medicae orderlies and the regimental band to protect our hides from a frothing swarm of homicidal lunatics wasn't exactly comforting. (Though it was marginally more so than the idea of the enginseers being issued with lasguns and shown which end to point forwards; being cogboys they could tell you every detail of how they worked, but couldn't hit the side of a starship if they were standing in one of the cargo holds. The sight of a group of white-robed tech-priests holding factory-fresh small-arms as though they were incredibly delicate works of art, being bawled at by Sergeant Lustig as he attempted to impart the rudiments of their use, will remain with me to the grave.)

'Contacts closing, fifty kilometres out,' the auspex operator droned, her voice as emotionless as a servitor. 'Descending rapidly. Forty-three kilometres and closing…'

The crimson blips crawled slowly across the hololith, heading straight for us and Glacier Peak. I tried to calculate the number of enemy soldiers that eight civilian shuttles might contain, then wished I hadn't. If they were packed out, each one could hold as much as a full company, which meant that in a worst-case scenario we could find ourselves outnumbered by two to one.

'On the plus side, they've probably forgotten their cold-weather gear like the last ones did,' Kasteen said, clearly doing the same piece of mental arithmetic I was.

'Let's hope so,' I said. It seemed likely; in my experience Chaotic troops tended to rush headlong into combat heedless of the suitability or otherwise of the equipment they had, or even if their weapons were adequate. And Khornate cultists were the most reckless of all. 'With any luck the cold will do most of the work for us.'

'It did before,' Broklaw said hopefully.

'Thirty-eight kilometres and closing,' the auspex operator chimed in. 'Maintaining descent vector…'

'Can you approximate an LZ yet?' Kasteen asked, her voice brittle with tension.

'It could still be any of the targets,' the operator responded. 'Thirty-two kilometres and closing...'

'Great.' Kasteen's hand closed on the butt of her bolt pistol, a reflexive response to stress I was long familiar with; indeed I tended to reach for my own weapons in moments of unease.

'Twenty-nine kilometres and closing,' the chant went on. 'Descent vector steady...'

'Regina, look.' Broklaw pointed to the chart table, relief evident in his voice. The potential landing zone was projected into it, a steadily shrinking circle, diminishing as the approaching shuttles neared the ground. The majority of it was now well to the west of both Glacier Peak and our own position. 'You were right!'

'Emperor be praised,' Kasteen said fervently, relief evident in both her posture and voice. There could be little doubt now that the site of the hab dome was the heretics' main target. If they just kept going on the same course, they'd come down inside our noose neat as you please. Our trap was about to be sprung.

'Three contacts veering off,' the auspex operator said. 'The rest maintaining course and speed, eighteen kilometres and closing...'

'Veering where?' I asked, a tingle of apprehension beginning to run through me. It had all been going so neatly. By way of answer, subsidiary landing zone circles began to shrink in the chart table.

'Where do you think?' Broklaw asked grimly, and I bit down on a couple of choice underhive epithets. Two shuttles were heading for the town, and one was unquestionably targeting us. It seemed that the enemy had learned something from their first attack, probably from vox traffic, and wanted to pin us down while they took care of their primary target. Well they were in for an unpleasant surprise, of course, but that wasn't going to help us or the citizens of Glacier Peak.

'First company, stand by. You've got two shuttles inbound, ETA...' Kasteen glanced at the auspex operator for confirmation before continuing, 'three minutes. Engage on sight.'

'Understood.' Sulla's voice was crisp and confident, but then it always was with combat imminent. Well, there was no point worrying about it now, she'd just have to do the best she could. I just hoped to the Emperor we hadn't made a big mistake. 'We'll be ready for them.' She switched channels to her platoon command frequencies and began chivvying up her subordinates. I listened in for a moment, but she seemed to know what she was doing, so I returned my attention to the chart table.

'How long have we got?' I asked.

'Four minutes, give or take,' Broklaw said. I nodded tensely. It could have been worse, I supposed.

A single shuttle couldn't hold much more than a company's worth of enemy, I reminded myself, so even if it was packed we were in for a fairly even fight. Assuming our rear echelon troopers were up to the job, which they most certainly should be. And if push came to shove we still had a company of front-line combat troops in reserve.

'Should I disembark second company?' Broklaw asked, almost as if he could read my thoughts. 'Bolster our defences here?'

Kasteen shook her head. 'Leave them aboard the dropship.' She indicated the main hololith, where contact icons were springing up all over the planet. 'All hell's breaking loose. Emperor alone knows where they'll be needed before long.'

It was hard to disagree. From what I could see, bitter fighting was beginning to erupt in nearly every population centre and the PDF were being hard pressed throughout the shadow zone, even where they were being supported by the Kastaforeans. It was credits to carrots that Zyvan would be calling his mobile reserves into action any time now, and he wouldn't be at all thrilled to be told that they'd be with him as soon as they could but something else had come up.

'We should be able to handle them,' I agreed, hoping I was right.

'Contact at LZ one in one minute,' the auspex operator chimed in. 'Contact at LZ two in two.' That would be us, and I watched the descending blip in the chart table with a kind of weary resignation. 'Contact at LZ three in four minutes thirty.'

'Fourth and fifth companies, stand by,' Kasteen ordered. 'Five shuttles incoming, ETA four minutes. They've taken the bait.'

'They might be landing, but they won't be taking off again,' the commander of fifth company promised, and Kasteen nodded in satisfaction.

'I don't doubt it.' She looked across at Broklaw and me. 'Good luck, gentlemen.'

'Let's hope we don't need it,' I said.

What we really needed was some serious firepower, but the sentinels had all been deployed with the ambushers out at the hab dome, so the best we could muster was small-arms and a few man-portable heavy weapons. Unfortunately, the number of people on the base capable of using the heavy stuff, apart from the specialists in second company who had been strapped into their crash webbing aboard the dropship since the first alert, were few and far between. Not for the first time I began to think things might be a little healthier somewhere else.

Or not. A worrying thought was beginning to nag at me, all the more insistently the harder I tried to ignore it. I turned to the nearest vox operator.

'I need a channel to the lord general's office,' I said. 'Highest priority.' Just to make sure, I added my commissarial override code.

'Ciaphas.' Zyvan sounded harrassed, which I suppose was inevitable under the circumstances. 'This isn't really a good time.'

'I know,' I said. 'And I'm sorry. But this is important.'

'I don't doubt it.' Zyvan sighed. 'What's the problem?' Behind his voice I could hear the unmistakable rumble of heavy ordnance detonating in the background. It sounded like things were getting pretty rough in Skitterfall.

'Kasteen was right,' I told him. 'The heretics here are definitely targeting the ritual site.' The distant crackle of lasgun fire became audible in the distance, seeping through the walls around us. 'Mainly,' I added, in deference to the prevailing circumstances.

'Interesting.' Zyvan was no fool, of course, and could see the implications as clearly as I could. 'I'll check with the Tallarns and Kolbe's mob here in the city. Just to confirm. But that does seem significant.'

'It's still our best chance of finding out what the sorcerers are up to and stopping it,' I pointed out. 'If the invaders are concentrating anywhere we need to get in there fast. Preferably ahead of them.'

'I'll look into it,' Zyvan promised. I glanced at the gently rotating globe in the hololith, struck by the number of enemy icons clustering along the shoreline of the larger sea, in some areas it looked as though the entire coast was bordered in blood.

'I'd concentrate on the shoreline,' I said. 'There has to be something there whatever Malden thinks.'

'I'll take that under advisement,' Zyvan said diplomatically, which is general-speak for 'I'll make up my own mind, thank you very much.'

'We're missing something,' I said, turning to Kasteen. The sound of gunfire was a lot louder now.

'All the military intelligence we've got is on the hololith,' she pointed out. The coin dropped, and I turned to the vox operator so fast the man flinched.

'What about the civilian channels?' I asked.

'I'm sorry, commissar, I haven't been monitoring...'

'Of course you haven't,' I said patiently. 'It's not your job. But you can connect me to someone who has.'

'Hekwyn.' The arbitrator sounded as though he was out on the street somewhere, talking into a comm-bead. To my distinct lack of surprise there was gunfire in the background. 'What can I do for you, commissar?'

'I need to know if there have been any unusual incidents around the equatorial sea,' I told him.

He laughed briefly, without humour. 'One or two enemies of humanity wreaking havoc, I'm told.'

'Something more specific,' I said, filling him in rapidly on the situation.

His tone changed. 'I'll get back to you,' he promised. 'But it might take a while.'

'Let's hope we've got long enough,' I said, cutting the link.

Becoming aware of a familiar odour at my elbow, I turned to find Jurgen standing there, the melta in his hands as always in times of trouble. It had been fired recently, the actinic tang of scorched metal hanging around the barrel. I raised an eyebrow in wordless enquiry.

'I thought you might be wanting to step outside again, sir,' he said. Well, not likely, with the compound being overrun with heretic foot soldiers and all, but I nodded anyway for the benefit of anyone who might be around to take notice.

'I'm afraid I'm needed here for the time being,' I told him, with the best air of frustrated martial zeal I could muster. It was at that point that I became aware that the gunfire outside had become very loud indeed, and that Jurgen's hat and greatcoat were covered in melting snow. 'What exactly is going on out there?' I asked.

Before my aide could reply, there was a loud explosion from the direction of the main door, which blew in, taking a couple of nearby troopers with it. Kasteen, Broklaw and I drew our side arms so fast it would have been all but impossible to tell who had been first, and turned to face this unexpected threat. A knot of red and black uniformed fanatics stormed into the room, heedless of the hail of las and bolter fire which cut them down as they rushed at us.

'Blood for the Blood God!' one more fortunate than most screamed, charging forward as las rounds gouged chunks out of his flak armour and the flesh beneath, so carried away he barely seemed to register his wounds. I switched aim, shooting him in the leg, and he crashed to the floor in front of me, reaching out with a red-stained combat blade. 'Blood for the Blood God!'

'Fine, he can have yours,' I snapped, stamping down hard on his throat and crushing his larynx. It wasn't a particularly elegant kill, but at least it shut him up.

'They're all over the compound,' Jurgen said. I glanced around the room as Kasteen rallied her motley collection of vox and auspex operators and began to beat back our assailants. It was clear the command centre wouldn't be much of a refuge now; even if we could clear it again it would remain wide open, and I didn't feel at all comfortable with the idea of remaining in an enclosed space under siege from a swarm of homicidal lunatics. I turned to Broklaw, who seemed more or less unharmed apart from a gash in his forehead.

'I'd better get outside,' I said, 'and try to rally our people.'

'Good idea,' he said, apparently unaware of the blood seeping down his face. 'If we lose vox contact with four and five now, our trap's pretty much frakked.'

'We'll keep 'em out,' I assured him, salving my conscience a little with the thought that at least someone would if I had anything to do with it. I turned to my aide. 'Come on, Jurgen. We've got work to do.'

'Right with you, sir,' he responded as phlegmatically as ever. I drew my chainsword and began hewing my way to the door, blessing whatever it is about Khornate fanatics that makes them run at you with blades yelling their heads off instead of shooting their guns like any sensible opponent would, potting the odd one with the laspistol whenever I got the opportunity. It wasn't often, to be honest. Kasteen was clearly revelling in the chance to get her hands dirty for a change instead of directing operations from a distance through a chain of subordinates, banging away happily with her miniature bolter as though she was racking up the prize tickets at a fairground shooting booth. The explosive projectiles were making short work of both heretic troopers and their armour, leaving the walls decorated in abstract designs I didn't want to look at too closely.

'Not enough of them in here for you?' she asked as Jurgen and I swept past, my aide having switched to his standard-issue lasgun in deference to the confined space and the number of friendly soldiers in the vicinity. I plastered my best devil-may-care grin on my face.

'It seems churlish to take yours while you're having so much fun,' I said. 'Besides, you and Ruput are needed here.' I stepped aside to give Jurgen a clear shot at a red and black trooper running through the door and realised as the man dropped that there were no more behind him.

Kasteen re-holstered her weapon, looking vaguely disappointed. 'Which leaves me to keep any more from getting in here,' I finished.

'I guess so.' The colonel turned back to the bank of vox units, already assimilating reports from the other battlefronts. A few of our people were down, but damn few considering, and several of those were walking wounded. Broklaw was rallying the others and returning them to work.

As I hurried down the corridor with Jurgen trotting at my heels, a party of medicae passed us going in the other direction. I felt a strong sense of relief at the sight. They were carrying lasguns, true, but slung across their shoulders, and if they were able to respond so fast to a call for aid from the command centre they couldn't have been needed to help defend the place. My spirits began to rise.

'Commissar!' A young corporal greeted us as we broke through into the open air, and I pulled the scarf over my mouth and nose without breaking stride (bumping the side of my face with the butt of my laspistol as I did so, but I wasn't about to relinquish either of my weapons under the circumstances). His face seemed vaguely familiar, and after a moment I remembered having him flogged on Kastafore for starting a brawl with some civilians over the favours of a joygirl. I dredged his name out of the depths of my memory.

'Albrin,' I said, nodding, and the fellow looked absurdly pleased that I'd recognised him. 'Who's in charge here?'

'I think I am, sir.' He waved vaguely out into the darkness beyond the light leaking from the doorway behind us, where the scorched and blackened remains of the thick metal portal which used to protect it gave mute testimony to the fact that at least a few of the heretics hadn't been so far gone with bloodlust that they'd forgotten how to set a demo charge. 'My section saw a bunch of traitors heading this way, so we followed up and took them from behind.'

'Good work,' I said, picking out a number of mounds in the snow which had probably been enemy troopers a few moments ago. It made sense: Khornate fanatics would be so fixated on breaking into the building and massacring everyone inside, it probably hadn't even occurred to them to watch their own backs, even when Albrin's team opened fire on them.

The corporal flushed. 'After we cleared them out, we started fortifying the breach. It seemed the most sensible thing to do.'

I nodded again. For a quartermaster's clerk he had a pretty sound grasp of tactics. 'It was,' I said. They'd begun piling up cargo pods and other odds and ends into a makeshift barricade, which seemed reasonably defensible. I tried to find some more of the defenders on my comm-bead, but none of them had tactical communications kit, so it was a futile gesture; in the end I had to make do with voxing the command centre and letting them know what was going on.

'Are you staying with them?' Kasteen asked.

'No,' I replied, conscious that only my end of the conversation would be overheard by the ad hoc defenders. 'They seem competent enough.' As I'd expected, a ripple of pride and renewed resolve went round the little group of men and women. 'I'll head on out and try to find another squad or two to send back to reinforce them.' This was not only good tactical sense; I stood a much better chance of avoiding the enemy than I would if I stayed put at an obvious target point.

'Good hunting,' Kasteen said, completely misreading my motives, and after a couple of encouraging remarks to the defenders, Jurgen and I moved on into the darkness.

The truth was that by that time the battle for the compound was all but over, the superior training and skills of the defenders and the bone-chilling cold combining to cut the attackers down like grain before a harvester. But at the time, as you'll readily appreciate, I had no way of knowing that, and was as cautious as I might possibly be in my movements. I did have time to scan the tactical frequencies, discovering *inter alia* that our trap at the hab dome had worked as well as we could possibly have hoped, fourth and fifth companies having encircled their prey and now well advanced in the process of squeezing the life out of them, while Sulla's new command was still, to my mingled surprise and relief, doing a sterling job of defending the town from the depredations of the invaders. (Though not without some collateral damage, of course.)

'Commissar.' Jurgen was little more than a silhouette in the endless night, although my eyes had now adjusted enough to make him out without undue difficulty. Which was just as well, as the freezing temperatures and the scarf across my nose was depriving me of my usual method of keeping track of my faithful companion in the darkness. 'Movement.'

I followed the direction of his gesture, wondering for a moment what the whining sound in my ears was, until I remembered that the dropship engines were still running. Well, good, at least we'd still be able to respond when the lord general's call came. That was probably the main reason our base here had been attacked, I thought. If the first wave had reported the presence of the orbital transport to their masters in the invasion fleet, someone, probably one of the Traitor Marines, would have had the sense to realise why it was there.

There was no time for further thought on the matter though, as the movement Jurgen had spotted began to resolve itself into a mass of moving darkness, occulting the few low-lying stars I could see between the buildings. At first I took it for a squad of troopers, but as it moved out into more open ground I realised it was far too massive for that.

'Emperor on Earth!' I said, a faint vibration beginning to reach my feet and an all-too-familiar grinding and clanking sound beginning to build through the all-pervasive whine of the dropship engines. 'They've brought a bloody tank!'

'Say again?' Kasteen said, a tone of surprise in her voice.

'It's a Leman Russ,' I said. 'Or it used to be at least.' The familiar outline had been blurred with icons and trophies I was heartily glad not to be able to make out in the darkness surrounding us, and what looked like a strip of park railing stuck to it for no readily apparent reason. 'They must have taken a while to get it unloaded from the shuttle.'

'Confirm that.' Kasteen conferred with the captains of the other companies for a moment. 'They've got a couple of armoured units at the hab dome as well. None in town, thank the Emperor.'

'We can take it, commissar,' Jurgen said, unshipping his prized melta. We probably could too, it was what the weapon was designed for after all. The flaw in that plan, at least from my point of view, was that attempting to do so would probably attract the attention of its crew, and that in turn would undoubtedly be manifested in a hail of heavy bolter fire from the nearest sponson.

I was saved from having to find a plausible reason to keep our heads down by a sudden intervention from our left, where a squad of Valhallans broke from cover without warning to unleash a hail of ineffective lasgun fire against the metal hull. The engine growled and its turret turned, bringing its main cannon to bear.

'Oh, frak this!' I said, as heavy bolter rounds began chewing up the snow all around us, punching holes through flakboard buildings and generally making an unholy mess of everything in sight. 'Take the bloody shot.' In truth it was our best chance of survival, since there was no way we could get out now without being cut to pieces.

'Very good, sir.' Jurgen squeezed the trigger, aiming for the thinner armour of the flank, and the idiots who'd attacked it in the first place cheered wildly (at least, the ones who weren't thrashing around in the snow bleeding to death did). The blast of superheated plasma punched through the side skirts, shredding the tracks, and the metal leviathan slewed to a halt, its engine screaming.

'Come on, men! Do you want to live forever?' The noncom in charge of the squad must have been on something, I thought. Nobody spoke like that outside badly-written combat novels. It seemed to work, though: with a banshee howl the whole damn lot of them were up and running, scrambling all over the blasted thing, trying to lever the hatches off and drop frag grenades inside.

Good luck to them, I thought. The turret swung again, as though it were trying to shake them off, and then I realised it was trying to aim at something. I jerked my head around, my gaze meeting the vast metal slab of the side of the dropship.

'Frakking warp!' I yelled. 'They're going for the dropship!' I began waving at the troopers still swarming all over the crippled tank. 'Get out of the way!'

Jurgen couldn't fire again with those idiots blocking his shot, and if the traitors managed to get a shell off at this range they'd hit the orbital transport for sure. I tried to picture the size of the ensuing explosion if they managed to penetrate its hull armour, and failed; all I was sure of was that there'd be precious little of the compound left, and I'd be a small cloud of drifting vapour.

There was no help for it. Grabbing Jurgen by the collar, I started to run for the dropship, frantically retuning my comm-bead to find the pilot's frequency.[1]

'Get in the air now!' I shouted.

---

1. Interestingly, it never seems to have occurred to him to order Jurgen to take the shot anyway, sacrificing the impetuous troopers for the good of the majority, a decision which most commissars would undoubtedly have taken without a qualm.

'Say again?' The pilot was on line, at least, but sounded bewildered. 'Who is this?'

'Commissar Cain,' I said, the breath beginning to rasp in my throat from the cold. 'You're in imminent danger. Lift now!'

It was even worse than I thought. The main cargo ramp was still down, warm yellow light spilling out of it, and if the traitor tank managed to get a shot off there wouldn't even be the hope of the hull armour stopping it. I redoubled my efforts, and after what felt like an eternity of slithering though the treacherous snow, but was in all probability no more than a handful of seconds, was rewarded by the clanging solidity of metal underfoot. Jurgen, of course, had no such difficulty and had outdistanced me easily. As I turned to look back he was already at the controls, stabbing at the closure rune with his fingers.

With a grinding hum the ramp began to rise, cutting off my view of that deadly battle cannon. My last sight of the tank was as the Valhallans who had assaulted it began scattering away, apparently having found a vulnerable point to chuck a grenade into. Whether it had any effect I don't know, as a sudden lurch underfoot knocked me to my knees.

For good or ill we were now airborne, and Jurgen and I were on our way to Emperor knew where. However, had I known our eventual destination and what we'd find there, I'd probably have charged the bloody tank myself and thought I was lucky.

Editorial Note:

At which point we find ourselves once again having to turn to other sources for a proper appreciation of the bigger picture. The first of which, at least, is readable.

The second is as painful as the rest of Sulla's assaults on the Gothic language, but I've included it for its summation of what was happening to the rest of the regiment while Cain was otherwise occupied. As Tincrowser summarises events adequately enough, readers of a refined sensibility may skip it if they wish, although it does provide a first-hand account of an aspect of the conflict which he, along with most Adumbrians, remains unaware of to this day.

From *Sablist in Skitterfall: a brief history of the Chaos incursion* by Dagblat Tincrowser, 957 M41.

As THE ENEMY battleship continued to bear down on the flotilla of merchant vessels and the defiant

Indestructible, which seemed all that stood between
them and certain destruction, the surviving transport
ships remained in orbit, pouring their cargo of traitors
and heretics onto the planet below. Many of the beleaguered defenders still hoped for the mighty Imperial
vessel to intervene, but it remained resolutely in place. In
truth it could do little else by now, since to turn away in
pursuit of a handful of scattered targets would achieve
little beyond exposing itself to the guns of the enemy.
Furthermore, there were the merchant ships to consider,
a little over a thousand of them at this point, all helpless
against the predator closing in on them.

Though no one wanted to admit it, the protection of
the merchant vessels was the battleship's highest priority. These ships would be needed if the worst were to
happen and an evacuation became necessary, so they
had to be defended, while the now empty transport
vessels, having succeeded in their fell design, presented
little further threat.

Nevertheless, we can still appreciate the frustration
felt by the crew of the *Indestructible* and the apprehension of the merchant crews as the Chaos Leviathan
continued to coast towards them.

If the battle in space had become a waiting game,
however, the battle for the planet below had reached
fever pitch. The invaders had struck almost everywhere
at once, concentrating, as one might expect, a considerable proportion of their force against the planetary
capital. Skitterfall became a grim battleground, where
PDF and Imperial Guard elements fought for control
of the streets against apparently inexhaustible numbers
of fanatical heretics, whose only imperative appeared to
be to cause as much death and destruction as possible.

Making no apparent distinction between defenders and civilians, they slaughtered their way into the city centre, while the gallant defenders withdrew to regroup in the northern suburbs. Here the fighting became even fiercer, as the invaders' confederates emerged from hiding to wreak further mischief of their own.

And this pattern continued all over Adumbria. On the coldside, hidden renegades appeared, intent on hampering the defence of Glacier Peak, although the Valhallans prevailed over them as easily as the invaders themselves. On the hotside, the Tallarns were hard pressed, as before, despite the lack of any obvious targets of strategic value, their rough riders galloping to the defence of the inhabitants of the scattered desert hamlets. And throughout the shadow zone the battle to cleanse the soil of our home world from the taint of the unclean continued unabated.

From *Like a Phoenix on the Wing: The Early Campaigns and Glorious Victories of the Valhallan 597th* by General Jenit Sulla (retired), 101 M42.

NOTWITHSTANDING THE IMPRESSION of imperturbability I took such pains to present to my subordinates, my readers will, I am sure, readily appreciate the apprehension I felt at the colonel's warning. I had scarcely had time to come to terms with my sudden and unexpected elevation, let alone come to know my new subordinates as anything other than the casual acquaintances of the officers' mess that they had until so recently been. Nevertheless, we were all soldiers of the Guard, the finest and most noble exemplars of humanity, so my confidence in their abilities was as high as it could be,

and for my part I was quietly determined to provide
them with the leadership such heroic women and men
deserved.

With but a handful of minutes before the enemy
onslaught was upon us, I checked the dispositions of
the platoons under me in the tactical display of the
company command Chimera, finding the routine com-
fortingly familiar. Indeed, were it not for the extra
datafeeds and vox links surrounding me, I could almost
have fancied myself back in command of my old platoon.

To my relief, our units were responding well to the
alert, the platoon commanders as efficient as I could
have wished, and glancing at the image in the hololith I
was left in no doubt that our readiness to meet the
heretic threat was as high as it was possible to be. All
we could do now was wait for their shuttles to ground
and move in as rapidly as we could to contain them.

And we weren't to be left waiting long. Within
moments I heard the shriek of their engines, even
through the thick armoured hull of the Chimera, a
sound which was shortly to be terminated by the ice-
shaking impact of their landing. One shuttle at least
would not be returning to the vermin-laden vessel
whence it came, as it had the misfortune to fly in
directly over the heads of third platoon, who welcomed
it as warmly as one might expect with the combined
firepower of their heavy weapons and Chimera-
mounted bolters.

'It's down and burning,' Lieutenant Roxwell
reported, unable to keep a note of satisfaction from his
voice, and under the circumstances I could scarcely
reprove him for that. Even before I could give the

order, he began moving his squads in to mop up the survivors, of which there were to prove far too many for comfort. Like the ones who had attacked us before, they fought like men possessed, heedless of their own safety or sound tactical doctrine. The fight became bloody, but their overconfidence was our strongest weapon, save for our faith in the Emperor of course, and it wasn't long before our superior competence and fighting spirit began to tell.

The second shuttle landed over two kilometres away, near the mine workings, but we had anticipated that, and first platoon were waiting for them, ready to give them the bloody nose all who dare to raise arms against the Emperor so richly deserve and invariably receive. Nonetheless, their charge was ferocious and our line buckled in places, allowing them to break through into the town itself before fourth platoon could move up to reinforce the gallant warriors of first.

Thus it was we found ourselves faced with two hordes of fanatics rampaging through Glacier Peak from opposite directions, firing indiscriminately at Guard troopers, praetor riot squads and unarmed civilians alike. Indeed, some even seemed to prefer the slaughter of innocent victims to facing our guns, cowards that they were.

The time was right for a bold initiative, and I ordered my unengaged units to consolidate around my command vehicle in the town square, where the twin thrusts of the enemy could be met simultaneously and held apart. For were they to meet and converge, the combined horde would undoubtedly have been able to wreak far more damage than either had managed alone. In this we were aided by two circumstances no one could have readily anticipated; the single-mindedness of the invaders, which allowed first and third platoons to wrap around their flanks and harass them all the way in, and the unexpected intervention of the underground cult we had spent so much time and effort attempting to expunge since our arrival on Adumbria.

It may be recalled that, as Commissar Cain was the first to point out, the invaders and the insurgents we had been engaging prior to their arrival appeared to owe their allegiance to rival Chaos Powers, and this was to be confirmed in the most unexpected fashion, as motley groups of armed civilians appeared in the streets to harass the invaders. I'm pleased to report that our women and men made no distinction between them, gunning down this breed of heretic whenever they appeared as eagerly as they did the crimson-uniformed foot soldiers of the traitor infantry, but the insurgents never retaliated in kind, concentrating all their efforts on killing the minions of their hated rivals even as they fell to the cleansing las bolts of the Guard. For my part, it must be said, I was considerably taken aback by their fixity of purpose, finding in it proof of the insanity which must surely be the state of mind of all who turn their gaze from the Emperor's light.

Nevertheless, they served a noble purpose, however base and corrupt their souls, for their intervention must surely have hastened the inevitable victory of the heroes I had the privilege to lead.

At the risk of appearing immodest, I have to say that my strategy worked: both arms of the invasion force met our solid centre and were successfully repulsed. Unable to break through, they were easily surrounded by the pursuing elements of first and third platoons, who used the superior mobility afforded by their Chimeras to good effect, and were utterly annihilated in gratifyingly short order.

It was, it must be admitted, our great good fortune that all the invaders who attacked Glacier Peak were on foot, since many of their other units were equipped with vehicles of their own. Indeed, the group which assaulted our base was supported by a battle tank, which Commissar Cain disabled single-handedly during his inspirational marshalling of our forces there, and the main force which landed west of the town, to be met by the bulk of our own troops, had a couple of tanks and a handful of armoured transports. These were disabled in pretty short order by fourth and fifth company, who had concealed their heavy weapons teams in ambush prior to the traitors' landing, and their victory, I'm gratified to report, was no less complete than ours, despite the greater numbers involved on both sides.

SIXTEEN

'Life's a journey. Shame about the destination.'

– Argun Slyter,
'Well What Did You Expect?', Act 2 Scene 2

SUCH WAS MY relief at our deliverance from imminent destruction that for a moment or two I did little more than catch my breath, slumping to the cold metal floor of the cargo bay as the surge of skyward acceleration continued. I had precious little time to reflect on it, however, since my comm-bead was full of voices demanding to know what in the warp was going on.

'We're aboard the dropship,' I told Kasteen as quickly as I could, conscious that my short-range personal vox wouldn't be able to stay in contact with her for very long. 'It was the only way to keep it safe.' And myself, of course, which I must admit had been my main priority.

'Better stay airborne,' she advised. 'Things are still a bit hot around here.' As we were later to discover, the battle below us was almost over, but at the time no one had the benefit of hindsight, and discretion seemed the most prudent course of action. The dropship and the troopers it contained were a vital part of Zyvan's defensive strategy, and losing it now after it had escaped destruction so narrowly would have been embarrassing, to say the least.

That was advice I was happy to follow, you can be sure, the traitors having neglected to bring any aerospace support, so everything in the sky apart from their landing craft belonged to us; a fact which the PDF fighter pilots appreciated no end, enjoying themselves hugely at the expense of the lumbering shuttles. Predictably they ran out of targets before very long, and reverted to strafing the traitors on the ground with scarcely less enthusiasm.

'That might be best,' I conceded, with as much reluctance as I could feign. 'Although I must admit it rankles a bit to be sitting on the sidelines while you do all the work.'

Kasteen laughed. 'I'm sure the lord general will find something to keep you busy before long.'

The pleasantry punctured my happy mood, you can be sure of that; up until then I'd been too concerned with feeling relieved at having escaped the worst of the fighting to think any further ahead, but of course she was right. Any time now we'd be on our way to a war zone. Oh well, there was no point in fretting about it, I'd just have to take things as they came, just as I always did, and trust to my well-honed survival instinct once we got there.

The pilot was still yammering away on another channel, demanding to know precisely what was going on, so I responded to him next, if only to shut him up.

'Stay in a holding pattern for now,' I said. 'I'm on my way up to the flight deck to brief you.' Not that I needed to see him in person, of course, but it was damned uncomfortable in the cargo hold, and I had to retune my comm-bead to use the ship's vox as a relay instead of the rapidly-receding set in the regimental HQ. Besides, it made him feel important, which is always a good way to get what you want out of people.

As I might have predicted, my presence aboard made a considerable impression on the troopers we passed as Jurgen and I made our way through the passenger compartments. The news rippled ahead of us, so that by the time we arrived at Detoi's command group, seated next to the flight deck as they had been on our eventful descent from the *Emperor's Benificence*, the captain was smiling in our direction.

'I thought you might not be able to resist tagging along,' he said, jumping to the conclusion which my reputation tended to encourage. 'So I saved you a seat.' And indeed the ones Jurgen and I had occupied when we first arrived on Adumbria were still vacant. (Which isn't as surprising as it sounds. The dropships were designed to carry a full company, which in some regiments can mean six* platoons instead of the five the 597th habitually fielded, at least during my time with them, and our platoons normally consisted of five squads instead of the six theoretically allowed for by the SO&E).[1]

---

1. *Slate of Organisation and Equipment, a slightly archaic term still in use by the 597th to refer to their personnel disposition. The so-called 'ghost squads' could be filled in by fresh recruits when the regiment returned to Valhalla to replenish its numbers, or, should sufficient inductees be found, an entire new company added to the roster. In practice, most commanders would prefer to have the new men dispersed among experienced platoons where they could learn from the veterans by example. It's by no means unusual for Imperial Guard companies to consist of fewer platoons, and the platoons of fewer squads, than their theoretical full complement; indeed, it was only the administrative error alluded to earlier which kept the 597th at a relatively steady number of soldiers despite their combat losses.*

'Very kind of you,' I responded with a carefully composed smile, and deposited Jurgen in one of the vacant chairs.

'So where are we going?' Detoi asked. He looked surprisingly fit, considering, but I suppose the prospect of action had perked him up. That, or the realisation that Sulla was out of his hair for good.

'Not entirely sure,' I admitted. 'I'm on my way to talk to the pilot now.'

The flight deck was cramped, of course, which was why I'd decided to leave Jurgen outside. Apart from the fact that I had no desire to be fending his elbow or the barrel of the melta away from my ribs every five minutes, being in a confined space with him was trying enough at the best of times, and I was used to it; for all I knew the pilot might be sufficiently distracted to plough us into a mountain or something.

'Commissar.' He glanced up from the polished wooden panel, inlaid with winking runes of inordinate complexity, and adjusted a large brass handle which I took to have something to do with our altitude as I felt the deck shift subtly under my feet as he did so. 'What's going on?'

I filled him in, while one of the tech-priests sitting at lateral panels of their own made the necessary adjustments to my comm-bead. (The other kept up the constant round of prayers and incantations apparently necessary to keep the engines functioning smoothly.) When I finished my account, resisting the urge to embroider it as I knew from long experience that a plain tale, plainly told, impresses people more than any amount of heroic posturing, the pilot nodded.

'Lucky you were there,' he said. 'A shell through the cargo hatch would have finished us all for sure.' He

shrugged, dismissing the thought. 'I still need a destination, though.'

'Better maintain the holding pattern,' I said, playing
for time. There were precious few significant targets on
the coldside, which meant we were as far from combat
as possible under the circumstances, and I wanted to
prolong that happy state of affairs for as long as I could.
'I'd hate to inconvenience the lord general by sending
us off on a wild pterasquirrel chase.'

It was at that point, of course, that fate chose to intervene. I'd no sooner tucked my comm-bead back in my
ear than a vaguely familiar voice began trying to raise
me.

'Cain,' I responded, still trying to place it.

'Commissar. Glad to hear you're still in one piece.'
The voice was drowned out for a moment by what
sounded like an explosion. 'Sorry about that. They're
trying to get across the bridge by the starport.' There was
a short rattle of bolter fire. 'Of all the choke points in
Skitterfall I have to end up back here. Ironic or what?'

'Kolbe,' I said, placing the young praetor at last. 'What
can I do for you?'

'I thought it was the other way round. Excuse me a
minute…' He was interrupted by a burst of incoherent
screaming which sounded like the warcry of a Khornate
fanatic and which terminated abruptly in a thud of a
power maul on full charge and a gurgle which sounded
distinctly unhealthy. 'Well he's not getting mine… Sorry
commissar, where were we?'

'You seem to have some kind of message for me,' I
prompted.

'Oh yes. Arbitrator Hekwyn said you wanted to be
appraised of anything unusual around the equatorial
sea. I had a quick skim through the reports, but there's

nothing you wouldn't expect, given the current state of emergency. I was just starting on the maritime stuff when we were mobilised to back up the PDF here.'

'What maritime stuff?' I asked, a faint tingle of apprehension beginning to work its way up my spine. My palms were beginning to itch again too, always a bad sign.

'There's quite a lot of shipping on both seas,' Kolbe said, sounding surprised. 'Didn't you know?'

It hadn't occurred to me, being a hive boy born and bred; I'd just assumed the seas were large areas of open water, of no real use to anyone, and dismissed them as dead ground. But of course as they both stretched between the hotside and the coldside going around them, particularly the equatorial one just opposite Skitterfall would be more trouble than it was worth, and bulky cargoes wouldn't travel by air or suborbital. In short, the Adumbrians needed ships, and that meant the sorcerers could get to where they needed to be to complete their plans without any trouble at all.

'Can you transfer the maritime datafiles?' I asked, sprinting back into the passenger compartment and snatching a slate from a startled Detoi. Fortunately, young Kolbe wasn't too busy splatting heretics to transmit the information, and it began to scroll across the screen with startling rapidity.

'What are we looking for?' the captain asked.

'Anything anomalous.' I shot him a rueful smile. 'Not a lot of help, I know.'

'If it's there we'll find it,' Detoi promised, and started working through the list with the aid of his subaltern. I hurried back to the flight deck and tapped the shoulder of the cogboy who'd adjusted my comm-bead.

'I need a channel to the lord general's office,' I told him. To my pleased surprise he didn't argue, inputting the priority codes I'd given him as though it were a purely routine operation.

'Ciaphas.' Zyvan greeted me with the faintly abstracted air of a man who's really hoping that you haven't got bad news for him because he's got enough of that to deal with already. 'I hear you've hijacked one of my dropships.'

'It's a long story,' I told him. 'But I think we might need it. There are ships in the equatorial sea. The sorcerers could use one to get right where they needed to be in order to complete the ritual pattern.'

'Believe it or not that had occurred to us,' Zyvan said. 'But Malden said it wouldn't work. There needs to be some physical connection with the solid surface of the planet. It's a psyker thing.' His voice took on a tinge of amusement. 'I'm afraid you're whistling up the wrong fungal pod this time.'

'If you say so,' I said, far from convinced. The pattern was far too neat and I trusted my paranoia; it had kept me alive this long after all.

Zyvan's voice took on a harder edge. 'I do. Our immediate priority has to be the defence of the capital. I'm bringing in you, the Tallarn and the Kastaforean rapid reaction companies, and dispatching a tank squadron from the 425th Armoured. If you can deploy behind the invaders and cut them off we can put an end to this.'

'Until the Slaaneshi raise their daemon again and finish doing whatever the hell they're doing to the warp currents,' I said. I still had no idea what that might be, which was probably just as well, but I was pretty sure that would be the end for all of us in any case. 'I can't believe you're just going to ignore the possibility.'

'Of course I'm not going to ignore it.' An edge of frustration was entering the lord general's voice. 'But we've still got nothing to go on. Once we do, we'll take them down. But I'm a soldier, not a bloody inquisitor. I can only fight the enemies I can see!'

I couldn't really argue about that. After all, it was his army, and we were visibly up to our armpits in Khornate loonies. And after all those weeks of trying to uncover hidden enemies, he probably wasn't the only one to feel something of a sense of relief at finally having a target to shoot at.

'Transmit the coordinates,' I said. 'Our pilot will lay in the course.'

I returned to my seat surprisingly troubled. On the one hand, the assignment seemed easy enough, and I've never had any problem about shooting enemies in the back. In fact, I prefer it: it's safer. But I couldn't shake the nagging feeling that the real danger lay elsewhere and if we didn't seize the initiative soon we'd never get the chance.

'What's a mineral dredger?' Detoi asked, looking up from his data-slate, still ploughing through the reports I'd inflicted on him.

'Haven't a clue,' I told him. 'We don't get them in the hives, that's for sure.'

'Or on iceworlds,' the captain said. He busied himself for a moment, calling up the briefing files on local customs and culture I hadn't been able to summon any interest in reading aboard the troopship. 'Oh, that's interesting. They're floating manufactoria, which scoop up mineral deposits from the floor of the ocean and process them on the spot. Apparently they can do that here because the seas are so shallow.'

'Physical contact with the solid surface of the planet,' I said, a chill of nameless dread working its way unpleasantly up my spine.

Detoi nodded. 'I suppose so, technically speaking...' his voice trailed off as he noted my expression.

'What drew your attention to the dredgers?' I asked as evenly as I could.

'The Arbites logged a mayday from one, about the time the invasion started. Under the circumstances they didn't have time to follow it up.'

'Show me,' I said.

The transmission had been short and abruptly curtailed, but whoever had been on the other end of the vox had just had time to mention pirates before they'd been cut off. I pointed to the transcript. 'See that? Pirates. Not soldiers, not invaders. Someone either boarded them, or there was a mutiny among the crew.'

'I see.' Detoi nodded slowly. 'Sounds more like the cultists we were fighting before.' Then he shrugged. 'Unless it really was pirates, just out to loot the place.'

'Not the sort of thing that happens on Adumbria,' I pointed out. 'Where would they go to sell the ore? There's only one starport, and that's locked tight at the best of times.' I found the co-ordinates from which the mayday had been sent, and the palms of my hands tingled more strongly than ever. They were almost exactly on the opposite side of the planet from Skitterfall. Precisely where Malden had said the final ritual would have to take place if the sorcerers were to succeed in their heinous plans.

I tapped the comm-bead in my ear and contacted the pilot.

'We're changing course,' I said. 'Here are the new co-ordinates.' I'd expected him to argue, but he'd evidently been around Guard personnel for long enough to know that a commissar's authority outweighs even a lord general's.[1] After a brief acknowledgement I felt the subtle shift in my inner ear which told me the dropship was turning. Jurgen swallowed hard, his face white.

'Cheer up,' I told him. 'We'll be down before you know it.' And facing one of the most terrifying ordeals of my life to boot. But at the time, of course, I had no inkling of that.

---

1. *The Imperial Navy also has commissars attached to it, though in lesser numbers than the Guard. Even if he hadn't encountered one of them, the pilot would certainly have come into contact with a few of those travelling aboard the* Emperor's Benificence *with their regiments.*

SEVENTEEN

'If you go looking for trouble, you're sure to find it.'

– Gilbran Quail,
Collected Essays

IF YOU'VE BEEN reading these memoirs with any degree of attention you're probably thinking that this apparent willingness of mine to rush headlong into danger is uncharacteristic to say the least. Well, perhaps it is. But the way I saw it, whatever the Slaaneshi were up to was the real threat, and seeing off a bunch of loony berserkers too carried away with bloodlust to use sensible tactics or even fire their guns half the time was little more than a sideshow. And, as I've said before, I knew from bitter experience that the only way to deal with warpcraft is to get in there straight away, before the witches or whatever's behind it have had time to finish what they've started.

So although I was as petrified as you might expect, I hid it with the ease of an experienced dissembler, and reflected that however alarming the prospect of facing sorcery might be, the consequences of not doing so were bound to be a damn sight worse. As so often in my life, it all came down to picking the course of action which offered the greatest chance of getting out with my hide intact, however great the immediate risk might be.

Besides, I had an entire company of Guard troopers to hide behind, and Jurgen's remarkable ability to chuck a spanner into whatever dark forces might be about to be unleashed, so all in all the odds seemed reasonably in my favour. And if they turned out not to be, at least I had a ship capable of making orbit.

On the whole I thought it might be polite to let Zyvan know his plan to disrupt the invasion was going to be short a company after all, but when I tried to raise him over the vox all I got was one of his aides.

'The lord general is unavailable,' he told me, with the unmistakable tone of a man who's making the most of the chance to be a pain in the arse. 'He's gone to inspect our forward positions.'

'Well, patch me through to his comm-bead,' I said.

The aide sighed audibly. 'Our orders are to maintain vox silence. If the enemy were to learn of his where-abouts–'

'Fine,' I said, making a mental note to find out exactly who I'd been talking to and make his life excessively unpleasant as soon as I got the opportunity. 'Then get me Malden.'

Fortunately, the young psyker was still at headquarters, and his familiar dry tone in my earpiece was surprisingly calming. If anyone on the lord general's staff could appreciate the danger we were facing it was sure to be him.

'Commissar.' He paused for a moment. 'I take it this isn't a social call.'

'I've found the fourth ritual site,' I said without pre-amble. 'It's a mineral dredger in the middle of the equatorial sea. I'm diverting a dropship full of troopers there now.'

'A dredger.' His voice was so flat that for a moment I thought he hadn't believed me, and was about to tell me not to waste my time. 'I wasn't aware that the Adum-brians use them. But then no one ever tells Adepta Astra Telepathica anything.' He sighed audibly. 'That does put a different complexion on things.'

'So the ritual could take place on one?' I asked.

'Without a doubt.' An unaccustomed edge of uneasi-ness entered his voice. 'I can only pray to the Emperor that you'll get there in time.'

Not the most comforting thing he might have said, I'm sure you'll agree.

'There's a time factor involved?' I asked.

'Probably.' The hint of emotion was draining away from his voice again as he became immersed in the problem at hand. 'My colleagues and I have been analysing the warp patterns and the timing of the pre-vious shifts. It's very likely that the next and final one will take place within the next few hours.'

'Oh good,' I said, wondering if I should just tell the pilot to head for space now, commandeer a warp-capable merchant ship and have done with it. But then there was supposed to be an enemy battleship up there, or so I'd heard, so that didn't seem like a terribly healthy option either. Better to stick to the plan we already had, at least for now. 'No pressure then.'

'Not so you'd notice,' Malden said dryly.

'We need to inform the lord general at once,' I said.

'I quite agree. Unfortunately, I don't have any way of getting in touch with him.' A faint trace of amusement, almost imperceptible, seemed to enter his voice. 'However, I'll try to prevail on one of his aides to pass on a message. They can be surprisingly amenable if I talk to them in the right way.' Knowing how nervous most people were around spooks I could well believe it.

'I'll leave it with you then,' I said, and settled down for a long, tense wait.

THE SKY BEYOND the armourcrys viewport in the flight deck had lightened to twilight, the stars overhead fading to invisibility as the colour gradually brightened from the familiar blue-black through purple to a greyish blue which put me in mind of the pre-dawn quiet on some nice normal planet with a proper day-night cycle.

Only the brightest stars were still visible over our heads. Were we in the opposite hemisphere, we would have been able to see a great many more pinpoints of light, dancing like the sparks from a bonfire as the invisible sun reflected from the hulls of the hundreds of starships in orbit (at least away from the streetlights of Skitterfall), but here only a handful of genuine stars shone in the sky.

With difficulty I tore my mind away from the struggle taking place on the opposite side of the planet. Here, where the only things moving were the waves on the cold grey water below, it was hard to credit the scale of the carnage going on a few thousand kilometres beneath my bootsoles.

I'd listened in on some of the signal traffic, and it wouldn't be much of an exaggeration to say that things were looking grim. Zyvan's counter-attack had checked the main body of the invaders well enough, driving a wedge through their heart and scattering them even despite our absence, but incredibly the Khornates had rallied and were making a grim and desperate last stand which looked like becoming a long and bloody affair. Scattered reports spoke of a giant in power armour leading them, so at least one other Chaos Marine had made it down to the surface unscathed, and I didn't envy whoever it was who finally got to take him out.[1]

I'd also gathered in the course of my eavesdropping that Beije had tagged along with the Tallarn company who'd joined the assault, no doubt spouting pious platitudes and getting in the way of the fighting men, and couldn't help wondering how he'd react if he came face to face with the Tainted Marine, which after his snide comments about my own encounter would have been poetic justice at least. (It never happened, of course; although if it had things would undoubtedly have worked out with far less fuss and bother all round.)

'There it is.' The pilot pointed, and I was just able to make out a glint of metal and a hint of solidity in the moving mass of water below us. I'd been in the flight deck for some time, trying to get Zyvan on the vox (with a complete lack of success so far) and exchanging messages with Malden about what we might expect to find when we landed (which essentially boiled down to 'your guess is as good as mine'.)

If I'm honest, I was doing this mainly to keep my mind occupied in preference to sitting and brooding,

---

1. *The World Eater leading the assault on Skitterfall appears to have been killed with gratifying thoroughness by an anti-tank squad from one of the Kastaforean regiments. (Two krak missiles and a lascannon not having left an awful lot to identify for sure.)*

but it also had the advantage of keeping me out of Jurgen's way. The prolonged flight wasn't agreeing with his stomach at all, and even though he'd managed to hang on to his last meal so far I'd rather not take the risk of being in the vicinity if his willpower gave out. 'Landing in five minutes.'

'Five minutes, everyone,' I voxed over the company command net, trying to think of a stock text to cover this and failing.

I moved to lean casually against the jamb of the cockpit door, where everyone in the forward compartment could see me, and looked into a row of tense, nervous faces. 'I can't honestly tell you what to expect when we get down there. But I do know that the fate of this world probably hangs on our actions when we do.' I paused, searching for the right words. 'All I can say is that I've faced warpcraft before, and I'm still here to brag about it.' A few nervous laughs rippled around the rows of seats as I played off my reputation for quiet heroism; Cain the Hero never boasted about his exploits, of course.

'Psykers and warpsmiths aren't to be taken lightly,' I went on, 'but in my experience they die just as easily as anyone else. I've yet to meet a witch who didn't find a las bolt in the head a severe inconvenience.' More laughter, a little louder and more confident this time. I shook off the mental image of Emeli, her green eyes filling with outraged astonishment as I shot her, and hesitated, my train of thought momentarily derailed. 'The Emperor protects,' I finished, finding refuge in a familiar platitude.

'We're on the final descent,' the pilot called. 'Better get strapped in, commissar.' I took a final glance back through the viewport and felt my breath still in my chest. The dredger was vast, filling the whole of the pane, and we were still some distance away from it.

In my ignorance I'd expected something not too different from a conventional ocean-going ship, maybe a little larger, because after all they had to process the ore they extracted somewhere, but my guess had been a long way wide of the mark. It loomed out of the sea ahead of us like a stranded hab block, fully a couple of kilometres from stem to stern, about half that wide and several hundred metres in height. And that, I suddenly realised, would just be the part above the waterline, there would be almost as much of the thing below the surface too. Even with a full company of troopers, searching a structure that size could take hours. Days even...

Well, in my experience, enemies were never hard to find once the shooting started, so I deferred that problem until we had to face it and staggered back to my seat to find Detoi engrossed in a set of schematics he'd managed to pull up from the files in his data-slate.[1] With a quick glance at my white-faced aide, who seemed no worse than before, I leaned across to look at them.

'Where do you think they'll be?' Detoi asked. I took in the bewildering array of compartments, ore processors and connecting passageways, trying to get a sense of the layout in my head.

'I'm not sure,' I admitted. In my experience, heretic cults tended to go underground, literally as well as metaphorically, so somewhere below the waterline, down by the keel, seemed like a good bet. On the other hand, there seemed to be a lot of machinery down

---

1. *Or, more likely, had had transmitted from somewhere. The plans of the dredgers would have been readily available to anyone with an appropriate security clearance.*

there, which might get in the way, and I had a vague memory that water was supposed to disrupt sorcery somehow.[1] I tried to picture the chambers I'd found in the hab dome and the bawdy house, hoping to find some clue in their layout. 'They'll need somewhere large and open, with a high ceiling.'

'Doesn't narrow it down much,' Detoi said thoughtfully. 'We've got the hangars next to the shuttle pad on the upper decks, a few recreation rooms, a chapel for the tech-priests, docking facilities for the cargo boats down by the waterline, and some of these manufactoria are vast.'

'Eliminate those, and the hangars, and the boat docks,' I said. 'At least for now. The rooms I saw before were big, but not that big.'

Detoi nodded. 'Still leaves us with a lot of ground to cover,' he said.

I couldn't dispute that. 'Well we'll just have to trust in the Emperor to show us a sign,' I said, with rather less sarcasm than I usually would.

'Brace for landing,' the pilot said, and all around me men and women tensed for the impact, readying their weapons and preparing to release their crash webbing. Jurgen cradled the melta like a juvie with a favourite toy, looking happier than he had done in several hours. The retros kicked in suddenly, compressing my spine with the abrupt deceleration, and a loud metallic clang rang through the hull. 'We're down,' he added unnecessarily.

'Third platoon, deploy and secure,' Detoi said, picking the unit nearest the cargo ramp. Lustig's voice responded, calm and confident, and the captain shot

---

1. *A widely-believed piece of folklore, but quite baseless according to the psykers I've asked.*

me a sudden and unexpected grin. 'Jenit's going to be sick as an ice weasel about missing this,' he said.

'Sulla's got enough to worry about in Glacier Peak,' I assured him, having used the vox to keep abreast of the rest of the regiment while we were in the air. But his mind was already on the deployment of our own troopers and I doubt he even heard me.

'Come on, Jurgen,' I said, turning to my aide. 'Let's see if a little sea air can perk you up.'

'Very good, sir,' he responded, looking a little better already (which, with Jurgen, was something of a relative term, of course).

I turned to Detoi. 'See you outside,' I said, and hurried to the nearest debarkation point. Landers on the ground are horribly vulnerable if the enemy has sufficient firepower, and I wanted to be out in the open if we were going to be taking any incoming.

Not that that seemed particularly likely, of course, as we hadn't had a sniff of any anti-aircraft fire on the way in, but I found it hard to believe that the heretics we were hunting hadn't even noticed the arrival of a dropship; they're not exactly stealthy after all. Besides, if there were any abnatural forces at work here I wanted to get Jurgen where his peculiar gift would begin to disrupt them as quickly as possible; under the circumstances there was no way in the galaxy I was going to move far from his protective aura.

As we left the shelter of the dropship, I became aware of a keen wind whipping across the vast steel plain that surrounded us, bringing the unmistakable oceanic tang of ozone and salt. Next to the blood-freezing temperatures of the coldside, however, it felt positively balmy and I inhaled it gratefully, moving upwind of Jurgen as I did so.

If I hadn't seen the place from the air, I would probably have imagined we were in an industrial zone somewhere rather than aboard a floating construct. Structures the size of warehouses rose in the distance, looming threateningly in the perpetual twilight, and even the vast bulk of the dropship seemed shrunken to the size of an ordinary shuttle by the sheer scale of our surroundings. I'd seldom felt such a sense of insignificance, even in a titan maintenance bay (well, perhaps then).

Third platoon were moving out to secure the landing pad, the squads separating with practiced precision, advancing a team at a time to keep one another covered as they scurried from one piece of cover to the next. I saw Penlan jog past, shepherding her new squad with calm deliberation, and reflected that my confidence in her seemed to have been well placed. Lustig was standing at the base of the ramp, watching her go with an air of quiet pride.

'Good job all round, sergeant,' I said.

'She'll do.' He nodded. I indicated the rest of the troops, deploying with equal efficiency.

'I meant the whole platoon,' I said.

Lustig nodded again. 'We won't let you down, sir.'

'Fourth squad at the mark. No sign of hostiles.' I recognised the voice of Sergeant Grifen, and nodded.

'Stay put for the moment. And keep your eyes open.'

'No problem, commissar,' she assured me. I was pleased to have her squad on point. Grifen was a good leader who looked after her troopers but wasn't afraid to take the occasional chance when necessary. I'd been impressed by her qualities on Simia Orichalcae, when our routine recon mission had gone so spectacularly ploin-shaped, and in the years since she'd more than justified that confidence.

'Pad secured,' Lustig reported after a moment, and the other four platoons began doubling down the ramp to join us. As you'll appreciate, all those boots ringing on metal made a hell of a noise, and it took me a moment to realise that Detoi had joined us.

'Under the circumstances I don't think the vehicles will be much help,' he said.

'I think you're right.' There was undoubtedly enough open space to make use of them; indeed there were a few cargo haulers scattered around on the fringes of the pad, some of them still loaded with crates and bundles. But the noise they'd make on that metallic surface would be the Emperor's own row, and we'd soon have to venture into some tight spaces where they'd be far too vulnerable. Far better to advance on foot.

'Lustig', the captain went on. 'Detail a squad or two to cover the pad. I don't want us cut off from the dropship if we need to pull back in a hurry.' That was a sound precaution to my way of thinking too. Normally the lander would have pulled back, either returning to orbit (or in this case our staging area) to deploy another company of troopers, or remaining in a holding pattern overhead once we were satisfied there was no danger to it from ground fire, but under the circumstances neither option seemed terribly attractive. We were surrounded by water, with nowhere to go, and the dropship was our only lifeline.

'First and third squads, cover the pad. Second and fourth, stand by,' Lustig ordered at once.

Like it or not, I found myself thinking, he looked like getting a commission for sure if he kept this up.

Detoi briefed his platoon commanders quickly, giving each of them an area to reconnoitre, and I watched our troopers disperse with mixed feelings. True, we'd cover a

lot more ground that way, but two hundred and fifty-
odd soldiers seemed barely adequate to the task of
searching an installation that size. I'd been counting on
the idea of safety in numbers more than I'd realised, and
as most of our complement disappeared into the shadows around us I began to feel uncomfortably exposed.

Well, standing around here wouldn't help much, so I
began to jog forward, intent on attaching myself to the
nearest squad (which, as it happened, was fourth,
under Grifen). As I did so, I glanced across the landing
pad, where Penlan was leading second squad from the
front. She'd just reached the next mark, a light cargo
hauler laden with something I took to be bins of
processed ore, when she glanced back to wave her second team on, tripped on something at her feet and
stumbled a pace before recovering her balance. Something about the way she and the troopers with her were
looking down seemed vaguely disturbing.

'Second squad,' she reported a moment later. 'We've
found a body. Civilian, shot in the back. Autogun by
the look of the wounds.'

'Any sign of a weapon?' I asked.

'No sir.' Even at this distance I could see the angry set
of her shoulders. 'This was murder, pure and simple.'

'It looks like he was running away,' one of the troopers chipped in helpfully. 'Rolled under here for cover,
maybe.'

'Well it didn't help him,' Penlan said. Something
about the tone of her voice promised bloody vengeance
on behalf of whoever it had been. 'He must have been
working up here when they landed.'

'If they landed,' I said.

Jurgen looked at me quizzically. 'There's nothing else
on the pad,' I pointed out.

'Perhaps they took off again,' he suggested. It was possible, of course, but somehow I couldn't see our shadowy enemies leaving here until they'd done whatever they set out to do, and it all seemed far too normal for that to have been the case.

'First squad,' a new voice chimed in, on fifth platoon's channel.[1] 'We're in the boat dock. Looks like there's been a serious firefight down here. Lasgun and autogun damage mostly. Maybe a couple of stubbers.'

Well that answered that. The raiders had come in aboard one of the scheduled supply vessels, probably after hi-jacking it on the way, unless at least some of the crew had been cultists to begin with.

'Any survivors?' Lieutenant Faril asked, his habitual good humour absent for once, which was hardly surprising under the circumstances.

'No,' the sergeant replied. 'Just bodies. Security personnel mostly, judging by the uniforms. It looks like they were trying to hold the attackers off while the workers got out.'

They didn't seem to have got very far, judging by the complete lack of any signs of life we'd seen since our arrival. According to the data Detoi had pulled, there should have been nearly three thousand workers

---

1. *Each platoon would have their own vox channel assigned, to which their troopers' personal comm-beads would be tuned. Their platoon commander would have access to this and the company channel, through which they would report to Detoi. In larger engagements the company commanders would have access to the regimental tactical net, through which they would report to Kasteen and Broklaw, and this arrangement would be repeated for higher levels of command right up to the lord general's staff. Cain, as a commissar, would have complete access to all the channels, enabling him to get an overall impression of the whole battlefield, albeit a somewhat confusing one on occasion. No doubt his training and years of experience would enable him to pick out any salient information from the rest of the traffic.*

aboard. It was hard to believe that the attackers could have taken quite so many, but as the search continued and the body count rose, it became increasingly clear that this was precisely what had happened.

'In other words, we're wandering around looking for a frakking army,' Magot said, apparently none too perturbed at the prospect. I nodded, flattening myself into the shadow of a companionway, while Grifen and her team moved ahead to the next mark.

'It's beginning to look like that,' I said. An army would be something of an exaggeration, but it had taken a good few dozen raiders to fight their way out of the boat dock. Not all had made it either, I was pleased to learn, the outlandish clothing (or more often lack of it) of some of the corpses indicating that the dredger's crew hadn't gone down without taking a few of their assailants with them. After that, hunting down and murdering the panicked workforce in small groups would have been easy, especially if they already had confederates aboard who could point them at the most likely hiding places.

I had little time to muse on this bleak prospect, however, as my thoughts were interrupted by the distinctive crack of ionising air which accompanied a lasgun discharge. It was followed an instant later by others, the harsher bark of an autogun and what sounded like a couple of pistols.

'Contact,' a voice said in my comm-bead. 'Level twelve, sector two.' A moment later Lieutenant Luskom, the officer in charge of first platoon, chimed in on the company frequency.

'Third squad's in a firefight,' she reported. 'Sector two, level twelve. I'm moving first and fourth in to support.'

'Sector two,' I said, recalling the map Detoi had shown me and mentally comparing it with our own position. 'It must be down that way.' I pointed, although there was no need to really, the sound of gun-fire intensifying in that direction as the fresh squads joined in the battle.

'Shall we go in to support them?' Grifen asked, and I shook my head.

'They seem to be handling it. I'm more interested in what the traitors are trying to defend.' And with any luck first platoon would be keeping them looking the other way while we went to find out.

Unfortunately, while the enemy might have been mad, they weren't stupid. As we rounded a row of stor-age tanks, finally moving out of the constant wind into some degree of shelter, a crackle of las fire sent us scur-rying for cover. An itchy rain of dislodged rust pattered on my cap and greatcoat, leaving a stain on the sable fabric that would be the Emperor's own job to remove, and I inched forwards on my elbows to peer cautiously around the corner.

'Frak!' I said feelingly. The heretics had erected a makeshift barricade which looked solid enough for all that, crouching behind a rough assemblage of girders, packing crates, metal drums and other detritus. More to the point they'd set up a heavy stubber to cover the open space in front. Any attempt to get closer would simply get the whole lot of us killed. As if to emphasise the point it opened up, gouging a line of dents in the deck plating.

'Well we're not getting in that way,' Grifen said as I wormed my way back hastily to join her.

'We could work around and try to flank them,' Magot suggested. 'Lob a few frag grenades over the barrier. That'd give them something to think about.'

'It might,' I said. 'The problem's going to be getting close enough.' By luck or by judgement the heretics had chosen their position well, without much cover for a flanking attack. The storage tanks we'd taken refuge behind were the nearest piece of solid cover; I could only hope that whatever they contained wasn't volatile. Even Jurgen's melta couldn't help us this time, the range was too great. He got off a couple of shots, which at least kept the heretics' heads down, but the thermal energy dissipated too much for the metal of the fortification to be anything more than mildly scorched.

I sighed with frustration. 'We haven't got time for this. We'll have to go round another way.'

This was easier said than done and looked like getting harder. As we pulled back, the mocking catcalls of the cultists echoing in our ears, I was getting a steady stream of tactical reports through the comm-bead. By now practically every squad in the company had encountered resistance, and the few which hadn't (apart from the ones Lustig had guarding the dropship) were being rushed in to reinforce their fellows.

From training and habit I compared the positions of the firefights with the memory of the schematics I'd seen and nodded grimly. The heretics had sealed off sector twelve, reinforcing their perimeter to withstand a siege. Whatever they were up to was happening somewhere in that part of the dredger.

'Detoi,' I said. 'We have to find a weak spot. If we don't break through soon it'll be too late.'

'I know.' His voice was tight with frustration. 'But we don't have the numbers. The way they're dug in they can hold us off indefinitely.'

'We can call for reinforcements,' I said, without much hope. Even if Zyvan was reachable now it would take far too long for any other units to get here. 'But I doubt they'll arrive in time.'

'Maybe if we concentrate our forces,' Detoi said, his voice heavy. 'Pull everyone back and consolidate, try to force a breach in one spot.'

His lack of enthusiasm for the idea was evident in his tone, and I could appreciate why. Not only would we be bottlenecked trying to get to a single fortification, the enemy would have time to reinforce the point we attacked. The fighting would be vicious and bloody and we'd take massive casualties. Even then the chances of succeeding were low.

'There must be something else we can do,' I said, reluctant to commit us to so desperate an action unless we had to, but right then I couldn't think of an alternative.

'Then we'd better think of it fast,' Detoi said, the flatness of his tone revealing that he was under no illusions about our ability to do so.

'I've an auspex contact, inbound,' the dropship pilot cut in. 'Closing fast.'

'Any vox contact?' I asked, the sinking feeling in my gut already providing the answer.

'Not yet,' the pilot confirmed. 'But the IFF[1] says it's Imperial.'

A sudden flare of hope lit within me. Malden must have been able to get through to the lord general at last, and with extra troops at our disposal we stood a chance

---

1. *Identification, Friend or Foe: a beacon fitted to most military craft which transmits a code identifying it as a member of the Imperial forces. Generally reliable, but occasional malfunctions have led to unfortunate incidents of fratricide; it's not unknown for such devices to fall into the hands of enemies, deviants and heretics, enabling them to masquerade as servants of the Emperor for their own nefarious purposes.*

of breaking through the heretics' defences and foiling their foul design. Whatever that might be.

'Lustig,' I voxed. 'Keep it covered anyway, just in case.' Things were dicey enough right now as they were and the last thing we needed was to fall for some heretic stratagem using a stolen shuttle.

'Acknowledged,' the stoic sergeant said, and I turned my attention back to Detoi. By this time the troopers, Jurgen and I were halfway back to the dropship, our boots ringing on the surface of the pad, and I could clearly see the captain and Lustig standing on the cargo ramp, shielding their eyes as they gazed to the west.[1]

'Better get everyone primed to disengage,' I said, 'just in case.'

'Already on it,' he responded. 'Their orders are to keep the enemy pinned, not expose themselves to fire, and be prepared to pull back.'

'Sounds good to me,' I said, with some relief. That kept our options open, at least for a little while longer.

I turned my head, looking in the same direction as the captain and the sergeant. The scream of an engine was audible now, closing fast, and ahead of it darted a sleek courier shuttle. I felt a sudden jab of disappointment. Another dropship with a full company would have been a bit much to hope for, but I'd been counting on a cargo shuttle with a platoon or two at least. The courier couldn't have held more than a squad.

I watched it touch down with a curious mixture of emotions I can only describe as inquisitive apprehension. Things were beginning to get out of hand again, and I didn't like the feeling. Its engines died down to an idle and I walked towards it, obscurely grateful for the

---

1. *Quite why they would have bothered to do this in perpetual twilight I have no idea; perhaps it was just out of habit.*

familiar presence of Jurgen at my shoulder. Grifen and her troopers stayed at my back, a few paces behind, their hands on their weapons. As we got closer the ramp descended and a squad of Imperial troops disembarked at the double, lasguns held ready.

'Tallarns,' Griffen said, surprised. I have to admit I shared her emotion. Behind the desert warriors came a familiar figure in commissarial black who pushed his way through the knot of troopers to stand in front of me. He was fighting to keep his face impassive, and losing badly; something akin to a smirk kept writhing to the surface of his pudgy features.

'Beije,' I said flatly, sure that whatever he was here for was bound to be bad news. 'This isn't a very good time.'

'Ciaphas Cain,' he responded, bouncing on the soles of his feet with an excess of self-importance. 'You are hereby charged with desertion, cowardice in the face of the enemy and misappropriation of military resources.' He gestured to the squad of Tallarn warriors, beckoning them forward. 'Arrest him.'

Editorial Note:

Without more background information much of what follows will appear to make little sense. Accordingly I have inserted another extract from Tincrowser's account of the campaign as a whole, which ought to go some way towards explaining what would otherwise appear to be a coincidence so huge as to stretch the credulity of even the most open-minded of readers. Cain, of course, concentrates purely on his own experience, barely bothering to speculate about the wider causes and implications of what's going on around him.

From *Sablist in Skitterfall: a brief history of the Chaos incursion* by Dagblat Tincrowser, 957 M41

WITH THE INVASION force now apparently stalled, thanks to Lord General Zyvan's bold and incisive strategy, the tide at last began to turn in favour of the beleaguered defenders. Encircled by no fewer than four companies of Imperial Guard, landed by dropship to fall on their undefended rear, the invaders attacking Skitterfall faltered and began to consolidate to no avail; bolstered by units of the PDF the Guard began to tighten their cordon, slowly but surely winning back the streets of the capital step by step and corpse by corpse.

In space, however, things still appeared grim for the lone cruiser standing guard over Skitterfall highport, and the frightened huddle of merchant ships which looked like easy prey for the twisted leviathan bearing down on the besieged planet below. At ranges almost too great for the mind to grasp, combat was eventually joined, ravening energies of barely conceivable power reaching out to strike at the Imperial vessels in orbit.

The *Indestructible* was to live up to her glorious name, however, despite the grievous wounds she suffered from that first strike, retaliating with her dorsal lance battery which alone could match the range of the formidable firepower unleashed by the Chaotic vessel. It was a heroic gesture, but seemed to some observers to be futile, since it was far less powerful than the shots she'd received, but if nothing else it served to goad the battleship into reckless action, increasing its speed in an attempt to close and decide the matter. To the astonishment of all, however, the *Indestructible* reversed her engines, giving ground and retreating slowly in the face of the aggressor.

The despair which must have been felt by those merchant crews at such a sight is something we can only imagine, since it must surely have seemed that the Imperial cruiser was damaged beyond all reasonable effectiveness and hoping to withdraw. That was certainly the impression the marauder got, for rather than concentrating its fire on the limping *Indestructible*, its auxiliary weapons began striking out wantonly at the merchant shipping and it continued to accelerate towards the tempting array of targets laid out before it.

This was precisely the intention of the *Indestructible*'s heroic captain, Igor Yates, whose tactical brilliance finally began to become clear. Just at the moment her looming attacker was overcommitted, the *Indestructible* launched a volley of torpedoes, which impacted on the Chaos vessel with most gratifying results. Too badly damaged to launch torpedoes of its own, and with its dorsal armament now out of action, the cumbersome behemoth began burning retros in an attempt to bring its broadside to bear on the Imperial vessel. However the turn was too ponderous and the momentum it had built up too great; Captain Yates's trap was sprung.

Still trying to turn, the crippled leviathan drifted into the middle of the fleet of merchant ships which, until now, it had considered nothing more than easy prey to be picked off at leisure. The feeble armament of a cargo ship would normally be no threat at all to such a mighty engine of destruction, but now it was surrounded by nearly a thousand of them, which, instead of attempting to flee as the murderous cowards aboard the battleship would no doubt have expected, began to swarm towards them, bringing their puny defensive batteries to bear as they did so. Just as a lumbering grox can be stung to death by a nest of maddened firewasps, the mighty warship died by increments as the sheer number of its assailants began to take their toll. Though its powerful weapons lashed out again and again, swatting one or two at a time, it could never hope to make much difference to so mighty a host, and once the *Indestructible* had returned to the fray, crippling its engines, the end was inevitable.

For a moment, they say, a new sun blazed in the sky over Skitterfall, bright enough to dazzle the observers on the ground, and at that sight Guardsmen and PDF soldiers alike cheered in unison, knowing the back of the invasion had been comprehensively broken. All that remained was the scouring of the stain inflicted on our fair world, a task they set to with a will.

In the years since, that engagement has been studied and considered by many, and a few have wondered at the Chaos captain's apparent recklessness. Surely, they ask, he must have had some reason for acting as he did, some compelling reason to continue on so suicidal a course?[1] Such speculation is, however, as futile as it is fruitless. What this undoubtedly teaches us is that the Great Enemy's greatest weakness is overconfidence, nothing more.

---

1. *A question Cain's narrative answers beyond all doubt, but not in any fashion suitable for the good citizens of Adumbria to learn.*

EIGHTEEN

'Well, that was unexpected...'

– Last words of the Chaos Warmaster
Varan the Undefeatable

THE PHRASE 'UTTER astonishment' barely begins to convey my emotions at that moment. No doubt I would have stood there completely stupefied with Emperor alone knows what results, if it hadn't been for the troopers with me. But as the Tallarns stepped forward to obey Beije's order, Grifen and the rest of her squad brought up their lasguns to forestall them. The desert warriors hesitated, looking to their commissar for a lead.

'This is mutiny,' Beije said, completely lost in a world of his own by now. He drew his laspistol and began to aim at the Valhallan sergeant. 'You're hereby sentenced to death under section–'

'Oh be quiet you absurd little man,' I snapped, bringing my own weapon up to cover him. 'No one's executing any of my troopers unless it's me. And if you even so much as think about pulling that trigger you'll be dead before she hits the ground, I promise you.'

'Too right,' Magot agreed, stepping between Grifen and the outraged commissar. 'You want her, you'll have to go through me.'

'Shoot them all!' Beije waved a peremptory arm at the Tallarns, who began looking from one to the other with the unmistakable air of men who've suddenly realised that they've walked blithely up to the brink of a precipice.

'No one's shooting anybody,' I said calmly. 'Unless it's the heretics we came here to cleanse.' I gestured in the direction of the sounds of battle, still clearly audible, as the sergeant in charge of the Tallarns nodded almost imperceptibly to his squad. They lowered their weapons a fraction, and to my relief the Valhallans did the same.

'In case you hadn't noticed, there's a battle going on here, and if we don't win it pretty damn quick, all hell's about to break loose. Literally.'

'You can't hide behind posturing and rhetoric this time,' Beije snarled, taking a step forward and bringing his laspistol around to point at me. 'You ran away from the battle for Skitterfall and you took a whole company of soldiers out of the field with you. You've been obsessed with finding some excuse to hide out here as far from the fighting as you can get ever since that petticoat colonel of yours came up with her ridiculous theory–' He broke off, suddenly aware of the naked anger on the faces of the Valhallans facing him, and the lasguns in their hands.

'You can accuse me of anything you like,' I said, playing to the emotions of the troopers with me with the ease of long practice. 'But you will not disparage Colonel Kasteen in my presence. She's one of the finest soldiers I've ever had the privilege to serve with, and the regiment she leads is among the best in the galaxy.'

I holstered my pistol with what I considered to be a suitably theatrical gesture. 'No doubt this farcical situation has warped your judgement, along with your manners. When you calm down I'll expect an apology on her behalf. Failing that, I'm sure we can settle the matter quite amicably on the duelling field.'

If I'm honest, I didn't expect to be going so far as to call him out, but as so often happens in these situations my mouth gets ahead of my brain. The results were quite satisfying, in any event; he went several colours I had seldom seen in nature in rapid succession, and rallied as best he could. The troopers loved it, though, and I could tell it would be all round the regiment within minutes of our return that I'd challenged the pompous little squit to a duel over an insult to the colonel, and, by extension, the rest of us too.[1]

'Once this is over you'll have no time for duelling or anything else,' Beije snapped.

'Commissar.' Detoi's voice was a welcome distraction in my comm-bead. 'We need to decide what we're going to do. The heretics are still holding firm along the entire perimeter.'

'There must be a weak point somewhere,' I replied, noting with interest that Beije was surreptitiously retuning his own comm-bead to listen in. 'Try checking the

---

1. *As so often in the sections of the archive dealing with his service with the 597th, Cain appears to have been so close to the troops, particularly the senior officers with whom he had a personal friendship, that his technical status as an outsider becomes blurred not only in their minds but in his own as well.*

schematics again. Maybe there's a cable shaft or an air duct we can infiltrate a kill team through.'

'I already thought of that,' the captain said. 'Everything's sealed tight.' He sighed. 'Barring a miracle it'll have to be a frontal assault. And it's going to be bloody.'

'I'm afraid you're right,' I said, my gut curdling at the thought. 'But we're out of alternatives.' I turned back to Beije and the Tallarns, my face as grim as I could make it. 'You heard that. We don't have any more time to waste on these ridiculous fantasies. If you're going to shoot us you'll have to do it in the back, and you'll be doing the work of the Emperor's enemies for them if you do.' It was a risk, I don't deny it, but I was pretty sure that taking that tack would disconcert a bunch of Emperor-botherers enough to shake their resolve. The sergeant, at least, looked as though he had enough sense to realise he was in way over his head.

I turned away, a little theatrically, the Valhallans at my heels. The Tallarns hovered uncertainly, looking to Beije for a lead and wincing visibly as Jurgen passed upwind of them. For a moment I tensed, anticipating a las bolt in the back and hoping the carapace armour under my greatcoat would hold, but they continued to hesitate just long enough for me to seize the initiative beyond all further doubt.

'If you want to face a real enemy and do His Majesty's work, you're welcome to join us,' I added over my shoulder. The Tallarns began to take a step forward, intent on following us, then hesitated, looking to Beije for a lead. The pudgy commissar looked after us, clearly at a loss and wondering how best to regain his authority.

'Go with them,' he snapped at last, petulanty. 'I'm not letting that posturing traitor out of my sight.'

'Good,' I said, wondering if I'd get the chance to nudge him into the line of fire before this was over. 'Let's get the job done before we convene the tribunal,[1] shall we?'

To my relief, Beije kept reasonably quiet while I consulted with Detoi, the two of us huddling over his data-slate while we tried to formulate a strategy for storming the heretics' makeshift stronghold.

'If we can breech the walls here,' I said, pointing out a workshop with a long expanse of steel hull plating in a patch of dead ground between two firing posts, 'we should be able to get inside before they respond.'

'Assuming they haven't thought of that and left us a surprise or two,' Detoi agreed. 'We'll concentrate our forces against their positions here and here. With any luck you'll be able to get your kill team into the dead ground while we're keeping their heads down.'

'How are you going to breech the walls?' Beije asked. 'Did you bring demo charges with you as well?' It was beginning to dawn on him that we were in deadly earnest and that we really were preparing to lay down our lives for the Emperor. Or quite a lot of other people's, anyway. I was going to stick close to Jurgen and hope that somehow we'd manage to escape the effects of whatever hellish sorcery the Slaaneshi were planning to unleash. That was why I was planning to go in with

---

1. *Since Beije had no direct authority over Cain, or any other commissar for that matter, his accusations would have to be looked into by a tribunal of senior members of the commissariat. (Commissars not having a structure of rank in the conventional sense, seniority would be determined by length of service and number of commendations.) If found guilty, Cain would be executed or remanded to a penal legion by the authority of the tribunal as a whole rather than any one individual; in this manner the Commissariat is able to regulate itself reasonably effectively, despite its members being essentially autonomous in most regards.*

the assault team, despite the risk; that way seemed marginally less suicidal than charging a fixed position with Emperor alone knew how many fanatical heretics pouring fire into our ranks.

'Jurgen's melta,' I said. 'It'll do the job.' And provide the perfect excuse for him to be there, of course.

My aide nodded and hefted his favourite toy. 'That it will,' he agreed.

'Who are you taking?' Detoi asked.

I nodded at Grifen's squad, who were still eyeing the Tallarns with mutual distrust. 'Fourth squad, third platoon,' I said. 'I've done this sort of thing with them before.' Some of them, anyway. Only a few familiar faces were left from the group I'd led into the ice caverns of Simia Orichalcae, apart from Grifen and Magot. I caught the eye of Trooper Vorhees, who flashed me a grin, and returned to conversing in an undertone with Drere, his girlfriend, who had been badly chewed up by an ambull on that expedition but who'd survived (to my surprise, I have to admit) thanks to my decision to send back the wounded as quickly as possible. Since then Vorhees had considered me something of a hero, and I have to admit it hadn't hurt my standing with the regiment to seem so concerned with the welfare of the common troopers. (Which made the fact that so many of them were about to die uncomfortably ironic.)

'They're understrength,' Detoi said.

I nodded, conceding the point. 'Only by one.' Smitti was still in the infirmary in Glacier Peak, and I have to admit to feeling to a momentary stab of envy at the thought. 'And they're here. Besides, Jurgen will more than make up the numbers.'

'Will one squad be enough?' Detoi persisted.

'They'll have to be. We'll need everyone else for the diversionary assaults if we're to have even a hope of getting away with this.'

'We're coming too,' Beije announced, indicating the Tallarns. 'I don't trust you and I'm not letting you out of my sight.' He smiled maliciously, turning my own words of a few moments before back on myself. 'Until we can convene the tribunal, of course.'

'Of course,' I replied, determined to seem unruffled, and turned back to Detoi. 'Have you been able to narrow down the objective at all?'

The captain nodded. 'My guess would be here.' He pointed out a chamber deep in the heart of sector twelve. 'The chapel of the Omnissiah. It's about the size you specified, and it's about as far inside their perimeter as it's possible to get.'

'Makes sense.' I nodded. 'If anything, profaning a consecrated chamber would only increase the power of their ritual.'

'And how would you know that?' Beije asked, glaring at me suspiciously. 'You seem very familiar with the secrets of warpcraft.'

'I've faced it before,' I said shortly, not wanting to recall those occasions or waste time recounting them. 'If you haven't, count yourself lucky.'

'The Emperor protects,' Beije countered. 'The pure of heart have nothing to fear.' Which pretty much ruled me out, of course, but under the circumstances I thought a good strong dose of trepidation was the only sensible option in any case.

'Well bully for them,' I said, ostentatiously checking my weapons. I turned to Detoi, reluctantly about to give the order which would condemn so many brave souls to death.

'Better start pulling them back,' I began. 'We'll need about ten minutes to regroup, which should be long enough to get the assault team in position. After that you can start the attacks at your discretion...'

I was interrupted by a sudden tingling sensation which washed over my body like the moment before a thundercrack, and a feeling of almost intolerable pressure inside my head which left my ears ringing with tinnitus. Beije glanced around wildly, swinging his laspistol, looking desperately for something to shoot.

'Sorcery!' he gasped, his face draining of blood.

'Take cover!' I yelled to the troopers. The Valhallans did so with alacrity, long accustomed to trusting my paranoia in situations like these, and the Tallarns followed their lead after a moment's disorientation, recovering fast like the good soldiers they were. 'Enemy incoming!'

'Where?' Detoi asked calmly, with a disdainful glance at the other commissar.

'We'll see in a moment,' I said. I indicated an open area near the Slaaneshi defensive perimeter. 'Somewhere over there would be my guess.' I'd been close to teleportation fields a number of times over the years, and had even been through one on a couple of occasions during my time with the Reclaimers, so I'd had no difficulty identifying the unpleasant sensations which accompanied exposure to the fringes of one. It had to be an enemy making use of the arcane device; there was certainly no such thing in use anywhere in our makeshift battlefleet.

My guess was proven correct a moment or so later, as with a thunderclap of displaced air five crimson and black- armoured giants appeared more or less exactly where I'd anticipated.[1] My ears popped and cleared, the abnatural pressure created by the presence of so much naked warp energy dissipating as suddenly as it had come.

'Fire!' Beije screeched, waving his chainsword in the general direction of the Traitor Marines. 'Cleanse them in the name of the Emperor!'

'Don't waste the las bolts,' I said, and the crackle of lasgun fire from our lines (which had been almost entirely unleashed by the Tallarns in any case) dwindled to nothing. They were ineffective at this range, and the last thing we needed was to attract the attention of the Tainted Marines. 'We can use this.'

'Use it how?' Beije asked, narrowing his eyes suspiciously. I gestured at the World Eaters, who had unleashed a hail of bolter fire against the Slaaneshi barricade which had so frustrated our own efforts such a short time before. The cultists were falling, their return fire being shrugged off by the ceramite armour of the superhuman warriors who had so unexpectedly joined the fray.

'They're doing our work for us,' I pointed out, remarkably mildly under the circumstances. I turned to Detoi. 'Leave our people where they are, keep as many of the cultists as possible pinned at the other weak points. If any pull back to reinforce against the Traitor Marines, they can follow up and force a breech. Fourth squad

---

1. For the World Eaters to have mounted a successful deep strike by teleporter through the bulk of the entire planet would have been a remarkable feat to say the least; we can only speculate about how many attempts this would have taken, and how many would have ended up entombed in the core of Adumbria or drowned in the sea surrounding the dredger before this particular squad made it through. Or perhaps the distortion of the warp currents initiated by their enemies were what made it possible.

with me, we'll follow these lunatics at a distance and get in through the gap they're making.'

I took a few cautious steps out of cover, prepared to dive back in an instant if any of the crimson giants so much as glanced in our direction, but true to form they ignored us, intent only on charging home against the Slaaneshi. Sure I was safe, I turned a disdainful look on Beije. 'Coming?' I asked. 'Or would you prefer to wait for the noise to stop?'

Without a backward glance, sure he would be goaded into following, I led the Valhallans in the wake of the Chaotic killing machines. To my silent relief, Grifen and her team took point, leaving Jurgen and I between the two fireteams, theoretically a little more protected from both directions. To be honest, I'd have preferred to put the Tallarns in front, where they'd catch the first fire from the enemy, but it was even more essential than usual to appear to be leading from the fore as my unmerited reputation would have everyone expecting. Besides, I didn't trust Beije any further than I could throw a baneblade, and the further away from me the conniving little weasel stayed the better I liked it.

A quick glance back confirmed that the Tallarns were double-timing in our wake, Beije huffing a little as he scurried to keep up, and then my attention was entirely on the Traitor Marines ahead of us.

'Golden Throne preserve us,' the Tallarn sergeant muttered. I could see his point. The World Eaters had reached the barricade, tearing it apart in their eagerness to reach and slaughter the cultists sheltering behind the makeshift barrier. As before, they seemed to disdain the use of their bolters once they'd closed, striking out with the peculiar chain axes I'd seen all too closely when their colleague had led the attack on our compound;

wherever they went blood fountained and Slaaneshi cultists screamed ecstatically as they threw themselves forward to be slaughtered, hoping no doubt to take their assailants with them.

'They're not invulnerable,' I assured him. 'I've fought them before.' He nodded dubiously, and I noticed with a flare of malicious amusement that Beije was visibly smarting at one of his own troopers having his morale boosted by me.

'And kicked 'em good,' Magot added. 'Hand to hand. You stick with the commissar here, you'll be fine.' For a moment I thought Beije was going to spontaneously combust, but the universe isn't that helpful, and I had to content myself with the strangulated gurgle he was unable to suppress.

'Wait one,' I said, flattening myself against the storage tanks we'd sheltered behind before. 'Let's make sure they're through before we commit.'

'I knew it.' Beije smirked triumphantly. 'Cowardice, pure and simple. A true servant of the Emperor never hangs back.'

'After you, then,' I suggested politely. 'Show us how it's done.' I gestured towards the vicious melee continuing by the devastated barricade. The crimson giants had almost run out of degenerates to slaughter, but their enthusiasm was undiminished so far as I could see.

Beije licked his lips. 'It's your mission,' he said at last. 'Do as you see fit. It's all extra rope to hang you with.'

'Then let's wait until we stand a chance of completing it,' I said, checking my comm-bead to see what was going on elsewhere along the perimeter. The rest of the company were following their orders, so far as I could tell, successfully keeping the majority of the cultists pinned down and occupied. That was good; the more of them they kept busy the fewer there would be to get in our way, and hinder the World Eaters in their drive for the centre of this poisonous place.

The Tainted Marines weren't getting things entirely their own way, though. As I watched, one of the Slaaneshi, a youth of indeterminate gender dressed in flowing silks, flung him or herself at the leading giant, laughing hysterically, to catch the twisted parody of humanity's finest in what seemed like a lascivious embrace. The sight was so grotesque it was almost a relief when the hermaphrodite exploded in a rain of offal, taking the Marine with it, and I realised he or she must have had a demo charge strapped somewhere under that voluminous garment. The stricken Marine tottered and collapsed to the deck, where the clang of ceramite against steel echoed almost as loudly as the explosion.

From my time with the Reclaimers, I had expected the remaining World Eaters to break off once the last of the defenders was dispatched to administer the last rites demanded by the traditions of their Chapter[1], but instead they ignored their fallen colleague, no doubt carried away on a tide of bloodlust, merely continuing their berserk charge into the depths of sector twelve.

'Time to move,' I said, suiting the action to the word, and we moved out at a brisk trot. As we reached the tumbled remnants of the barricade, I couldn't help breaking stride to check for some sign of life, but where the servants of Khorne had been there was no hope of that; I glanced at the shattered corpse of the dead

---

1. *Cain presumably witnessed a Reclaimer or two recovering the geneseed from their fallen battle brothers after a skirmish, but appears not to have understood the significance of what he saw.*

Marine and shuddered. Even in death it gave off a powerful aura of malevolence and dread. Beije, I was amused to note, was staring at it as though it were Horus himself risen from the dead.

'Ugly frakkers, aren't they?' I said cheerfully, patting him on the back.

'Did you really kill one with a chainsword?' the Tallarn sergeant asked, a note of awe creeping into his voice. Behind him, I was gratified to note, his squad mates were looking quietly agog and trying not to look as though they were listening.

'These stories get a little exaggerated,' I said, confirming it in their minds and consolidating my reputation for modesty at the same time. 'But they're not quite as tough as they look.'

'I'm glad to hear it,' he said dryly.

We pressed on, following in the wake of the World Eaters. Their trail wasn't hard to track, being blazed in the corpses of the cultists who'd resisted them. At every fork in the passageways, every junction in the service tunnels, the path to our ultimate destination was clear to see.

'It's definitely the chapel,' I reported to Detoi, who in turn informed me that resistance was weakening in several places as cultists withdrew to meet the new threat. 'They're heading straight for it.'

The interior of the dredger was as big a surprise to me as the outside had been. I'd been expecting a maze of corridors, like the interior of a starship, but the passageways were as wide as city boulevards, and the ceilings so high that the rooms leading off them were more like small buildings. Indeed, it was only the presence of the luminators overhead and the subtle sense of enclosure no hive boy could miss which reminded me that we weren't still outdoors. Many of the street-sized intersections had been hastily defended, the bodies of variously-armed cultists lying around in varying states of disassembly, and the marks of bullets and las bolts clear to see on the walls and floor.

It was also apparent that the Traitor Marines, for all their martial prowess, weren't getting things entirely their own way. Even conventional weapons would be a threat to them in sufficient numbers, and the heretics they faced were able to marshal a few heavier pieces in support. To the eyes of experienced warriors, like the Valhallans and myself, and the Tallarns too I suppose, it was obvious that they'd been finding the going harder as they went, a plethora of small, minor wounds slowing them down.

'Wait.' Vorhees was on point at this juncture, and gestured emphatically with his hand to reinforce the hissed instruction over the comm-bead. 'There's movement ahead.' We closed up, moving cautiously over the intervening distance, to peer round the next junction. As before, there was a barricade there, hastily thrown up to meet the advance of the tainted supermen, and just as casually thrown aside. But this time one of the defenders appeared to be moving.

'A survivor,' Beije said. 'We can interrogate him and find out exactly what's going on around here.'

'Be my guest,' I said dryly, knowing better than to expect any useful information; torturing a masochist is singularly unproductive, as Zyvan's interrogators had already found out. But if he wanted to try, at least it would keep him out of my hair.

We moved forward again, hugging the edge of the thoroughfare from habit and sound common sense; just because the cultists we could see were in no fit state to fight it didn't mean that there weren't others, comparatively uninjured, lurking in ambush behind what remained of the barricade.

'Clear,' Magot reported at length, having lobbed a couple of frag grenades over the barrier to make sure. We rounded it, and I found myself looking down into the face of another of the cultists. As Vorhees had indicated, he was still alive, but only just, and I was sure the detonation of Magot's grenades hadn't exactly perked him up. He twitched feebly, bits of metal stuck through parts of his anatomy which looked extremely uncomfortable clinking against the deck plating, and reached out a hand to grab my ankle.

'She comes,' he said, an expression of imbecilic rapture on his face; by that point I don't suppose he had a clue who we were. 'The new world is at hand!'

'Who's coming?' Beije bustled up, kicked the hand away and squatted next to the fellow. 'What are you talking about?' He aimed his laspistol at the man's stomach, which was a bit of a waste of time given the fact that most of his intestines were already spread around the floor, then evidently realised the fact as he switched his aim to the man's hand at the last minute. The gun cracked, blowing a hole through the palm. 'Tell me!'

'Listen to you.' The cultist giggled, hoisting himself up Beije's chest with a sudden surge of strength which left the pudgy commissar gasping with surprise, and kissed him hard on the mouth. Beije leapt backwards, astonishment and outrage mingled on his face in a fashion which I have to admit struck me as extremely comical. Magot, Vorhees and a couple of the other Valhallans stifled audible snickers. 'You'll find out.'

'Vile degenerate!' Beije spluttered. 'How dare you... I'm not that sort.... Disgusting.' For a moment I thought he was going to shoot the man in a fit of pique, but the cultist saved him the bother, expiring before he could exact his petty revenge.

'When you've quite finished enjoying yourself,' I said sarcastically, 'do you think we might get on? Planet to save, daemon-summoning to stop, remember?'

'Do you think that's what he meant, sir?' Jurgen asked, hefting the melta as though it might actually be of some use against a hell-spawned abomination. 'When he said she's coming?'

'It's possible,' I said. My previous encounters with daemons had been mercifully brief, thanks to their inability to remain in the physical world for very long, and I'd had other things to worry about at the time than whether concepts such as gender had any real meaning for them. 'In which case he could have meant that the ritual has already started.'

'We've no time to waste then, have we?' Grifen began rounding her squad up. 'Move it people, clock's ticking here.'

'Better do the same,' I advised the Tallarn sergeant. 'What's your name, anyhow?'

'Mahat. Sir.' He saluted me, earning a black look from Beije, and turned away to follow Grifen's lead.

All at once the apprehension I felt, which had become a dull ache in the pit of my stomach so familiar that I'd almost been able to ignore it, redoubled, shaking me with its intensity. Jurgen looked at me curiously for a moment, then rummaged in one of his pouches for a flask of tanna tea.

'Bit of tanna, sir? You look like you could do with it.'

'I could indeed.' I swallowed a couple of mouthfuls of the fragrant liquid, feeling it warm its way slowly into my stomach. 'Thank you Jurgen.' There was no point putting it off any longer; for if I was right about the summoning being underway there was no hope at all of survival if we delayed here. And everyone it seemed was ready, except for me. (And probably Beije, who was so far out of his depth it was a miracle he hadn't drowned by now, which just went to prove the truth of the old adage that the Emperor takes care of the feeble-minded, I suppose.) I nodded to Grifen. 'Move out, sergeant.'

It wasn't even the thought of facing a daemon which had me so spooked, I realised, as we double-timed through the echoing passageways, heedless now of anything except the necessity of reaching our destination as quickly as possible. It was the dying cultist's other words. What was this new world he'd mentioned? Nothing good, I was sure.

So it was, torn between the growing fear of what we'd find at the heart of this lair of iniquity and the cast-iron conviction that not to face it meant death or worse (and I've seen enough over the years to know that there are plenty of things worse than dying), that we hurried on towards a confrontation which would shape the destiny of not only a world, but the entire sector.

NINETEEN

'The past is always with us.'

– Gilbran Quail, *Collected Essays*

THE DEEPER WE penetrated into that heart of darkness, the greater became the carnage we witnessed. The Slaaneshi cultists had obviously been intensifying their efforts to defend the site of their ritual, bringing in reinforcements from the perimeter in ever-increasing numbers, despite fatally weakening their defences there in the process. Detoi reported that all our squads were now making headway, and in a couple of places the barricades had fallen entirely.

'We can get reinforcements to you in a matter of minutes,' he said, and despite the flare of relief which accompanied his words, I found myself demurring.

'Better leave them to secure the perimeter for the moment,' I counselled.

Tempting as the prospect of more troopers to hide behind was, if I was right about what was waiting for us in the desecrated chapel, they wouldn't make any difference anyway; numbers had meant nothing to the PDF troopers in the bordello in Skitterfall, and I had no doubt that the daemon, if it was allowed to materialise again, would slaughter our people just as easily. Our only hope against it was Jurgen, and the fewer witnesses to that the better.

'If you say so,' Detoi replied, sounding vaguely disappointed, and I threw him a bone to cheer him up.

'We've still got the Traitor Marines to consider,' I reminded him. 'I'd feel a lot happier knowing they're bottled up tight if push comes to shove.'

It was at about that point we ran into one, almost literally. I'd noticed the scarring on the walls from weapons fire had grown more intense at the sites of the last couple of firefights we'd found the remains of, but quite how much firepower the heretics were able to bring to bear still hadn't consciously registered with me until I saw the wounded World Eater staggering along the corridor. His once-gleaming armour was pitted and stained by innumerable weapon impacts, and some had evidently taken their toll – his left leg dragged, the armour joint stiff, and he kept one massively-gauntleted hand on the wall for support, where it pressed dents into the steel every time he put his weight fully on it. His weapons had gone, Emperor knew where, and blood was leaking from several of the rents in his armour, forming sticky pools on the floor before hardening to the consistency of tar within seconds.

'Don't touch it,' I cautioned, as one of Mahat's men bent to examine the patch ahead of him. 'It might be toxic.'[1] He sprang upright at once, looking alarmed.

'Baseless superstition,' Beije scoffed, giving the patches a wide berth nevertheless.

'If you say so,' I said, quite happy to let him be the one to find out. At which point the Traitor Marine seemed to become aware of our presence for the first time, turning aside from his dogged progress towards the desecrated chapel.

'Blood for the Blood God!' he roared, lurching forwards, arms outstretched to grab and tear.

'I'm getting really sick of hearing that,' I said, bringing up my laspistol and cracking off a few rounds. The troopers with me, Valhallans and Tallarns alike, followed suit, and the front of the giant's armour rang like a foundry with the impact of scores of las bolts. Nevertheless, on he came, swinging wild punches which caught a couple of unfortunate troopers, slamming them against the walls. I ducked a massive fist, shaking off a peculiar sense of *déjà vu* as I did so, and stepped inside his guard, hoping Jurgen could get off a shot with his melta as he had before. But this time there were too many of us in the way, and my aide hovered indecisively.

I had only one chance: my laspistol seemed useless against the giant, but by great good fortune my

---

1. *Many Marine Chapters have the advantage of tainted blood, so that even in the act of wounding them the enemy harms themselves, and even if not actively toxic, the amount of alchemical and genetic enhancement in the modified blood which flows through their veins is unlikely to make it particularly healthy for the rest of us to be around for very long. Cain's caution is therefore quite understandable, particularly as a World Eater's bodily fluids are bound to have been even further altered by the mutating touch of Chaos.*

chainsword was in my other hand. Spying a rent in the ceremite armour, made by a krak grenade if I was any judge, I rammed the humming blade deep into the gouge, feeling to my intense relief the whirring teeth bite home on sinew and bone.

The giant roared in pain, shock and fury, and I ducked another wild swing of those sledgehammer fists, driving the blade deeper with all my strength. Abruptly he fell, shaking the deck, enabling my aide to run in close and dispatch him by vaporising his head.

'Two for two! Well done, commissar!' Magot shot me a wild grin and went to check on the wounded. Mahat stared at me, an expression I can only describe as awe on his face, as I retrieved the blade from the corpse (taking very good care to make sure none of the blood from it touched my skin). Beije simply stared, his jaw slack, as though unable to credit what he'd just witnessed.

'How are the wounded?' I asked, more to keep up appearances than anything else, but acutely aware that if I didn't find something else to concentrate on I'd end up undermining the moment with some snide and petty-seeming aside to the little weasel about his scepticism over my previous clash of arms with a World Eater.

Magot shook her head. 'Not going anywhere, that's for sure.'

The Chaos Marine's berserker charge had incapacitated three of the Valhallans (although they'd all be up and around again after the medicae had finished with them, a fact I could only attribute to the World Eater's astonishing degree of debilitation) and one of the Tallarns. There was only one thing for it; I detailed the squad medic to look after them and we proceeded as rapidly as we could towards the objective.

As we moved on, with a final glance back at the casualties and a call to Detoi to send someone in to collect them, I took in our diminished band with a sense of foreboding I tried very hard to hide. Apart from me and Jurgen, there were only five of us left now: Grifen, Magot, Vorhees, Drere, and Revik, a trooper from Magot's team I knew little about as he'd joined the regiment in the last batch of replacements and had so far committed no serious infractions. (Although with Magot as a role model, that happy state of affairs was unlikely to continue for long.) The Tallarns and Beije I more or less discounted, despite Mahat's obvious confidence in my leadership I couldn't bring myself to trust them, and the thought that we were now outnumbered should they stoop to some form of treachery was far from comforting.

So you'll understand my mind wasn't exactly easy as we hurried along in the wake of the World Eaters, afraid to get too close in case we attracted their murderous attention, but also acutely aware that time was of the essence if we were to stop the cultists at the heart of this web of corruption from completing their blasphemous task.

'Almost there,' I told Detoi, my knack for finding my way in enclosed spaces proving as reliable as ever, which the captain acknowledged with audible relief.

'We're still holding the perimeter,' he reported. 'All the defenders have withdrawn to meet the Traitor Marines. We could move in and mop up at any time.'

'Stay put for now,' I told him, not wanting his understandable eagerness to get in the way at this late stage. 'We'll vox you as soon as we know for sure what's going on down here. I'd hate to blow this by falling for a feint just when we're so close.'

'That would be a shame,' he agreed, almost managing to hide his disappointment.

'Listen.' Grifen held up a hand, and we paused, trying to distinguish the sound she'd heard. The dredger was full of background noise, of course, most of it barely noticeable – the hum and clangour of distant machinery, the moaning of the wind through the interstices of the vast structure, and, rather more obtrusively, the reverberations of weapons fire and dying screams as the Khornate Marines went about their butchery. I tried to filter them all out, along with the continual hiss of Drere's augmetic lungs, and after a moment I nodded.

'I think you're right,' I said grimly. It was a low, droning sound, which I felt as a vibration through the deck plates as much as I heard it directly. Chanting, which rose and fell in cadences no human throat should have been able to produce, and which raised the hairs on the back of my neck.

The troopers, Valhallan and Tallarn alike, looked uneasily at one another.

'What?' Beije asked, looking baffled.

'Come on.' I broke into a run, quickly, before my resolve could evaporate. 'We don't have much time.' How I knew this I couldn't tell you, not even after all these years, but my survival instinct had kicked in with a vengeance, and I trusted it. If we didn't face the enemy now we'd be too late, and death and damnation would follow. I knew that as unarguably as I knew that a dropped object would fall to the floor, or that Beije was an idiot. To my bemused surprise I found myself out in front as the Valhallans fell in behind me, and registered their presence with relief.

'Don't just stand there, get after him!' Beije shrilled. 'Can't you see he's trying to get away?' The Tallarns followed close on our heels, though more from the prospect of getting to grips with the enemy than because they believed a word of his idiotic accusations, I'm quite sure. The pudgy commissar huffed in their wake, his face crimson.

Up ahead the sounds of combat grew louder, and a confused melee was filling the street-sized passage ahead of us.

Detoi had been right, I could see; every cultist on the dredger had apparently converged on this one place with the evident aim of defending the chamber ahead of us. The cogwheel sigil of the Adeptus Mechanicus was embossed, taller than a man, on a pair of vast brazen doors beyond the mass of struggling bodies, and with a thrill of horror I realised that the sacred symbol of the priesthood of the machine had been profaned, lines added in a substance I didn't care to identify to warp and pervert it into the symbol of the unholy god of sensuous excess.[1] That was undoubtedly our goal, but reaching it would be more easily said than done: the full might of the Adumbrian cult of Slaanesh had been mobilised to defend the objective from the remaining World Eaters, and neither side expected or was capable of giving quarter.

For a moment, it seemed, even those superhuman warriors had met their match. The sheer weight of numbers ranged against them seemed to be telling; there must have been over a hundred of the cultists still on their feet, and at least half as many again already wallowing in their own blood. I've seldom witnessed carnage on such a scale, at least in a skirmish, and the sight affected even the veteran warriors with me.

---

1. *Something Cain would be able to identify instantly, thanks to his previous encounters with the deluded minions of the Dark Powers.*

'Emperor on Earth,' Grifen said. 'Where did they all come from?'

I presumed the question was rhetorical, as we'd already established that some at least had fought their way in from the boat dock, but it was plain that many had been part of the dredger's crew. Some were still in their work clothes, contrasting bizarrely with the outlandish costumes of their perverted confederates, and hard though it may seem to credit I even glimpsed the white robes of a tech-priest or two among their number.

Their victory over the tainted Marines should have been assured, their numbers telling against even so doughty a foe, and no doubt had they been Guardsmen or PDF troopers they would have prevailed without taking a tenth of the casualties they had. However, these were civilians, not warriors, and barmy to boot. They threw themselves heedlessly at the armoured giants without the faintest hint of coordination or tactics that I could see, and consequently died in droves. Worse, they got in each other's way, so half the shots aimed at the Traitor Marines killed or wounded their own.

Not that the Khornates were getting it entirely their own way. Even as I watched, one was seized from behind by a cargo-handling servitor fully as large as he was,[1] its metal hands closing relentlessly on his helmet. For a moment, augmented muscle strained against ceremite, then the armour gave way under the pressure, bursting like a ripe molin. The thing's victory was short-lived, however, as the two surviving Marines turned on it as one, tearing it apart with their chain axes.

Incredibly, the remaining pair of World Eaters managed to break through the line of foes opposing them,

---

1. *Presumably under the direction of one of the treacherous tech-priests whose presence Cain had noted before.*

so drenched in the blood they'd shed that it was impossible to tell now which parts of their armour had once been red and which originally black, to slam against the great bronze doors with an impact so great as to reverberate even over the screams and weapons fire. However strong and impressive that stout portal had seemed, though, it was no match for the accursed axes they bore; ceramite teeth squealed against metal, fountaining sparks like a firework display, and bronze tore and twisted like tissue paper as they ripped away at it with their gauntlets.

'What now?' Mahat asked, and with vague surprise, not to mention a certain degree of self-satisfaction, I realised he was addressing me directly, effectively ignoring his own commissar.

'We have to follow them,' I said. 'No matter what.' The Tallarn sergeant nodded grimly, reflecting the expression of the Valhallans, who seemed equally determined to see our errand through to the end (which looked uncomfortably close about now, let me tell you).

'That lot'll take some breaking through,' Grifen replied, hefting her lasgun and snapping a fresh power pack into it with practiced precision. Most of the others followed suit, no doubt reflecting that the middle of a glorious banzai charge was a pretty bad place to run out of ammunition.

'Maybe not,' I said, motioning Jurgen forward and acutely aware that the World Eaters had disappeared inside the chapel by now. Most of the surviving defenders attempted to pile in after them, choking the portal and getting in each others way, looking about as coordinated as a bunch of drunken orks. 'They're all bunched up and looking the other way.'

'Traki[1] shoot,' Magot said happily. 'I love it when the enemy's on our side.'

With a suitably dramatic flourish of my chainsword I rushed forward, making sure a couple of the troopers outpaced me a little, and we fell on our unprepared foe like the wrath of the Emperor himself. Jurgen's melta ripped a ragged hole through their lines, vaporising flesh and bone, to leave a narrow corridor of flash-burned victims writhing and screaming on either side where the air around the superheated plasma burst had scorched and seared them, and the rest of us opened up on the survivors to widen it. The first wave fell, barely aware of our presence, and we had almost made it to the ravaged portal before they began to turn and regroup.

'Again!' I ordered Jurgen, and he happily complied, clearing the way entirely to the doors and widening the gap created by the Chaos Marines.

'Having fun yet?' Magot asked Mahat, hosing down a group of cultists with a burst of las-fire as they turned and began to raise their weapons.

'Doing the work of the Emperor is its own reward,' the Tallarn admonished. 'But this is quite satisfying.'

Inevitably, though, the heretics began to get their act together and return our fire, although with a gratifying lack of accuracy; if we'd tried the same tactic against even a moderately organised foe, even one of the calibre of an underhive gang, it would undoubtedly have been a different story, but most of their fire went as wild as it had done against the World Eaters. Some, however, hit; Revik went down, blood leaking from a jagged rent

---

1. A large, slow-moving creature native to Valhalla, much prized for its succulent meat and soft pelt. Most hunters find them too easy to kill to be much of a challenge, hence the local expression employed here by Magot.

in his torso armour, and Vorhees and Drere picked him up by an arm each, barely breaking stride as they did so. They even kept firing, although aiming their lasguns one-handed didn't do a hell of a lot for their accuracy. A couple of the Tallarns went down too, being retrieved by their squad mates with similar dispatch and efficiency.

Abruptly I made it to the haven of the brazen doors, scuttling inside with a sense of relief I didn't even bother trying to hide, las bolts and slug rounds pinging off the metal behind me. A thick, cloying scent, like the one I'd noticed in the hab dome on the coldside, invaded my nostrils, and I was obscurely grateful for a full-strength whiff of Jurgen as he fell into place at my shoulder.

'Cover the others,' I said unnecessarily, as he was already turning to do so and they were only a couple of paces behind me.

I glanced around the antechamber we found ourselves in, looking for something we could use to our advantage. The bronze doors would afford us little protection now, having been forced by the World Eaters and thoroughly scorched by Jurgen's melta, but to my immense relief a polished steel side table stood nearby, covered in devotional candles and brightly coloured machine parts no doubt of great significance to the tech-priests who normally worshipped here.

I hurried over to it and tried to push it into the gap, my muscles cracking with the strain.

'Help me with this!' I called, beckoning to Beije and Mahat. They stood where they were, looking indecisive, while most of the troopers from both squads found what cover they could and poured fire through the gap. The only other exceptions were Magot, who was ripping

Revik's body armour away in an attempt to find his wound and stem the bleeding, and a couple of Tallarns doing the same for their colleagues. Jurgen's melta belched its cleansing plume of white-hot air again, disrupting the incoming fire for a moment or two.

'That would profane these holy symbols,' Mahat said doubtfully, and Beije nodded smugly, like the most pedantic of schola tutors. (And until I became one myself I wouldn't have believed quite how petty some of them could be. But I digress...)

'We can hardly profane them any more than the heretics already have,' I pointed out, somewhat forcefully, and with a few extraneous adjectives which I needn't record at the moment. 'And in case you haven't noticed, this place isn't even dedicated to the frakking Emperor, it's a cogboy chapel to their clockwork one.'

'Well that's an interesting theological point,' Beije began. 'Some would argue that the omnissiah is simply another aspect of His Divine Majesty, which would mean–'

'Well you can ask him about it in person if you don't shift your arses and help me move this bloody thing,' I snapped, 'because the heretics outside will be all over us in another couple of minutes if you don't.' I'd be the first to admit I'm not the most likely man in the galaxy to win a theological debate, but I took this one hands down. After an uneasy look passed between them, Beije and the Tallarn sergeant hurried over to join me and between us we manhandled the cumbersome slab of metal into the gap, turning it over onto its side for good measure. (Which of course sent the candles and the ironmongery flying, to their evident consternation, but that couldn't be helped.) After that I set Drere and Vorhees to reinforcing the makeshift barrier with

anything else readily portable they could lay their
hands on, and took stock of our position.

'How's Revik?' I asked Magot, wondering if he was
going to be in any fit state to hold a lasgun.

'Pretty bad. Seen worse,' she said, not bothering to
lift her head and applying a pressure bandage. 'Lucky
it was a las bolt.' As I've had occasion to be grateful for
myself more than once, they tend to cauterise the
wounds they make, cutting down the amount of
bleeding considerably. A solid round will leave a hole
you can bleed to death from frighteningly fast. Neither
of the Tallarn wounded was getting up any time soon
either.

'Grifen,' I said. 'You're in charge.' I glanced at Beije and
Mahat, expecting some objection, but there was none
from either of them; which, as you'll readily appreciate,
I found all the more unnerving. 'Hold them off at all
costs. If they manage to get in now and prevent us from
stopping the ritual...' I had no need to complete the
sentence.

'We'll keep 'em off your back,' the Valhallan sergeant
assured me. 'You can count on us.'

I turned to Jurgen. 'Come on,' I said, overwhelmed by
the sense of fatalistic detachment which often descends
in those moments when you know your chances of survival are minimal, but still a damn sight better than if
you do nothing at all. 'Let's get this over with.'

'Mahat.' Beije beckoned. 'You're with me. Bring Karim
and Stoch.' The two troopers he'd indicated left their
posts at the firing line at once, leaving Vorhees and
Drere to plug the gap as best they could, and all the Valhallans to look collective murder at the overweight
commissar.

'They're all needed here,' I said tightly.

Beije smiled without humour. 'I thought you had complete confidence in your people. After all, they're one of the finest regiments in the galaxy, aren't they?'

'We'll manage,' Grifen said, picking off a couple of heretics who were incautious enough to raise their heads as she spoke.

'We haven't got time to argue,' I said, turning on my heel and leading the way out of the antechamber. The route was obvious, the World Eaters having been as subtle as ever in their approach, a pair of ornately engraved brass doors buckled from their hinges in one corner. The chanting was louder in here too, the direction unmistakable, and as I listened it became overlaid with the unmistakable whine of chainblades and the gleeful roar of the Khornate Marines piling into more victims.

'Sounds like the big red buggers are saving us a job,' Jurgen said at my elbow as we ran towards the sound. I'd expected the chanting to falter as the acolytes died, but if anything it seemed to swell, resonating in my very bones. I wasn't sure what that meant, but I'd bet a year's tarot winnings that it was nothing good.

'Golden throne!' Beije bleated as we burst through a ripped curtain into the main chapel. For once I could sympathise with him. I'd had some idea of what to expect, having seen the ruins of the ritual chambers in the hab dome and the bordello, but the full sanity-blasting horror of the intact symbols on the walls surrounding us completely was new to me, and sent my senses reeling. I'm sure it was only the presence of Jurgen and his peculiar talent, which insulated my mind from the worst of it.

'Don't look at them,' I cautioned, trying to focus on the carnelian giants wading through the congregation of degenerates with single-minded determination, slicing and hacking with their chainblade pole arms. 'Stay focussed.'

My warning came too late for one of the Tallarn troopers, though, Stoch I think – he curled up into a foetal position, bleeding from the eyes and whimpering something which sounded like the first line of the Emperor's benediction over and over again. Beije paled and threw up, but rallied, to my surprise, reciting one of the catechisms of command in a faltering voice.

'What should we do, sir?' Jurgen asked, as phlegmatic as ever, his voice as unconcerned as though he was asking if I wanted another cup of tanna. 'Take them all out?'

In truth it looked as though that would be the only way. I nodded.

'Concentrate on the cultists,' I shouted, trying to make myself heard over that hellish chanting. 'Leave the Chaos Marines for last.' There must have been at least as many acolytes in the chamber as had been defending it from the outside, and we were going to need all the help we could get to be sure of killing the lot before their ritual reached its climax.

But we never got the chance. Almost as soon as the words left my lips, the chanting ended, a sudden silence pervading the chamber, broken only by the sounds of slaughter as the World Eaters went about their grisly work, and Stoch's ravings.

'She comes! She comes!' Five score throats abruptly yelled, a few of them breaking off with a gurgle as the Khornate chain axes ripped through them. Then even these suddenly ceased, their owners stopping abruptly, like servitors with their power supplies cut. A sickly glow began to suffuse the air, spreading through the crowd, and wherever I looked, expressions of imbecilic ecstasy slithered across faces, distorting them in ways beyond the physically possible.

'Frak this,' I said, my eyes darting around the chamber for a target, any target, skittering away from the symbols daubed on the walls and ceiling before they had a chance to register on my forebrain. 'Let's kill something.'

'Oh, Ciaphas.' Mellifluous laughter rippled through the room. 'You haven't changed at all, I see.'

Several of the cultists close to us began to shiver, ululating in ecstasy, the flesh of their bodies flowing together like melting wax. The sight was more hideous than I can describe, and all I can say is if you think that's disappointing count yourself lucky you can't picture it.

'Emperor preserve us,' Beije gibbered, grabbing my elbow. 'This is sorcery, sorcery most foul...'

'It's worse than that,' I told him, a chill of pure dread rippling through me. The mound of flesh in front of us was changing by the second, smoothing out, taking on a clearly defined outline. Fully twice the height of a man, with limbs inhumanly lithe, a body curved and rounded in a manner indisputably feminine, yet for all that both hideous and attractive in a manner utterly inhuman. The face too was completely different from anything remotely familiar, but for a pair of eyes, emerald green, cool and disdainful, which regarded me with detached amusement.

'It's been quite a while,' the apparition said, addressing me directly. 'I hope you're well.' It reached down, picked up the stupefied Stoch, and bit his head off, chewing thoughtfully for a moment before discarding the body.

Mahat and Karim twitched, trying to raise their lasguns, but they seemed as paralysed as the World Eaters.

'That's better. So impolite to run off at the mouth while somebody's talking, don't you think?'

My nightmare came flooding back to me then, and with it a sense of recognition I couldn't ignore. It was impossible, I knew, but I couldn't prevent myself from blurting the name out.

'Emeli,' I said.

The daemon nodded. 'I told you I was coming back,' it said.

TWENTY

'Then the prophet spake: saying "Frak this, for my faith is a shield proof against your blandishments".'

– Alem Mahat, *The Book of Cain*,
Chapter IV, Verse XXI[1]

WELL I MIGHT not be the biggest bang in the armoury, but I can put two and two together as well as the next man.

'Those dreams,' I said slowly. 'They weren't just dreams, were they?'

---

1. *This is the only quotation I've used which doesn't come from Cain's commonplace book. The thought that there's a fringe sect on Tallarn which reveres him as a prophet of the Emperor, and a physical conduit of His Divine Will, is a truly terrifying one. Nevertheless, in my more whimsical moments I must confess that I do find the idea somewhat appealing, if only for the fact that he would have been so utterly appalled at the idea if he'd ever found out about it.*

'What dreams?' Beije asked, gazing at the apparition in awestruck horror, as unable to tear his gaze from its repulsively fascinating visage as the rest of the congregation. The daemon and I ignored him, continuing our conversation as though we were completely alone. Only Jurgen showed any sign of animation, although his habitual expression of vague bafflement concealed it nicely, and I tried to keep the thing's attention focussed on me. Once it realised what he was, and that there was still a chance of us derailing whatever plans it had, we'd have seconds at best to react before we became an unpleasant stain on the decking, or another impromptu snack.

'We have a connection,' the daemon said, its voice as low and seductive as I remembered from my encounter with the human it used to be. 'When the warp currents were favourable, or I was physically present on this drab little world, I was able to caress your mind from time to time.' It laughed again, a long, sinuous tongue moving about its lips like a grotesque parody of a flirting courtesan.

'I don't understand,' I said, playing for time. If Jurgen could edge a little closer and nullify whatever power the thing had to hold our companions in thrall, there was just a chance we could take it by surprise. I didn't expect a couple of lasguns to make much difference, to be honest, but Jurgen's melta might just be enough to hurt it, and if we could do enough damage to disrupt its physical presence here it would be drawn back into the warp. It wouldn't exactly be harmless there, but at least it would be out of our hair.

The daemon laughed again, and despite myself I felt a shiver of delight running through me, like the sensation you get on a crisp autumn morning when the sun is bright and the world seems full of simple pleasures. 'When we met before, I took you for human.'

'I was, silly.' The daemon glided away from us, just as I was about to signal Jurgen to act, and I stilled the gesture, biding my time. Emeli, and Emperor help me I still couldn't help thinking of the thing as the woman who had almost cost me my soul on Slawkenberg, moved between her acolytes, slinking around them, bestowing tender caresses with fingers, tongue and lithely twitching tail. And wherever she touched bodies fell, leeched of their souls, with cries of terminal ecstasy. 'But I served our prince well in life, and he received my soul gladly. I grew strong in the warp, and after a time I became able to affect things in the physical world too.'

'But not for long, thank the Emperor,' I said, and the daemon bristled, a naked and terrible anger marring the sensuous perfection of its hideous features for a moment.

'You dare to invoke the name of your corpse god in this holy place?' It tore one of the World Eaters in half in a fit of pique, which still seemed somehow coquettish and grotesquely endearing, his ceramite armour crumpling like paper. The other she picked up and threw against the wall, which deformed into a dent the depth of my forearm under the impact, leaving the corpse to bounce randomly and fall to the metal floor beneath with a sound like somebody dropping an armful of buckets (crushing a couple of her own cultists in the process, but I don't suppose she was too bothered about that).

'It was his first,' I pointed out. Well, technically I suppose it was the Omnissiah's first, but I'd had enough of that argument from Beije.

Emeli giggled, a grotesque echo of the flirt she used to be, and began moving back towards us, a smile on her face again. Provoking her was a risky gambit, but if I could only keep her mind focussed on me for long enough to lure her into range of Jurgen's strange abilities we might just be able to get out of this alive.

'Finders keepers,' she said, slithering around another group of deliriously expiring cultists. 'Now it's mine, and soon I'll be the queen of the whole world.' An expression of distaste flickered across her face. 'Dreary little place at the moment I know, but I can soon fix that. What do you think of violet for the sky? Or maybe pink.' A beatific smile spread across that terrible face. 'I love decorating.'

'Are you sure you'll have the time?' I asked, still trying to lure her in. 'As I recall, your kind doesn't stick around in the physical world for too long.'

A tidal wave of mellifluous laughter washed over me, leaving me tingling with joy, and despite the terrible danger we were in I felt a smile begin to play over my face at the sound.

'Poor Ciaphas. You really don't understand, do you?' Gleeful mischief danced in her eyes, as captivating as they'd been all those years before when she'd been the preternaturally seductive woman who'd almost lured me to my doom. 'I'm not going back to the warp this time. I'm staying, and my friends are coming out to play too. The energy I've absorbed from these playthings will be enough to break the barrier between the realms for good.'

The thrill of horror which shot through me at those words was enough to dispel the unnatural glamour the daemon had been able to exert on me, and I found the air curdling in my lungs. It was closer now than it had ever been, and the scent of her body washed over me, compelling and enticing, threatening to enthral me once again.

'You're opening a warp portal,' I choked out, and behind me I heard Beije moan in terror at the thought. Emeli's smile spread, that inhuman tongue flexing against her lips again.

'No, silly. I'm making the whole planet into a portal. Half in and half out of the warp, where my friends can come and go as they please and we can shape reality as we see fit. Won't that be fun?'

'For you, maybe,' I said, my head growing fuzzy with the nearness of her physical presence.

Despite the fear and revulsion still consuming me, the desire I'd once felt for her human form was stirring too, and the inhuman sensuality of her daemon body was somehow amplifying that. I fought against the impulse to open my arms to her, my skin tingling in anticipation of her touch. But still my survival instinct clung on, as it had in her bedroom the first time she tried to seduce me and claim my soul. To yield, I knew, meant extinction. 'Not so much for the rest of us.'

'You have no idea,' the daemon breathed, warm musk washing over my face and clouding my senses. 'The pleasures I can show you, the bliss we can share. I told you before, you could be one of us. Have powers no mortal can conceive, experience an eternity of rapture. All you have to do is take it. Take me...'

'Frak this!' I said, a sudden familiar smell displacing the one which had so bewitched me, and I thanked the Emperor for Jurgen's presence. He'd edged a little closer while Emeli was concentrating on seducing me, although why she should have been so concerned over claiming my little soul while there was a whole world stuffed with them up for grabs I've no idea. Perhaps she was just a sore loser and wanted to make some kind of point after our last ill-fated encounter. 'My soul's my own, and I'm keeping it!' Reflexively I brought up my laspistol and fired.

'You really are remarkably tiresome,' the daemon said petulantly, apparently unphased by the detonation of the las bolt, which did nothing beyond marring the pale flesh of her skin. 'Have it your own way, then.' The blemish disappeared, fading into invisibility in the space of a heartbeat. 'Let's see how you like being killed for a change, shall we?'

She charged forward, beautiful and terrible, scattering her few remaining acolytes as she came. I fired again, repeatedly, the las bolts just as ineffective as before, flinching as the daemon reached out for me...

And then reeled back, an expression of confusion and doubt clouding her strangely elongated eyes.

'What?' She glanced around in perplexity, and began to back away. 'What are you doing?' I fired again, and this time the las bolt left a real wound, a faint pockmark which leaked some ichorous fluid. I nudged Jurgen's arm, urging him forward. We had to stay close to her.

'Come on!' I yelled. 'It's now or never!' I swung my chainsword, eliciting a gout of ichor from one of the reaching hands, and a squeal of outrage which rang in my skull like an opera singer hitting and holding a perfect note. Mahat and Karim snapped out of their stupor and began firing, fortunately proving good enough marksmen to hit the huge target in front of them without endangering Jurgen or myself. More wounds began to open across that pale and sensuous skin.

'You can't do this, it's not fair!' the daemon howled, bounding forward again. I dodged frantically, opening a slash across its leg with the chainsword, and Jurgen leapt to one side, raising the melta but before he could fire, the thing's long, sinuous tail snapped round against the side of his head. He dropped to the ground, stunned, the precious heavy weapon falling with him. 'Stop it! Stop it, you horrible little man!'

It backhanded Karim, sending him flying backwards in a tangle of limbs and lasgun, but Mahat kept firing doggedly. Beije, I noticed, was still standing there, his mouth open, like a half-witted shop dummy.

'Shoot it, you moron,' I yelled, diving for the fallen melta, praying to the Emperor that they could keep the daemon occupied long enough for me to reach it, and that it would stay pinned within the radius of Jurgen's peculiar aura. My aide stirred, staggering to his feet, shaking his head groggily, and stumbled a step forward, trying to unsling his lasgun.

'What?' Beije seemed to become aware that he still held a laspistol, and cracked off a couple of badly-aimed shots, which at least attracted Emeli's attention. Her head snapped round towards him, that long, sinuous tongue lashing out to entangle his arm. Squealing in terror, Beije was pulled inexorably towards her gaping jaws.

'Good! Keep her busy!' I shouted encouragingly, while the pudgy commissar scrabbled frantically for his chainsword. I rolled to my feet, hefting the weight of the heavy weapon, marvelling for a moment at the ease with which Jurgen seemed able to lug the thing around, and pulled the trigger.

A bright, actinic flash seared through my closed eyelids, leaving dancing afterimages on my retina, I blinked my vision clear and found the daemon reeling, a hole punched clear through its torso. Any mortal creature would surely have found such a wound instantly fatal, but Emeli simply staggered, rallied and turned back to face me.

'Not this time,' she said, an expression of utter malevolence washing across her inhuman features, dropping Beije in the process. She bounded towards me with preternatural speed, failing to see Jurgen in her eagerness to close her hands around my neck.

'I'm coming, commissar,' my aide said, still dazed and entangled in the sling of his lasgun. He stumbled into the daemon's leg, and it screeched as though he was white hot, leaping away with an expression I can only describe as terror on its face.

That was all the opening I needed. I fired the melta again, blowing a chunk of its head away. The daemon howled, all pretence of civilisation gone, and rushed at me, intent on murder. I worked frantically to bring the heavy weapon round, cursing its weight and mass, sure I couldn't make it in time...

And it staggered, its entire body erupting in spatters of ichor. The crackle of lasguns echoed around the chamber, deafening me and drowning out even the shrieking of the doomed warp entity. For a moment it writhed, tormented, unable to decide where to go, then it vanished with a thunderclap of imploding air. Dazed, I stared around the room, finding it packed with Valhallan uniforms.

'You forgot to vox,' Detoi said laconically from near the door. 'So we came to see how you were getting on.'

'Not so well that we're not pleased to see you,' I said, sagging with relief. I indicated the handful of feebly-twitching acolytes still scattered around the chamber. 'Bring them, and let's get the frak out of here. And try not to look at the walls, they fry your brain.'

'No problem.' The captain beckoned a couple of troopers armed with flamers forward. 'Burn it all down.'

'Works for me,' I said, wondering for a moment what Malden would say, and deciding I didn't give a frak. I turned to Jurgen, who was looking as alert as he ever did, and handed him the melta, which he accepted with as close as he ever got to enthusiasm. 'You dropped this,' I said.

'Sorry about that, sir,' he responded.

'You think you've won, don't you?' One of the cultists turned to me, glaring defiantly for a moment before Magot jabbed him none too gently with the butt of her lasgun to get him moving again. There was something vaguely familiar about his face, and after a moment I recognised him as one of the aristocratic by-blows infesting the Council of Claimants, although if I ever knew his name I couldn't recall it.[1] 'But she'll be back. Slaanesh is eternal, and so are his servants.'

'Yes, but you're not,' I snapped, fighting the urge to put a las bolt through his head there and then. 'And you'll hang long before I do.' I turned to Beije, who was staring vacantly at the daemon slobber on his sleeve as though it might be about to sit up and bite him. 'See you at the tribunal,' I said.

---

1. *Umbart Segundo of House Yosmarle, the first of the conspiritors to be positively identified. The Ordo Hereticus spent several months cleaning house on Adumbria, and as so often in these affairs many of the prime movers in the cult turned out to be minor aristocracy in search of exotic thrills or hoping to gain some measure of power through the connections their membership of a secret society opened up for them. Only a few were sufficiently deluded to hope to gain more than this through currying the favour of their daemonic mistress, but as always those were the ones who did the real damage.*

TWENTY-ONE

'Revenge is a dish best served with mayonnaise and those little cheesy things on sticks.'

– Osric the Loopy, planetary governor of Corania (appointed 756 M41, removed from office by the Officio Assassinorum 764 M41)

As IT TURNED out, I didn't have to wait long for my day in court. Under the circumstances, Zyvan graciously allowed the Commissariat to convene the tribunal in his headquarters on Adumbria once the warp currents had stabilised enough to put the astropaths back to work, and a brisk exchange of signal traffic had established that no one could be bothered making the trip out from the subsector office on Corania for what everyone involved seemed to think was an open and shut case.

By that time the rest of our fleet had finally arrived, metaphorically red-faced and panting, just in time to play a couple of quick rounds of hunt the heretic. The last survivors of the Khornate invaders were picked off in pretty short order once our reinforcements arrived, leaving the five regiments who'd borne the brunt of the fighting to grab some much-deserved R&R, and Kasteen and Broklaw had found time to meet me in Skitterfall and sit in on the proceedings.

'I appreciate this,' I said, making myself as comfortable as I could on the bench outside the conference suite where the two Kastaforean commissars and the Valhallan from the 425th were concluding their deliberations. Beije sat on the opposite side of the lobby, alone save for Asmar, still rubbing absently at his arm where the daemon had licked him; I suspected he'd acquired a lifelong nervous tic from the experience.

'It was the least we could do,' Broklaw assured me, cracking his knuckles and stifling a yawn. 'You've put yourself on the line for us any number of times.' This was true, albeit never from choice.

'Quite.' Kasteen shot a venomous glance at the other commissar. 'Is it true you challenged him to a duel for insulting me?'

'I thought of it more as an insult to the regiment,' I said, playing things down as usual.

Kasteen nodded, apparently not fooled for a moment. 'Thank you anyway,' she said.

'So how are things with the lord general?' Broklaw asked, breaking the awkward silence.

I shrugged. 'Pretty much as usual. Still not much of a regicide player.' Nevertheless, the social evening I'd spent with him the previous night had been a pleasant one, only slightly overshadowed by the possibility that it could have been our last. Neither of us expected Beije's ridiculous charges to stick, especially as Zyvan had quietly seen to it that the triumverate of commissars comprising the tribunal had been given access to some very highly classified files and been left in no doubt what would have happened if I hadn't acted as I did, but there was always the possibility that one or other of the Kastaforeans would apply the letter of the regulations rather than a dose of common sense. (Which, I've observed, is remarkably scarce in most cases.)

'I thought you might care for some refreshment,' Jurgen said, materialising a few paces behind his bouquet and passing round a tray full of tanna bowls.

I took one gratefully. 'Thank you, Jurgen,' I said, taking my first sip of the fragrant liquid.

'Commissars.' One of the lord general's personal guard appeared at the door to the conference suite. 'The tribunal is ready to announce its verdict.'

'Typical,' I said with heavy humour. 'Wait all afternoon for a decent brew, then…' I replaced the bowl on the tray.

'I'll keep the pot warm for you sir,' Jurgen said, which was as close as he would come to wishing me luck or expressing concern, and I nodded.

'I won't be long,' I said, stilling a sudden fluttering of nervousness which took me completely by surprise. Damn it all, I'd just faced down a daemon, and not for the first time either; a few minutes listening to my colleagues huffing with self-importance couldn't hold a sconce to that. So outwardly, at least, I was completely impassive as I walked into the conference room, Beije at my side, and stood at parade rest in front of the trio of black-clad commissars seated behind the polished wooden table.

Dravin, the commissar of the Valhallan tankies, was chairing the tribunal by virtue of his length of service (roughly twice that of either of his colleagues), and rested his elbows on it, cupping his chin on steepled hands.

'This has been an unusual case,' he began without preamble. 'And one which my colleagues and I have had to regard with the utmost seriousness. Fortunately, our verdict was unanimous in all particulars.' He paused for dramatic effect. Beije licked his lips nervously, and I remained impassive with the ease of the practiced dissembler; you don't play as much poker as I do without learning to mask your feelings. Dravin indicated the data-slate in front of him. 'We have no hesitation in finding all the charges made against Commissar Cain completely baseless and without foundation.'

I inclined my head, in what I calculated would be a sufficiently restrained response for a man of my reputation, and savoured the mew of disappointment which escaped from Beije's tightly clenched lips.

Dravin returned the nod. 'However,' he went on, 'we feel that under the circumstances we have had no option but to introduce new charges of our own. Charges I'm bound to say which disappoint us, and which reflect badly on the reputation for scrupulous conduct for which the Commissariat has always stood.' This was a surprise, I must admit, and a thoroughly unwelcome one at that. But I kept my feelings from my face just as easily as before, did my best to ignore the look of vindictive triumph on Beije's, and nodded gravely. No point in panicking just yet.

'I await your verdict with interest,' I said levelly.

'No doubt.' Dravin glanced down at his data-slate again. 'Tomas Beije, you are charged by this tribunal with conduct unbecoming to a commissar. Your unwarranted interference in Commissar Cain's pursuit of his

duty could have had the most catastrophic of consequences not only for the world of Adumbria, but the
entire sector.'

I glanced across at Beije. He seemed to be hyperventi-
lating, incapable of making any sound other than
'Wha... Wha... Wha...'

'Under the circumstances we have no option but to
recommend your immediate removal from field duties
pending further enquiries. I'm sure you're aware that
the most severe penalties may be deemed appropriate
once properly formulated charges can be brought.'

So as you'll appreciate, it was with a light heart that I
rejoined Kasteen, Broklaw and Jurgen in the corridor
outside. Beije tottered out after me a moment later,
looking as though he could already see the firing squad
taking aim, and I took him gently by the arm.

'If it helps,' I said, with all the sincerity I could muster,
'I intend to testify that in my opinion you acted
throughout from the best and most noble of motives.
I'm sure you would have done the same for me.'

'Of course,' he said insincerely. He began to pull away.
'Now if you'll excuse me I really must break the news to
Colonel Asmar...'

'Of course.' I nodded sympathetically. 'As to our other
meeting, Jurgen will be acting as my second. When
you've had time to appoint one, perhaps he would be
so good as to convey a time and place convenient to
you.'

'That, ah, won't be necessary.' Beije licked his lips,
glancing at my chainsword, no doubt remembering I'd
last used it on a Chaos Marine and a daemon. He
turned to Kasteen. 'I may have passed certain remarks in
the heat of the moment. If any offence was caused, I
most sincerely apologise.'

'None taken, I can assure you,' Kasteen said graciously.

'Good. Well then…' Beije tottered away, and I smiled with satisfaction. I'd let him sweat for a couple of days before I pulled a few strings to get him off. I'm not really a vindictive man, for all my other faults, and there was no point in letting them shoot the man. He might just have learned something from the experience, and even if he hadn't, it was going to be far more fun watching him squirm every time he was reminded that he owed me his neck.

'Well then,' I echoed, turning back to my friends. Despite the damage the battling Chaos cults and our own forces had done, life in Skitterfall was returning to normal, and I felt I had something to celebrate. 'I seem to recall a rather pleasant little restaurant not far from here. Care to see if it's still standing?'

[At which somewhat self-satisfied juncture, Cain's account of the Adumbria incident comes to a natural end.]

WARHAMMER
40,000

Basic training: four months. Planetary transportation:
seven weeks. Life expectancy...

FIFTEEN HOURS

Mitchel Scanlon

*Coming soon from the Black Library: an incredible
slice of war-torn action, from a devastated planet
where the average life expectancy of a new Imperial
Guardsman is just...*

FIFTEEN HOURS

by Mitchel Scanlon

'BEARING ONE EIGHT degrees one five minutes,' the navigation servitor's voice croaked, the parchment thin tones of
its voice barely audible in the lander's crew compartment
over the roar of engines. 'Recommend course correction
of minus zero three degrees zero eight minutes for opti-
mal atmospheric entry. All other systems reading normal.'

'Check,' said the pilot, automatically pushing his control stick forward to make the adjustment. 'New
bearing: one five degrees zero seven minutes. Confirm
course correction.'

'Course correction confirmed,' the servitor said, its
yellowing sightless eyes rolling back in their sockets as
it rechecked its calculations. 'Atmospheric entry in 'T'
minus five seconds. Two. One. Atmospheric entry
achieved. All systems reading normal.'

'Look at that glow, Dren,' Zil the co-pilot said, his
eyes lifting from his instruments for a fraction of a

second to look out the view-portal at the nose of the lander as it was surrounded by a nimbus of bright red fire. 'No matter how many planetary drops we do, I never get used to it. It's like riding in a ball of flame. It makes you thank the Emperor for whoever first made heat shields.'

'Heat shields reading normal,' said the servitor, gears whirring inside it as it mistook the comment for a question. 'Exterior temperature within permitted operational thresholds. All systems reading normal.'

'That's because you've only got a dozen drops behind you,' the pilot said. 'Trust me, by the time you've done another dozen you won't even notice it. How's the signal from the landing beacon? I don't want to miss the drop point.'

'Beacon signal reading strong and clear,' Zil replied. 'No air traffic, friendly or hostile. Looks like we've got the sky to ourselves. Wait! Auspex is reading some–'

'Warning! Warning!' the servitor interrupted, the whirring of its mechanisms reaching an abrupt crescendo as it burst into life. 'Registering hostile missile launch from ground-based battery. Recommend evasive manoeuvres. Missile trajectory eight seven degrees zero three minutes, airspeed six hundred knots. Warning! Registering second missile launch. Missile trajectory–'

'Evasive manoeuvres confirmed!' the pilot said, pressing his control stick forward as he pushed the lander into a dive. 'Servitor: belay hostile trajectories and airspeeds until further orders. Zil, deploy chaff!'

'Chaff activated. Instruments reading chaff successfully deployed,' Zil said, his voice growing suddenly hoarse as he looked at one of the screens before him.

'Wait. The chaff, it's not done any good. It's as though…
Holy Emperor! None of the hostile missiles have guidance systems!'

'What do you mean?' the pilot asked as he saw Zil's
face go pale. 'If that's the case we have nothing to worry
about. If they're firing blind there's not one chance in a
thousand of them being able to hit us.'

'But that's exactly it,' said Zil, his voice frantic. 'I'm
reading a *thousand* hostile missiles as airborne already!
And hundreds more are being launched every second!
Holy Throne! We're flying into the biggest shitstorm
I've ever seen!'

'Emergency evasion procedures!' the pilot said, bark-
ing out orders as he pushed the lander forward into an
even steeper dive while from outside they could hear
the first of the missiles exploding. 'Servitor: override
standard flaps and navigation safety protocols – I want
full control! Make sure your strapped in tight, Zil –
we're going to have to go in hard and heavy! Looks like
this is going to be a *close* one…'

Falling.
They were falling.
With nothing to slow or stop them.
Like a comet.
Falling headlong from the stars.

In the lander's troop compartment, slammed back
in his seat by the force of acceleration, it felt to Larn
as though his stomach was trying to push its way up
from his throat. Around him he could hear men
screaming, the sound all but drowned out by the dull
thud of explosions from outside the lander. He heard
cries for pity and muttered oaths, all the while the

skin being pulled so tight across his face he was sure it was about to rip free from his bones. Then, sounding much louder than any noise he had ever known before, there came the boom of another explosion and with it the gut-wrenching sound of tearing metal. With those sounds he found himself forced back against his seat with even greater force as the fall began in earnest.

We've been hit, he thought, overcome with sudden panic while the world began to spin crazily around him as the lander turned over and over on its axis out of control. *We've been hit*, the thought crowded his mind and held him at its mercy. *We've been hit! Holy Emperor, we are in freefall!*

Suddenly he felt himself struck in the face by a warm and semi-solid liquid, the acrid smell and the taste of the droplets dribbling past his lips telling him it was vomit. Half mad with desperation, he found himself wondering incongruously whether it was from his own stomach or someone else's. Then another thought forced its way fearfully into his mind and he no longer cared whom the vomit belonged to. A thought more terrible than any he had ever considered in his seventeen years of life to date.

We are falling from the sky, he thought. *We are falling from the sky and we're going to die!*

He felt his gorge rise in a tide of sickly acids, the half-digested remnants of his last meal spewing uncontrollably from his mouth to soak some other unfortunate elsewhere in the lander. Certain he was on the brink of oblivion he tried to replay the events of his life in his mind. He tried to remember his family, the farm, his homeworld. He tried to think of fields of flowing wheat, magnificent sunsets, the sound of his father's voice. Anything to blot out the terrifying reality around him. It was hopeless though and he realised the last moments of his life would be spent with the following sensations: the taste of vomit; the sound of men going screaming to their deaths; the feeling of his own heart beating wildly in his chest. These were the things he would take with him to death: the last sensations he would ever know. Just as he began to wonder at the unfairness of it all the world stopped spinning as, with a bone-jarring impact and a terrible screech like the death-knell of some mortally wounded beast, the lander finally hit the ground.

For a moment there was silence while the interior of the lander was plunged into total darkness. Next, Larn heard the sound of coughing and quiet prayers as the men in the lander drew a collective breath to find, despite some initial misgivings, they were very much alive. Abruptly, darkness gave way to dim shadowy light at the activation of the lander's emergency illumination system. Then, he heard a familiar strident voice begin to bark out orders as Sergeant Ferres sought to re-establish control of his troops.

'Fall in!' the sergeant shouted. 'Fall in and prepare to disembark! Get off your arses, damn you, and start acting like soldiers! You've got a war to fight, you lazy bastards!'

Releasing his seat-restraints Larn staggered unsteadily to his feet, his hands warily prodding his body as he checked to see whether any of his bones were broken. To his relief, it seemed he had survived the landing little the worse for wear. His shoulders were sore, and he had the painful beginnings of a bruise where the clasp of one of the seat-straps had bitten into his flesh. Other than that, he had escaped from what had seemed like certain death remarkably unscathed. Then, just as he began to congratulate himself on surviving his first drop, Larn turned to retrieve his lasgun and saw that the man sitting in the seat next to him had not been so lucky.

It was Jenks. Head lolling sideways at a sickening angle, eyes staring blankly from a lifeless and slack-jawed face, Jenks sat in his seat dead and unmoving. Staring at his friend's body in numb disbelief, Larn noticed a thin stream of blood trickling from Jenks' mouth to stain his chin. Then, spotting a small bloody-ended piece of pink flesh lying on the floor of the lander beside his feet, Larn realised that with the force of the landing Jenks must have inadvertently bitten off the end of his tongue. As horrified as he was by that discovery, Larn could not at first understand how Jenks had died. Until, looking once more at arrangement of seat-restraints around Jenks' body and the way his head lolled sideways like a broken puppet, Larn realised the restraints had been improperly fastened, causing Jenks' neck to snap at the moment of their landing. The realisation brought him no comfort. Jenks was dead. Understanding how his friend had died did nothing to lessen Larn's grief.

'Fall in!' the sergeant shouted again. 'Fall in and get ready to move out!'

Still numb with shock, Larn grabbed his lasgun and stumbled past Jenks' body to join the rest of the company as they lined up in one of the aisles between the upper deck's endless rows of seating. As he did, he became aware for the first time of the sound of distant ricochets clanging off the exterior of the hull. *We are being fired at*, he thought dully, his mind still reeling at the sight of Jenks' corpse. Until, noticing an almost palpable sense of unrest among the other Guardsmen as he took his place in the line and waited for the order to move out, Larn realised he could smell smoke and with it, there came an unwelcome realisation that cut through the fog of his grief and seemed to grip at his heart with clutching icy fingers.

The lander was on fire.

Spurred on by horror at the prospect of being trapped in a burning lander, the Guardsmen began to hurry for the stairwell while behind them Sergeant Ferres shouted profanities in the vain hope of maintaining some form of order. No one was listening. Frenzied, they rushed down the stairs towards the lower deck, treading on the corpses of those already killed in the landing. Running with the others, Larn caught a brief glimpse of their company commander Lieutenant Vinters sitting dead in his seat with his neck broken just like Jenks. He had no time to dwell on the Lieutenant's death; caught in the crush of fleeing Guardsmen he could only run with the crowd as they made for the lower deck, to the assault ramp and freedom. As they came within sight of it they found that the assault ramp was still sealed shut, while from all around them the smell of smoke grew ever stronger.

'Open that ramp!' screamed Sergeant Ferres, pushing his way through the crowd of milling Guardsmen to where a small group stood studying the control panel governing the ramp's mechanism. Seeing the group raise their eyes to look at him in confusion, he pushed them aside and stretched out a hand towards a metal lever set in a recess by the edge of the ramp. 'Useless bastards!' he spat in contempt, his hand closing around the lever. 'The master control panel must have been damaged in the landing. You need to pull the emergency release lever – like this!'

Pulling the lever Sergeant Ferres shrieked in sudden agony as one of the ramp's explosive release bolts misfired, a bright tongue of yellow fire bursting from the side of ramp to engulf his face. Screaming, a halo of flame dancing around his head, he stumbled blindly against the assault ramp as the other bolts fired and the ramp fell open behind him. Falling into the suddenly vacated space, his body rolled down the ramp and came to a stop partway down it as one of his legs caught on a protrusion at its side. For a moment, seeing the strugglings of their sergeant's body grow still as the life left him, his troops stood gazing at him in shocked silence, hypnotised by the brutal calamity of their leader's death.

'We have to move!' Larn heard someone say behind him as he realised how warm it had grown in the lander. 'The smoke is getting closer. If we don't get out of here now we'll either burn to death or choke!'

As one, the Guardsmen burst forward to rush down the ramp, the light outside seemed blinding in its intensity after the shadowed dimness of the interior of the lander. Barely able to keep his feet as the men behind him pushed to get out, Larn stumbled down the ramp with the rest, his first experiences of the new world before him registering as a disconnected jumble of sights and sensations. He caught snatches of an empty landscape through the press of bodies around him, saw a grey and brooding sky above them, felt a savage chill that bit gnawingly into his flesh. Worst of all was the sight of Sergeant Ferres's burnt and disfigured face. The fire-blackened sockets that had once held his eyes glimpsed briefly at the edge of Larn's vision as he followed the others down the ramp. Then, as the first ranks of Guardsmen reached the foot of the ramp and apparent safety, the frenzied herd instinct of a few moments before abruptly abated. Released from the crushing pressure of the crowd as the Guardsmen in front moved to take advantage of the open space before them, Larn was relieved to find himself able to breathe properly once more. Then, standing uncertainly with the others as they milled leaderless in the shadow of the lander, he turned to take his first clear view of the planet around him.

This is it, he thought, his breath turning to white vapour in the cold. *This is Seltura-III? It doesn't look much like they talked about in the briefing.*

Around him, as endless as the wheat fields of his homeworld, was a bleak and barren landscape; a flat treeless vista of frozen grey-black mud, punctuated here and there by shell craters and the rusting silhouettes of burned-out vehicles. To the east of him, he saw a distant cityscape of ruined buildings, as grey, foreboding and abandoned as every other aspect of the landscape around it. *It looks like a ghost town*, he thought with a shiver. *A ghost town, hungry for more ghosts.*

'I don't understand it,' he heard a questioning voice say as he realised Leden, Hallan and Vorrans had come to stand beside him. 'Where are the trees?' Leden asked. 'They said Seltura-III was covered in forests. And it's cold. They said it would be summer.'

'Never mind that,' said Hallan, terse at his side. 'We need to get to cover. I heard shots hitting the hull when we landed. There must be hostiles around here some–' He paused, stopping to look up with anxious eyes at the sky as, overhead, they heard the whistle of a shell coming closer.

'Incoming!' someone screamed as the entire company raced frantically to seek shelter at the side of the lander. Seconds later, an explosion lifted up dancing clods of frozen mud thirty meters away from where they were standing.

'I think it was a mortar!' Vorrans said, an edge of panic to his voice as he huddled with the others beside the lander. 'It sounded like a mortar,' he said, jabbering uncontrollably in a breathless rush of fear. 'A mortar, don't you think? A mortar. I think it was a mortar. A mortar!'

'I wish to the Emperor that was *all* it was,' Hallan said. Around them, more shots and explosions rang out. A fusillade that seemed to ominously increase in volume with every instant, as the noise of bullets and shells striking the hull on the other side of the lander grew so loud they had to shout to be heard over the roar. 'Lucky for us whoever's shooting is on the other side of this lander but we can't stay here forever. We need to find better cover, or it's only a matter of time before their artillery finds the range and starts to loop shells over the lander to land right on top of us!'

'Maybe this is all a mistake?' Vorrans said, his face alive with the glimmer of desperate hope. 'That's it, mistaken identity. Maybe it's our own side doing the shooting and they don't know who we are. We could make a white flag and try to signal them.'

'Shut up, Vors. You're talking like an idiot!' Hallan snapped. Then, seeing Vorrans look at him in shock, he softened his tone. 'Believe me, Vors, there's nothing *mistaken* about it. There's a ten metre tall imperial eagle painted on each side of the hull of the lander. The people shooting at us know *exactly* who we are. That's why they're trying to *kill* us. Our only way out of this is to try and make for our own lines. Though we'll need to find out where they are first.'

'There!' Leden said, his finger pointing eastward. 'You see it – the eagle in the distance. Sweet Emperor, we're saved!'

Turning to follow the direction of Leden's jabbing finger, Larn saw a flagpole rising from the rubble-strewn outskirts of the city. At its top a worn and ragged flag: an imperial eagle, fluttering in the breeze.

'You're right, Leden!' Hallan said, the excitement in his voice drawing the attention of the rest of the company as dozens of eyes turned to look toward the flag. 'It's our own lines, all right. If you look close you can see the outlines of camouflaged bunkers and firing emplacements. That's where we should be headed!'

'But it's got to be seven or eight hundred metres away at least, Hals,' Vorrans protested. 'With nothing between us and that flag but open ground. We'll never make it!'

'We don't have any choice, Vors,' Hallan said. Then, seeing the eyes of every other Guardsman in the company were on him, he turned to them, his voice raised loud enough to be heard among the din of gunfire. 'Listen to me, all of you! I know you're scared. Zell knows, I am too! But if we stay here we are as good as dead! Our only chance is to make for that flag!'

For a moment there was no response as the Guardsmen cast frightened eyes from the now burning lander to the wide expanse of open ground before them. Each man weighing an unwelcome decision: to stay and risk an undetermined death sometime in the future, or to run and risk an immediate death in the present. Then, suddenly, a shell landed on their side of the lander no more than five metres from where they were standing and the decision was made for them.

They ran.

Breathless, terror dogging his every step, Larn ran with them. He ran, as from behind them there came a remorseless tide of gunfire as the unseen enemy tried to shoot them down. He saw men die screaming all around him, red gore spraying from chests and arms and heads as the bullets struck them. He saw men killed by falling shells, bodies torn apart by blast and shrapnel, heads and limbs dismembered in an instant. All the time he kept his eyes glued on the flag – his would-be refuge – in the distance before him. His every breath a silent prayer in the hope of salvation. His every step one closer to making that salvation a reality.

As he ran, he saw friends and comrades die. He saw Hallan fall first, his right eye exploding from its socket to make way for the bullet passing though it, his mouth open in a cry of encouragement to his fellow Guardsmen that would never be finished. Then Vorrans, his torso ruptured and mutilated as a dozen pieces of shrapnel exploded through his chest. Other men fell: some he had known by name, others he had known only by sight. All of them killed as, just as breathless and desperate as he was, they ran for the flag. Until at last, with most of his comrades dead already and the flag still a hundred metres away, Larn realised he would never make it.

'Here! Over here! Quickly, this way! Over here!'

Suddenly, hearing shouting voices nearby Larn turned to see a group of Guardsmen in grey-black camouflage appear as if from nowhere to beckon him towards them. Changing direction to head for them, he saw they had emerged from a firing trench and raced towards it with enemy bullets chewing up the ground around him. Until at last, reaching the trench, he leapt inside to safety.

Trying to catch his breath as he lay at the bottom of the trench, looking about him Larn saw five Guardsmen standing around him in the confines of the trench: all clad in the same uniform of grey-black patterned great-coats, mufflers and fur-shrouded helmets. At first they ignored him, their eyes turned to scan the killing fields he had just escaped from. Then, one of the Guardsmen turned to look down towards him with a grimace and finally spoke.

'This is Vidmir in trench three, sergeant,' the Guardsmen said, pressing a stud at his collar as Larn realised he was speaking down a comm-link. 'We have one survivor. I think a few more made it to the other trenches. But most of those poor dumb bastards are dead out there in no man's land. Over.'

'I can see movement on the ork side,' one of the other Guardsmen said, standing looking over the trench parapet. 'All this killing must have got their blood up. They're getting ready for an attack.' Then, while Larn was still wondering if he had really heard the word 'ork', he saw the man turn away from the parapet to look towards him. 'Assuming that uniform you're wearing is not just for show, new fish, you might want to stand up and get your lasgun ready. There's going to be shooting.'

Pulling himself to his feet, Larn unslung his lasgun, stepping forward as the other Guardsmen moved sideways to make space for him on the trench's firing step. Then, as he checked his lasgun and made ready to put it to his shoulder, he saw something that caused him to wonder if his first combat drop might have gone even more badly wrong than he could have thought. As, from the corner of his eye, he spotted a bullet-riddled wooden sign erected behind and slightly to one side of the trench. A sign whose ironic greeting gave him pause to wonder if he really was where he thought he was at all.

A sign that said:

Welcome to Broucheroc.

'THEY'RE GETTING READY to move all right,' the Guardsman said next to him, spitting a wad of greasy phlegm over the trench parapet. 'They'll hit us hard this time, and in numbers. It's the blood that does it, you see. Our blood, I mean. *Human* blood. The sight and smell of it always makes 'em more willing and eager for a fight. Though, Emperor knows, your average ork is usually pretty *eager* to begin with.'

His name was Repzik: Larn could see the faded letters of the name stencilled on the tunic of the man's uniform under his greatcoat. Standing beside him on the firing step, Larn followed the direction of his eyes to look into the landscape he now knew as no man's land. No matter how intently he stared across the bleak fields of frozen mud before them he could see no movement, nor for that matter any other sign of the enemy. Ahead, no man's land seemed as flat, featureless and devoid of life as it had when he had emerged from the lander to his first view of it barely ten minutes ago. The only difference now was the addition of the burning shell of the lander itself, and with it the bodies of his company strewn haphazard and bloody across the frozen landscape. Abruptly, as he looked out at the remains of men he had known as friends and comrades, Larn felt the beginnings of tears stinging wetly at the corners of his eyes.

Jenks is dead, he thought. *And Hallan, Vorrans, Lieutenant Vinters, even Sergeant Ferres. I don't see Leden. Perhaps he is still alive somewhere. But nearly every man I came here with from Jumael is lying dead out there in no man's land. All of them slaughtered within minutes of landing, without even having fired a shot.*

'It's a pity about your comrades,' Repzik said, his voice almost kindly as Larn clenched his eyes to try and stop the other men in the trench from seeing his tears. 'But they're dead and you ain't. What you need to start thinking about now is how you're going to stop yourself from *joining* them. The orks are coming, new fish. If you want to live you're going to have to keep yourself hard and tight.'

'Orks?' Larn said, trying to concentrate his mind on the practical in an effort to lay his grief aside. 'You said "orks"? I didn't know there were any orks on Seltura VII?'

'Could be that's true,' Repzik said, as beside him one of the other Guardsmen looked to the sky in silent exasperation. 'Fact is, you'd have to ask somebody who's actually *been* there. Here in Broucheroc though we generally have more orks than we know what to do with.'

'Wait,' asked Larn, confused, 'are you telling me this planet isn't Seltura VII?'

'Well, I wasn't specifically commenting on it, new fish,' Repzik said. 'But since you ask, you'd be right enough. This place isn't Seltura VII – wherever in *hell* that is.'

Stunned, for a moment Larn wondered if he had somehow misunderstood the man's meaning. Then, he looked out again at the treeless landscape and was struck by all the troubling inconsistencies between what he had been told to expect on Seltura VII and the stark brutal realities of the world he saw before him. They had made the drop three weeks early. There were no forests. It was winter rather than summer. The war here was against orks, not PDF rebels. A catalogue of facts that, with a dawning horror born of slow realisation, pushed him inexorably toward a sudden and shocking conclusion.

Holy Throne, he thought. *They sent us to the wrong planet!*

'I shouldn't be here,' he said aloud.

'It's funny how everyone tends to think that when they're waiting for an attack to begin,' said Repzik. 'I wouldn't worry about it, new fish. Once the orks get here you'll soon find yourself feeling right at home.'

'No, you don't understand!' Larn said. 'There has been a terrible mistake! My company was supposed to be going to the Seltura system. To a world called Seltura VII, to put down a mutiny among the local PDF. Something must have gone wrong because I'm on the wrong planet!'

'So? What is that to me?' Repzik said, his eyes as he looked at Larn seemed little warmer than the landscape around them. 'You are on the wrong planet. You are in the wrong system. Not to mention probably the wrong war. Get used to it, new fish. If that is the *worst* thing that happens to you today, you will have been lucky.'

'But you don't understand–'

'No. It is *you* who does not understand, new fish. This is Broucheroc. We are surrounded by ten million orks. And right now some of those orks – maybe only a few thousand or so, if we are lucky – are getting ready to attack us. They don't care what planet you think you should be on. They don't care that you think you're in the wrong place, that you're wet behind the ears, or that you're probably not even old enough to shave. All they care about is *killing* you. So if you know what is good for you, new fish, you will put all this crap aside and start worrying about killing them instead.'

Shocked at the man's outburst Larn said nothing, his reply dying on his tongue as he saw Repzik turn away from him to gaze darkly into no man's land once more. As though by some sixth sense the other Guardsmen in the trench had already done the same: all of them staring hard into no man's land as though watching something happening out there of which Larn was entirely unaware. No matter how hard Larn tried, he could see nothing. Nothing except grey-black mud and desolation.

Frustrated, wary of asking the others what they were looking at for fear of drawing another angry outburst, Larn turned to glance around him. Behind him, hidden from his sight when he had first landed by a gentle sloping of the ground, were a series of firing trenches and foxholes. All of them led down towards sandbag emplacements that covered the entrances to a number of underground dugouts set among the shattered husks of buildings at the outskirts of the city. Now his eyes had become accustomed to the relentless grey of the landscape, Larn could see other firing trenches around and to the side of their trench – their parapets cunningly camouflaged to look no different from the countless chunks of crumbling half-buried plascrete and other detritus that lay scattered across this wasteland. From time to time a Guardsman would suddenly emerge from one of the trenches to run half-crouched, zigzagging from one piece of cover to the next until he reached the safety of either another trench or the entrance to one of the dugouts. Behind them, in the distance, the main body of the city stood brooding across the horizon as though watching their lives and labours with disdain. A city of ruined and battle-scarred buildings set against a grey and uncaring sky.

This is Broucheroc, Larn reminded himself. *That is what they said the city was called.*

'There,' one of the Guardsmen said beside him. 'I see green. The bastards are moving.'

Turning to gaze once more into no man's land with the others, for a moment Larn found himself vainly struggling to see anything among the wearying grey of the world about them. Then, suddenly, at ground level perhaps a kilometre away he saw a brief glimpse of green flesh as its owner stood upright for a split second before abruptly disappearing once more.

'I see it.' Larn said, the words jumping breathless from him, unbidden. 'Holy Emperor! Is that an ork?'

'Hhh. I only wish orks were as small as that, new fish,' Repzik said, spitting over the parapet into no man's land again. 'That's a gretch. A gretchin. Keep looking and you should be able to see some more.'

He was right. Ahead, Larn saw the creature stand upright once more. This time it stood where it was unmoving, its green flesh plainly visible against the contrast of the grey backdrop of the landscape behind it. Then, after a moment, Larn saw another dozen creatures appear beside it, all of them standing still and motionless as though trying to smell something on the wind. Each of them perhaps a metre tall at most, their stunted green bodies appearing curiously hunched and misshapen inside their rough grey garments. Watching them, Larn felt himself recoil in instinctive horror at his first sight of an alien species. Until, before he even knew what he was doing, his finger was on the trigger of lasgun at his shoulder as he sighted in on the *Xenos*.

'Don't bother, new fish,' Repzik said, laying a hand across his barrel. 'Even if you did manage to hit one of the gretch at this range, you would be wasting your ammo. Save it 'til later. Save it for the orks.'

'I don't like it,' one of the other Guardsmen said. 'If the orks are sending their gretch out like that it means they're planning on hitting us with a frontal assault. Another one. What is that now? Something like the *third* one today?'

'Third time is right, Kell,' the Guardsman called Vidmir said, his face grim as he pressed a finger to his ear to listen to something on his comm bead. 'You'll have to remember to remonstrate with the orks about their lack of originality when they get here. From the reports I'm hearing over the tactical net, you should soon be getting the opportunity to do so.'

'What is it?' the other Guardsman – Kell – asked, while the rest of the men in the trench turned to look at Vidmir. 'What have you heard?'

'Sector Command says auspex is reading a lot of movement in the ork lines,' Vidmir replied. 'Sounds like Repzik was right. They're going to be hitting us hard, and in numbers. Though, from the sound of it, I think there's more to this than just a matter of the orks getting excited over killing the new fish's friends. Could be they were already getting ready to launch an offensive. Which would be bad enough, except it sounds like our own side is trying to get us killed as well. Battery Command are refusing to give us artillery support until they are sure this is really a full-blown assault and not just a feint.'

'A feint, my arse,' Kell grunted. 'When have you ever known an ork to do anything by halves.'

'Agreed,' Vidmir said. 'But, irrespective, it looks like we're going to have to repel the orks on our own. Emperor help us.' Then, turning towards Larn, Vidmir gave him the cold flash of a graveyard smile.

'Congratulations, new fish,' he said. 'Looks like not only did you manage to get yourself dropped right into the middle of Hell. But you picked a bad day in Hell besides.'

REPZIK, VIDMIR, DONN, Ralvs and Kell. These were the names of the five men who shared the trench with him. Larn had learned that much about them at least in the quiet time as they waited for the battle to begin. They were from a planet called Vardan, they told him. They and their regiment, a group of hardened veterans known as the 902nd Vardan Rifles, had come to the city of Broucheroc more than ten years ago and had been here even since. *Ten years!* He could hardly believe it. Nor where those the only things that Larn had learned from the Vardans.

'I don't understand it,' he said, looking out at the group of gretchin on the other side of no man's land. 'What are they waiting for?'

Ten minutes had passed since the first alien appeared. Though the numbers of those waiting with it had now increased to perhaps a couple of hundred, still the ranks of gretchin stood exposed and out in the open on the other side of no man's land. Occasionally a squabble would break out, two or three of the aliens suddenly breaking away from the main group to fight a bloody battle with tooth and claw while their fellows watched with lazy interest. For the most part the aliens simply stood there unmoving, their feral faces turned to stare unblinkingly towards the human lines. It was an unnerving spectacle. Not for the first time, Larn found himself fighting the urge to take his lasgun and fire at them. To shoot over and over again until every one of the ugly inhuman faces he could see before him had been obliterated.

'It's an old trick, new fish,' Repzik said. 'They're waiting for us to shoot at them and give away our positions.'

'But that's suicide,' Larn said. 'Why would they be willing to sacrifice themselves like that?'

'Hhh. They're gretch, new fish,' Repzik replied. 'Willing doesn't come into it. If their Warboss tells 'em to go stand out in no man's land and wait to get killed, it's not like they get much say over it. 'Course, even the fact that their boss is smart enough to think of using his gretch that way tells us something. It means the greenskin leading the assault is likely to be one crafty son of a bitch, relatively speaking. And that's likely to be bad news for us, believe me. There's not much worse than a crafty ork. Now quiet down, new fish. There will be plenty of time for questions later, after the attack. Assuming, of course, we survive it.'

At that Repzik fell silent once more, his eyes staring into no man's land with the rest of the Vardans. Denied the distraction of further conversation, Larn began to realise just how tense the atmosphere was in the trench. *An attack is coming,* he thought. *Although these men have faced dozens, perhaps even hundreds of such attacks in the past, still the tension is plain on every line of their faces for anyone to see.* Briefly, he tried to find comfort in that thought. He tried to tell himself that if hardened veterans like these felt queasy in the face of the impending assault, there was no shame in the churning of his own stomach but he remained unconvinced. *Am I a coward,* he thought. *I am afraid, but will my nerve hold so I can do my duty? Or will it fail? Will I fight when the attack comes or will I break and run?* But as forcefully as those questions rebounded around inside his head, he could find no answer.

The waiting was the worst of it. Abruptly, as he stood there on the firing step, Larn realised that until now he had been inoculated against fear by the sheer breathless pace of events since the lander had been hit. Now, in the silence of the lull before battle, there was no hiding place from his fears. He felt alone. Far from home. Terrified that he was about to die on a strange world under a cold and distant sun.

'Ready your weapons,' Vidmir said, as more gretchin began to appear on the other side of no man's land. 'This is it. Looks like they got tired of waiting.'

'We hold our fire until they're three hundred metres away,' Repzik said to Larn. 'See that flat grey-black rock over there? That's your mark. We wait 'til the first rank of gretch reach that before we fire.' Then, seeing Larn looking in confusion into no man's land as he tried to distinguish which of the thousands of grey-black rocks was the mark, Repzik sighed in exasperation. 'Never mind, new fish. You shoot when we do. You follow orders. You do what we tell you to do, when we tell you to do it, and you don't ask any questions. Trust me, that's the only way you going to survive your first fifteen hours.'

Ahead, the group of gretchin out in no man's land had swelled to become a horde several thousands strong. They seemed agitated now, jabbering to each other in incomprehensible alien gibberish while the more brave or foolhardy among them pushed their way to the front of the group as though restless for their wait to be at an end. Then, finally, the waiting was over as for the first time Larn heard the sound of massed alien voices screaming a terrifying war cry.

Waaaaaaaghhhh!

As one, firing their guns into the air, the horde of gretchin came charging towards them. As unnerving as the sight of the aliens had seemed to Larn earlier, they were nothing compared to the horrors he now saw emerging into view in their wake. Just behind the onrushing gretchin he saw countless numbers of much larger greenskins rise up to join the charge. Each one of them a grotesquely muscled broad-shouldered monster more than two metres tall, screaming with ferocious savagery as they took up the battle cry of their smaller brethren.

Waaaaaaaaghhh!

Sweet Emperor, Larn thought, half-beside himself with terror. *Those must be the orks. There's so many of them and every one of them is huge!*

'Eight hundred metres,' Vidmir said, sighting in on the enemy with the targeter clipped to the side of his lasgun, his calm voice barely audible above the sound of approaching thunder as the greenskins charged ever closer. 'Keep yourselves cold and sharp. No firing until they reach the kill zone.'

'Don't fire until you see the reds of their eyes,' Kell snickered, as if he had found some grim humour in the situation that eluded Larn.

'Six hundred metres,' Vidmir said, ignoring him.

'Remember to aim high, new fish,' Repzik said. 'Don't worry about the gretchin – they're no threat. It's the orks you want to hit. We open up with single shots at first – continuous volley fire. Oh, and new fish? You might want to release the safety catch on your lasgun. You'll find killing orks is easier that way.'

Fumbling at his lasgun in embarrassment as he realised the Vardan was right, Larn switched the firing control from safe to 'single shot'. Then, remembering his training and the words of *The Imperial Infantryman's Uplifting Primer*, he silently recited the Litany of the Lasgun in his mind.

Bringer of death, speak your name,
For you are my life, and the foe's death.

'Four hundred metres,' Vidmir said. 'Prepare to fire.'

The greenskins were closing. Looking past the scuttling ranks of gretchin, Larn could see the orks more clearly now. Close enough to see sloping brows and baleful eyes, while thousands of jutting jaws and mouths filled with murderous tusks seemed to smile towards him with eager and savage intent. With every passing second the orks were coming closer. As he watched them charging towards the trench, Larn felt himself suddenly gripped by an almost overpowering urge to turn and flee. He wanted to hide. To run away as far and fast as he could and never look back. Something deep inside of him – some mysterious reservoir of inner strength he had never known before – stopped him. Despite all his fears, the dryness of his mouth, the trembling of his hands that he hoped the others could not see, despite all that he stood his ground.

'Three hundred and fifty metres!' Vidmir shouted, while Larn could hear the distant popping sound of mortars being fired behind them. 'Three hundred metres! On my mark! Fire!'

In the same instant every Guardsman on the line opened fire, sending a bright fusillade of lasfire burning through the air towards the orks. With it came a sudden flurry of airbursts as dozens of falling mortar and grenade launcher rounds exploded in mid-air in a deadly hail of shrapnel. Then came the blinding flash of lascannon beams; the rat-a-tat crack of autocannons; the flare of frag missiles streaking towards their targets. A withering torrent of fire that tore into the charging orks, decimating their numbers. Through it all, as the Vardans in the trench beside him ceaselessly worked the triggers of their lasguns to send more greenskins screaming to *Xenos* hell, Larn fired with them.

He fired without pause, as merciless as the others. Over and over again, his fears abating with every shot, the terrors that had once assailed him replaced by a growing sense of exultation as he saw the greenskins die. For the first time in his life, Larn knew the savage joy of killing. For the first time, seeing orks fall wounded and dying to be trampled under the heedless boot heels of their fellows, he knew the value of hate. Seeing the enemy die he felt no sorrow for them, no sadness, no remorse for their deaths. They were *Xenos*. They were the alien. The unclean. They were monsters, every one of them. Monsters. With a sudden insight, he finally understood the wisdoms of the Imperium. He understood the teachings he had received in the scholarium, in the sermons of the preachers, in basic training. He understood why Man made war upon the *Xenos*. In the midst of that war, he felt no pity for them.

A good soldier, he felt nothing but hate.

Then, through the heat and noise of battle, Larn saw something that brought all his fears rushing back to him. Incredibly, despite all the casualties inflicted by the Guardsmen's fire, the greenskins' charge had not wavered. Though the torrent of fire continued from the Vardans' positions, the orks kept on coming. They seemed unstoppable. Abruptly, Larn found himself uncomfortably aware just how much he wanted to avoid having to face an ork in hand-to-hand combat.

'One hundred and twenty metres!' he heard Vidmir yell through the din. 'Change cells and switch to rapid fire!'

'They're getting closer!' Larn said, his hands clumsy with desperation as he struggled to change the cell in his lasgun. 'Shouldn't we fix bayonets – just in case?'

'Hardly, new fish,' Repzik said, his cell already changed and firing with the rest. 'If this battle gets to bayonet range we've as good as lost it. Now, shut up and start shooting!'

Out in no man's land the charging orks came ever closer. By now most of the gretchin were dead, winnowed away by blast and shrapnel. Though the ranks of the orks had also been thinned, from where Larn stood there looked to be thousands of them left. All bearing down across the battered landscape of no man's land in a relentless and barbaric tide hell bent on slaughter.

There's no stopping them, Larn thought. *We're going to be overrun!*

He saw orks armed with short bulbous-headed sticks running at the head of the mob, the sticks covered in a lethal profusion of spikes, blades and flanges. At first he took the weapons in their hands to be some form of primitive mace or club. Until he saw the front rank of orks suddenly throw the same 'clubs' to land in the frozen mud before the trenches, each one exploding in a shower of shrapnel. Instinctively, seeing one of the stick-grenades land a few metres from his trench, Larn ducked his head to avoid the deadly fragments whistling through the air above it. An action that drew a terse reprimand for Repzik.

'Damnation, new fish. Keep your fool head up and keep on shooting!' Repzik yelled. 'They're trying to make us keep our heads down so they can get in close.'

Doing as he was told, Larn resumed firing. Only to look on in horror with the rest of the men as, flying through the air so slowly it might almost have been moving in slow motion, another of the stick grenades hit the parapet and bounced inside their trench.

'Stikk bomb!' Vidmir screamed. 'Bail out!'

Rushing to evacuate the trench with the others, Larn scrambled over the trench wall behind him, stumbling over his own two feet as he made it to ground level and turned to run for cover. He tripped, his body already falling towards the ground as the blast of the stikk bomb ripped through the air behind him. He felt a pain in his shoulder and a sudden pressure in his ears.

Then, he hit the ground and everything went black.

The story continues in
FIFTEEN HOURS
by Mitchel Scanlon

Coming soon from the Black Library

Read till you Bleed

Do you have them all?

WWW.BLACKLIBRARY.COM

Coming Soon...